EYE
OF THE
UNICORN

Morag Higgins

Fisher King Publishing

Eye of the Unicorn
Copyright © Morag Higgins 2013
ISBN 978-1-906377-65-6

Fisher King Publishing Ltd
The Studio
Arthington Lane
Pool-in-Wharfedale
LS21 1JZ
England

Cover design by Sam Richardson

To my loving husband Mark who
supports me in all that I do.
Thanks also to my family and friends
and especially to my publisher Rick
Armstrong, who, despite thinking that
the nice men in white coats should cart
me off to the rubber room, stuck with it
and helped me get my novel in print.

Chapter One

Dawn.Time was counted in heartbeats as the adversaries faced each other, the dwellers of darkness and the lover of light, no mercy would be shown and bloody death would most certainly greet the new day.

The cool stare of the San wavered as he looked deep into the red orbs of the Cuc. Fearful of the terrible heat of the twin suns yet unwilling to provoke an attack the San motioned to his group to edge around their adversary. Sensing the strategy the monstrous form lazily swung its massive bulk across the intended path and waited. It was one of the few living creatures on the burnt out planet that was capable of withstanding the terrible heat of the sister stars. It could endure the discomfort of direct sunlight if it provided the additional entertainment of watching the sensitive San fry.

Realising that a direct attack was inevitable the San gathered his strength and lunged at the towering form, on his cue the others of his group sprang into action. Several razor sharp axes met their mark, slashing a ragged line across the great neck and down the Cuc's side. Black liquid oozed from the wound, dribbling across the thick scales that armoured the Cuc's hide. Taken off guard the Cuc squealed its protest, a surprisingly high pitched sound from a creature so large. It lashed out at its main attacker, the hooked claw swinging through the air to be parried by the axe's head.

With a neat side step, the leading San completed his stroke by burying the axe deep into the soft pad of the foot.

Furious, the Cuc shook its leg trying desperately to free itself from the weapon, in doing so it snatched the axe from the grip of the San, throwing him a considerable distance across the rough ground. The others backed off and re-grouped. The lead San gasped as his sensitive night skin was

1

sandpapered off his back by the rocky surface, allowing blood to seep and sting down his spine. Climbing quickly to his feet he motioned to the others to draw the Cuc towards the rocky outcrop of the mountain range.

By now the day was beginning to brighten with a searing light. Protective inner lids closed across the Sans' eyes eliminating much of the glare, but they could feel their skin tingling with the heat. The Cuc, meanwhile, had finally managed to free its foot from the axe and was limping towards them, hissing its rage, intent on finishing off its enemies.

The group of San turned as one and ran. Squealing shrilly the Cuc followed, its speed considerably impaired by the injuries it had already sustained. The San were racing not only the Cuc, but also the life threatening heat of day. Without the protection of the shaded mountains, they would die, burned by the fierce sister suns. The cool of the mountain outcrops seemed frustratingly near, teasing them with their promise of safety. The stifling heat of day was already beginning to thicken the atmosphere, snatching the very breath from their lips. Looking up, the lead San could see they were only a short distance from their mountain haven. Being careful not to let the Cuc become disinterested with them he slowed the pace slightly.

Finally the cool shade of the first of the strewn rocks gave a welcome reward for their efforts. They did not rest, for the Cuc was relentlessly following, furious as it saw its foes disappearing into the rocks.

The change in temperature of the shade had revitalised the San and they split up, nimbly clambering over the rocky surface, instinctively keeping out of the harsh light. The Cuc began to slow, uncertain if it should follow, the San were smaller and surefooted in this mountain terrain, and a truce had been called. The vast mountain range that circled the Northern half of the planet belonged to the San, the flat plains that stretched to the equator was the Cucs. No creature, not even the Cuc, could survive the terrible heat that lay south of the Equator. If a member of either race found the other within their borders then, and only then, would an attack be provoked. It wasn't just war, it was survival! Food was scarce, the planet was dying and only one race could survive. This Cuc had been content to let the group of San die in the heat of the day and then feast on the remains. However, the San had struck the first blow injuring not only its hide, but also this particular Cuc's pride and it intended to make its enemy pay dearly for that indignity.

The Cuc stopped and sniffed the air, the San had disappeared. It swivelled its head searching for a scent. Fear gripped its heart, it had not realised it had followed the San so far up the mountain side and now it had managed to get itself jammed in a narrow gorge. It began to run backwards, panic overtaking what little sense it had. The great body quivered as it reversed over a small circle of stones not noticing the opening between them.

As the Cuc's sensitive and unprotected belly skimmed across the hole a San struck from his hiding place, thrusting a sword deep into the creature. Screaming in agony the Cuc ran back even faster and succeeded in ripping its own belly open. Staggering, it backed a few more feet before ramming its hind quarters into the canyon wall. Another San leapt onto its head, thrusting a dagger deep into one crimson eye. Hissing and scrabbling with its claws against the dirt, it writhed in spasmodic bursts.

Finally it collapsed, the blunt nosed, shovel-shaped head thumping into the ground, blood trickling from its nostrils and gurgling through its teeth.

As the massive flanks heaved and sighed its dying eyes saw the hated San standing together, their leader watching from the hole in the ground. It tried to squeal its fury but only succeeded in choking on its own blood. It shuddered and lay still.

Out on the plain each sibling from the Cuc's nest stopped in their tracks. Each one knew that their nest mate lived no more. Each one knew that the killers were the San. They raised their heads and hissed in fury, the truce had been broken.

The leading San grinned. At least they would not return empty handed, judging by the size of the Cuc there would be more than enough meat to feed their families tonight. He watched while the others butchered the carcase with practised skill and took as much meat as they could carry. Once their gory task was completed he lifted his share of the meat and nodding to the others, they turned to go.

"Would you like some help?" The enquiry echoed in the lead San's head. He turned to see a figure emerge from a rock shadow. The cloak that covered the newcomer's body was pulled back and he removed the hood and mask that enveloped his head, protecting the skin from the searing heat.

"Curmer," thought the lead San in jubilation as he laid down the meat and grasped the newcomer's arms in greeting. "I'm glad you are here, now you can help us bring back this food."

"Not so loud Remruc," answered Curmer, mentally blocking some of the force of his brother's greeting. "First I must see to your wounds or do you want to be scarred for the rest of your life?"

Curmer firmly pushed Remruc back against the shadow of the rock and deftly applied healing salve to the raw flesh of his open wounds. Remruc growled as the salve stung his skin but soon its cooling properties began to relieve his pain. "How did you know where we were?"

"You forget brother that I am a healer and more sensitive to the pain of others, and besides, you scream like a Cuc when you're injured; a mind numb Lemath could find you blind folded."

Remruc smiled and the others of his group shook their heads in mock disdain. "I must try to control my output in future", he thought to himself. It was to be expected that Curmer could sense him so easily being his brother, but it would be bad if an enemy could hear him too.

The San rose and hefted the meat into bundles. Curmer waited as Remruc took a cloak, hood and mask from a pack attached to his belt and put them on.

Remruc grinned and gingerly wriggled until the weight of the pack rested on the least skinned portion of his sensitive back. With an anxious glance at the ferocious Suns they set off, instinctively staying in the shadows.

"The Cuc are coming further north," thought Remruc, "we met this one only ten sharr from our range."

Curmer paused and looked at his brother, "the Cuc grow fat and strong on the carcases littering this world. They are many in number; perhaps it will not be long before they wish to feed on us."

Remruc grimaced and motioned for his brother to continue. If that was the case then his people would have nowhere left to hide.

Once the San had been a nomadic race of humanoids roaming the planet's surface guarding their various tribal tracks of land jealously. When the sun Emur had changed from burning gold to blood red, so too had their life changed. They had become almost nocturnal, travelling in the cool of night. They soon learned that they must not be caught in the open in the full force of Rume and Emur's cruel heat and radiation.

They travelled less and finally settled in a range of mountains that spanned the northern circumference of the planet; they called these mountains the Sanlands. For generations they had lived in these ranges, still guarding family strongholds with vicious intensity. The San were divided, but they still thrived. Thrived, that is, until the sickness. A mysterious illness was sweeping through the San with horrifying results. Every family, cut off from each other, struggled to combat the disease, each thinking the other clans had somehow caused the plague. As a result, the race known as the San were nearing extinction. Food had always been difficult to come by, now it was nearly impossible to find anything to hunt. There were not enough workers strong enough to tend the crops and so they died. The animals could not be brought water. They died. Any food to supplement the meagre diet scratched from small gardens and pets had to be caught on Surn's burning plains. This meant risking an encounter with the Cuc. The San and Cuc had never competed before. They treated each other with the respect that hunters and scavengers deserve. Each served a purpose, but now the Cuc were finding that they were becoming prey, and they were not pleased. They had moved far to the south almost to the equator. No other living being on Surn could stand that intense heat. There they waited and multiplied, now this plague had spread among the San, weakening them and the Cuc were returning.

Remruc and Curmer paused at the summit taking the opportunity to scan the territory of their neighbours. Two of their group automatically scouted the surrounding area, a standard search formation. This was the closest border area, it had moved frequently in the past when one family would become more powerful than the other, as a result both sides normally kept sentries posted along its length. Remruc and Curmer's clan had been stricken with the sickness and could no longer guard their borders. They lived in constant fear of invasion, alert for the first conquering soldiers to stroll across. But none had come.

Remruc shaded his eyes from the suns and gazed across the red crags, wavering in a shroud of heat. They dipped and twisted across the border tearing at the sky with clawed peaks of purple and gold. Burning and smouldering like the spines of a great dragon wallowing under the skies. There was a single pinnacle of red, orange rock that towered above the rest. That was the lookout for the Nemn, the neighbouring tribe. It was unmanned. Remruc set his jaw grimly and wondered if perhaps, contrary to his clans belief, that they too had the sickness. That would explain the lack of attention they were paying to their borders.

The back of his hand began to burn as the relentless heat of Rume and Emur baked his skin. He signalled for the scouts to return to the main group and they turned to descend into the indigo depths of a deep chasm that slashed itself into the very heart of the mountain range. Now they were shaded from most of the glare from the sky and they paused as their eyes changed from day vision to sensitive night vision, glowing with a cold blue iridescence. As they journeyed down through the monochromatic chasm, the temperature also began to change cooling to a more comfortable degree. Moisture now dared to exist, darkening the porous rock with its presence, giving plant life an excuse to cling desperately to the surrounding walls.

Finally the gorge narrowed to a point and before the travellers began their final descent they scanned the area cautious of being followed by the Nemn. Ahead of them two great shelves of rock a millennium ago had strained against each other fighting to win supremacy, until one had collapsed and crumbled leaving the victor to rise above and overlap as the planet's mantle edged ever onward on its journey. Between them a narrow opening to a cave had been formed. It appeared to be a nothing more than a small cleft precariously placed between the warring shelves of rock. At least a casual observer may think that the case. However, if time was taken to study the rocky walls, they would be surprised to see the chipped and gouged granite where massive excavations had been conducted. The walls were skilfully sculptured into natural supporting beams. This was the main entrance of an artificially dug tunnel, a tunnel that led to the subterranean city of the Chai clan. Remruc and Curmer descended into the inky depths, moving by instinct as even their night vision was useless. The floor dropped at a gradual angle, seeming to go on for miles before it finally levelled out. It was at this point that a wall of rocks blocked the way.

To an unknowledgeable stranger, it would seem a dead end, but to the Chai, the narrow, hidden stairwells to the left and right were the last means of defence against intruders. The stairs opened out in a funnel shape and at the top they expanded onto a well lit rocky platform. Here Remruc and Curmer waited for their patrol to be checked by the entrance guards. They all knew each other, but the formalities had to be followed; there must be no risk of infiltration by the neighbouring tribe. Once acknowledgements had been made Remruc and Curmer were free to descend into their subterranean home.

The city of the Chai had been hewn by generations out of the heart of the mountain. It had once been an underground cavern carved by a long gone lake of modest size. Now it sprawled into the distance, its buildings cut out of solid rock. The structural architecture took on strange, aesthetic forms as the constructors had followed the grain and flaws in the rocks themselves. The winding streets and alleys seemed to follow no set pattern but meandered where they pleased between the dwellings. Shafts of light beamed down through bore holes in the ceiling. These holes had been laboriously drilled directly to the surface angling every so often to lessen the strain on the roof. At each angle in the hole, a polished plate of metal was placed which acted like a mirror reflecting the light from above down to the heart of the mountain. It was the surface entrance to one of these bore holes that Remruc had wedged himself into to hide from the Cuc. The holes themselves had to be wide enough to allow the San to clean and polish the reflecting mirrors. This maintenance was generally done at night, for although the intensity of the heat and light on the metal surface could be tolerated in the early morning or late evening, by midday it was phenomenal. It was this heat that warmed the cavern above the sub-zero temperature to a comfortable degree. The bore holes also served the double purpose of ventilation. Torches on pillared stands solved the problems of night lighting, blackening the walls with their tarry smoke.

Once Remruc and Curmer's clan had been healthy and thriving, the streets full of jostling crowds going about their business, laughing, cajoling, bargaining furiously with market sellers pedalling their wares. There was once life in their city. Now there was only silence. The patrol's footsteps echoed hollowly against the walls, their boots crunching on the gravel pavements. As they passed a dwelling they glanced through the opening. Sitting on the mats were three children. In the corner lay the covered corpses of their parents. All of them had famine in their eyes and one of the boys had the fever of

9

the sickness. The girl looked up with pleading eyes. Curmer smiled and gave her his share of the meat. At least they would not die of hunger. Remruc clenched his jaw in frustration, wishing that his patrol had brought more food for his starving people. He pulled his brother away. It was a familiar sight now in his city; no family had been spared the sickness. There were too many corpses now to even merit a decent ceremony to send the life essence into the voids as the people found it hard enough to take the bodies to the pit. Their group walked on in grim silence. As they passed the corridor that led to the gardens of the city Curmer paused and stared into the cavern beyond. An intricate matrix of bore holes in the ceiling gave the impression that the cavern was open to the sky. It had plenty of light for plant and animal life with the added bonus of protection from the heat. The Cavern was gargantuan and covered miles. In better times enough crops were grown here to feed the people and support for animals and pets. Constant attention was needed for irrigation and crop care. When the sickness came the care was lost as more people fell. Now the withered brown stems of drought-choked plants were all that remained. A lone figure wandered pitifully among the desolation, a water canister on his back. But the dry crops were beyond even this desperate act of revival.

Here Remruc dismissed his patrol, giving them their orders to distribute what little food they had. Taking a small share, the brothers moved on, a quickness in their step as their goal was in sight. A curving, gracefully spiralled dwelling grew out of the ground in front of them. It was one of the largest buildings in the city. The home of the chieftain, the home of their sire. As they approached the doorway a sled drawn by two beasts pulled up alongside them. The animals hung their heads in exhaustion, the flesh on their bodies not enough to hide the bones that jutted out at extreme angles. They gazed at Remruc and Curmer emitting sad hungry tones which filled their minds with clouds of emotion. Their legs trembled with fatigue. The animals' owner appeared from the back of the sled. "I have come for the body. A chieftain must have a decent ceremony even in these desperate times".

Grief and shock struck Curmer's mind as Remruc struggled to question him. Through the haze he managed to relay that their sire had felt unwell when he left that night. The family had put this down to weakness through hunger. He had been sent to bring Remruc's hunting expedition back as quickly as possible, but he had never thought that Storn would succumb to the sickness. He could not believe that such a strong and powerful warrior could have died in so short a time. As one they ran into the house scaling the stairs three at a time they burst into the master room.

Sadelna, Cupe, Lenta and Musi sat quietly and gravely by Storn's sleeping platform. The San could not weep, but they did not suffer grief any the less and their minds shouted the turmoil that they felt inside. Sadelna held Storn's hand and gazed at her sons with stricken eyes. Sadelna was Storn's first mate and the mother of his pride and joy. She had borne him twin sons, a very rare thing in the San.

They had been given, as was traditional for any kind of twin, the same name; one spelt forwards and one spelt backwards. While they were apart then they were only half the person they should be. Their talents complimented each other and it was only when they were together that they were truly whole. Storn had left his clan two powerful leaders-to-be and now was the test of their strength.

Cupe and Lenta sat either side of Sadelna. They were Storn's second and third mates. Cupe, a warrior and huntress, sat in full battle dress, her sword lain across her knees. Lenta comforted her daughter Musi.

"My sons," Sadelna's mind whispered, "come and bid the Chieftain farewell".

They walked slowly forward and knelt by Storn's body. Cupe rose and stood between them.

"Your father was the strongest warrior and wisest leader ever born to this clan. I taught and trained you as best I can. Your father was very proud of you. You will not have an easy task ruling our people in these troubled times, but I will guide you as best I can and I pledge my loyalty to you." She drew her sword above her head, "hail Remruc and Curmer, may the fortune of two leaders take us to better days." Cupe re-sheathed her sword and walked from the room.

Gently Sadelna took Lenta's hand, "do not grieve Lenta, not even a healer as skilled as you could save our mate. Perhaps his death was necessary to give us two leaders who shine like our two fierce suns."

Sadelna drew her to her feet, "take little Musi away, I do not want her to see Storn leave."

Lenta managed a weak smile and squeezed Sadelna's hand. "Thank you," she said, "hail Remruc and Curmer, I pledge my loyalty to you", she continued, resting her hands on their shoulders.

Musi ran to Remruc and clung tightly to him. Her young mind was not able to control the pain that she felt.

"Don't grieve little sister, Storn has gone to lead an army against our enemies, even as we speak he fights the creatures of the sickness that kills our people. He is a hero." Remruc whispered into her mind, desperately controlling his own grief. Musi gazed at her brother and kissed him lightly on the cheek.

She turned to Curmer and hugged him tightly, she murmured "hail Remruc and Curmer my brothers."

Lenta gently pulled her away from Curmer and walked quietly from the room. There were a few moments silence as they paid their respects, Sadelna stood gracefully and rested her hands on her sons' shoulders, "a great burden has been placed upon you, and your skills will be put to the test in these troubled times. I know in my heart that you were given to me for a special purpose and I know that it is only you who can save our people." She turned and led the silent procession. They placed the body on the sled. It would be prepared for the ceremony. That night the San would send Storn into the void and greet the new leaders who must save them from extinction.

It was a tragic sight that filled the eyes of the new chieftains. All of the Chai who were not sick or dead had formed a procession that followed the sleds of corpses to the void. The main sled was drawn by four mantelos, the beasts were nearly dead on their feet with starvation, but they bravely pulled their burden determined to fulfil their duty to the dead chief before they themselves passed into the void. At one time a procession like this would have stretched for miles, all the people dressed in their finest clothes. The warriors and hunters carrying their weapons high and chanting a mental lament for the dead leader. Now it was pitiful, the sleds of the dead outnumbered the living mourners. There weren't enough mantelos to pull all of the sleds. Family and friends helped each other drag the burdens over the well-worn path to the land of the dead. Remruc guessed that the Chai clan that was once hundreds of thousands strong was decimated to barely three hundred starving souls.

They passed through underground chambers with passageways leading off into the inky depths. These underground roads would lead eventually to the two sister cities of the Chai. These cities were now completely deserted.

When the sickness first started refugees flocked to the city that was the stronghold of the healers. They came from all of the small outlying caverns. The story was the same - sickness, fever, death. So far there had been no cure.

The passages were now completely dark, the only light given by the torches carried by the Chai. The walls were painted black giving the illusion that you were walking through nothing. This was the void.

As they neared the pit, there were inscriptions painted in white on the walls. These varied from dots to spirals representing the stars in the night sky miles above them. They were the guardians of the world of the dead. An oppressive atmosphere descended on the sad column of people. Not a sound was uttered as they progressed to the edge of the pit. The air was stale and very cold. They rounded a corner and there before them was the doorway to the dead world.

A vast gaping chasm screamed its voiceless anger to the blank stare of the rock walls. The length of this chasm was unknown. The depth could not be perceived. It was said that a healer once cast a stone into the pit and waited for the sound of it hitting the bottom. The sound never came. If you stared at the black gaping hole then you would experience a strange swirling sensation the edges of the pit would become blurred and it would draw you into its cold embrace. This was a place of mystery, it was the window to the other world. The people of the Chai were afraid. They tried not to look directly or too long at the beckoning darkness as they slowly lined the sleds along its edge.

Lenta stood on a plinth of rock near the sheer drop. "People of the Chai. we have come here to send the dead on their journey to the void. There are some of us here who will follow soon to join our comrades. Those who wish to go with them now and spare themselves the suffering of the sickness may do so. I am a healer who has lost the ability to heal. I am defeated; I do not deserve to stay with the living. I could not even save the life of my mate. However, I cannot join Storn until I have completed my sworn task to train his son to be a master healer. So I will stay until my task is done."

Cupe stepped to Lenta's side and drew her sword, "I am a warrior who has been defeated. I could not destroy the sickness that attacked my mate. I would like to go with him into the void, but I am sworn to protect his sons and guide them in their difficult task. I must remain until I am sure that they can learn no more from me." Sadelna slowly walked forward and grasped the arms of Cupe and Lenta,

"My sisters, I am glad that you have decided to stay and I know I can trust my sons to your care. My task in this world is complete; I wish to go with Storn into the void." There was a gasp of surprise from the gathered crowd. No one had expected Sadelna to go.

Curmer, Remruc and Musi ran forward as one. "Sadelna, you must stay. Your wisdom and compassion are needed here now. Help us to make the right decisions for our people," thought Remruc. "We will be lost without you. Our grief will be too much to bear."

"My proud, brave sons," she thought gently, "you have already learned more than you know. I cannot teach or guide you anymore, my mind is empty without Storn and I long to feel his presence again. The only path left for me is to follow my mate to the dead world, please, let me go."

Musi gave Sadelna one last embrace and left the platform. Curmer and Remruc could not move. Both were struggling to control their emotions and looked at Sadelna in utter desperation. She closed her eyes and held out her arms, "people of the Chai. These are the new Chieftains. Our clan is blessed. Together the Chieftains are stronger than any other

San, they are wiser, they are braver warriors and they shine like Emur and Rume. Follow my sons, the legacy of Storn, and they will lead you to better days."

The crowd silently knelt and swore allegiance to Remruc and Curmer. The mental hail was subtly coloured by the emotions of the clan, but the strongest, brightest feeling was that of hope. With two leaders perhaps the Chai would thrive once more. The ceremony was over. Sadelna turned and closed her mind to the people of the Chai. She was dead. She walked to the sled of her mate and lay down beside him. Curmer felt his legs give way as he lost the mental touch with Sadelna. That soft murmur that had been there all his life was gone and a void took its place. Remruc grasped his brother's arm and steadied him. He too felt the bond break, but he was a warrior and not as sensitive as his brother and it hurt him less. What caused him more pain was the agony of Curmer, he sent his strength into his brother's mind and Curmer stood tall once more. They moved to the sled, one on either side and pushed it over the edge, into the void. Along the edge of the Chasm, the people of the Chai sent the bodies over the edge. Those few who chose to go with their loved ones also cast themselves into space. In silence the Chai returned to their decimated city.

Later, as the family of the Chieftains were gathered in the main chamber, Remruc and Curmer retired to one side and stood for a time in private conversation. Finally Remruc turned, "I want to call a council of all the surviving healers," Remruc looked grimly at Lenta, "I wish to know their thoughts on this plague."

Lenta bowed her acknowledgement and left the main chamber of the Chiefs quarters.

Curmer glanced at his brother, "what do you suspect?"

Remruc moved to the opening and looked out across the

silent city, "I do not believe that this plague was caused by our neighbouring tribe. In fact, I strongly suspect that they too have suffered great losses."

Curmer did not, as Remruc expected, protest to this line of thought. He was silent for a few moments considering the implication of what had been said. "If that is the case, then it is possible that every tribe of the San may have been struck. Perhaps, another of the clans has found a cure and they may help us."

Remruc looked at his brother, "do you believe that any other tribe would help its neighbour? You know our people's history as well as I do, they would be glad of the demise of a rival clan and they would claim the land as their own."

"That may have been true in the past brother, but this sickness has brought about many changes."

Remruc regarded him carefully as he spoke, "I wish I could believe what you say, but it is my belief that the San do not have compassion in their nature." Curmer's mind was coloured with outrage.

"That may be true from a warrior's point of view, but remember Remruc that I am a healer, I have witnessed the suffering caused by this plague and I believe that every healer in every clan would wish to bring an end to the sickness. I speak now as a healer and not a chieftain. I know that I would gladly give anything to find a cure. If another clan has been successful in fighting the plague then surely you can trust me when I honestly say that our healers and yes, their healers, would want to help any others who suffer, irrespective of their clan. I am not a warrior like you Remruc. I do not live to fight, I live to give life, and I do have compassion!"

Remruc slowly smiled at Curmer, "I am glad my brother that you feel so passionately about helping others, for if my reckoning is correct then the San will have to learn to work together and exchange their knowledge. Your reaction was exactly what I was looking for. I take it our senior healers would feel as strongly as you?"

Curmer nodded. "Good. For if I can motivate our people into contacting our neighbouring clans and convince them that there is no shame in asking for help then perhaps the Chai can survive. You know as well as I do, Curmer that even if the sickness was cured there are not enough of us left to re-populate our city."

Curmer swallowed hard, "are you suggesting that any survivors should seek inter-marriage with the Nemn?"

Remruc shifted in his seat, equally uncomfortable with the idea. "I'm not suggesting anything at the moment, but we may have to consider the possibilities of such an event." He stifled his brother's reply, "initially let us try to get the healers to co-operate, we will take it from there.

The first obstacle would be our own people. The warriors would do as I say Curmer, but it will be up to you to help me convince our healers. If both of these professions are on our side, then the rest of our people will follow our decision, despite their own personal beliefs."

Curmer relaxed and laughed realising that he had been skilfully manoeuvred into a line of thought that was against all of his teachings as a youngster. To ask for help from a neighbouring clan was unheard of.

The Chai were, or had been, the most powerful of the San tribes, their pride alone had prevented any outside contact so far.

Their father was very strict in his traditional duties; he obeyed his clan's laws to the letter and would have forbidden any such notions.

Storn was dead now, and it was up to Remruc and himself to save their people. Perhaps now it was time to change their ways and swallow their pride. "You will not find the council of healers so easy to convince my brother, they may not be swayed by your thoughts".

"That is what I suspected and so I will need your help. Remember what Sadelna said, 'together we are stronger than any other San and we cannot be defeated'. This, Curmer will be our first test."

The Chieftains entered the main hall of the house. It could accommodate several hundred people if need be, but now it was empty save for the few surviving healers huddled around the main podium as if afraid of the shadowy walls. "Are these all that are left of the Chai healers?" asked Remruc discreetly using a mental frequency that was used for personnel communication between Curmer and himself and well above the common speech frequency used by the Chai.

"There are some missing, probably left to tend the sick at the healer dwelling," answered Curmer.

"Show respect for the Chiefs." declared Lenta as she saw them enter. The circle of healers bowed low to the young leaders. As Remruc and Curmer seated themselves on the platform, so the circle of grave faces sat down.

"What news do you have of the sickness, Munta?" inquired Remruc politely.

"We believe that a solution may be imminent. However all we can really do is care for the ill and ease their suffering," he replied carefully. His guarded comment did not hide the feeling of hopelessness colouring his thoughts.

"Have you no opinions as to the cause?" Curmer pressed.

"The cause is common knowledge! It was sent to us by the Nemn those treacherous neighbours." Munta was unusually vehement for any of the healer ilk. They were normally of a passive and caring disposition and not normally prone to angry outbursts. The fact that strong emotions were being displayed showed the desperation amongst the healers and mirrored their feelings of inadequacy.

"Calm yourself healer Munta." Remruc spoke gently - a rare occurrence from a warrior of his ferocity, "may I ask, how the Nemn sent the sickness to us, and why?"

"By spies of course!" said Sorta, a junior healer who often came to the Chiefs abode to help Curmer with his studies. "They sent spies who poisoned our land and contaminated our supplies. That is how they must have done this terrible deed."

"If spies were sent, how would they get past the guards Remruc?" asked Curmer looking pointedly at his brother. A feeling of uneasiness rippled through the circle of healers they did not want to be witness to a confrontation between their young chiefs, it would bode ill for the Clan. Unknown to them the entire conversation had been carefully orchestrated and it would soon reach its crescendo.

"They could not. There is only one way into this city from the outside and the only other access is via the outlying cities and strongholds. All paths are carefully guarded and my men would not be fooled by a Nemn spy," he replied firmly.

"But Lord Remruc, if there is no other way that an enemy could enter our city and wreak havoc on our lives, then perhaps one of your guards was not careful enough," said Munta in a neutral tone.

"How the sickness got into the city should not be the issue!" exclaimed Sorta in exasperation, her eyes flashing in anger, "we must concentrate our efforts in curing this terrible plague."

Caught off guard and annoyed at such an outburst from her junior healer, Lenta forgot herself and quickly shot back a reply, "there is no cure Sorta, you should know that, haven't we tried everything!" There was a hushed silence as the circle of healers realised that too much had been said, aghast at her indiscretion, Lenta clenched her teeth.

Remruc regarded Curmer carefully, "did Lenta ever let on to you the extent of their worries?" he asked on their private frequency.

"Never, she was very guarded with her thoughts. Remember, I am not a fully trained healer and I was the chief's son. Perhaps she was worried that I may have passed their anxieties on to Storn. He would have been very angry and would have taken terrible revenge on both them and the Nemn." They turned to the shamefaced group seated before them.

"So," Remruc said slowly, "the master healers of the Chai cannot find a cure for this sickness. If this plague was sent by the Nemn why would they have waited so long before sending their armies to destroy the last remnants of us".

"Perhaps they are frightened that they too may catch this plague," suggested Munta tentatively. "They may be waiting till the Chai are no more".

"Why would they wish to destroy the Chai?" Remruc pressed.

"To capture our lands of course," said Lenta, glad that the subject had been changed slightly. "It is common knowledge that the Chai are... were... one of the wealthiest Clans."

"What use are lands that are infected by an incurable disease?" stated Remruc. The healers were lost for words. They had never considered this line of thought before. They had been frightened to mention any of their thoughts of the sickness to anyone outside of the healing profession. Alone they had strived to control it spreading. The warrior cast of the Chai were not normally concerned with the healers' methods or motives. Their job was to protect the Clan and make sure no intruders entered their domain. Now the warriors were angry, their pride had taken a severe blow. It was commonly believed that the Nemn had caused this plague and that meant that the guards had failed in their duty.

Even when the plague had reached epidemic proportions and it became obvious that something was very wrong, the hierarchy of warrior lords had not questioned the authority of the healers and had left them to their own devices. They had been convinced that eventually a cure would be found. Finally Storn had begun to demand results from his healers. All of the Chai, even the warriors, had feared the sickness, but they feared Storn's wrath even more. The healers therefore continued to report that a cure was imminent and a little more time was needed. They tried to play down their fears and divert Storn's thoughts of revenge for the terrible curse that was believed to have been brought on them by the Nemn. Even though the healers were angry and frustrated, they did not wish to prompt the massacre of more people.

Storn certainly would not have rested till every last Nemn was dead, and because this line of thought had occupied the minds of most of the warriors in the Chai, the healers were left in peace to strive for a cure.

Now even the warriors' authority had no bearing in the city of the Chai. The people were broken, their spirit to survive was waning, they did not care who or what had caused this sickness, they did not even want revenge any more, they only wanted it to be over and the healers could not promise them this.

"Did you know that the Nemn have had no border guards on patrol for ten journeys of our suns?" said Remruc.

"How do you know this? After all, our own borders have been unattended for so long," Munta replied.

"I know because I have seen the empty watch towers." Remruc paused as he watched the healers shocked faces at the news that their precious Chieftain had been risking life and limb on the surface of Surn. "Tonight I will take a band across the border and seek the entrance to the city of the Nemn," he continued.

There was a gasp of concern from the collected group and they consulted with each other on their own private thoughts. Finally Lenta spoke, "Lord Remruc, I ask you not to risk yourself in such folly. Our forces are not able to deal with any conflict, we will be overrun by the enemy."

"Indeed Lenta we will not," Curmer cut in, "you see I do not believe that the Nemn are the cause of our plight."

"Not the cause! What do you mean, Curmer, what do you believe?" Lenta exclaimed.

"Work it out for yourself, Lenta! Why have the Nemn not placed border patrols? Why have they not invaded our city and what could they possibly gain by poisoning the land next to theirs and so risking infecting their own people?"

She thought and conferred with her colleagues, they thought and conferred with her. Finally they came up with an answer. "The only explanation that is possible from what you say is that they too have some problems, possibly even some sickness as well."

"Exactly! That is what I have come to believe, and tonight Remruc will know for sure," Curmer smiled.

Sorta looked up, her brow furrowed with anxiety. "Lords, if the sickness was not caused by the Nemn then where did it come from?"

"That we do not know Sorta, but perhaps the healers of the Nemn do know," Curmer answered.

"The healers of the Nemn," sputtered Munta in outrage, "they know nothing! Their knowledge is inferior to ours!"

This was a reaction that Remruc and Curmer had hoped to avoid. Acting quickly and hoping that Remruc would follow his lead, Curmer spoke, "you have not found a cure Munta, perhaps they have." he snapped.

With a barely noticeable pause Remruc jumped into the argument. "Impossible, I told you this was a foolish idea! Munta is right, even if they did know they would not share their knowledge with us. After all they are only Nemn and would delight in our anguish and the suffering of our people." Both of the young Chieftains stood up facing each other, poised for a fight.

The healers were stunned. They did not like to witness a conflict between their leaders it made them uneasy. They glanced at each other unsure of what to do.

"Please Lord Remruc, that is not entirely true," said Lenta quietly. She looked to the other members of her profession for support, "any healer, from any Clan would gladly fight a sickness, even if it meant helping an enemy. Of course, the Chai are skilled in healing and if we cannot cure the plague then there is little hope of the Nemn being able to. However, we cannot bear suffering; we would even, if pressed, help a Cuc."

There was a murmur of discontent at Lenta's last claim, but the overall tone was one of approval to her statement.

"Surely you don't believe that, Lenta? No Clan would gladly help another," Remruc countered. There was an embarrassed silence and all of the healers had difficulty in meeting the Chief's eyes.

"Well if the truth be told, Lords Remruc and Curmer," Munta said in quiet tones, "it has been said that in the past there was some trading done between the healers of each of the Clans, you know an exchange of ideas such as medicines. A ridiculous idea I know, but these stories are only legend now and I suppose even a legend has some basis of fact".

Struggling to control his own feelings of disdain he continued, "perhaps considering the seriousness of the situation, we might try to revive this custom, at least for the time being." Munta leaned back apprehensively searching Remruc's face for any hint of disapproval.

Curmer spoke to Remruc on their private thoughts, "well done brother you have even managed to plant the seeds of change in old Munta's mind. I hope your gamble pays off."

Remruc gave no indication of Curmer's statement, but he nodded slowly to the healers, "you have all given me some serious thoughts on this matter. I find it hard to believe that we could ask our neighbours for help, or that they would give any willingly. I am not convinced". There was a murmur of protest and reassurances from the council, "however," Remruc stated, "if you are as convinced that it may be possible to seek help from the Nemn, as I am sure that they too are suffering from the plague, then I will try my best to help. Tonight I will take a select group of my men and enter the city of the Nemn." Remruc and Curmer rose and indicated that the meeting was at an end. They strode out of the room barely controlling the smiles on their faces.

Chapter Two

Six black shadows oozed over the night clad mountains. They paused listening. Five moved onwards slipping over the ground as silent as the darkness until they reached the safety of a rocky overhang. Remruc looked back towards the rear guard they had left behind to protect their escape route. He had merged completely with the black rock, the only sign of his existence were the two glowing blue orbs of light that were his eyes. The five continued. It was unfamiliar territory and progress was slow, each step had to be carefully planned, all minds scanned the area ahead listening for the mental murmur of a Nemn guard. There was none.

They reached the base of the watch tower for the Nemn and glanced into its hollow belly. The pitch black of the interior stank of age, the silence could be felt, like a force that crept towards them reaching out with noiseless claws, trying to capture some living souls to end its lonely vigil. The Chai shuddered.

"Carsh," Remruc whispered into his mind, "I need you to stay near here, but keep away from this tower, it has a bad feeling." Carsh did not need to acknowledge this order, he simply vanished from the group into the inky depths of the mountains. The four carried onwards. They looked for any signs that a passing Nemn may have left as they moved back and forth from the watch tower. There were faint signs that someone had been here but the tracks were very old. It was beginning to look like a hopeless task when one of the group stumbled over a water carrier lying on the ground. The noise he made, although slight, seemed like a thunder clap in the still, silent air. The group scattered instantly like grains of sand blown by a sudden gust of wind.

In the blink of an eye there was noone to be seen anywhere

near the water carrier and the air was quiet once more.

An age seemed to pass before any of the Chai reformed their group. The tracks around the water vessel were very clear, someone had either not bothered to be careful so far into their lands, or were beyond caring about the consequences. The Chai moved on with greater speed, the tracks were so obvious that they began to doubt whether they were genuine or not. Finally, as the invaders rounded a sharp turn, they saw the gaping entrance to a cave. Remruc motioned to Cupe to climb above the cave entrance, this she did with nimble ease belaying her age. She was looking for signs of boreholes, this would mean that the cave was the entrance to a dwelling and not a blind alley. None of the Chai used their telepathic communication. They were too near to the Nemn and the possibility of their being overheard by a lone Nemn guard was too great.

Cupe re-emerged behind the group and by using hand signals she explained that there were a number of boreholes in the rocks above and behind them. This meant that the cave must double back in a loop and enter a dwelling of the Nemn.

The group split into two teams, one led by Cupe slipped into the gaping hole of the cave, the other, led by Remruc clambered to the top of the rocky mound and unwrapped the ropes from around their waists. Remruc secured the metal hook into the gravelly ground and pinned it down with rocks, this also served to disguise the rope and hook. He slowly let the rope down into the borehole and bracing his back against the wall of the hole, he began to slowly 'walk' down the tube. Meanwhile Cupe and Moorker edged their way into the blackness - one on either side of the tunnel.

They came to a split in the cave, one branch veering to the right, the other to the left. They both chose the left tunnel; it would double back in the direction they had come and in the direction of the boreholes. The right must be a trap.

It took the first team about thirty minutes of climbing to reach the first bend in the borehole. By that time they had virtually run out of rope. They rested against the mirror to get their breath back. The next slope was not vertical and ran at quite a lazy angle, making it easier to climb down without ropes. Once more they descended listening all the while for any sounds that may indicate the end of the shaft. Four bends later they finally saw a glimmer at the end of the bore hole and the faint murmur of Nemn thoughts drifted towards them. Both Remruc and Garn automatically put up mental shields, to block any of their thoughts being detected by Nemn guards but still allowing them to listen in to what was being said by their neighbours. They slipped down to the very end of the ventilation shaft and crouched on the lip, just within the opening peering down into the brightly lit cave.

Although the distance to be covered by Cupe and Moorker was less, they took longer to reach the entrance to the Nemn city because of their careful, stealthy progress. It was easy enough to creep to the edge of the pool of light that indicated the entrance because of the lack of guards. Cupe was surprised at the inefficiency of their policing system and found herself thinking of the ways in which it could be improved. With their mental shields up they remained in the darkness at the edge of the light, listening to the talk between the entrance guards.

The dwelling of the Nemn was not nearly as large as that of the Chai. The Nemn still retained the ancient custom of living in tent like structures made from the hides of animals, animals that now no longer could survive on the plains of Surn. Many of the skins were very ancient and the technique of preserving hides to such perfection was a secret known only to the Nemn. The Chai, who were renowned for their beautifully woven cloths and fine garments, prized any hides that had been successfully stolen from the Nemn in raids over the centuries.

The tents themselves were no longer complete units with roofs etc, but merely complicated structures of partitions forming rooms and framing a large enclosure within each family group. They were open to the roof of the cave and as a result Remruc and Garn had a bird's eye view directly into a large family tent. It was obvious from the conversations of the inhabitants that this was a small out holding some distance away from the main Nemn city. The family that Remurc and Garn were watching were gathered in one of the sleeping chambers of the enclosure. The floor and walls of the chamber were richly decorated with furs, hides, and Cuc scales. There was a body lying on a cushion of soft fur. Whoever it was had not been long dead and the mourners were still decorating the corpse with rich gifts to take into the next world. From the conversation overheard it quickly became apparent that the Nemn were also stricken with the plague and that this was just the latest victim from this small holding, the survivors were now making plans to leave and travel to their city. From the tone of the conversation it was obvious that they had little hope of finding many survivors even there.

A strangely dressed Nemn entered the dwelling and made for the sleeping chamber. It was impossible to tell if the Nemn was male or female for the stranger was completely covered in fine skins that were so soft and flexible that they moved like woven cloth. Their head was covered with an elaborate hood and decorated with bright gemstones. When the stranger entered the dwelling all present bowed low and saluted. Once inside the chamber the newcomer removed the hood and revealed a very beautiful Nemn woman of obvious high ranking and breeding. Her reddish brown hair was swept back from her face and was decorated with strings of brightly coloured stones. On her forehead was a pendant of bright blue crystal, sparkling in unison with her dark eyes. She motioned the people present to sit and explained to them the reason for her visit.

From what Remruc and Garn could gather, she had been sent to this smallholding as a messenger from the Nemn city. She was a high ranking healer and was one of the daughters of the Nemn Chief. In soft tones she explained that she had been sent to round up all survivors of the plague and bring them back to the city. The healers of the Nemn had discovered a method of preventing the disease from spreading. It was not, she hastened to add, a cure for the sick. But, she explained, that a serum had been developed from those who had recovered from the illness and was being administered to those who still lived.

Remruc smiled grimly, this was the kind of information that he had hoped for, so far there had been no survivors in the Chai clan but this life saving serum may be the solution to the problem. With a quick gesture he motioned to Garn to move back up the ventilation shaft, he had heard enough.

It was several hours later that they rendezvoused with Cupe and Moorker and they moved off immediately, being careful not to leave any signs that they had ever been there. They travelled back to the watch tower, moving quickly and with less caution now that they knew the weakened condition of the Nemn. Carsh joined them in a state of obvious agitation. He did not explain the reason behind his nervousness because the group were maintaining mental silence. Remruc would question him later as to his odd behaviour; Carsh was a solid warrior who did not scare easily.

Once they had crossed the borders of their territory they

moved with great speed. Silence and stealth was not necessary now, but they still did not speak. They reached the rocky overhang and were stunned. There was no sign of the rearguard. The ground around the rock was badly cut up, showing signs of a struggle, a few spots of blood splashed around the area confirmed Remruc's worst fears. Instantly the group split up and hid. The listened intently for any stray thoughts by an enemy. Cupe crept forward and studied the ground, her brow furrowed in confusion. She moved outwards and searched the surrounding area, the rest of the group watching for any attack, she returned to Remruc shaking her head. He had to think quickly. Obviously the Nemn were not so helpless as he had believed. To go straight back to the Chai city would be folly, they may be followed and their guards could not withstand a full scale attack. Remruc reached a decision. They struck out and headed in the opposite direction of the main entrance running at full speed. It would be dawn soon and they had to reach safety as quickly as possible.

It was not long before they reached a cave entrance. It was more like a cleft in the rock than a real cave, but Remruc knew that it lead to a long deserted outpost of the Chai. There they could defend themselves easily if they had been followed.

It was only when they had reached the entrance platform of the old fortress and torches had been found and lit that Remruc questioned his warriors, his thoughts burning with the fury that he felt.

It was Cupe that spoke first, "Lord Remruc, I looked at the ground surrounding the rock, there were no other tracks within a considerable distance. I do not know what attacked our rearguard, but the only tracks visible were his own. I swear Remruc, I could find no other signs." Her face reflected the fear in her mind and her confusion. Remruc had never known Cupe to be either afraid or confused, he trusted her tracking abilities completely and he knew that she had been known to find signs over the bare rocks themselves. He turned to Carsh, "why were you so afraid?"

Carsh regarded them, his face grave, "I think I heard the death of Soll. He never uttered a sound, but I am sure that I heard a struggle, like rocks being kicked, but it was very faint and I could not be sure. It was then that I felt a dread, like nothing I have ever experienced; I hid in a cleft between the rocks and waited. A presence passed me, I cannot explain what, but I know that it was not a San and I know that it killed Soll".

"How could anything have passed you Carsh, there were no tracks to be found?" said Moorka, "we would have seen them on our way back."

"I do not know how it passed me, but the very air hissed as it sped by, it seemed to come from everywhere, even above."

"What do you mean above? Was it bigger than you like a Cuc?" Garn tried to control the fear that coloured his question.

"I don't know! I don't know what I mean, I just know that for the first time in my life I felt really afraid and helpless. I am sorry, but that is all I can tell you."

Remruc put his hand on Carsh's shoulder, "you have told us enough Carsh. Whatever it was has gone now and not followed us. I doubt if we will need to prepare for an attack, let us rest and eat our travel food and tonight we will go back to our homes."

The weary warriors gratefully sat down and Moorka lit a fire by the side of the platform and started to cook the combined field rations. Remruc motioned Cupe to one side and they sat in silence staring out at the old crumbling homestead lurking beyond the circle of light.

Finally Remruc spoke to Cupe alone, "if it wasn't a Nemn

attack, or a Cuc then what else could it have been? You are the oldest amongst us, Cupe, you have seen creatures that are now extinct, do you know of any that could leave no tracks?" Cupe frowned and considered carefully all of her vast knowledge of prey animals.

"Lord Remruc, I personally do not know of any living creature that could leave no tracks. There were some who knew more about the dead species than I, but all who possessed this knowledge are now themselves dead. I cannot help you, but I can advise you. There were definitely no tracks made on the ground, save those of Soll, but what if this creature did not use the ground? What if it could move through the air, that is the only way that Soll could have been taken? I think that he heard a strange sound and had crept from his hiding place to investigate, he would never think of looking towards the sky for an attack."

"You have no memory of any creatures that could move through the air, do you believe that such a thing is possible?"

"I believe, Remruc, that anything is possible," she looked at him and smiled, "even the continued existence of the San."

Remruc returned her smile at her and relaxed, if what she said was true then the Chai would just have to learn to deal with this new menace, right now they had to destroy the plague and that would be the topic of conversation for dinner. The aroma of hot food signalled the end to their private discussion and they joined the others for a welcome meal.

"So, Cupe what did you learn from the entrance guards?" asked Garn.

"Well, for a start, I learned that they are highly inefficient when it comes to guarding their tribe and outposts, but I suppose that with so little of them left it is hard to co-ordinate warriors. That much I could learn from the conversation spoken publicly. However, I noticed two of the guards move aside and change to a different level to speak, it took me a while to find the frequency and I think I only caught the tail end of the conversation. Apparently the Nemn are even worse off than us, they are only beginning to round up all survivors and take them back to the city and from what I could gather it has been a distressing task. Whole outposts and smallholdings have been entirely wiped out, but amongst some of the survivors are those who have had the plague and lived to tell the tale. This I feel is important news." The listeners all nodded in agreement. "I do not know why they are being taken back to the city, but it is so important that the Chief sent one of his own family to escort them back."

"I know we saw her", said Remruc. Cupe looked at him sharply and he quickly closed his private mind. "Anyway," she continued regarding Remruc thoughtfully, "if some have survived perhaps a cure has been found."

"It is not a cure Cupe", said Garn, "It is a..." he looked to Remruc for the explanation.

"It is a method of prevention", finished Remruc, "somehow they have found a way to stop the plague from spreading, but they cannot guarantee a cure for those who are ill."

"But surely that is all we need, a prevention," said Moorka, "if we can stop this plague from spreading and protect the survivors then we can repopulate our cities." They all agreed.

"The next problem we have to discuss is how to obtain this medicine," prompted Remruc.

"The only option open to us is to capture their city, and the only way to do that is to use the members of the outpost as guides for our warriors," suggested Garn.

"No, that would mean risking a battle and we could lose too many of our people," said Remruc.

"Then how do you propose we get what we want? Should

we just walk in and use harsh thoughts?" snapped Cupe.

"In a way yes, we will ask them to give us the medicine in return for something they value greatly", smiled Remruc. "We will take their Chief's daughter as a hostage."

There was laughter and agreement for this option and although Cupe felt that Remruc was hiding something she agreed that it would be a good plan. It all depended on speed. If they returned to their city as soon as night fell, gathered their warriors and made for the Nemn smallholding straight away, they would be able to catch the group of survivors before they had gathered all of their belongings and organised their evacuation. They settled down to rest and let the baking heat of the day pass.

Chapter Three

The rich, warm stench of rotting flesh crept around the chamber. It clung to the very walls, mixing with the aroma of excrement. There was movement at the far end as a skeletal shape uncurled itself from a raised platform and leisurely scented the air. It savored the smell of the decaying flesh on the floor and it crawled lazily across to one of the still forms. The fresh kill was not ripe enough to eat, but the San that it had found a few days earlier was just right. The flesh peeled easily from the bone and melted in the mouth. A faint sound far away alerted the creature. It listened intently for a few moments and was rewarded by a definite noise. It slipped towards the entrance of its nest and gazed with blood red eyes across its chosen domain.

Far away in the corner a bright light broke the gloom of the nest and movement disturbed the perpetual stillness of the deserted homestead. The creature's eyes burned like the fire on the platform, the hated San had dared to enter its territory. He paused and considered the new situation. There were five San on the platform, it was dangerous to tackle one live San let alone five, but if they discovered its nest then he would be killed. The creature gazed soulfully around the chamber; it was such a lovely nest, not too hot and not too cold, just right for a new generation of Cuc. Anger and hatred filled its heart. He would not be driven from this land, the San had broken the truce, they had entered the plains of Surn and now the Cuc will make them pay. He hissed his agitation, and spread his new wings. Like the Cuc from the nest he came from he had the memories of his siblings, but unlike them he had wings and could mate with a female from another nest. He wasn't a clone from the Queen Cuc and he was determined to hold his new found territory.

Carsh paused and listened, he was sure that he had heard something echoing across the deserted homestead. He glanced at the others but they seemed unconcerned and were lazing around the platform. He shrugged his shoulders, he was still jumpy. A small rock was dislodged from its place somewhere off in the distance and it skittered down a slope and came to rest at the foot of a building. The noise was like a scream in the silence of the cave. All of the San were fully alert and on their feet. Each gazed intently across the dim landscape their minds open to catch any passing thoughts. What entered their heads chilled them to the very bone. There was no real coherent pattern to the emotions that crept towards them, only a mixture of hate and aggression. A mindless form of fury with a cruel and unforgiving heart. The San closed their minds to the foul feelings and prepared themselves for battle.

"Cupe, what did you make of that?" asked Remruc.

Cupe frowned and looked thoughtful, "it felt similar to a Cuc, but different somehow. As though all of the negative traits of that race had been collected in one creature."

"I didn't know that the Cuc had any positive sides to their nature," said Remruc.

"Even the Cuc have some redeeming qualities. Not many I grant you, but you would only prompt such as strong a reaction as this if you entered a Cuc's nest..." her thoughts trailed off and she looked at Remruc with a horrified expression. "Surely they would not dare make a nest in our mountains!" she exclaimed.

Remruc grimaced. So the Cuc had decided to take advantage of the weakened state of the San. This would give him a legitimate argument for seeking help from the Nemn. In fact, it may even be useful to consider the possibility of the unification of the Nemn and the Chai survivors, to boost their numbers. Safety depended on strength of numbers.

37

Unfortunately he would have preferred a different means of persuasion. Quickly he directed the group to split into two, this they did, keeping a mental touch for instructions. There was no need to shield their thoughts from a Cuc, those creatures could only hear siblings from their own nest.

The San climbed stealthily along the tops of the crumbling dwellings. They would attack the Cuc as it crawled along the streets. In silence they formed a V formation that would drive it towards the sheer wall of the entrance platform.

He sniffed the air cautiously. The San had formed two lines and they were high up. Well, he could go higher still. The Cuc backed away from the San and climbed the rough wall of the cave. Once he had reached the curving ceiling he spread his powerful wings and dropped into the black air of the cavern. With swift beats he streaked across the ruins towards his victims. As he neared he lowered his forelegs, the single razor sharp claw arched in readiness, glinting like a giant scythe. The San did not have time to react, they were gazing down towards the ground when death swept over them, slicing through one row scattering severed bodies like sticks. The survivors closed their minds to the death cries of their comrades and leapt from the roof of the building. They instantly ran for cover, each in different directions.

In the relative safety of an old homestead Remruc assessed the situation, they had lost Cupe, Garn and Moorka, but this was no time for sorrow, their grief must wait.

Curmer paced anxiously along the platform wall. His brother should have returned by now, even if there had been trouble the rearguards of the group should have made it back. The guard group at the entrance watched him with bated breath. Curmer reached a decision, "alright, I want you to search the main pathways around the border crossing. DO NOT cross the border! Look for signs of fighting, tracks, or messages hidden along the way. You have until mid-day."

The guards sprinted eagerly down the narrow stairwell determined to find or avenge their Chief.

Curmer walked slowly back to his home, he could be of no use at the entrance, he must prepare his people for possible bad news. He searched inside himself. He knew that Remruc was still alive, he could feel that much, but he was very far away. There was no way he could touch or catch his thoughts and there was no way he could leave his people alone and chiefless to search for him. A niggling worry gnawed constantly at his stomach. Remruc was in trouble. On impulse he changed direction and headed for the main healers building. This was the busiest part of the city. The overspill of sick Chai and their relatives had occupied most of the surrounding dwellings. Everywhere you looked there were people some sitting dejected, others anxiously rushing about trying to relieve some of the suffering. Even here, in the most hopeless of atmospheres, the Chai visibly brightened when they saw their new Chief walk among them. Even in their plight he felt the greetings and wishes of good fortune to the youth on whom the weight of responsibility was almost too much to bear. Desperation welled up inside of him, he must save his people, even if, as Remruc had suggested, they must seek help from another clan. He would not let his people die. He ran up the steps to the main entrance of the healer hall, two at a time and made his way down familiar corridors to Lenta's study.

"Then you must find more volunteers to carry water, go out into the street and drag those that sit in despair to their feet. We must have water to cool the fever!" Curmer inadvertently walked in on a heated argument between Lenta and one of the junior healers he discreetly shut out any further thoughts and entered the room. The exhausted junior struggled to her feet and bowed to the Chief, she was obviously embarrassed that he may have heard the conversation. Curmer made no indication that anything was amiss and smiled at her. He knew how she must feel, a lot of the more senior healers were dead or dying and, as a result, the full responsibility for the running of the hall had been placed on the juniors. They did not have the experience to cope with such a large scale demand on their services and were rapidly falling ill themselves.

Lenta relaxed when she saw Curmer and she looked at her junior healer as if for the first time. The girl was obviously exhausted and frightened. She should not have lost her temper, but even she felt tired sometimes, "off you go and do as I have said." She spoke in gentler tones and smiled kindly. The junior gratefully exited.

"What news has Remruc brought?"

"Remruc has not returned yet."

Lenta's face grew ashen as she slowly lowered herself into the seat. She forced herself to sound calm but she could not hide the growing panic within her. "Has he sent any news?"

"No." Curmer sat down opposite her and waited.

Finally Lenta looked up, "can you hear him at all Curmer?"

"I cannot hear him, but I can feel him. He is in trouble but he is so far away and very faint."

"If you can feel him he must be somewhere near our city. That means he was not captured by the Nemn. You must send out a patrol to look for him . . ."

"I have already done so," said Curmer.

Lenta smiled, "… and we will try to contact him together."

"Will just the two of us be enough? Perhaps Musi should join us."

"No, Curmer, she is too young but you are right, we will

need three minds at least."

At that moment Sorta burst into the room,"we have lost another healer Lenta," she blurted out before noticing Curmer. She hesitated in her mind and bowed to Curmer feeling abashed that she had not checked to see if anyone else was in the room. "I am sorry Lord Curmer I had no idea that you were here."

"Perhaps in future you will check girl, before charging through a door like a Cuc," Lenta replied icily. Sorta squirmed inside. It was bad enough that she had disturbed a conversation between her superior healer and her Chief, but to be reprimanded in front of Curmer was almost too much to bear.

Curmer glanced at Lenta, he knew that she was not really angry, but it was necessary to instill good manners in all of her charges. "Now that you are here Sorta you may be of some use to us." His mellow tones eased the tension within Sorta, but she was careful to guard her thoughts should some of her inner feelings become known. "Lord Remruc has not as yet returned from his trip across the border," he continued,"and we require to locate him. You can help us call him, that is if you're not too busy?"

"I...I..." Sorta looked anxiously to Lenta for approval.

"I take it that you have been studying the technique to mind merge?" asked Lenta.

"Yes Lenta. I have practiced several times."

"Good, then you may join us. You will only be needed to strengthen the touch, Curmer will direct the proceedings. Do you understand?"

"Yes, I think so."

"It is very important that you do not interfere with the search! You could cause us to lose control."

Lenta tried desperately to control her exasperation, but she was beginning to lose her temper again.

Curmer intervened tactfully, "Sorta," he said gently, "all you have to do is give me your strength. Nothing more will be asked of you. Try not to think of anything, this will help me more than anything else. Alright?"

Sorta nodded quickly, a turmoil of emotions boiling inside of her. She desperately wanted to help Lord Curmer, but was terrified of making an awful mistake and ruining everything.

"Good, that's settled then," said Lenta brusquely, "we shall begin now."

They seated themselves in a circle and joined hands. The Chai did not need to touch each other for normal communication, but when joining minds it was better if physical contact was maintained. For the first time Sorta felt Curmer and Lenta's presence instead of just 'hearing' what was being said. She became fascinated by the distinct patterns of their consciousness. There was from Curmer a strength and resoluteness that she had not been aware of before. She also sensed his love for Remruc and the deep bond that tied them together. Lenta, she was surprised to find, had a gentleness that was not always apparent in her everyday manner.

There was a very compassionate and patient core to this woman who tried her best to appear firm and stern, as a master healer should be, but whose love for her people was unequalled among the Chai. Sorta caught herself thinking, "what must they think of me?" when Lenta's command, "be quiet girl!" flooded her mind. The thought seemed so loud, it was as though Lenta was sitting inside her head. She quickly suppressed any further meanderings and concentrated on the task ahead. She 'listened' very carefully to Curmer as he began to call for Remruc. Instinctively Lenta willed her strength to him but Sorta was inexperienced in the technique and Curmer had to draw on her mental powers. She felt as though her energy was being sapped from the extremities of her body, drawn through her mind and absorbed by Curmer. She fought down the natural panic that screamed in the back of her head as her body seemed to lose all feeling and power. Curmer sent a piercing thought along the frequency used by him and his brother. The call was amplified by the two women. A murmur of recognition reverberated back to him and he struggled to bridge the gap of distance that separated him from Remruc.

Curmer opened his eyes, but he did not see Lenta's room, instead he was looking through Remruc's eyes, out from a dark and crumbling building into a dim street. Curmer felt his stomach lurch when he saw what was lying in the street. A severed arm, sword still clutched in its hand, oozed blood into the dry dirt. It was the arm of a woman. It must belong to Cupe. Remruc deliberately scanned the whole street, allowing his brother to see their predicament. The shadowy remains of several bodies were scattered along the length of the street. Curmer's eyes were carried upwards towards a faint outline gliding through the air above his brothers hiding place. The image changed as Remruc shut his eyes and visualised their location. Curmer only managed to get a glimpse of the surrounding area before the link was broken.

When he finally focused his eyes and mind he looked with alarm towards Sorta. She had collapsed and lay sprawled on the floor. Lenta was bending over her anxiously.

"Is she alright?" he asked.

"Well she is completely exhausted and will have an excellent headache when she wakes, breaking the link so suddenly is dangerous. Here help me get her onto the sleeping platform."

Curmer lifted Sorta's light weight with ease and gently placed her on the platform. Lenta went to one of her storage bottles and prepared a pain killing draft that would ease Sorta's discomfort when she finally woke. This done she turned to Curmer, "Let's go into the other room and discuss what you saw."

She listened with grave concern to what was said. If Cupe had lost a limb then she could well be dead through shock or loss of blood. It was always better to expect the worst. "Where are they Curmer?"

"Well that is the point. The link was broken before I could get an exact location. It is definitely an old Chai settlement. I don't know precisely where, but it must be close to the border." Lenta nodded solemnly.

"We will require a map of the Chai holdings old and new. There are several stored in the guards' hall that will be of use to us. When did you tell the patrol to return?"

"They will be back by mid-day".

"Good. You go and meet the patrol at the entrance and bring them back to the guards' hall. Perhaps they will have found some clues as to where Remruc is."

Curmer turned to go, "just one more thing..." Lenta pulled Curmer back, "what was the thing in the air that you saw?"

"I have no idea Lenta, but whatever it is, it means to destroy us."

Chapter Four

Remruc reeled as the link with his brother was suddenly broken. He hoped that Curmer had managed to receive enough information to find them before it was too late. He glanced across the street to see Carsh tentatively peering upwards and edging out of the building. A hideous scream shattered the air as the winged Cuc swept down towards its intended victim.

Carsh leapt backwards trying to reach the safety of the building, but losing his footing on a loose stone he stumbled and fell. Desperately he swung his axe high, trying to ward off the dark shape plunging towards him.

The Cuc backwinged at the last possible moment, avoiding the arc of the axe. It landed next to the San, hissing its outrage and snapping at Carsh's attempts to strike a lethal blow. Carsh could not get to his feet, if he dropped his guard for a second the Cuc would have him. All he could do was parry the whipping forelegs whilst trying to crawl back through the doorway. As the creature circled round its victim it turned its back on Remruc's hiding place. Remruc seizing the opportunity sprang forward and struck at the monster. He chose his target well, the armour-plated hide of the Cuc would have deflected his blow, but the wings were fine shreds of skin and easily damaged. Another shrill scream echoed in the cavern, this time not in anger, but agony. The Cuc wheeled round to face this new source of danger giving Carsh time to crawl into the building. Remruc managed to strike a few more blows but none were more successful or damaging than his first. He too backed off into the chamber and he fervently hoped that the walls would be strong and thick enough to hold off an enraged Cuc.

The Cuc was livid. Both of the remaining San had

outwitted him, spinning wildly he tried to leap into the air to safety but the searing agony in his wing was too much to bear.

He hissed his fury, snapping his jaws and gurgling at the shadowy figures that were frustratingly out of reach, his eyes glowing red like the fire that burned in his beautiful new wing. That San had injured him deeper than the mere cut in his flesh. He felt the hatred grow within his dark heart, they had defeated him in this fight, but one battle did not win a war. He lowered his head and peered into the gloomy interior of the building. The San that had dared to strike him was backing off into a corner; he could smell the tension from its frail body.

Their eyes met and the Cuc burned his hatred into the very being of creature before him, he memorised the face, yes, he would not forget this San, he would make him pay dearly for this deed. Finally he spun round and ran swiftly along the street looking for a place to hide and review his tactics. His wing was damaged, but not permanently, if he ventured into the open air, the burning suns would cauterise the open wound within seconds. It galled him to leave his nest, driven out by the San intruders, but he had no choice. He could not fight the San effectively if he could not fly, so with furious strides and revenge already fermenting in his brain, he made his way to the borehole that he had enlarged for his entrance. He scrambled up the slope of the hole, digging his large claws into the gouged earth, hissing whenever he accidentally knocked his injured wing, which would not fold properly, against the rough wall. With every step he cursed the San and vowed he would return to drive them from this nest. It did not take him long to reach the surface and as he did a screech of pain shattered the still air as the wound sizzled and dried in the searing heat of a Surn midday. The Cuc quickly backed into the mouth of the entrance a gurgling hiss reverberating in his throat, it would not take long for the pain in his wing to pass, and then he would be able to fly again.

As he sat brooding over his predicament a hot wind swept past the hills. It came from the plains slightly to the south-east racing across the desolate lands, gathering up grains of sand and carrying them high in a dizzying dance of hot death. As it careered past the San lands sandpapering the rocks with its gritty passengers, a scent mingled with the hot particles and it brought the Cuc to immediate attention. He lifted his massive head and inhaled, strong membranes in his nostrils barred the grit from ripping joyously down his windpipe, but the hot wind insisted on burning its way to his lungs. He was rewarded with a definite perfume. Somewhere, far to the south-east was a female Cuc, and she was inviting prospective suitors to join her and start a nest.

Slowly and painfully a thought emerged in his dim brain, this process was almost alien to the Cuc, but he had already proved himself to be unusual in many other respects. He came to a decision. He would wait until his wing regained its strength and the air to cool. Then he would seek out the sender of this tempting message, but she would not find him as biddable as the other males. No. He had revenge in his heart, and he was not about to be dominated by a nest queen. She was going to be in for an unpleasant surprise. He would use her to produce a ruthless army of mindless workers, and they would be the instrument of destruction for the hated San. This line of thought surprised even him. Normally the Cuc mind was not capable of coherent planning. In the past it was only necessary to use the memories of the nest, built up through thousands of years by the experiences of the siblings. The conditions to produce male and female Cucs had not been right for several centuries, and this latest batch were surprisingly different from their predecessors.

47

Perhaps it was a mutation due to the increased radiation showered on the planet, or perhaps it was a natural step in evolution, but, whatever the cause, the Cuc were rapidly becoming a force to be reckoned with. This particular Cuc was learning fast. He would not be so easily outwitted when he next encountered the San, and he would advise his worker army of such tactics. No, he would not be defeated next time, he would destroy the hated San and the Cuc would replace them as masters of this world. He growled contentedly with himself, carefully folded his injured wing and lowered his head onto his massive forepaws. This would be the beginning of the end for the San.

Remruc and Carsh lay for a long time their breathing rapid as they listened to the diminishing sounds of the Cuc heading towards the planet's surface. Even when they were sure it was gone they remained hidden, their minds searching for the thoughts of a second creature that may be in hiding.

"Can you hear or see anything, Carsh?" Remruc asked.

"Not a thing, I think it was alone and has been frightened off."

Tentatively they crept from their hiding place and dusted the grime from their torn clothing. They viewed the scene of devastation with dismay and horror, revulsion and grief choking them. Scattered along the street were the remains of their companions. It took several minutes before either of them could bring themselves to look at each other. When they did their mutual pain did little to lessen the effects of this lightning and ruthless attack. Together, and in silence, they dragged the bodies into one of the buildings.

"We must leave them here and return to our city. We will come back with guards to bring them home tonight". Remruc tried to control his thoughts, knowing that his anger at this misfortune must be overwhelming Carsh's mind. They had lost Cupe, his mentor and probably the best tracker that the Chai had ever known. These feelings that he felt inside were stronger than the grief over the death of his father and almost as strong as the pain over the loss of his mother. Why had so many disasters followed so close to each other? What had the Chai done to deserve this?

"Lord Remruc, we cannot return tonight, we must go to the Nemn city and capture the girl." Carsh was careful to bathe his statement with neutral tones. He knew exactly how angry and distraught Remruc was over the loss of his father's mate and he did not want to provoke an outburst. It was not as though Remruc was prone to lose control of his temper, but with the present pressures placed on the young Chief it was always wise to be cautious. Remruc spun round sharply and glared at Carsh, "do you suggest we just leave them here! These are our friends, and this is my father's mate!"

Carsh stood his ground and spoke quietly, "Lord, we are the only ones left who can guide a guard patrol to the Nemn city. There are others we can send to collect the bodies. Please see reason."

Remruc's body tensed, poised to strike. He clenched his teeth and desperately fought to control this turmoil within him. It was not Carsh that he needed to strike, in a fury he stormed out of the building. He knew that Carsh was right, but it didn't take away the confused anger he felt. He lifted Moorka's axe above his head and buried it deep into the stone of a crumbling wall. "Carsh, be my witness. I swear that I will avenge this outrage and destroy all Cuc that dare to trespass the Sanlands. I will not rest till this is done."

"I understand lord. Come, we must go." Reluctantly the two warriors left their comrades and climbed slowly towards the crumbling platform. The torches and fire they had lit were almost burned out, the glowing embers casting barely enough light for them to see the doorway. Remruc gazed at the ashes within the hearth and watched fascinated as each glowing red coal finally puffed itself into oblivion, he did not see the coals dying in the fire place, but the red eyes of all the Cucs that he would destroy to avenge his patrol. Carsh pulled him gently by the arm and led him towards the doorway. Remruc looked for the last time at the dead settlement towards the temporary resting place of his friends and whispered once more his oath.

The search patrol stood dejectedly in front of Curmer, shuffling their feet in frustrated defeat. They had found tracks that had headed in to and returned from the Nemn country, that part had been easy, but what had worried and distressed them was the evidence of a struggle at one of the guard points at their border, and then nothing. One of the warriors had thought that he had seen a sign, pointing them towards the outskirts of the mountain range, but they did not have time to investigate. Curmer, however, was pleased with the results as they confirmed the rough location of his brother's group. He smiled encouragingly to the tired patrol and beckoned them to follow him at a brisk jog down the main thoroughfare of the city towards the guards' hall. Surprised Chai watched them from the doorway as they sped past, gossip as to their mission quickly passed through the crowd prompting even the most apathetic into curiosity.

They reached the large warrior dwelling, which stood as austere and grim as the warriors within. They were met by Lenta at the door and she ushered them hurriedly through the maze of corridors towards the map room. After listening intently to their report she ordered them to rest and refresh themselves with the food and drink she had thoughtfully provided.

Curmer entered the map room and scanned the cluttered interior. All around the room, on every conceivable surface, were maps of the land of the Chai. These maps, many of them etched in stone, were a detailed display of the history of the Chai, as they had spread out along the matrix of the underground caverns that riddled the mountains. Many of the settlements had been long empty, perhaps due to bad ground for growing crops, or too close to the border and attacked regularly. Even so they showed the impressive size of organisation that had once been the trademark of the Chai. On one of the few spare tables in the room, there were laid two maps. They dated back far into the Chai's history and they showed settlements that were potential sites where Remruc could be. After much 'humming' and 'hawing' as to which to search first, Lenta finally spoke,

"We will simply have to be systematic," she said, "and start at the nearest settlement." She slammed her fist down on the table, "if only Sorta had not broken the link so soon, we would have had a definite location".

"She is only young, and it was her first real mind meld. I don't think you should be so hard on her," Curmer retorted, surprised at the sharpness in his tone.

"I'm sorry, I know. It is just that I am so tired, Curmer." he put his arm around her shoulder.

"Do not worry Lenta, everything will be alright. I am sure that we will find Remruc and that he has brought us good news." Curmer tried his best to sound convincing, but deep down he felt a dreadful foreboding. They quickly drew up a plan of action and returned to the waiting guards. The men struggled to their feet as Lenta and Curmer swept out of the room determination shining in their eyes.

Curmer regarded the tired warriors before him, expectation on their faces, "I know that you are exhausted, so I will not be offended if any of you feel that you cannot go back out in search of the missing patrol. There was an instant outburst of reassurances from the guards as to their capabilities. Curmer hushed them to silence and continued, "I must warn you, they are under attack by a strange and terrible creature." There was a murmur of interest and curiosity, but not a single hint of fear from the brave band.

The patrol leader spoke for his men, "Lord Curmer, tired we may be, but warriors we are and if our Chief is in danger then we would gladly give our lives to aid him. None of us will stay behind."

Curmer felt relief and pride well up inside him, once more the Chai proved their resilience and determination to overcome all difficulties whatever the cost. He quickly filled them in on the shadow shape he had seen and also the predicament that their Chief was in. He and Lenta showed the map, and their plan of action that they had drawn up, to the quiet group.

Moving quickly and efficiently, they refreshed their equipment and water supplies, a new feeling of hope steeling their nerves for an arduous journey. Once ready they set out for the entrance platform, causing even more of a stir amongst the onlookers. A crowd had started to follow them, curiously matching the ground eating jog set by Curmer. Mental murmurs of questions and answers flashed back and forward between the guards and the crowd, but they did not reveal the danger that Remruc's party was in. When they had finally reached the platform most of the able bodied Chai had gathered around and were waiting to see what the commotion was all about.

Curmer felt more and more frustrated. He had tried his best to keep the search party quiet, but despite his best efforts it was now common knowledge that there was some problem with Remruc's patrol and they had not returned. He spent several minutes trying to sort out his guards on the platform and to keep the questioning crowd distracted.

Lenta managed to quell any immediate panic from the people and was successfully handling questions thrown at her by the inquiring people. It was while they were waiting for their clearance by the guards at the door when an alarm was raised. As they turned to see the cause of the commotion two dusty figures appeared through the doorway.

"Remruc!" Curmer could not control the relief in his mind, this quickly turned to shock as he noticed Carsh as the only other survivor. "Where are the others?" He already knew the answer before Remruc replied.

"We lost the rest of our patrol." Although Remruc's thoughts were neutral, Curmer saw the fire of pain, grief and fury burning deep in his eyes. He sent a private message of support and was surprised when his brother did not visibly relax.

"What happened Remruc?" Lenta asked gently. Remruc turned and stared at her with empty eyes and Lenta felt her blood run cold. She recognised the murderous quality of his mood and when she tried to question him privately she found that his mind was closed.

He moved to the edge of the platform and a silence fell upon the crowd. "People of the Chai. I have important news, but I will not discuss it here. I want a meeting of all the Chai, a gathering of all those who can walk. You will come to the Chief's hall, only then will I tell you of what we have seen and heard. You have one hour to spread the news." With that he motioned for Curmer to follow and strode towards their home.

Curmer sat quietly in the corner of their private quarters, arms folded and watched his brother stalk up and down the room. You did not need to be telepathic to know how furious and distressed he was.

Curmer had given up trying to speak to him and decided that it was perhaps better to let him calm down by himself, what was worrying him was the length of time it was taking his brother to control his temper.

Remruc finally stood by the window staring at the city with unseeing eyes. "How dare those filthy Cucs try to start a nest in our lands! To even have the gall to enter our mountains is bad enough, but to invade our homes is sacrilegious!" This was the latest of the many outbursts Remruc had subjected Curmer to within the last few minutes. He began to pace up and down again.

Finally Curmer broke the tense silence and speaking in deliberate tones broke into Remruc's mood. "Tell me again, did the Nemn woman say that they had really found a cure for the sickness?" Remruc stopped dead in his tracks and gaped at Curmer in amazement.

"Have you not heard what I have said? The Cucs are trying to invade our lands. We must stop them and now!" He sprang towards his brother. For a moment Curmer thought that Remruc would really strike him, but he forced himself to remain calm and motionless. He spoke in quiet tones, "tell me Remruc do you remember the last time we sat in this room and talked? You were right then to stress the most important objective for our people - to end this sickness. Even though there have been new developments, the cure for the plague is still the most important issue. You cannot think clearly until you accept the death of Cupe. I know she was your favourite, second only to Sadelna, as Lenta is my favourite, but she is gone now and we are still here. Do you think she would wish you to allow the Chai to die just to avenge her?" Curmer watched his brother carefully as his thoughts hit home.

Finally Remruc lowered himself into a chair and rested his head in his hands. "I am sorry. I miss her so much."

"We are all sorry Remruc, and we will all miss her, but let us honour her by finishing our quest. A quest that she died trying to fulfil." Curmer looked at his brother and felt frightened for him. He had never seen Remruc look so tired and vulnerable, but he knew his thoughts had not only comforted him, but had given him strength to reach a new goal.

"Ah, Curmer, where would I be without you? Your good sense has again saved the day. What Sadelna said is true, together we are stronger than any other San and together we can never be defeated." They both smiled at each other and began to discuss their plan of action.

The mood in the great hall was one of suppressed excitement and hope. The atmosphere was electric with the buzzing conversations of the Chai as they discussed the news they had been told. Remruc and Curmer had deliberately played down the attempts of a Cuc to nest in their lands and had stated only briefly the damage the Cuc had caused. They had felt it necessary though to stress that this new type of Cuc could travel through the air and that any Chai moving above ground should be wary of this new source of danger. There was no point in causing more distress than necessary to the already depressed population. The ploy worked and the Chai people paid little attention to the Cuc attack, pinning their hopes instead on the finding of a cure. It was decided that Remruc and Carsh would lead a full complement of guards into the Nemn City. They would block off the escape route to the surface with two patrols, a second patrol would descend down one of the air shafts as far back as possible, their job would be to locate any other exits and seal them. The third and main body of warriors would scatter themselves across the township and capture every Nemn they could find.

Remruc gazed with satisfaction across the vast hall, and

slowly began to relax inside. He still found it hard and sometimes frightening to think that Cupe had gone. She had taught him everything he knew, had drilled him constantly in fighting techniques, tactics and weaponry. She had always been there if he was unsure or confused, and she had always known the right course of action. Remruc searched inside himself, trying to find the main source of his distress, he knew now that he was alone. There was no one who would correct his mistakes, so he must not make any mistakes. It was difficult to face this, especially as he had now so much more responsibility, but, the thought comforted him, he had Curmer, his quiet counterpart. He realised that if at all unsure, he could turn to Curmer and that between them they would solve all problems. No, Remruc corrected himself, he was not alone, Curmer would always stand beside him. His eyes refocused on the crowd before him, their faces reflecting the mood of their thoughts. Even the hall itself seemed brighter somehow, the stones happily absorbing the atmosphere, retaining the feelings washing over them and radiating their own joy. It was filled from wall to wall by the Chai people, such a sight had not been seen for a long time.

The air was alive with active, energetic thoughts as each Chai enthusiastically discussed and planned the night's events. He glanced towards Musi and she rewarded him with a radiant smile. Remruc seemed to look at her with new eyes, and was surprised with what he saw, a young and beautiful lady, dressed in her finest gown, that, although sparsely decorated, was cut from the finest cloth into a simple and flattering shape, with a colour that complimented her fair skin. "She is growing up," he thought, "and into a beautiful Chai woman. I will make sure that she will have a future to look forward to and a mate to set up her own holding with." Curmer watched him, a smile playing on his lips. This was

Remruc in his element.

He could sense a change in his brother, a strength not physical, but in character had evolved and Curmer was glad and relieved. Remruc he knew would prove to be a powerful leader, controlling and directing his peoples thoughts and giving them hope and life for a better future. Remruc turned towards his brother, sensing his thoughts, his eyes flashed determination and gratitude for Curmer and he motioned him to his side. Together the Chiefs rose and silence descended.

"People of the Chai," they said in unison, "wish us success in our mission and we swear we will give you life!" They were almost knocked senseless by the tumultuous wave of cheering that flooded their minds. Grinning from ear to ear they saluted their people, grateful for their overwhelming support. Curmer's eyes fell on Sorta whose laughing face was suddenly lowered and embarrassment flushed her cheeks. Curmer noticed her plain and poor quality clothing and was shocked to realise that this poor girl had probably not even managed to change from her work clothes as she busily tried to keep the main healer hall in some sort of organisation. He made a mental note to speak to Lenta about giving her at least some time to rest. He would make the excuse that he needed to catch up on some studying, and that Sorta would be the best candidate to ensure his diligence. Curmer smiled inwardly, yes, that is what he would say, he would be glad of Sorta's company. He frowned at his feelings in puzzlement, but was instantly distracted as the crowd parted to allow them to lead the masses out towards the entrance and on to victory.

Every warrior left alive in the Chai clan was needed for the sortie. They were assembled en masse beneath the platform, armed to the teeth, they looked a daunting sight.

Remruc and Carsh inspected their troops, all wore protective clothing not only from the suns, but from potential resistance from Nemn guards.

The armour was lightweight, but tough, Cuc scales, shaved down to be almost transparent, they were fitted close to the body in sections. An overlay of black clothing provided invisibility for the night, and dark tunnels of the Nemn and each section wore face masks that were carved in the Chai style, with inlays of coloured metal to differentiate each section and individual.

Once satisfied with their warriors, Remruc issued final instructions then ascended the steep stairs to the entrance. It took a substantial amount of time for the full complement of warriors to leave the city as they had to descend into the tunnel in single file. By the time they reached the open air it was already evening. The party split into three sections and made off, there was no need to be cautious of Nemn guards, but each Chai kept a wary eye on the skies above. It did not take long to reach the Nemn holding, and each group was aware of their individual mission and they melted into their prospective positions and awaited the signal to attack. Each section leader remained in mental touch, they knew that the Nemn would not be able to hear them at this range. Once satisfied that each group was ready Remruc sent the word for the attack and with lightening speed the Chai stormed the Nemn holding.

All of the survivors of the Nemn holding were gathered in their main square. They listened carefully and with growing hope to their Chief's daughter as she explained the route they would take to the main campground of their people. Although the Nemn lived below ground, they still used ancient terms that had originated on the open lands of Surn. They had never quite converted to a settled way of life, and were prone to up camp and move to a different subterranean cave on the spur of the moment. They stood in the center square, their clothes of fine hides in bright colours giving a kaleidoscope display of culture.

They were excited not only by the news of the new medicine, but by the news that they would be going on the surface for part of the journey, this was a danger that their people had not experienced since the start of the sickness. It would be stimulating to feel the open air around them once more. Although this journey would be done in the hours of darkness, the real thrill lay behind the fear that winged Cucs once more darkened the sky of their world. The Nemn were renowned for their stringent maintenance of history and culture. They constantly told tales of ancient deeds, and species of animals that no longer existed. They also had a rare collection of the hides of these winged Cuc, preserved and displayed at the main camp, the Nemn were the only ones who realised the true significance of these evil creatures and were terrified of what could happen. They knew that the Cuc were on the move again, and this time the San were in no fit state to ward them off.

The people gathered up their belongings. Most of them carried prized hides and gemstones, possessions that were far too valuable to leave behind, even if they were planning to return later to this cave. Every tent had been dismantled and reformed into travois like structures. These were laden with the belongings of the Nemn. The Chief's daughter had done her best to dissuade them from carrying so many goods, especially as they would be required to go above ground, and rough going at that, but they would not listen. For all of them, these goods represented a past heritage that must be maintained and treasured at all costs. Frustrated that her advice fell on closed minds, she had reluctantly conceded to the bulky travois.

After what seemed like an age, the Nemn people were

ready to move off.

There was much bustling as they jockeyed for the best position in the procession, but it was as they turned to leave their cavern that an alarm was raised at the main entrance.

Within minutes their guards appeared, running full pelt, some of them wounded and helped by their fellows. They managed to blurt out that a full scale attack had been sprung on them and they could not hold the heavily armed and ferocious Chai. The Nemn people panicked. They dropped their travois and grabbed their back packs. Turning in the opposite direction they tried to make for one of the emergency exits, but to their dismay another mass of Chai warriors were charging towards them. Suddenly the air was full of their enemies, as they descended from the ventilation shafts swinging quickly down ropes and joining others already on the ground. The Nemn were paralyzed with fear. They were completely surrounded and unarmed. They cowered over their belongings as they were encircled by their old enemies. They expected no mercy, but hoped for a swift and as painless a death as possible. Slowly the realisation dawned on them that they were not being slaughtered but instead the Chai warriors were watching them carefully. One by one the Nemn got to their feet and gazed at the faces of an enemy that had been feared for generations. One of the Chai stepped forward, he was of high rank judging by the design on his face mask and the Nemn took this as a signal for the killing to begin.

"Stop! We are unarmed! Take our goods and leave us in peace." The Chief's daughter leapt forward blocking Remruc's path. As the daughter of the Chief, she must accept full responsibility for her people. Remruc stood where he was and gazed at this woman in front of him. She was breathtakingly beautiful. He had not had the opportunity to study her face in detail before but now here she was, her head held high and her eyes sparkling with a mixture of defiance and fear. Her hair reminded him of the reddish brown mountains of the San, her skin of fine silky cloth, pale almost translucent quality, but it was her eyes that moved his heart. They gleamed like the night sky of Surn a cool but comforting violet-blue and framed with long dark lashes. Not only was she beautiful, but she was brave to stand unarmed and try to block his path.

"We mean you no harm," he answered once he had finally got his emotions firmly under control.

At first his statement did not seem to sink in, the Nemn woman continued with her pleading. "There is no need to kill us, we will not stop you from taking what you want, please leave us alone..." she hesitated mid-thought, "did you say you mean us no harm?" Her brow wrinkled in confusion.

"That is correct. I only wish to speak to you."

Taken aback by this unusual situation she was not quick enough to control her fiery temper, "Do you always speak to people while holding a sword at their throats? I would have expected better manners, even from a Chai." Her mood changed as her aristocratic breeding took over, she was outraged by this unwarranted attack on her people and this quelled her fear faster than any reassurances. Perhaps there was a chance she could talk herself and her people out of certain death. She must be strong and show her authority. "Have you any idea who you are talking to?"

"Ah yes, I believe I do my lady." Remruc performed a graceful bow. "I know you are the first daughter to the Chief of the Nemn. Unfortunately I do not know your name?"

She felt herself bristle at this oh so charming Chai. How could he possibly know who she was? Unless, of course, they had been spying on her people since her arrival. Her fury rose at this thought, "my name is of no importance to you. I will speak only to your Chief, not to some common warrior and spy." She instantly regretted her outburst as the surrounding army moved forward quickly at her insults, anger in their thoughts. Whoever this commander was he certainly had the respect of his troops.

Remruc raised his arm and calmed his soldiers, a smile was playing on his lips, he liked this Nemn woman despite her arrogance. He removed his mask and gave her an equally arrogant stare, "if you will not tell me your name then I will be forced to refer to you as woman."

This time it was the turn of the Nemn to be outraged and regardless of their situation they advanced on Remruc.

"You cannot speak to the lady Eriya in such a manner. It would be unforgivable!" an older woman piped up.

"My apologies Eriya." Remruc bowed once more.

"LADY Eriya if you please!" she retorted her fury barely controlled, she flashed a glowering look towards the woman who had given her name away and regarded this Chai coldly. He was of a high status within his clan, she could tell by his manners and attitude. He was obviously used to being obeyed, especially by women. Well, she would not be a simpering wench to run to his beck and call. He may be handsome but she would teach him that the Nemn women were stronger.

Remruc laughed and nodded. This infuriated Eriya even more, how dare he treat her so flippantly! She clenched her jaw and glowered at this arrogant Chai. He signalled to two of his warriors and they singled out two Nemn soldiers and dragged them forward.

"I take it that you two can find your way back to your main city?" The frightened guards nodded frantically.

"Good. I want you to give this message to your Chief. Tell him his daughter is enjoying the hospitality of the Chai and that there are some matters that we feel should be discussed.

Do you understand?" Again the guards nodded. The crowd of Nemn looked at each other nervously. Why were they being taken to the Chai's city? What will happen to them once they were there? They looked to the Lady Eriya for direction. Eriya quickly assessed the situation. If they were taken to the Chai city then they would be enslaved not slaughtered. If they chose to fight here they would definitely die. At least while they were still alive they had hope. She regarded this officer in front of her coolly. Her people would show no fear.

The Chai could not possibly know how little of the Nemn remained. She knew her father could not send warriors to attack the Chai and free them, her only option was a negotiated release and she could do this better if they co-operated with the Chai for the moment.

"My people will go with you Chai, but do not think that we will tolerate any abuse. We would surely die before such an insult."

Remruc looked approvingly at Eriya, she had conducted herself well. He motioned to the Nemn to gather up their belongings and escorted by his warriors they made their way back to the Chai city.

Chapter Five

It took the mass of San the rest of the night to complete the journey across the rough terrain and down through the dark Chai tunnels. They had extreme difficulty in negotiating the narrow staircase at the entrance to the Chai city and there was much discussion as how best to move their burdens. They dismantled the travois and carried each item up the steps in single file. Eriya could not understand why the Chai were taking so much trouble to ensure that her people did not lose any of their personal belongings.

From early childhood she had been conditioned to believe, through stories and teaching hides, that the Chai were ruthless killers, who would stop at nothing to get what they wanted. Her imagination had been fired by stories of old warriors who had participated in raids and skirmishes with the Chai and they told of the ferocity of these warriors in battle. The sight of a Chai could send fear into the heart of the best Nemn hunter, it had even been said that the Chai lived in stone chambers because the heart of a Chai was also made of stone and knew no mercy. No Nemn warrior had ever seen a Chai city, the farthest they had ever reached were small outholdings close to the border, so Eriya's imagination had run riot as she pictured the kind of world in which her enemies lived, but even her vivid imagination did not prepare her for the sight that lay before her eyes as she stepped out onto the platform. The shapes and colours of the city that spanned out across this vast cavern destroyed the cold grey image in her mind. Graceful structures weaved their way almost as far as the eye could see, dipping and merging in a kaleidoscope of colours. Here was something of such awe-inspiring beauty that she was almost glad that she had been taken prisoner, even if she were to lose her life she would be grateful to have glimpsed this spectacle. Eriya regarded the Chai warriors around her.

To construct such a thing of wondrous beauty required a sensitivity of spirit and nature that was contradictory to all she had been taught. Perhaps the Chai were not as cold as they appeared? Perhaps they could be swayed to consider compassion? As she turned once more to admire the spectacle, a deepening realisation crept into her mind. There was something very wrong with this city, but what? A feeling of terrible sadness washed over her consciousness. As she looked across the cavern she realised what was wrong. This wonderful, beautiful city that spoke so much of life and joy was almost completely empty. Where were the crowds of people to greet the returning raiding party? A thought came to mind almost unbidden. Could the Chai also have the sickness? She did not have time to dwell on this notion as the guards began to move the group of Nemn down into the labyrinth of wondrous structures.

Throughout the journey along the streets, the party were joined by more and more Chai. At first the Nemn bowed their heads, ready to shut out the expected ridicules and oaths, but slowly they realised that the Chai were not regarding them with disdain or hatred, but with respect that carried an undercurrent of hope. It was as if the Chai were welcoming them tentatively as friends and were inviting them to stay. This was very confusing for the Nemn. They had been brought up to mistrust anyone outside their tribe, and more especially to fear their neighbouring clans. The Chai had the dubious reputation of being the most viscous and warlike of the San, and the sight of a Chai warrior would strike terror into many of the Nemn. To see them like this was contradictory to all they had been taught. Suddenly, they came to the end of their journey. They passed through a large gateway which opened out into a cavern that was as big, if not bigger than the first. At first the Nemn were completely disorientated, for they felt as though they had stepped out onto the surface of the planet. There was even the faint glowing light of a Surn dawn, as another baking day began on the surface. Eriya gazed into the distance and could make out faintly on the horizon the far wall of the cave, but what impressed her more was the feeling of space. There was not a building in sight, instead there were the remains of crops arranged in neat rows and stretching from wall to wall of this extraordinary structure. Looking up, Eriya saw the source of the light. The surface of the roof was a honeycomb of boreholes that shed rays of cool sunshine into the farthest corners.

"You may set up your camp here and rest a while," said Remruc. "Guards will come to collect you and your escort at midday my Lady Eriya and bring you to a gathering of our councils. Perhaps you will be good enough to grace our Chief with your sparkling conversation."

Eriya scowled at the Chai commander. Why did he irritate her so much? It was not his manners, for he was very courteous, he simply managed to sound as though he was mocking her and this bruised her ego as surely as a blow would bruise her face. The Chai guards left them standing in the dust of a field and made their way out of the cavern. A compliment remained at the gate to deter anyone trying to leave or enter. The people of the Chai were curious about the Nemn and quite a large crowd hovered around the entrance watching the strangers. Eriya turned around irritably. This would never do. To be stared at in such a manner was most embarrassing. Directing her people into groups, the Nemn quickly cleared the dusty ground of debris and lay down tough Cuc hides as flooring. As the tents went up there were murmurs of amazement at the variety of brightly coloured hides.

Once the tents had been erected and there was a suitable degree of privacy available for the Nemn, Eriya called the elders to a meeting within her quarters.

Seated on a fur covered cushion, she surveyed the frightened people before her. "I suggest we try to find a solution to our predicament as quickly as possible," she said. "do any of you have any idea as to why we are here?" They looked at one another blankly.

Finally an old woman spoke up, "Lady Eriya, I think that we are going to be enslaved and forced to work for the Chai."

Eriya smiled a humourless smile. "That much is obvious. What we must consider is why the Chai require slaves. Have you noticed how empty this city is, and the feeling of despair among its people? I ask you to consider that perhaps the Chai have also had this sickness and they too are depleted in numbers." Each of the Nemn mulled this suggestion over at an irritatingly slow rate. Eriya could barely contain her impatience and she stared at the floor idly plucking at the fur blanket beneath her.

The old woman watched her with growing concern, finally she could remain silent no longer, "Lady Eriya, please! That is a very valuable fur stole, do not pick it bare."

Eriya stared at her dumbfounded then slowly and carefully smoothed the hair back into place laughing in a harsh tone, "I must apologise for damaging your property. You obviously regard it with high esteem, but I wonder how much longer it will be in your possession." She allowed the tone of her reply to rise to caustic sarcasm on her last comment. The woman was suitably abashed at her remark. Eriya had finally brought home to them the real priorities involved in their predicament. The other elders began to feel panic rise within them, what were they going to do? Eriya sensed the mood of her people and quickly raised her hands, "this is what I believe has happened," her cool voice calmed the group. "Somehow the Chai have discovered the medicine we have made. I think that they want to force the secret out of us and then enslave the rest of our people. It would be typical of the Chai to think that they can steal our cure. Rest assured, I will die before our secret is forced from me. If they want our medicine, then they will have to pay a suitable price."

"What do you mean Lady Eriya?" an elder asked.

"I mean we can use the cure as a bargaining tool for our release and the safety of our people."

"How can you be so sure that it is the medicine that they want?" the old woman retorted.

"Why else would they keep us alive? It would have been much easier to kill us all and simply take our belongings." Eriya saw with satisfaction the grim faces of her people as they considered her logical answer. Perhaps now they would be motivated to help her fight for their release. She looked around the tent at the carefully displayed hides. Was this what her people had become? Vain and material shells of the once proud and strong hunting clan. If they had to give up all of their wealth to save their lives would they do it? It was once said that the Nemn lived for their possessions and trinkets. She had not believed this until now. Looking back at the faces in front of her she saw her answer. From deep within themselves, the Nemn elders had drawn upon a strength and resolve that had not been needed for many years. They would stand by her, Eriya knew that for certain, and yes, if it was necessary, they would give up everything to save their people. She felt herself relax inside. That was one battle won. Now she had to face an even more daunting foe - the Chai Chief.

At midday a section of Chai warriors entered the

encampment. Eriya was waiting for them alone. She knew it would be better for her to show her strength by facing this Chief singlehanded. She had deliberately chosen a soft hide dress that flowed in graceful folds down to her feet. It clung to her slender frame in all the right places and was a deep and shining copper that flattered her complexion. It was decorated in suitable Nemn fashion with gemstones set in intricate designs. The effect was stunning and Eriya noticed with satisfaction the approving looks of the Chai guards. They had never seen any garment as richly decorated before. She was surprised to see that the commander was not among them, "perhaps he has gone to mock someone else," she thought to herself. Smoothing the folds of her skirt deliberately down her legs she followed her escort out of the encampment. Eriya knew that she was a beautiful woman and despite her pride she would, if the worst came to the worst, use herself as a bargaining tool to free her people.

It was a long journey to the Chieftain's house and throughout the walk Eriya noticed how empty the city was. Those few Chai that she saw observed her with the same awe and approval that the warriors had given her earlier. This encouraged her, she may well be able to use her charms to good effect on the Chai leader, but when she saw the enormous building of the Chai Chief loom before her all of her confidence drained from her mind. If the Chief was as daunting and impressive as the home he lived in then this was going to be a difficult task. She lowered her head and steeled herself for what she expected to be an arduous fight.

She was led along a confusing number of corridors that seemed to meander at will within the large structure. What struck Eriya was the lack of decoration within the building. Growing up as she had, constantly surrounded with wondrous artifacts, this spacious, bare interior was alien to her. As their journey progressed she began to notice how the stone had been fashioned and polished to show its natural grain and colour, with new eyes she saw the true beauty of the building. The Chai valued the simplistic nature of the rock itself, utilising the colours and flow of the stone and merging them into a dizzying display of shape and texture. She resisted the impulse to reach out and touch the cool walls, clasping her hands in front of her instead. Every so often they passed an alcove; displayed within these were life size figures of past Chiefs. There was something oddly familiar about the features of some of the Chiefs, but she couldn't quite place the niggling feeling. The doors of the main audience hall swept open to reveal a brightly lit aisle gouging a path between the pillars of a large and shadowy room. Her footfalls echoed back towards her, following her progress with empty steps, as she made her way to the end of the room. Seated before her in a semicircle were the Chai elders. Each was the leader of a service or industry in Chai society, and it surprised her to see how young some of them were. "Surely they were not the only ones left in their trade who could replace dead leaders?" she thought to herself. Her eyes moved to the dias in the centre of the semicircle. On its surface were two chairs. Eriya puzzled over this, but she soon discovered the reason.

"Stand and show respect for the Chiefs," commanded Lenta.

Eriya automatically performed a low bow, deftly flipping the folds of her dress out with a swish. A dance of colour was performed by the gemstones as they sparkled in the torchlight. She was so engrossed in her tactic of dazzling the Chief with her rich clothing that she did not see him enter.

She barely disguised her shock when she finally looked up and saw standing before her not one, but two versions of the irritating commander. They sat down and the council followed suit. "I must remain standing it seems," mused Eriya to herself. She looked closer at the spectacle before her. The Chiefs appeared to be physically identical, but there was a definite difference in their minds. She recognised instantly the aggravating arrogance of one, but the other was much different, more subtle, gentle and deeper thinking but with a similar edge to his character as the first.

"So, I see that not only do I need to put up with your comments, but they will be in duplicate from your brother. At least I assume that you are brothers? The Chai are indeed fortunate to be blessed with twin Chiefs." Eriya stared defiantly at Remruc and he, irritatingly, smiled back.

"I see your rest has not sweetened your tongue Lady Eriya. I feel I should remind you of your predicament and that you are speaking to Chieftains, perhaps it would be prudent to remember your manners, after all it is something for which the Nemn are known to be so proud." Remruc sent a personnel message to his brother, "I told you she was proud. It may be difficult to persuade her to help us, but I am sure her father will see sense, in the meantime if we cannot convince her then we must keep her out of harm's way."

"I agree with you brother, but you seem to be able to aggravate her in the extreme, perhaps if I try to talk to her she will listen."

"Feel free, Curmer, and good luck."

Remruc regarded the woman in front of him. She had obviously taken great care in choosing her outfit, he had never seen anything quite like it. "It may impress another Nemn," he thought, "but a Chai will look deeper than clothing to find what he likes." She was still fuming over his last remark, and knowing his brother's skill with words, he was going to enjoy the next few minutes.

"Lady Eriya, please do not think badly of my brother, he is

71

a warrior and so is used to direct thought. I must apologise for his not introducing us, my name is Curmer and this is Remruc. We are the leaders of the Chai." Curmer flashed a winning smile at Eriya, and she relaxed slightly.

"I accept your apology Lord Curmer, and I understand what you mean about the warrior mentality." She threw a sidelong glance at Remruc and smiled to Curmer.

This time it was Remruc's turn to be annoyed. At that moment he could have quite happily throttled the arrogant little upstart.

"Patience brother, do not let her provoke you," Curmer murmured to his brother, "she is going to be a difficult one to handle."

Curmer decided that flattery would be the way round Eriya. She was beautiful but arrogant and this was her weak spot. At the moment Remruc's stronger nature was only making her angry, he would therefore need to move carefully and keep her in an open frame of mind. He indicated that a chair be given to Eriya and he motioned for her to sit.

"My lady Eriya, I feel that I must put your fears to rest. No Chai will harm either yourself or your people. Please believe us when we say that we wish to end all conflict between our clans. In fact, we respectively request your aid in a matter of great concern." The Chai council visibly flinched at this remark, and healer Munta pointedly cleared his throat.

Eriya considered carefully what had not been said. The Chai must indeed be desperate if they needed the help of her people, however, she would not give her help for nothing and despite what Curmer had said she was not entirely convinced of their good intentions. She feigned ignorance and asked the obvious question, "what is this matter of great concern that has caused you to terrorise and drag my people by force into your city?"

Curmer ignored the acidity in her question and looked at her solemnly. "My lady Eriya, the Nemn are not the only clan of the San that have succumbed to the sickness. Our people are dying and our healers are at their wits end. We know that you have developed a method to prevent the spread of the disease, we need your help and expertise. Please work with our healers and save our people." Eriya studied the face of Curmer, she knew that he spoke the truth, and she knew he was desperate. It was apparent from the moods colouring his thoughts that he was deeply distressed, perhaps he too was a healer, or was training to become one.

"Tell me Lord Curmer, how can I believe what you say when we are held prisoner against our will. You have armed guards watching us. My people are terrified, but if you swear on your life that you will let us go then perhaps we will help you. The choice is yours let us go or lose our help." Eriya swallowed the fear inside her, this statement could provoke the Chai to kill her where she stood.

Remruc sprang to his feet, his face suitably outraged, "Let them go! We do not need the help of snivelling, terrified weaklings. They do not even have the strength of character to face a Chai on equal terms, but only if they are hiding in their holes!"

Eriya was infuriated and losing her decorum for a moment, she leapt onto the platform and stood face to face with the formidable figure of Remruc.

"You have the gall to call us weaklings! What right do you have to imprison my people, I am not afraid of you Remruc."

"LORD Remruc if you please LADY Eriya! If you and your people are so brave, why will they not stay here and work side by side with the Chai?"

"THAT IS ENOUGH!" Curmer stood between the two battling figures. "Lady Eriya won't you please sit down. Lord

Remruc, your chair." He looked pointedly at his brother. Still glowering at each other Eriya and Remruc sat down again. "Now that we have managed to calm down let us continue with our discussion."

Eriya was not satisfied. "Lord Curmer, if you allow all of my people to return to our land then we shall send some of our healers back to help you."

"That is not good enough!" said Remruc, "We know that you would not return. Your people would disappear into your mountains, we would never be able to find you again."

"I will give you my word that we would return." replied Eriya, her mind barely controlling her fury. "Or is that not good enough either!"

"Lady Eriya," healer Munta rose from his seat, "please... we desperately need your help. We cannot wait any longer, our people cry out in anguish and we as healers have failed in our duties. I beg you to reconsider our proposal." His old eyes reflected the pain he felt.

Still furious with Remruc's slanderous remarks, Eriya's smouldering reply sizzled its way across their minds, "I am not satisfied with your demands, however, I will discuss them with the elders of my people. Now if you would be so kind as to escort me back to the cavern, or do you intend to murder me where I stand?"

Realising that there could be no more reasoning with Eriya, Curmer stood and motioned to Remurc to do likewise, "Thank you Remruc," was his caustic thought, "I asked you to keep quiet but no, you had to butt in with your insults."

"She is an arrogant woman, Curmer. She would not respect us if we grovelled and begged in the dirt, we must have her respect before she will offer us her help. Trust me I know what I am doing."

Remruc smiled at Curmer's grunt at his comment,

motioning to his guards and trying to ignore the angry glances of the other elders, he spoke to his loyal troops privately. "Take Lady Eriya back to the caverns, but this time take a different route." He was very careful in his instructions to his guards, Eriya must not suspect a thing. Healer Munta drifted towards him, intrigued. On seeing him approach he decided to include him in this little plan, he could be very useful in persuading this contrary maid.

Without warning, the guards unceremoniously took Eriya by the arms and pulled her towards the door. She struggled to free herself, suddenly very afraid that she may have pushed the Chai too far with her manner and that they really were going to kill her.

"Guards! Please!" cried healer Munta, "remember that she is a Chieftain's daughter and deserves more respect."

Eriya looked towards the elderly man grateful for his interference and relieved somewhat when she was immediately released. Curmer and Remruc left the room as suddenly as they had entered, not even, much to her annoyance, giving Eriya a second glance.

"Lady Eriya," healer Munta continued, "I will escort you back to your people and ensure that you receive the treatment befitting your status." He bowed courteously and she nodded her acceptance, nervously watching the guards out of the corner of her eye.

They emerged from the Chieftain's building from a different entrance and it took Eriya a few minutes to get her bearings. There was total silence from the buildings surrounding her, their empty windows gazing sadly at the deserted street. They walked slowly along the smooth walkway, the beautiful polished marble of the pavement a joy to behold. It was upsetting for Eriya to see so many empty homes, to think of the people that had once lived there and to wonder as to their fate. Had they survived the plague? Or, as most of her own people, had they succumbed to starvation.

Munta watched her carefully. He sensed that this young girl had integrity as well as a fiery temper. Lord Remruc was taking a chance that her heart could be moved to pity and it was up to him to try to push her into that vein before it was too late. Gathering his thoughts he politely inquired, "I trust that you have not been too upset by our young Chieftains?"

Eriya bristled slightly at the memory of her encounter, but she replied, "I will survive their insults I am sure."

"They had no wish to insult you Lady Eriya, they are just, well, eager to win your trust."

On sensing her neutrality to his line of thought, Munta changed tactics. "Do you like the Chai buildings? This is perhaps one of the best areas of our city, the rock has many different hues and grain, don't you agree?"

Momentarily knocked off guard by this question, Eriya looked around in wonder at the enormous buildings reaching to the roof of the cavern. "Have these dwellings ever been filled with people?" she said almost to herself.

"Filled? Oh yes Lady Eriya, filled to the brim and overflowing once, but not now I am afraid and perhaps never again."

The pain in his last comment caused Eriya to look at him sharply and there in the lined face she saw a weariness shadowed by a terrible, terrible grief. Quickly she looked away and lightly replied,

"Are we nearly back at the cavern yet?"

"Not far now Lady Eriya, just past the healer halls and on for about one sharr," replied one of the guards.

It was as they approached the healer hall that Eriya began to understand the full impact of the plague on the Chai. The remaining members of the clan occupied all of the buildings surrounding the halls, but they were a sorry sight. Dejected they sat in huddled groups, waiting to fall ill with the plague, hoping only for a quick ending to their misery. Even the sight of the strangely dressed woman did little to rouse them from their apathy. A young healer stumbled down the steps of the building carrying a water canister, she was thin and weak, the fever of the plague beginning to moisten her brow as she staggered past them intent on completing her duties. As they passed her she swayed slowly and collapsed, one of the guards dropping his axe as he caught her before she hit the ground.

Forgetting herself Eriya rushed to her side and dampened the hem of her gown with the water. She gently mopped the brow of the young girl and looked on her piteously thin face as she moistened the parched lips.

The guard carefully lifted the girl and carried her up the steps to the healer hall, his face grim with the knowledge that there was little anyone could do for her. Eriya stood slowly and looked around her, the commotion had gone unnoticed by the mass of people and she realised that this was an all too familiar sight to the Chai.

Eriya relented. She understood how difficult it was for the Chai to admit defeat and how desperate they must be to resort to seeking help from a neighbouring clan. She knew now that the Nemn must help these people, it was time that their healers worked together to rid themselves of this terrible curse. Eriya also knew something that the Chai did not. There were not enough Nemn left to survive as a clan for any length of time, for her people the medicine had been discovered too late. It was obvious that there were many more Chai still alive, if she could save their lives then perhaps she could also persuade the Chai to allow the Nemn to live with them, to gain their protection and so ensure their survival.

Eriya studied the ground in front of her a frown upon her face. She must be very careful. It must have been a terrible humiliation for the Chai healers to resort to this, if she seemed arrogant or boastful she may provoke them, as she had done Remruc, beyond the point of control and that would be disastrous for not only the Nemn, but the Chai themselves. Munta stood with bated breath as he watched Eriya gather her thoughts. Finally she spoke.

"This is indeed a most distressing sight healer Munta, I understand now why you would wish the help of the Nemn, but, the healers of the Chai have the distinguished reputation of being the most skilled, diligent and resourceful of all the San. I am most surprised that you have not developed a similar medicine. Perhaps it was due to an overtaxing of your resources that has prevented you from examining the survivors of the plague. If you had, then you would have surely developed the serum from their blood." She paused and looked towards the old man his mind was still tinged sorrow at the sight around him but he was smiling at her gratefully.

"My Lady Eriya, you have chosen your thoughts carefully and well, it does you credit. Not only have you politely given us the answer that we seek, but you have strived to restore our self esteem and for that I thank you. I must confess that I was initially opposed to this line of action by our Chiefs, but having seen for myself your integrity, manners and bravery I am glad that Lord Remruc and Curmer persisted. It also saddens me to inform you lady Eriya, that we did not examine any survivors of the plague because there have been no survivors among the Chai."

Eriya stared at Munta in horrified disbelief. It was true that her people had been virtually wiped out by the plague, but they were not numerous to begin with. Proportionally there had been more survivors than deaths caused by this sickness.

What they had found was that more of their people had died of starvation because they were too weak to tend their crops. It was then that the sheer devastation of the Chai was brought home to her. These people had faced a horrifying sickness, they had fought with all of their knowledge to survive, but they had not even been comforted by the fact that there was hope and that their loved ones could live. It must have been similar to standing alone and throwing stones at a mass of Cucs charging down upon you, trying to stop them, but knowing that you will be killed. Her respect for the Chai was firmly founded.

She would not let this brave people be defeated after what must have been a long hard fight.

"Healer Munta, I do not know what to say. I am shocked to hear of your losses, we had no idea of the devastating effects of this sickness. Most of our deaths were due to starvation not the plague. As a fellow healer I humbly offer my services and knowledge to you so that you may end the misery of your people."

"You are most generous, Lady Eriya the Chai will be forever in your debt." Munta took her hand and bowed.

Chapter Six

The following day, Eriya and the elders of the Nemn were escorted back to the hall of the Chieftains. Eriya had sat through most of the night relating the events of the day and striving to persuade the villagers to help the Chai. It had not been easy. Old ideals and prejudices were difficult to change and Eriya had to content herself with convincing them to help the Chai by donating some of their blood to make a serum and leave her ideas about uniting the Clans for a later date.

She stood once again before the two Chai Chieftains, but this time with an understanding heart. She carefully presented her speech. "Despite your thoughts on the matter, Lord Remruc, my people are not afraid of the Chai and we will be happy to remain here to help your healers. There are many of us who have survived this plague and you may use our blood to make the serum. I am sure that despite our outward differences we are the same underneath." She looked at Curmer and smiled to take the edge off her final words. Remruc felt his heart leap at her radiant beauty, how he longed for Eriya to give her smile to him.

"We are most grateful to you and your people, Lady Eriya. Please remember that they are free to go anywhere they wish in the city and I am speaking for all of the Chai when I say that we would like you to remain here as our guests."

Eriya was pleased with herself and taking her courage in both hands she decided to press for a union of the clans, "Our price for this serum will be high Lords Remruc and Curmer."

The Chieftains visibly stiffened in preparation for what they expected to be extortionate demands in jewels etc made by the Nemn.

"We wish to come under the protection of the Chai tribe and to be granted living space within your lands."

It was an option that Remruc and Curmer had not even considered. "What do you think brother?" asked Remruc on their private line.

"It seems too good to be true, to get the cure and fresh input into our population for such a small price is fortunate indeed. I think we should accept before she changes her mind."

The shocked expression on the Nemn elders faces had not been lost on Curmer and he guessed that this was something even they had not expected.

Remruc was almost ecstatic at the opportunity of winning the heart of the beautiful Eriya. If she and her people were living in close contact with the Chai then anything would be possible. "Lady Eriya, your demands are high but are acceptable to us," he said as he struggled to control his feelings of joy. Curmer caught the muffled colours of emotion emanating from his brother and he looked at him curiously.

Remruc, suddenly aware of his brother's scrutiny covered his thoughts and distracted him with conversation, "well, I am glad that we managed to sway her, it would have been most annoying and inconvenient if she had to be imprisoned. I only hope that her father will be as easy to convince and he will not ask for more in payment."

"There is no need to congratulate me, it was your well timed bit of play acting that saved the day," quipped Curmer.

Remruc look at him innocently. "Oh come on, you can't fool me, I know that you were just trying to humiliate her into a fury and then play on her emotions as a healer to convince her to stay and help and that you really weren't angry."

Remruc laughed and shook his head, "is there anything I can hide from you, Curmer?"

"Not much," was the jaunty reply. A shadow flashed across Remruc's face, but he laughed again and made his way out of the hall. Eriya departed to instruct her people of the outcome and the council members went about their appropriate duties. Curmer lingered a while in the great hall, watching his brother disappear out of the door deep in conversation with Munta. "So," he mused to himself, "the proud Remruc has finally been besotted. He has made an excellent choice, but I fear he will have a fine fight to convince his chosen bride. Perhaps a little innocent help from me would be in order, after all that is what brothers are for." Curmer wandered back to his living apartments, deep in thought as to the best plan of action.

It was not until the cool of the evening had descended upon Surn that a runner was sent back from the guard post on the Chai border. He brought news of a large body of Nemn making their way towards Chai territory, they were armed but did not appear to be trying to launch an attack. Their approach was too open and obvious. The message was brought directly to Remruc and Curmer, disturbing their evening meal. "Trust the Nemn to turn up at the most inconvenient time," moaned Curmer, as he hastily finished his food. "I was looking forward to relaxing and digesting that."

Remruc drained his cup and grinned across the table. He rose quickly to his feet, his digestive system being used to having to work quickly, picking up his light-weight night-cloak he was half-way through the door before his brother was out of his chair. Curmer finally caught up with him as he was striding down the steps of their home, heading towards the healer hall. "Why are we going to the healer hall first? I would have thought that you would want to organise your guards," he said falling into step with his brother.

"My guards already have their instructions. I thought that it might prove useful to bring Eriya along with us, it would prove our good intentions and convince her father that we mean what we say." Remruc paused as they were crossing a street, some children playing on the corner had distracted him. Curmer turned and followed his gaze. There, outside one of the Chai dwellings, were two Nemn youngsters and three Chai. They were totally engrossed in their game and did not notice the Chieftains watching them; they laughed out loud, their minds echoing the fun they were having. "It would be good if the elders of our clans could learn so easily to live together." Remruc said, moving off again at a brisk walk.

As they neared the healer hall they were surprised by the number of Nemn mingling with the sick Chai. The whole atmosphere was alive with active conversation, as old barriers and pre-conceived ideas were slowly whittled away on both sides, it was most refreshing for both of the young Chiefs to see their dream begin to take shape. The corridors of the healer halls were no longer crowded with apathetic bodies drowning in their own misery, but were busy, bustling hives of activity as the Chai healers hurried about their life saving business. They found Eriya with Lenta and Munta in Lenta's study, discussing the best methods of distributing the newly developed medicine. The three healers turned as one as the Chiefs entered the room, all performed a bow of courtesy. Remruc was pleased to notice that Eriya had changed into more practical clothing for her task, although by Chai standards it was highly decorative, it was a simple design and quite short in length.

Most of the Chai women preferred a long flowing skirt or the leggings that men wore and it was at first quite disconcerting for both Remruc and Curmer to see as much bare leg publicly displayed.

"Lady Eriya has been most helpful and I must say I am very impressed with her knowledge and skill in the healing arts." Lenta stated, trying to drag Remruc and Curmer's stare away from Eriya's bare legs.

Healer Munta cleared his throat loudly and thrust a writing slate under Curmer's nose, "perhaps, Lord Curmer, you would be interested in reading the details of their discovery?"

"What? Oh, yes, thank you," replied Curmer hurriedly as he realised how obviously he had been staring and made a private comment to his brother. "You are staring at her Remruc, for goodness sake show your manners."

"I don't care, she thinks I am a barbarian anyway," he replied, a grin on his face. He bowed to Lenta and Munta then turned back to Eriya. "Lady Eriya, we have been informed that your father and a complement of his guards are approaching our border. I thought perhaps you would like to accompany us as we go out to meet him, it would relieve some of the worry he must have over your safety."

"That is most thoughtful and kind of you, Lord Remruc. I would very much like to see my father and try to make him understand this unusual situation," she replied lightly. The reaction of the two Chiefs as to her manner of dress had not gone unnoticed by her and it pleased her to think she could tease the two Chai as easily as any of the Nemn suitors her father had suggested for her.

"Thank you Lady Eriya, we will leave as soon as you are ready," replied Remruc.

"Ready?" she asked.

"Yes. I would advise you to cover up some of that bare flesh, it could prove to be quite uncomfortable if you were to get a chill in such a sensitive area." Remruc quipped as he turned and exited from the room.

Lenta stared at him in shocked disapproval while Munta suddenly became fascinated with the ceiling. Curmer was struggling to keep a straight face as he followed his brother into the corridor, but he managed to mumble a quick apology before he made a hasty exit. Eriya looked ready to explode and Curmer was grateful that he was out of range of her sharp temper.

"You really know how to infuriate her, Remruc," he said as he laughed at his brothers side, "it will take her a good few minutes to calm down. I pity Lenta and Munta."

"I only stated a simple fact. I was not trying to be aggravating in any way. Is it my fault that her arrogance makes her see every statement as an insult?" Remruc could not disguise the humour in his mind, he could not explain why, but he certainly enjoyed teasing this proud woman and besides, it was better if he was the outlet of her aggression and not the Chai clan.

They had to wait for more than a few minutes for Lady Eriya to join them at the entrance platform. The Chai guards were restless and paced up and down checking and rechecking their armour.

All of them wore lightweight night clothing but underneath their shirts the clicking of the Cuc scale body plates could be heard, none of them would be taking any chances. Finally Eriya appeared accompanied by three of the Nemn village elders. All four were wearing bright white hide overshirts and leggings. The shirts were, as in the usual Nemn fashion, decorated with precious stones. Curmer, however noticed that each elder had a distinct and different pattern displayed on the front of their shirts, but identical patterns on the back. He pointed this out to Remruc who was pre-occupied with his guards. He turned to see the group of Nemn standing quietly at the edge of the platform, "ah, Lady Eriya, I see that you are better dressed to keep out any draughts." Eriya threw him a frozen stare then turned and smiled to Curmer.

"I do hope I have not kept you waiting too long, Lord

Curmer," she said sweetly.

"Not at all, Lady Eriya and I must say that I admire you and your companions' clothing. Tell me, what is the significance of the different patterns? Is it purely decorative?"

"Each pattern is associated with a different skill or labour within our clan, the pattern on the back of the shirts identifies an elder in each of these areas. We have chosen the white shirts to make us more visible to our people at night, after all, we do not want to surprise them by suddenly appearing from nowhere, do we?" she said looking pointedly at the black clothing of the Chai.

"You are most thoughtful and of course correct Lady Eriya," replied Curmer carefully. "Perhaps it would be better if you walk at the head of our guards in case there is any misunderstanding. We of course will not wear our masks, as an indication of our open and good intentions."

Eriya smiled and nodded her approval of this diplomatic answer. She was beginning to have a great deal of respect for this young leader. They moved off into the inky depths of the tunnel, the Nemn were led slowly and carefully down the narrow staircase. Eriya losing her footing, slipped and nearly fell headlong down the treacherous stairwell, but a strong pair of arms secured themselves quickly round her waist, concern emanating from the owner. At first she thought it was Curmer that had caught her and she felt unusually exited with the notion. The mind that she felt so acutely because she was so close had only her safety occupying it, then almost as suddenly as the arms had caught her, she sensed the strong undertones that were distinctively Remruc. Angry with herself for being so foolish she wriggled free of the firm grip, quickly closing her mind as strains of amusement from the Chief began to filter through. For the benefit of the Nemn visitors, and to aid faster movement, torches were light once they had reached the tunnel.

Eriya was impressed by the size of this roadway to the surface, the walls were highly polished and gave no indication that they had been hewed manually from the mountain itself. They had not travelled far along the tunnel when Eriya noticed an opening in the wall to her right. It had been fashioned in such a way that the grain of the rock in the tunnel matched perfectly with the wall of the offshoot tunnel. The effect was such that if you looked directly at the opening or from the side as though you were coming from the surface, it appeared to be a solid wall, the only angle at which it was obviously an offshoot was from the Chai city side.

"Very clever, and very impressive," thought Eriya to herself as they were all ushered along this new tunnel.

The side tunnel would bring the party out closer to the estimated rendezvous point with the Nemn group. It was seldom used by the Chai and Eriya noticed the roughness of the walls and the dust underfoot, which rose in billowing clouds around their boots. They passed several other offshoots along the way each one leading to a now abandoned settlement. Eriya shivered at the thought of so many empty homes, alone and desolate in the heart of this mountain. It also brought home to her the enormity of the disaster that had struck these people. The original numbers of the Chai must have been in hundreds of thousands and now only a few hundred remained. She sympathised with their losses and once more vowed to herself that she would help save the survivors.

Suddenly, without warning, she found herself on the planet surface, the jewel-bedecked sky glistened in unison with the Nemns' gemstones. Eriya drew her breath in sharply and looked back at the tunnel entrance, it was barely visible from the outside, appearing to be a cleft in the rocks, her mind was still reeling with the surprise of the open air after the claustrophobic closeness of the tunnel and she sat down gingerly on a still warm rock, watching the troops silently emerge from the blackness of the shadow. The speed and silence of their movements brought to her mind the childhood tales of these ferocious warriors and she found herself grateful that, for the moment at leas,t they were both on the same side. It did not take long for the guards to assemble themselves, standing in neat rows, awaiting orders. They suddenly split into two sections, one hanging back at the entrance the other forming a column behind Remruc and Curmer. Eriya was fascinated, she had heard no command being given, her mind searched the different 'wavelengths' to try to find the 'frequency' they were using.

Inadvertently she stumbled across Remruc and Curmer's private line of thought, although intensely curious as to what they were saying, she knew that it would be extreme bad manners if she were to 'listen', but before she could switch elsewhere, Curmer sensed her thoughts, whirling round to face her, his eyes blazing with indignation at such a social insult he instantly moved their conversation to another level.

It was in that instant that Eriya saw the similarity between the two brothers. Although Remruc was a warrior and was naturally aggressive, he could normally control his temper. Curmer, on the other hand, was more passive and it took a lot to make him lose his temper, however, if riled, Curmer could be equally as dangerous as his brother. She cast her eyes downwards, away from the accusing stare, humiliation filling her being. How could she have made such a grave mistake. All Eriya wanted to do was to apologise profusely for her indiscretion, but to do that would make public her social disgrace, and she could not bear that insult on her character. Instead she hoped that Lord Curmer and Lord Remruc would forgive her and not mention the incident to anyone.

Strangely enough, Remruc appeared to be less annoyed than his brother, instead he simply regarded her with a dry stare, the sort that one might give a child who had committed the same offence. Eriya cringed inside. It was bad enough to have angered the Chai Chiefs, but to be seen as an immature child in their eyes was the ultimate disgrace. Suitably chagrined and completely subdued, Eriya led the column of people along the path indicated, towards the rendezvous point with her father.

The Nemn party stopped at the border. The warriors were acutely alert, ready for a surprise attack at any second, slowly and carefully they spread themselves out, forming a protective circle around their Chief. Eskara gazed with anxious eyes across the rocky ground, every muscle in his old body complaining about the unaccustomed exercise, his heart trembling at what might have happened to his beloved Eriya.

Although a great age, he still stood tall and proud, his hair, almost white, was interwoven with beads, ornaments made of precious metals and gemstones, his eyes the same colouring as his daughter's were keen and sharp, with a gaze that could wither the most precocious youngster. One of his bodyguards alerted him to the approach of a company of Chai, led by four figures bearing the emblems of the Nemn village elders. The rest of his bodyguards moved restlessly, they were nervous about the close proximity of Chai warriors and they looked with apprehension towards the mountains, hands straying inadvertently to their sheathed weapons. Eskara gave a short, stern command for restraint from his people, any show of aggression could be fatal for them all. He called two of his servants to him and they proceeded to lay a ground sheet and open tent in the centre of the circle, providing rich furs for seating for their Chief, and the expected Chief of the Chai.

Eskara seated himself, fighting down the knot of fear in his throat and forcing himself to be calm for his daughter's sake. An instant tension ran like an electric current through the surrounding guards as the column suddenly appeared over the rise, moving quickly and almost silently towards them, like a black shadow creeping across the ground. The one reassuring feature was the prominent white clothing of the Nemn elders, standing out like a beacon in a dark night.

As they drew closer Eskara let out a sigh of relief as he recognised Eriya at their head, striding towards them her head held high, her eyes searching the face of her father.

"My daughter, you are safe!"

"I am well father, the Chai mean us no harm." Eriya stressed her final statement, looking pointedly at her father's bodyguards who had begun to draw their weapons. Eskara sent an order streaking towards his guards, stinging their minds with its intensity. They instantly dropped their hands to their sides, but maintained a watchful eye on the approaching column.

The Chai warriors stopped a short distance away from the Nemn circle and two Chai accompanied the Nemn elders across the final few yards to the tent of the Chief.

Eskara's face and public mind did not show the surprise he felt when he saw the twin Chai flanking Eriya. It was a good omen for the Chai to have twin leaders, this would make them even more powerful and dangerous especially with his clan so few in number, he sent a private message to Eriya, suggesting that he should try to cooperate with the Chai and not risk a battle. To his surprise he received an encouraging prompt from her, then she moved to her public mind and introduced the Chai leaders.

"Lord Eskara, leader of the Nemn, most beloved father, I have the honour and pleasure of introducing to you Lords

Remruc and Curmer, the leaders of the Chai." She used precise and neutral tones to convey her message, all of her thoughts were geared now to a fair and diplomatic settlement. Eriya was determined to use her skill to the utmost in order to redeem herself in the eyes of the Chai leaders, and she finished her introduction with a low bow first to her father and then to the Chai Chiefs, in traditional Nemn fashion.

A second seat was quickly brought in to accommodate the extra guest while Eriya gracefully moved to one side. Again, to Eskara's surprise, she pointedly stayed on the side nearest the Chai, at first he thought that this was a warning that the Chai had some power over her and she was their prisoner, but, according to San tradition, meetings like this, although uncommon, had been carried out in the past and the area selected was always neutral territory. It was expected that any hostages could then move back into the protection of their own clan. Eriya's actions were an indication of the unusual mood of this meeting.

"Lord Eskara, it is a pleasure to meet you, I trust that you are in good health?" Curmer's polite inquiry caused Eskara to flinch visibly and his eyes narrowed to slits as he viewed the youngsters in front of him. The subtle undertones of the greeting were not lost on the wise Chief and he carefully framed his answer with his own inflections.

"I am and I wish the same good fortune on you and your people, Lords Remruc and Curmer." He shifted position slightly, a subtle indication to his guards to move fractionally closer. Remruc sensed the movement and tension in the surrounding Nemn, he quickly smiled and replied to the disguised threat in honest and open tones.

"Thank you Lord Eskara for your generosity, I only wish that you had sent your blessing to our people earlier, perhaps then we would not have resorted to such drastic and reckless action to seek your help." He watched the Nemn Chief carefully as he mulled over his thoughts. A slight relaxation of Eskara's shoulders eased the alertness of his guards, and the Nemn soldiers backed away.

"I am sorry to hear that your people are not well. Perhaps you would care to expand on your thoughts and how my people can help the mighty Chai clan." There was no hint of sarcasm in Eskara's reply, he was paying an open compliment to the Chai and he waited with interest for an appropriate complimentary reply from the young leaders. Curmer smiled softly and motioned for Eriya to join them.

"I feel, Lord Eskara, that the best explanation would be given by the beautiful Lady Eriya. My feeble attempts would be lost beside her skill in describing our predicament and superior knowledge with regards to the solution."

Eskara smiled and regarded the two Chai. "Very good." He was impressed by these two young Chieftains, they knew how to handle themselves in a diplomatic way, he was sure that they were more than capable when it came to armed conflict. He motioned for Eriya to join him by his side and, moving to his public mind, he asked her to begin. Eriya drew a deep breath, she knew that it was up to her to convince her father and she was grateful for the opportunity, she would not disappoint Lord Curmer.

All present listened intently to Eriya's thoughts. She moved skilfully from the recital of her capture, to the discovery of the reasoning behind the Chai's actions. Her tone and inflection were strategically placed to move the listeners and stir the appropriate feelings of compassion. The San were enchanted, they watched her graceful figure, as she used her posture to emphasis her points. They sat in silence long after she had finished her tale and had seated herself quietly beside Remruc and Curmer, her eyes downcast.

Eriya was exhausted in mind and body, she had excelled herself and she fervently hoped that her father would be swayed by her.

Finally Eksara gave an answer. "I have listened to what has been said, but it is too great a decision for me to make alone. I will return to my people and they will decide what they wish to do and, if we decide to help you, what compensation must be given. Lady Eriya, will you return with me and give your thoughts to our people as you have here?" Eskara watched her carefully, the indecision within her was obvious to him alone, he knew that there was something holding her to the Chai, making her loath to leave and he suspected that he knew what it was.

"I will return with you Lord Eskara, beloved father..." she began. Curmer sent a strong personal command to Remruc as he sensed the instant tension in his body and mind at her reply. "... and I will request that our people help the Chai, but on one condition." This time it was Eskara's turn to sit up and take notice. "That is, irrespective of the decision of our people, I will be allowed to return to the Chai and work with their healers in administering the serum."

The outrageousness of her demand caused all of the Nemn to look at each other in disbelief. Eskara on the other hand had expected as much from his strong willed daughter and much to the surprise of his people he agreed.

The meeting was over. Remruc and Curmer rose and bowed to Lord Eskara and Lady Eriya, they moved quickly and fluidly away from the meeting ground, their actions belaying the inner battle that they were having with each other. Curmer had his work cut out to steer his brother away from the Nemn tent, he constantly reassured Remruc that the Nemn were honourable and that Eskara was likely to keep his bargain, he only wished that he believed his thoughts himself.

"It does not take three days to make a decision Curmer! We have been tricked out of our bargaining prize, I should never have let her go." Remruc gripped the frame of the window, digging his fingers into the stone in frustration, a low growl forming in his throat. He was about to launch into another flurry of thoughts, when Curmer stopped him.

"For once brother I must agree with you, but how will we find them? They are bound to have moved camp by now, it could take months of searching and time is a factor that we do not have."

Remruc swung round and strode to his brothers chair. He sat down opposite him, staring at the floor, carefully organising his thoughts. Curmer was silent, he sensed that Remruc was going to say something shocking and he was worried about what it might be.

"There are still the Nemn from the village in our field cavern. They have been most helpful in donating blood and helping our healers, but there are not enough of them to give us the blood we need, that is, if we take blood in small amounts." Remruc raised his eyes and looked carefully at the shocked expression on Curmer's face.

"Remruc, you are suggesting that we drain the blood from every Nemn in our city?" was the quiet reply. A sudden mixture of conflicting emotions clouded the mind of the Chief.

Curmer felt the uncertainty and loathing for this course of action wash over him, surely there was some other way. They could not kill innocent people to save themselves.

"I can see no other way. Our main concern is for our people, we must save the Chai clan we must carry out our obligations, even if that means sacrificing a small number of Nemn." Despite Remruc's cold thoughts, he was struggling with his conscience. It was repulsive to him, to kill in cold blood, there was no honour involved and the warriors of the Chai would die before dishonour.

"NO REMRUC! I will not allow it. We cannot betray the people who have tried so desperately to help us, it is not right, none of the healers would condone such an action."

"Then brother, we will be sentencing our people to certain death. According to our laws we must both agree on any decision, I need your support, do not let our people die!" Remruc reached across and gripped his brother's arm. To his surprise Curmer pulled away violently and leapt to his feet, knocking his chair over with a heavy thud. He looked at the face towering above him, it was dark with anger, the eyes blazing in fury. It was not often that Curmer was moved to such aggression, but Remruc knew that he felt passionately about the lives of others, irrespective of their clan.

"If we are destined to die, then we will die, but I will not agree to the slaughter of the Nemn villagers." Curmer swept across the room, his body tense with anger. He paused at the door, unable to look at Remruc but determined to finish his thoughts, "do not try to carry out this act without my agreement brother. If you do, I swear not one of the healers will use the blood provided. Do I make myself clear?" There was an eternity of silence before Remruc's quiet response.

"Perfectly."

Curmer marched along the cold corridors, his boots clicking on the flagstones in staccato accompaniment to his thoughts. The turmoil of feelings within his body raged in confusion as he tried to analyse the situation and come up with another solution. Moods and emotion clouded his brain and leaked into his public mind, startling the occasional guard dutifully patrolling their quarters. He burst into his private study, the door swinging wildly, striking the wall and rebounding with a shudder, leaving chips of stone to fall lightly onto the floor.

"My Lord Curmer, I am sorry... it is better that I leave..."

Curmer looked up and saw Sorta rising from one of the wall benches, her face flushed as she hurriedly tried to collect her study slates.

"What are you doing here?" The anger within Curmer gave his thoughts an edge he did not intend and he instantly regretted his mood as Sorta recoiled from him as though she had been struck, the slates slipping from her grasp and shattering on the floor. She looked at the pieces in dismay her hands trembling.

"Lord Curmer, I... I... was sent by Lenta. She said that you wished to study our healing practices. I should have asked you first, I am sorry." Sorta was picking up the pieces of her work slates as she hurriedly explained her reasons for disturbing the Chief's private quarters. A razor sharp edge sliced deeply into her hand and blood trickled down her fingers, dripping in pale blue drops onto her gown. She let out a gasp of pain and quickly grasped her hand, squeezing the folds of the cut together to stem the flow.

Curmer moved quickly to her side, taking her hands in his he led her to a shelf in the corner of the room and reaching up he brought down a container with an assortment of bandages and healing salve. With deft movements he quickly cleaned and sealed the wound covering it in a light dressing.

Sorta kept her head down while Curmer treated her hand, struggling to control the turmoil of emotions that swirled within her, lest any thoughts leaked into her public mind. To be so close to Curmer and feel his touch was almost more than she could bear, her heart was beating so loudly that she feared he might hear. Sternly she reminded herself that Curmer was now the Chieftain and she was no more than a trainee healer. He had the choice of any of the most beautiful women in the Chai, he would not look twice at her, she was not even pretty, just plain old good-hearted Sorta. The most she could content herself with was their friendship. They had started training together and had shared many joys and disappointments. Sorta had loved Curmer from the minute she had set eyes on him, even before she knew who he was and she was determined to keep that love a secret in case she destroyed the friendly bond between them.

She was concentrating so hard to keep calm that it was several moments before she realised that, although Curmer had finished, he still held her hands firmly. Looking up she saw his face watching her, all the anger gone, a soft glow in his eyes and a smile on his lips.

"What thoughts do you try so hard to keep from me Sorta?"

"Thoughts... nothing, I was just eh... thinking about the lessons I had lost on the slates..." she gasped and tried to remove her hands from his grasp, but he held onto to her, pulling her closer.

"You never could lie, Sorta, that is what I like about you. I know I will always hear the truth in your mind. I am sorry I frightened you, but you should know by now that I could never hurt you Sorta." He watched her face carefully. "Now, tell me the truth. Why are you afraid of me? You have seen me angry before so I know that is not the reason; trust me Sorta, I do not ever want you to run from me, I need you, I need your friendship and your judgement."

She looked down at her hands and saw them tremble within the gentle grip of Curmer. How could she tell him how she felt? Did he not say that he needed her friendship, not her love? Sorta was slowly tearing herself apart, she could feel the pain within her like a sharp knife cutting away her heart. His hand gently stroked her hair then lifted her chin and forced her to look at him.

When Curmer saw the pain, fear and uncertainty shining in her eyes he felt a knot of anguish within him.

"Sorta! What is it that hurts you so? I cannot bear to see you this way, tell me!" He let go of her hand and held her face, unconsciously seeking contact points that would allow him to enter her private mind without her consent.

She could bear it no longer, she closed her eyes and opened her mind to him. Curmer automatically closed his eyes and received her thoughts. Their minds merged in a kaleidoscope of colours and emotions as each was drawn into the others being in a dizzying, swirling cloak of feeling. Finally Sorta closed the door of her private mind, exhausted and drained, convinced that she had lost not only her secret love, but her closest friend. She felt her legs starting to tremble and was afraid that she might collapse, suddenly and without warning Curmer took her in his arms and pulled her close to him.

Holding her tightly, a soft croon in his throat, he quietly spoke to her, "my sweet, gentle Sorta. Why did you not tell me? Did you really think I would desert you? Surely you knew me better than that? Do you not know how strong my feelings are for you?" He let her move back slightly and looked at her surprised and unbelieving eyes.

"But Curmer, I am only an insignificant trainee healer, I'm not even pretty, how could I possibly be of any interest to you, other than as a fellow student?" she murmured, afraid to believe what was happening.

Curmer led her over to the wall seat and sat down beside her. Taking her hands firmly in his he searched her eyes and thought gently but firmly. "Sorta, you are the most important person in my life, next to my brother. I look at you and your beauty shines from within, radiating happiness and love for all life. You are truly the most beautiful woman in all the Chai, and I would be proud to take you as my first mate. Will you stand by my side and take my family name?" He looked at her anxiously, his private mind open to show his true feelings and intent.

Joy filled all of Sorta's being, she did not need to answer Curmer, her mind was overflowing with her soul deep happiness.

Remruc spent much of the day walking through the streets of the city deep in thought. He never liked to quarrel with Curmer and he felt that this time he had perhaps pushed his brother too far, but he could not see any other course of action. He was angry with himself for not being a bit more diplomatic but, he smiled inwardly, diplomacy had never been his forte. Although Remruc felt that all the odds were against finding another solution, there was a niggling feeling at the back of his mind that perhaps he had not given the Nemn the benefit of the doubt. Perhaps it did take them three days to consider their position, after all, they were being asked to save the lives of their ancient enemies.

His steps unconsciously headed towards the field cavern as he brooded over the problem. There was a tangible change of mood in the air, so obvious that it filtered into the closed thoughts of Remruc prodding him back into his surroundings with an insistence that bordered on annoying. He began to take notice of the streets and the people around him. There was something different, at first he could not decide what, then it struck home. The dwellings of his people were fully occupied.

They had managed to drag themselves away from the healer hall where they had huddled in fear of the dreadful sickness. All around him the hustle and bustle of everyday life was returning, his people were happy. For the first time in a long while the people of the Chai were busy as they tried to rebuild their shattered lives. Remruc felt his heart miss a beat, there, moving among them, helping, chatting, gossiping were the Nemn villagers. He stood for a moment and watched two women, one Nemn, one Chai discussing their children and laughing at mutual problems with their upbringing, actively suggesting to each other solutions and sharing their traditional ways. Across the street, were two men. Remruc recognised one of them from his own personal guard, the other was a Nemn warrior. They were deep in conversation about hunting techniques, the Nemn hunter was teaching the more battle orientated Chai methods of killing the few remaining wild species of animals roaming Surn's surface.

As he watched, Remruc slowly began to realise just how obscene his solution to the problem had been. Curmer was right. They could not kill the Nemn villagers, for in these few short days they had become welcome additions to the members of the Chai clan. To kill them would be to kill their own kin and that would be inexcusable. The Chai guard looked across and recognizing Remruc eagerly made his way over, dragging the Nemn amiably along with him.

"Lord Remruc!" he excitedly burst into Remruc's thoughts, "I would like you to meet Herka, he is the best hunter from the Nemn village and he has been teaching me techniques that I know you would love to learn."

The guard's enthusiasm was catching and Remruc felt his spirits lift despite the desperation of his situation. He grinned at the Nemn and was surprised when the warrior bowed formally and introduced himself.

"Lord Remruc, Chief of the Chai. It is an honour to meet you at last, I have heard so much about you from Rarl here. It would be a pleasure to talk to you about our hunting methods, that is if you are interested and have the time?"

Remruc thought to himself, "Do I have the time? Does the San race have any time left at all?" He sighed and nodded, it would do no harm to listen to this willing teacher and perhaps he would find an answer in the thoughts of another.

It was drawing close to evening mealtime before Remruc returned to his home. He had a most informative lesson with Rarl and Herka, they had ended up by sampling some excellent beverage illicitly brewed by the Nemn villagers and it was having an unusually quick effect on him. He made a mental note to acquire the ingredients of this brew, as it definitely made the world seem a lot better and eased your worries away. As a result, Remruc was feeling relaxed and at ease with everyone by the time he reached the dining hall. He peered inside and was surprised to see that although the table was set, there was no evidence of his brother. With a frown creasing his forehead, he was finding it increasingly more difficult to think straight, he pondered on this unusual occurrence, then, in blinding light of inspiration he concluded that Curmer must still be in his private quarters, brooding over their earlier argument.

Well then, he thought to himself, I'll just go along and apologise for what I said earlier. How could I have possibly suggested killing people who have such a civilised culture. With an inane smile on his face, Remruc made his way unsteadily along the corridors, which seemed to be moving slowly from side to side, to his brothers apartments. He paused outside the door to Curmer's study, mentally announcing his presence on their private line.

When there was no reply, he opened the door slowly and swayed into the room, glancing quickly around to be sure that it was empty.

With an amiable sigh he continued his journey towards Curmer's living and sleeping quarters, by the time he arrived at the appropriate rooms he had given up announcing his presence, feeling sure that the joviality within him would be reciprocated from Curmer. With a surprisingly accurate movement he managed to open the door and bounced into the main living quarters of his brother. Curmer was at that moment entering the room from his adjacent sleeping quarters, quickly finishing his dressing, his shirt still opened and loosely hanging around his shoulders, his hair wet from a recent bath, he was caught mid-stride, his mouth open in surprise, which quickly gave way to amusement when he saw the ridiculous figure standing in front of him.

"Curmer, Curmer, I have come to apologise for what I said earlier. I was wrong and you my brother were right." Remruc's thoughts were fuzzy round the edges and it was obvious that he was trying very hard to think straight.

"Are you unwell brother?" Curmer could not hide the amusement in his enquiry.

"I am fine, it is just this room that insists on moving around. How do you put up with it?" he quipped back, "You know, the Nemn have this extraordinary drink, it really is quite good, I think that you should try some too." Each thought tumbled quickly one after the other as he in turn tumbled casually into a conveniently placed seat.

"Oh dear! I think that you have sampled more than enough for both of us," laughed Curmer as he strolled back into his bathing chamber. Looking amongst a small selection of herbs he picked one that had a suitably stimulating effect, guaranteed to sober up the most inebriated of San.

Normally the unpleasant tasting herb was concealed in a flavoured drink, but as there was nothing immediately available Curmer decided to be ruthless and put it in plain water.

By the time he had returned to the living room, Remruc

was staring glassy eyed at the ceiling, an inane smile on his face. "Here drink this." he placed the cup into his brothers hand and watched as Remruc drank the contents in one gulp. He stood back and waited for the delayed reaction to the taste of the herb and he was not disappointed in the result.

It took several seconds before Remruc's befuddled brain translated the frantic signals that his taste buds were sending out, but when it did, it regretted the action. The fixed smile on Remruc's face instantly vanished to be replaced with an opened mouth choke, his eyes which had been slightly glazed became very alert, in fact one would almost say panic stricken. He frantically waved his arms in the air, coughing and trying to spit the lingering flavour from his mouth. Curmer listened with satisfaction to the increasingly more coherent thoughts, albeit curses, that flashed from the chair in front of him.

"Are you trying to poison me brother!" was the most clear statement to emerge, along with,"I think I'm going to be sick!" After a few minutes, the taste in Remruc's mouth vanished as quickly as it had arrived and he was left staring in wonder, the room that had formerly seemed fluffy and comfortably bright was now hard edged and decidedly harshly lit.

"Feeling better?" asked Curmer.

"That was a very nasty trick brother. I was quite contented and relaxed now look at me, my body feels like it has been run over by a Cuc." Remruc ran his hand through his hair giving his temples a good hard rub. "There I was trying to improve my understanding and relationship with the Nemn people, meeting with one of their best trackers, sampling their beverages and in general enjoying myself. Then you bring me back down to earth with a thud."

"I take it then that you have seen sense and have

disregarded your original solution to our problem?" Curmer asked tentatively. Remruc looked up and smiled.

"Yes, I have. I will be honest, Curmer, I fear for the survival of not only our clan, but the whole of the San. If the Nemn had the plague, why then not the Doona, Tarl and Jenta. Our border with the Doona territory has been deserted for nearly a year and we have not been attacked by them.

Yes, yes I know that the Doona never really fight and that their cities are much further away than the Nemn's, but even they must have been curious of our absence? What if Curmer... what if we are the only ones left?" Remruc's face echoed the distress and fear that coloured his thoughts, a bleakness and deep sense of hopelessness filled his being. "Perhaps, Curmer, the Nemn will cause us all to die if they do not return."

Curmer sat down slowly his mind racing, quelling the joy inside him about his proposed marriage to Sorta. Taking a deep breath, he tried to drag courage up from the depths of his heart. He knew that for his peoples sake at least, he must be hopeful and show a brave face.

"Remruc, listen to me. Our people seem destined to be faced with one trouble after another, but it cannot go on forever and we will win. I think that you have been too quick to condemn the Nemn, I feel they will come back and help us, they may ask a high price for their services, but, if we speak to them as openly as we speak to each other and explain our fear, then I know they will join us. Their Chief, Eriska, he is very old and I think very wise. He will see our good intentions; perhaps he will convince his people that what we say is true even if he doesn't believe it himself. After all, he knows that the Nemn would benefit from living with us." Curmer watched his brothers face, his mind open to receive any hint of mood or emotion.

"I hope you are right, Curmer, I really do," was the soft reply, muted with sadness which was washed away by deliberate and not entirely true cheerfulness. "Anyway, tomorrow is tomorrow, but today is today and right now I am very hungry. Let us go and eat." He stood up abruptly and instantly regretted his action as his stomach took a few minutes to catch up with the rest of his body, "What on earth did you give me to drink?" Curmer laughed and slapped him on the back, leading the still shaky figure out of the door and towards the food hall.

"It was only a pinch of Reeesa herb."

"Reeesa! I thought that was poisonous!" gasped Remruc,

"Only if taken in the wrong dosage, do not worry I know the correct amount to administer to bring dulled senses back to alertness. You will feel much better with food inside you." They walked along the corridor in amiable silence.

Curmer decided to wait for a better opportunity to tell Remruc about Sorta. They would need to organise a proper ceremony and invite the right people. When a Chief married, he must do it in style. It will be a celebration for all of the Chai, everyone will be happy, even if the San race is destined to die, they do not need to know straight away, if at all, he thought to himself.

Chapter Seven

In the cool hour before dawn, when the sky was beginning to lighten and warn of the impending heat of day, the Chai guard at his post alerted the runner at the base of the pinnacle of the rock. A cloud of sandy soil, thrown up by the tramping of many feet, appeared over the edge of the ridge, barely visible in the darkness and moving quickly towards the border. With well-trained swiftness, the runner set off heading for the nearest entry tunnel to the Chai complex.

She flew over the uneven surface, like a shadow of a cloud blown by the wind, her footfalls light, hardly marking the soil or disturbing rocks and pebbles. On reaching the cluster of boulders disguising an entrance, she quickly flashed her message to the guard stationed halfway along the tunnel; this in turn was relayed through several sources placed at strategic intervals until reaching the guards on the entrance platform. The whole process from start to finish took barely five minutes.

The knock on the door, accompanied by the guard's formal identification and request for entry, filtered slowly into Remruc's brain. He was still feeling the side effects of the Nemn brew and it took slightly longer than usual for him to respond to the summons. Once he had listened to the news however, he was completely alert and awake. Sending the guard on to inform Curmer, he dressed quickly in outdoor gear, lifting a mask and hood in anticipation of the dawn light. Marching briskly out into the street he paused briefly to wait for Curmer, gazing out across the street, trying desperately to suppress the gnawing anxiety in his stomach. He did not need to wait long. Curmer bounded down the steps to join him, his step vigorous and sickeningly energetic. "Do you have to look so awake and healthy brother?" was Remruc's dry response to the playful thump that Curmer gave him on the shoulder.

Curmer laughed at the still drowsy face in front of him. "Are you feeling the worse for wear? That will teach you to drink so much."

Remruc did not even bother to reply and simply grunted deep in his throat. They turned as one and marched towards the entrance platform, followed closely by the guard. When they reached their destination, Curmer was shocked to see a full complement of warriors fully armed and deployed around the doorway into the city. A second complement was waiting quietly for the Chiefs to arrive.

"Why have you armed your guards and called them out Remruc, this could provoke an attack!"

"We do not know for sure that the Nemn are not trying to attack us Curmer, it is perhaps better to be safe than sorry. I will only take one complement and believe me they will be discreet. Here, you better take this." Remruc thrust a mask and hood into Curmer's hands and he took them, reluctantly looking at the soldiers falling in silently behind them.

Emur and Rume were beginning to venture above the horizon, the glowing edge of their orbs sizzling with the promise of a baking day. The Chai warriors stood motionless along the edge of their border. Their masks down and hoods drawn tight, covering any exposed flesh. Their weapons were concealed within their cloaks, ready to be drawn should the need arise. The dust cloud that had heralded the approach of the Nemn had stopped just behind the last ridge. Looking up, Remruc asked the lookout at the top of the pinnacle of rock if any movement could be seen. The answer was negative. Remruc moved restlessly back and forwards between the rock and the troops, deep in thought.

Curmer moved to his side and pulled him back into a shaded area. "What do you make of it?" he asked, the tension in his mind sharpening his thoughts.

"It doesn't look good Curmer. They are behind that ridge, waiting. If their intentions are friendly why do they not continue and meet with us.

I am only going to give them a few minutes more, then we will attack." Remruc pulled away from his brother and motioned to his guards to fan out in flanking formation. The only sound to be heard was the clicking of the weapons and Cuc scale armour as the warriors moved into position.

Curmer sighed to himself, why can't the Nemn cooperate? They will lose many of their tribe today if a confrontation is provoked. He looked sadly towards the ridge, willing the Nemn to appear without their weapons drawn for an attack. No sooner had the thoughts passed his mind than an alarm was sounded by the lookout. All eyes turned towards the Nemn territory to see the ridge top, already beginning to waver with the heat haze, throw a plume of red-brown dust into the Surn sky.

As the cloud drew closer, the dusty silhouettes of many, many figures, slowly trudging forward, became gradually visible. The Chai lookout was straining his eyes against the glare of daylight and the choking density of the sand shroud that covered the advancing entourage, but he finally let out a happy confirmation to the tensely waiting group,

"Lords Remruc and Curmer, the Nemn appear to be dragging their travois and carts. I can see a long line of at least one hundred travel carts surrounded by Nemn, young and old. There are no obvious signs of warriors, or armed Nemn."

Curmer visibly relaxed at the joyful news, he had not realised that he had been holding his breath during the commentary until frantic signals from his lungs had penetrated his brain. Smiling and chiding himself over his foolishness he looked across to Remruc, who was already regrouping his guards in a less threatening pose. "Well Remruc, the Chai and the San race may yet be saved!" he said, the joy and elation he felt sparkling through his thoughts.

"Perhaps Curmer, perhaps," he countered, the happy colouring taking the pessimistic edge out of the reply.

It did not take long for the Nemn to cover the final leg of their journey, the remaining few beasts they had brought along were exhausted as they dragged their share of the burdens up to the waiting Chai. When the column finally reached the borderline Lord Eskara climbed down from the shaded travel cart, his head covered completely by a skin hood, decorated with precious stones, with slow stiff steps he made his way towards Remruc and Curmer.

"Lords Remruc and Curmer, I greet you on behalf of the Nemn people with open arms and open hearts." Eskara raised his arms, palms upwards to emphasise his statement and show that he had no hidden weapons.

Remruc stepped forward and bowed formally, "Lord Eskara, I as commander of all the Chai forces, welcome you and guarantee the safety of you and your people within our territory."

He was joined by Curmer who continued the formalities, "Lord Eskara, I as the official of all the Chai trades and services, welcome you and guarantee that all goods and services available to the Chai will be available to the Nemn on equal terms." They then joined thoughts and finished the ceremony as one. "Lord Eskara, we as the Chiefs of the Chai welcome you with open arms and open hearts."

Eskara looked at the two young Chiefs thoughtfully, Eriya had been correct in her opinion of them, they were indeed destined to become great leaders, although he felt that his daughter had been somewhat hard in her thoughts about this Lord Remruc, after all the San was a warrior and was expected to have a strong character. Eskara smiled inwardly, his own thoughts reaching a conclusion that may or may not come to pass. The three Chieftains moved towards the waiting mass of Nemn. Remruc and Curmer subtly slowing their pace to enable their elderly companion to carefully pick his way over the uneven ground. Once they had reached the lead travel cart they were joined by the Nemn elders, all graven-faced, their anxiety obvious by the tension in their bodies.

Eskara stood by his people and faced the two Chai, "Lords Remruc and Curmer, we the Nemn have agreed to aid you the Chai in this crisis. However, our terms of payment are high."

Remruc felt his stomach tighten as he waited for what he expected to be impossible requests. Curmer forced himself to look calm, but inside he felt the same churning sensation of expected disappointment that was emanating from his brother.

Eskara paused in his announcement and regarded the two leaders waiting patiently in front of him, barely resisting the urge to smile when he saw the look on their faces, he continued, "we will require all the food, shelter, animals, clothing and services needed to ensure a comfortable living within your city. We will require all the open space we need to set up our camps and if our people prefer to live in your stone tents, we will require the appropriate accommodation. We will require, the absolute guarantee that our high ranking people are treated on equal terms with your high ranking people, I understand of course that there may be some cultural differences at first, but I am sure that your people will learn to accept our standards. Finally, we require the assurance that all our goods, clothing, ornaments and so forth are safe from theft or plunder and should the occasion arise where an item goes missing, that my own people are allowed to deal with the offenders as we see fit. In return for all of these conditions our healers will work with you and save the Chai clan." He finished his proclamation and watched the Chai Chieftains mull over what had been said.

Remruc spoke to Curmer in private, "I cannot believe it. They have asked for nothing that we would not have given them anyway, yet they have made it sound like a major concession on our part."

Curmer replied, unable to hide the admiration in his mind, "I think you can thank our pretty little Lady Eriya for this brother. Her clever mind has been working overtime with her father and these Elders, it is she who has put these notions in their heads and worked them around to our way of thinking. Oh, I am not saying that her father has been duped as easily as the Elders, but even if he saw through her words, he has understood that this way no one loses any face, not the Nemn or the Chai. You know as well as I do brother that our people could not afford to pay a high compensation either in goods or food. All we can offer is our friendship, and that is what Eskara has accepted. Now, let me give an appropriate answer."

Curmer moved forward and laid his arms out palm upwards, "Lord Eskara, your people have demanded a high price for your knowledge. But, if the price to be paid reflects the value of your knowledge then I know that our people will be saved. I, Lord Curmer, humbly accept your demands."

Eskara placed his hands face down over Curmer's and they struck their palms together in a finalising of the agreement between the Nemn and the Official for the services and trades of the Chai. He then looked towards Remruc, who stepped forward to replace Curmer's position.

Taking a deep breath and hurriedly memorising the correct wording of his statement that had been flashed across from

Curmer he began, "Lord Eskara. What you ask from me is difficult. The warriors of the Chai and my own guards have maintained a disciplined society for many generations. Theft and plunder is unknown among our people. We share all things and covet nothing. However, I understand your anxiety for in the past, our people have raided your camps and taken furs and hides. I know that you think this may happen when you enter our city, but I give my solemn promise that no one will take what is not theirs by right, or agreement. I will therefore consent to one of your demands from me, that is for your own warriors to police the everyday interaction between our peoples, to ensure that no misunderstandings arise. If, however, an incident does occur it must remain up to the Chai to decide who is guilty and who is not. Although it troubles me, I will allow your people to enforce their own punishments if a guilty party is found. I can give no more concessions other than the guarantee that the Chai being powerful warriors will remain so, and our role as protectors will now engulf not only our people, but the Nemn as well."

Remruc regarded the impassive face of Eskara, hoping fervently that the Nemn would accept. Eskara replied after mulling over the thoughts of Remruc with not only his elders, but Eriya as well.

"Lord Remruc. It saddens me to think that you are troubled by our methods of justice and punishment. However, in light of the gracious offer by your warriors to protect the Nemn as one of your own, I am willing to accept this concession in our demands." He slapped the palms of Remruc, who had been holding out his arms since the speech making had started.

So it was finalised. The Nemn were accepted into the Chai clan. The first time in the bloody history of the San that such an agreement had been made.

As the twin suns rose to expose their full and awesome

heat, the last survivors of the Nemn were led by the twin Chieftains into the cool safety of the Chai tunnels, beginning a long journey towards a new future and the birth of a new race.

Within days, the Nemn had established themselves in the field cavern, their brightly coloured tents covering almost half with a patchwork quilt like effect that dazzled the eye with its vibrant colour.

The immediate problem was the shortage of food. The Chai had plenty of seed grain waiting to be sown, there had just not been enough people healthy or willing to attend to their duties, so the ground had been allowed to dry and the grain had withered to dry brown husks. Now, with the influx of new and strong hands, the Nemn and Chai set about the remaining half of the field cavern. It was tilled into neat rows, a cloud of dust threatening to choke the workers as they bravely turned the soil. Once this was complete the seed grain was sown, a particularly fast growing variety, not as nutritious as some but, in view of the emergency, vital. Water was brought up from the vast artesian wells that were fed by underground streams that had their origin in what used to be the polar ice caps which had melted and seeped below the surface of Surn.

The Nemn had brought with them their few remaining livestock animals, some bred for food and some for draught work. Although these creatures were weak from hunger and drought, a few days rest with the sparse dry fodder taken from the dwellings and stores of dead Chai inhabitants and their beasts, it was soon noticed that although they were skinny and malnourished, the animals had come from good breeding stock.

The Chai elder in charge of the breeding of livestock immediately sent out a request to the Chai people to release any remaining livestock that they had and allow a new breeding programme to be set up. It did not take long to organise such a project, but they soon realised that there was not enough space in the field cavern to allow for food, animals and Nemn. So it was decided by the Nemn elders to accept the empty dwellings of the Chai and they quickly selected the best of the remaining buildings for their purpose. The Chai and Nemn worked hard and well together towards a common goal for their common good. Both tribes were surprised at the comparative ease with which they merged, and how much they really had in common.

Initially the Chai shared what little food they had, the Nemn courteously forgetting for the moment their demands to be fed well by the people they were helping. Once the grain had been grown it would be a much easier and better standard of living for all.

It had shocked the Nemn at first, to learn of the total devastation of the Chai race and to see for themselves the vast and empty city. It chilled them to think of the other two completely deserted cities of the Chai with their darkened buildings and cold streets where only the spectres of the dead who had not been taken to the spirit world roamed and lived. It did not take long for pity and respect to replace the fear that they had once felt for the Chai. Many of the opinions of the Nemn were greatly influenced by Eriya. She was adored and worshipped not only by her father, but by virtually all of the remaining Nemn. It was not just her beauty that swayed their favours, but her dedicated skill in healing the ailing Nemn through the plague had given her a hero-like status. It was due mainly to her influence over the Nemn that they had been convinced to come on what seemed at first a suicide journey into the hands of their enemies. Eriya had had her work cut out to prompt their final decision and it was she who had drawn up what demands they should make on the Chai for payment.

She had seen for herself the preferred sparseness of the Chai dwellings and their lack of interest in jewellery and adornments. She knew that their textile industry was famous, had seen and felt the fine cloths and yarns in storage. She had even been given as a gift from Lenta, a beautiful soft dress, a light blue-green, that flowed to her ankles like water down a rock fall. However, it had been a long time since any yarn or cloth had been produced and it would take even longer to train new people to the trade. Eriya knew that the cloth that was stored would be essential to see the entire population through several seasons before the plants used for the textiles were mature. It had been obvious to her from the start, that the Chai did not have anything that the Nemn would not be given as rightful members of the clan, so she decided to sway their original decision for payment in goods, to payment in keep and status. Something that the Nemn valued greatly.

It took nearly a full Surn month, for the Chai and Nemn to organise their society into an efficient and well run order. Initially, Remruc, Curmer and Eskara were responsible for all orders and were the ultimate decision makers. The elders of both clans carried out their instructions to the letter and the system seemed to work in the short term, but Curmer knew that as the population of the cavern increased, so would the need for a more formal and fair system of ruling. He decided to bring this matter to the attention of Eskara and Remruc at their next meeting and to push for some formalising of a system to at least be started.

It was a very busy month for all of the San, the healers were working every hour that they could stay awake, dispensing the life saving medicine. Some of them even had time to try to inoculate the surviving livestock, although the beasts seemed to be less afflicted with the plague and had suffered more by the lack of care and attention from dying people.

Sorta was carrying out the duties of a full healer, although she was still officially only a trainee, with many of the duties and decisions as to who was treated and when falling on her shoulders. She threw herself into the task with a strength and determination that won her respect from every healer, both Chai and Nemn, striving to complete the programme before others fell sick and died. It was a race against time. Although the serum could prevent the illness from occurring, those who had already contracted the disease were at real risk. Lenta and Eriya had formed a close friendship and both concentrated on finding a cure for those already sick. They were having a limited success by using a mixture of serum and herbal remedies, administered at crucial points throughout the progression of the illness and, thanks to the work of Sorta and her team, there were fewer and fewer people falling ill. It would not be long they concluded before everyone was either inoculated or had survived themselves and that would herald the end of the plague.

By the end of the second month, things had quietened down quite considerably. The grain was almost ready to harvest, emergency rations and supplies were still above the quarter-line mark, the livestock were recovering rapidly, most of the females being pregnant and everyone who had not shown signs of illness had been inoculated. Those few remaining patients in the healer hall, seemed to be responding to a frightening mixture of medicines and treatments concocted by Lenta and Eriya. There was an atmosphere of hope and elation among the peoples of the Nemn and Chai and now a short period of relaxation before the first major harvest of food grain for a long time was due.

Curmer moved around his study, his arms in the air in a bone popping stretch. He absentmindedly shuffled a few slates on his desk and gazed out of the window, the buzz and noise of the city below was probably the most beautiful thing he had ever experienced. No, he corrected himself, the most beautiful experience is my love for Sorta and it pales this sight almost to insignificance. He smiled lazily, perhaps at last they could now announce their love and proposed marriage. They just did not have time before but at last things were beginning to improve and now Curmer dared to hope that their people had a future. Today he would see Sorta, alone, for the first time since their momentous meeting in this very room and he knew something she did not, a little surprise that would please her immensely.

His eyes flicked around the room, everything was tidied away into neat wall shelves, pocketed like pigeon holes around the perimeter. The floor was swept, the furniture arranged informally in fact Curmer had tidied the room at least three times in as many minutes. He nervously straightened his tunic and chided himself for being so uptight. On impulse he marched over to the polished metal plaque on the wall and viewed his reflection critically. He was clean, neat and tidy. Why do I feel like a child at an important reception? He mused, fighting down the knot in his stomach. He looked at the reflection of the room in the plaque and his eyes fell instantly on a small jar of antiseptic solution hiding in a corner nook by the window. That should not be there, he thought and immediately moved across intent on putting the rogue jar in its rightful place. As he swept the offending article from the nook there was a knock on the door, and the familiar soft, sweet thoughts announced her presence. The door was swung tentatively open and she quietly swept into the study. "Sorta!" he said, the elation and love colouring the thought with such a dazzling display that he almost knocked her off her feet, as he opened his arms to greet her, the jar of solution slipped from his gasp, shattering on the floor, splattering his new leggings with its brightly coloured contents, "Oh no!" he quickly bent down to gather up the pieces of jar and bumped heads with Sorta who had also moved down to help him.

"Oww, that hurt," she laughed delightedly, the amusement in her mind relieving the worry in Curmer's. "Look at us," she said, "as nervous as a mantelo in the claws of a Cuc!"

"Leave it," Curmer grasped her hands, the urgency in his mind startling Sorta at first, "and let me hold you." He picked her up and swung her round in his arms, "I have missed you so much!" He held her close for a few moments and she returned his embrace.

"And I have missed you my love. Perhaps now that things are improving we can spend some time together." She kissed his cheek softly and lent back in his arms, their minds merging and dancing together as one.

"I can do better than that, Sorta. I intend to announce our proposed marriage tonight, at the Council of Elders." He smiled delightedly at the pleasure in her mind, "and you will be there to hear it."

She pulled away from him a quizzical look on her face. "How can I be there? I am not an elder."

His smug expression and deliberately quiet mind told her that she would have to wait to find out the secret he held from her.

"Oh! How I hate it when you tease me!", her delight covering the annoyance in her tone. He dragged her back into his embrace and held her tightly.

"Now, where were we before I became distracted?" He grinned mischievously and she matched his intentions thought for thought.

A sharp knock on the door and quick announcement gave them barely enough time to move apart, Sorta bending to pick up the pieces of jar and hiding her face which she knew must be flushed.

"Lord Curmer, I just thought I would pop by and visit you now that I have a few moments to spare... Oh! Has there been an accident?" Eriya stopped short, barely avoiding tripping over Sorta who was fumbling around on the floor.

"Yes, yes, it was my fault, clumsy of me really... I... I am most sorry Lord Curmer, I hope I have not ruined your clothing," stammered Sorta quickly.

"No, not at all Sorta, I am sure it will wash out, here put the pieces on the desk and I will clear them later." His hand brushed hers lightly as he helped her with the sharp fragments. He turned to look at Eriya who was watching Sorta with mild irritation; on seeing his attention, she quickly flashed her most winning smile and gracefully moved to his side linking his arm with hers.

"I felt, Lord Curmer, that a refreshing stroll round the courtyards would be in order. Perhaps you would take me to see your wonderful grain? I would love to see how well it is growing." She was leading him towards the door before he could form a proper response. Curmer glanced back towards Sorta an apologetic air about him,

"Sorta. We can go over your report as soon as I return. Perhaps later tonight?"

Eriya tightened her grip on his arm ever so slightly and regarded the plain girl standing by the desk.

Although she wore a smile on her face, Eriya's eyes glinted with annoyance, that Curmer should waste time talking to a mere trainee when he should be paying attention to her.

Sorta regarded Curmer, smiled and nodded, she did not feel as happy as she looked and it distressed her deeply to see the interest that Eriya had for Curmer. She did not want that woman digging her claws into her beloved mate to be.

On that note, Curmer was dragged, albeit subtly, from the room, Eriya filling his mind with a constant babble of small talk.

The great hall was half full of elders of every profession in both the Nemn and Chai tribes, they were mingling, deep in conversation with fellows from both sides, filling the air with their hopeful chatter. The mood was jovial, spirits were high and an anticipation of promotions for juniors within the trades in attendance kept an undercurrent of excitement circulating. A signal was given by one of the guards at the side entrance, and the three Chieftains entered the room, each was dressed in their finest clothes, the Chai's plain and elegant uniforms contrasting with the intricate, brightly coloured tunic and leggings of the Nemn. All present bowed low to their leaders and remained standing till they were seated. A formal call was then given to the guards at the main entrance. They moved in unison, opening the great doors, revealing a host of juniors, trainees and apprentices waiting outside in the corridors. The juniors were moving restlessly, nervousness and tension emanated from them in waves. Each was dressed in the appropriate uniform and colour for the different trades that they were trained for and it was pleasing to the elders of the Chai to see so many newcomers to their textile industry. There were many junior healers and several apprentices to the other main trades of the Chai. A pleasant surprise for Remruc and Curmer were the number of Chai youngsters that had chosen to train in Nemn trades, it was a credit to the work of the elders that the merging of the two tribes had been so smoothly and uneventfully handled.

Once all the trainees had entered the room, standing respectfully at the back, the speech making could begin.

Eskara rose stiffly from his seat and moved to the front of the dais. "It is good to see so many people gathered for this happy event. There are many of you I recognise as old friends, just as there are many old friends who are no longer with us. Today we will celebrate a new beginning, a new life and the success of our combined people and, to represent this, we have decided to promote to full recognition of their chosen trades, the trainees, juniors and apprentices gathered here.

You were the best, most skilled and diligent of your class mates and are now worthy to obtain your full title. I hope that this will lead the way for a good and prosperous future." He smiled warmly at the youngsters at the back of the room and slowly eased himself back into his chair. Curmer rose to his feet and took his place at the head of the dais.

"Lord Eskara has chosen his words well and I feel that there is not much more I can say to express my happiness at this momentous meeting except that there will be a special celebration meal in the main dining hall. I am afraid the fare that is offered is poor compared to our usual standards, but I am sure you will enjoy it nonetheless."

There was a wave of subdued cheering at this news and the crowd moved restlessly, eager to get on with the proceedings. Remruc passed Curmer as he was sitting down and flashed a grin at him.

"It is now my turn to address you, and I have quite a lot to say." There was a barely suppressed moan at this comment as the crowd prepared themselves for a lengthy lecture, "however," Remruc continued unabashed, "I can sum it all up in one word... ENJOY!" There was a wave of cheering flying from the minds of all those gathered at this light-hearted humour.

With that, the ceremony began, each of the trades represented had their newly promoted trainees named and as they came forward, they were awarded with the official robes of their chosen profession. Curmer's eyes filled with pride as Sorta was named as a full healer and as she stepped forward to receive her robe he sent a private message of support and love to her, she almost dropped the robe in surprise at the unexpected message, but managed to compose herself before everyone noticed. Everyone that is except Eskara. He may have been old, but his sharp eyes and experienced mind never missed a trick. He smiled inwardly.

So... this young Lord has already chosen his first mate. I wonder if his brother has been so fortunate?, was the wandering thought that entered his brain. Perhaps I could prompt him along just a little bit.

The meal, although sparse, was a complete success. The Nemn had been very liberal with their beverage and almost all of those in attendance were well into the relaxed and friendly state that Remruc knew so well. Curmer decided that this was the time to announce his proposal of marriage to Sorta. He looked through the crowd and saw Lenta deep in discussion with Eriya, his brow furrowed. Eriya seems to be spending a lot of time with Lenta, perhaps I could use Lenta to deflect her attentions away from me and onto my brother, he mused as he sent a message floating over to his father's mate, "Lenta, would you care to join me for a moment, I feel the urge for a speech coming on!" Lenta laughed and excused herself from her friend. Curmer then sought the mass of faces for Sorta, he could hear her soft tones, light and bubbly as a rock stream, but he wanted to see her face as well. He loved to watch her face, that gleam in her eyes and the way she moved. He eventually found her amongst her classmates, showing off her new clothing and enthusing about the ceremony.

"Sorta" he thought softly, "come and be by my side my love." Her eyes met his, brimming with happiness as she excused herself from her eager listeners. Eskara was feeling jolly and relaxed. His mind was becoming slightly fuzzy, a phenomena he could not understand as he was well used to the potent brew in his goblet.

"Ah," he thought to himself, "this is a definite sign of age. When one cannot drink what one used to." He grinned and emptied the glass with a lip smacking, satisfied slurp. He looked across at the two Chieftains and considered his plan for the unison of the two tribes. He only had one daughter, but there was at least one of the twin leaders free to take a first mate. The problem was that Eskara seemed to be having difficulty in remembering which one of the Chieftains was available. They both looked identical and his old mind couldn't quite focus clearly on the different mental images of their minds. Coming to a decision he rose unsteadily to his feet and raised his arms, mentally calling for silence. Sorta was only half way across the floor when the Nemn Chief rose and she stood respectfully waiting to hear his thoughts. "Fellow Nemn. The Chai have welcomed us into their homes, as well as their hearts and I feel that it is time for us to show our total commitment to the unison of our two peoples. What better way is there than for me to offer the hand of my eldest and most beautiful daughter in marriage to the Chai Chief." Due to his befuddled state, Eskara omitted to mention which Chai Chief he had intended.

There was a gasp of astonishment from the crowd and a few cheers of well wishing. Eriya was taken completely by surprise. She of course had no objection to the arrangement, but she would have preferred to have pushed her seemingly reluctant intended into the decision herself. However, always the adaptable and opportunist, Eriya rose gracefully from her seat and flashed her ever so charming smile around the room her eyes rested on Remruc for barely second, his eyes were hopeful, his body tense.

Then she looked directly at Curmer, who was shifting uncomfortably in his seat, his eyes nervously straying around the room. She didn't hesitate.

"I am honoured and grateful beloved father, that you deem me worthy of such a compliment. As the Chai are so fortunate to have two leaders then I think that it is appropriate that I choose who to marry. Curmer, I would be more than happy to be your first mate."

The leaders were almost knocked senseless by the tumultuous cheering and well wishing. Curmer closed his eyes and clenched his jaw. What can I do, he thought. To refuse now would be a grave insult and would destroy everything we have built, but I cannot accept. I do not love Eriya, I love Sorta and I want her to be my first mate. He turned and looked at Remruc.

The face that regarded him was that of a man stricken. The pain in his eyes was frightening, his whole being spoke of frustration, anger and despair. Curmer tried desperately to speak to him on their private line but the mind of his brother was closed against him.

Remruc rose and walked purposefully toward him. "Congratulations, I hope that you will both be very happy." The thoughts came stiffly, and formally with no hint of the anguish that Remruc felt inside. With that he turned and marched from the room, having to push his way through the crowd of well-wishers. Curmer searched frantically for Sorta and caught sight of her as she ran from the room, her mind a turmoil of emotion. She understood the severe political damage that Curmer would cause should he refuse such an offer, but it did not help her to ease the despair that she felt.

Eskara listened to the cheering and happiness being conveyed around him, but still, in the back of his mind, there was a nagging voice that told him something was not right.

That something had happened that he had not intended. Something he had forgot to say perhaps. He could not put his mind on what that irritating doubt was, so he simply smiled and sat back enjoying the prospect of his daughter being married.

Curmer could not sleep that night. He paced the length of his private rooms, frantically racking his brain for any way that he could change the terrible event that had happened. It was difficult to think clearly, for his mind was tormented by the pain and awful knowledge that Remruc would not communicate with him except for public conversation and that Sorta was breaking her heart somewhere out there in the city. She had not returned to her quarters at the healer's hall, he had searched there first, but she was wandering aimlessly around the streets trying to rationalise and quell the turmoil of emotions within her. She didn't know, but Curmer could feel her pain as sharply as his own, his mind was open to her, but she would not accept him. He sat by the window staring with unseeing eyes his head resting against the smooth, cold stone. Why, why, why, did Eskara have to speak up at that moment, he thought to himself. If only he had waited a little longer, then Eriya would have had no choice but to accept to be first mate to Remruc and none of this would have happened.

"There is no point on dwelling on what should have happened son of my mate. You must try to deal with what has happened."

Curmer turned sharply to see Lenta standing quietly by the door, she had been listening to his unguarded thoughts, a privilege that only she was allowed. "Lenta!" his mind gasped, all the hurt and anguish released in that one exclamation. She moved quickly to his side as he all but collapsed in her arms, her mind trying to absorb some of the agony that was pouring from her beloved mate's son.

"I cannot stand it, Lenta, Remruc refuses to listen to me, Sorta will not hear me, but I can feel her pain and Eriya has been searching to try to find my private thoughts."

Lenta held him tighter and gently stroked his hair. "I know, I know." The thoughts came softly into his torn and stricken mind. "Listen to me Curmer, I am going to help you. I know Eriya better than anyone, she and I have become good friends and believe it or not, underneath that arrogant, superior shell there is a very insecure and loving person. Now I know you are not stupid and that you have guessed Remruc's feelings for Eriya, although he manages to hide them well. Eriya does not love you either Curmer, she is just playing a game, a dangerous one at that. She only decided to marry you to anger Remruc." Curmer looked up at her his eyes blazing.

Oh no, I don't think she has tried to deliberately hurt you or Sorta, she does not even know about Sorta, but she thinks that Remruc hates her and would be furious if his only beloved brother took the woman he hates as a first mate. Frankly Curmer, she does not know about Remruc's true feelings, just as he does not know of her real fascination for him."

The whole irony of the situation overwhelmed Curmer and he tried to pull away from Lenta's comforting embrace, but she only let him go far enough to bring her face level with his, her eyes locking his with their intensity, "we can sort this whole mess out Curmer, but it will take time. That is what we must bargain for, time."

"How Lenta? What possible reason can I give for not accepting the proposal instantly? If I do turn her down, I will not only insult the whole of the Nemn, but Remruc as well. I know him Lenta, in a perverse way he would be dishonoured if I did not marry the woman he loves, it would look as though I thought her below my status and not worthy of our family." The desperation in his mind struck Lenta to her core.

She knew that this anguish could destroy him. He could not bear to lose the two people he loved more than life itself. She gripped his arms fiercely, her own fear giving an angry edge to her thoughts, "listen and believe what I am going to tell you. This is the only way I can see where no one will lose face or be dishonoured." Slowly and calmly Lenta shared her plan with Curmer and he began to feel a faint sense of hope.

Chapter Eight

Remruc punched the wall in frustration. He had been prowling around the city, restless, distraught and very, very angry not only with Eriya, but with himself. He knew that Curmer was not to blame for this unfortunate turn of events; in fact, he suspected that his brother was involved with that young healer girl, her name eluded him as his distraught mind searched for the reference. Glancing down the quiet street as he marched across a fleeting shadow caught his eye. He looked around quickly for the Nemn guards who were responsible for patrolling the city and maintaining order, typically there were none in sight. Sighing deeply he decided to investigate the curious behaviour himself and turning on his heels, set off at a jog to catch up with the elusive shadow. As he rounded a corner he spotted his quarry slowly heading towards the stone garden that was the pride and joy of the Chai city. He crouched low and tried to assess who the person was. They were dressed in Chai clothing that much was certain, but many of the Nemn settlers had taken up the same form of dress, at least Remruc could tell that it was a female, by the light frame and soft motions. He followed quickly as the woman disappeared into the garden. Pausing at the arched doorway he peered into the interior, his eyes searching in the brighter enclosure.

The garden was aptly named. The Chai relished the texture, colours and nature of the rocks on Surn and they had delighted in designing a display that gave the impression that the rocks had grown from the gravely ground in the same way that crops grew in the caverns. Most of the features were unfashioned and shown in all their natural beauty, carefully positioned so that the light from the ever burning torches danced with a myriad of colours across their many-faceted surfaces.

Here and there were deliberately carved pieces, some in abstract form, spiralling in a wild eccentricity understood by only the artist, but appreciated by all, while others were more formal, depicting animals or people long dead. They were all set in a light gravel soil, made from the rare white rocks that were found only in Chai territory. The small granules reflected the light from the torches back up and off of their massive companions, giving the illusion that the rocks exuded the light themselves. In the centre of the garden was a natural waterfall. It bubbled up from an underground spring and cascaded down a steep sided gorge, forming a pool at the bottom. Steps led down to the edge of the pool, and in earlier days it was a popular spot for swimming and relaxing in the coolness of the rocks.

It was down these steps that Remruc's mystery woman was heading and so he followed her, at a discrete distance.

Sorta sat gazing out into the blackness of the rock pool. It seemed to beckon her with its promise of tranquillity, a chance to escape from the pain and turmoil of her present state. She felt herself drawn, slowly, subtly towards the edge, her movements stiff and puppet like, her mind watching herself with detached fascination.

A sound from her left broke the awful magnetism of the water and she looked round guiltily as a figure emerged from the shadow of the overhang. When the light fell on his face Sorta's mind raced with excitement, "Curmer!" she ran towards him, the joy that filled her colouring the name with a brightness that was almost painful. She had only travelled a few steps when she realised her mistake, the mind that met hers was not her beloved Curmer, but a pained and stricken shadow of the strong Remruc.

"No, I am sorry, you are mistaken," was the sympathetic

response. Sorta felt the words enter her mind like a knife, cutting deep into the elation she had felt and letting the despair and anguish spill out into her public mind.

"Lord Remruc, my apologies," she managed to form the reply with great difficulty as she tried desperately to control herself. Remruc had felt the joy in her original mistake and now the anguish in the realisation of the truth, it did not take much to know who this girl was and why she was behaving in such an unusual manner. He felt for her and his sympathy seemed to lessen the pain that he was feeling.

"There is no need to apologise, it is an easy mistake to make. I know your face, you are one of the newly appointed Healers are you not?" Remruc kept his thought light and as cheerful as he could and he was pleased to see the girl begin to relax.

"Yes Lord Remruc, I was at the ceremony earlier today." Sorta managed a half smile.

"Please no formalities," Remruc raised his hand and smiled to emphasise his thoughts, "I see that you like to visit this pool, so do I and I seldom have the chance to indulge in conversation. Would you care to join me? I feel that we both have a lot to talk about." Without waiting for an answer, he took her arm and led her to the nearest seat.

Sorta followed unresisting, bewildered and grateful for a friendly face.

It was dawn before Remruc and Sorta left the garden. They had discussed their mutual predicament and each was resigned to their fate. It had been refreshing for Remruc to be able to admit to someone the attraction he had for Eriya and Sorta had been sympathetic to his feelings considering the hurt that Eriya had inadvertently inflicted on her.

He in turn had tried to be supportive to Sorta and, after taking the time to talk to her, he understood why Curmer loved her so much. It was then that he realised how distressed Curmer must be with this unusual turn of events. He was angry with himself for being so childish and shutting Curmer out. He now realised that his brother had probably needed him more than at any other time in his life and he had let him down. A gentle squeeze on his arm disturbed his thoughts and he glanced down at Sorta.

"I must return to my rooms and rest. Today is my day off, so no one will be surprised if I sleep late. Remember what I have said and thank you, Remruc for your help, your secret will always be safe with me." Although her mind was tired and her thoughts still showing the hurt in her heart, Remruc knew that she was more than capable of drawing on her inner strength and recovering from the pain. They parted company and Remruc watched her till she had disappeared into the healer hall.

He slowly made his way back to his home, chagrin and fatigue dictating the pace he set. The city was coming to life; people were setting about their business with an efficient jovial air. There were many greetings and salutes by both Nemn and Chai as he wandered along the streets. Remruc made an effort and smiled and responded to the good humour with a joviality he did not feel. As he entered the Chieftain's home a wave of anxiety almost overwhelmed him. He considered that Curmer might not forgive his behaviour or maintained the distance that he had set? Frightened by his own thoughts, he tentatively sent out a tendril of thought on their private line. Curmer's mind was open, but he was asleep and Remruc quickly withdrew the inquiry lest he disturb him. Remruc was not sure if he was glad that Curmer was asleep, but he crept quietly to his own rooms to try to rest before he had to face his brother.

Emur and Rume were well on their way towards sunset

before Curmer stirred from his exhausted sleep. He stretched and yawned, not quite fully recovered from his night vigil that he finally had to give up. He washed and dressed quickly, determined to initiate as soon as possible Lenta's plan to save them from this terrible situation. As he made his way to the main hall, he passed Remruc's quarters, the door was slightly ajar, carefully Curmer opened it and glanced into the room. The living area was deserted. Curmer moved further in and looked through the archway leading to Remruc's sleeping platform. His brother was lying face down, fully dressed and sound asleep. Curmer could not help smiling at the ridiculous expression on Remruc's face which was squashed into the soft sheets that covered his platform. He backed out of the room, more determined than ever to right the situation and so hopefully gaining his brother's forgiveness.

He marched quickly towards the hall calling for Lenta to join him. To his surprise she answered his thoughts quickly and loudly, "I have been waiting Lord Curmer," she replied, her humour not entirely masked by the pretended acidity, "for some time." He turned into the hall to find Lenta deep in discussion with Eskara and his most trusted elder.

"Lord Curmer. I trust you are well rested?" Eskara rose stiffly from his seat and bowed. His thoughts were deliberately neutral, and Curmer wondered if he realised just how much trouble his speech had caused.

"Yes Lord Eskara I am. I expect Lenta has filled you in on our initial proposals. I do hope that you understand my reasons for delaying the proposed marriage that you so generously consented to." Curmer kept his mind clear of any emotion, but he did not miss the slightly embarrassed tinge to Eskara's reply,

"Yes, yes, I fully understand and I do agree that it would only be right that we at least attempt what you have proposed."

Eskara quickly moved the conversation along, only too pleased to try to alleviate the embarrassment that he had caused. "Should we not consult with Lord Remruc? After all it will be up to him to organise such an expedition." Lenta and Curmer exchanged glances,

"Lord Remruc is still sleeping. I wanted to ask your opinion before we raised the matter with him. As soon as he wakes we will ask him to join us. Now let us try to formulate a plan of action." Curmer skilfully manoeuvred the Nemn Chief away from the touchy subject of Remruc.

He was still not sure that Remruc would listen to him if he tried to approach him alone, but if Eskara, Lenta and this elder backed him up, then Remruc would have to listen.

A dull ache penetrated his brain, forcing him to full alertness. He opened his eyes carefully, flinching at the light from the torch which burned brightly in the corner. Rolling over onto his back, Remruc groaned at the stiffness in his neck and gently rubbed the offending muscles. All too quickly the events of the previous evening came flooding back and Remruc felt a sickening feeling in his stomach as he considered his impulsive actions. He slowly sat up, and judging by the amount of light in his living area he figured that it must be well into the daylight hours. With deliberate motions he bathed and dressed, pausing to look out at the bright, bustling, busy city beneath him. The torches were being reset for another night, and the sudden realisation that he had slept for most of the day hit home. With quicker movements, he finished dressing and hurried out into the corridor, a passing guard informed him that Lord Curmer, Lord Eskara, Healer Lenta, and Elder Kanar were meeting in the great hall. With a formal acknowledgement to the guard, Remruc walked briskly down to the hall, a mild irritation that he had not been awakened for this meeting lending urgency to his steps.

Barely pausing long enough for the announcement of his presence to be acknowledged, he strode into the hall, heading first for the dais then, realising that no one was sitting there, altered his direction to the informal group in the corner.

"Lord Remruc, I am glad that you have joined us, please sit down." Lenta rose, her thoughts pleasant and light, dispelling the annoyance in Remruc's mind. He allowed himself to be led to a chair and it was only after he had been seated that he realised Curmer was next to him, watching carefully. Remruc decided to be brazen and sent a message on their private line.

"Good morning brother. I trust you are well?" he sensed the initial shock from Curmer and then a relieved reply came bouncing back.

"I am now Remruc. Thank you for asking." Curmer glanced quickly at Lenta, who had noticed his surprised expression and had guessed the reason behind it. Eskara started the discussion by filling in Remruc with the proposed idea.

"Lord Remruc, we have been considering the possibility of sending an expedition across both our borders to contact the Tarl, Doona and Jenta. It is quite probable that the plague has devastated their populations as well and our healers are of the opinion that they should offer their serum to all and sundry. What are your thoughts on this matter?" Eskara watched Remruc and listened to his reply, ready to catch any hints of emotion or mood in his thoughts.

"Lords Eskara, Curmer, healer Lenta and elder Kanar, I am surprised that the idea did not occur to me earlier. I think it would be most generous of our healers to offer help to those in need and I can only see advantages for both our tribes.

Perhaps some of the other clans would wish to join us as well; together we can become a strong race once more. The Nemn and Chai have shown that it is possible for two clans to live together without cutting each other's throats therefore I can see no reason why the whole of the San cannot unite. Our peoples have suffered so much alone, perhaps together we can survive and thrive." The more Remruc thought his reply, the more eager he became with the whole concept. He and Curmer had only considered the unison of the Nemn and Chai, but now a whole new prospect was laid before him. Why could they not combine the talents of every tribe of San? He drifted into his private thoughts unaware of the group around him.

Eventually Lenta prompted the second point of their discussions. "There is one problem, Lord Remruc." He looked at Lenta sharply, drawn suddenly from his private calculations as to how to organise such an expedition. Lenta continued in careful, muted tones, "a journey of this enormity would of course take time and would draw on a vast amount of manpower and resources. Everyone would be needed to help coordinate communications, medications and supplies and sacrifices will have to be made by everyone. One of the most obvious being that of the proposed marriage of Curmer and Eriya."

The sudden tension and pained look that flashed across Remruc's face was not missed by Lenta and she quickly proceeded with her plan. "It would not be viable to carry out this marriage at the present time. It was planned to symbolise the union of our two tribes, but if the other clans of the San decide to join us, would it not be prudent to at least allow both yourself, Curmer and Eriya a choice of partners from suitably high ranking?" She paused and looked for support from Curmer he smiled and nodded for her to continue.

"In this way the other tribes, if they do decide to join us, would not feel left out. Just think how the other Chieftains would react if the Nemn and Chai were so obviously sided with one another. It could be possible that because of our alliance they would assume a plot against them and so not trust us. We feel that it would not help to convince them to stay with us. What are your opinions?"

Remruc looked at the ground, the emotions within him threatening to break free. He hardly dared to hope that perhaps he could win Eriya's heart while his soldiers were scouring the planet for survivors. This was an opportunity that he had not believed would come along, he could not let this idea be quashed, he must give his support. He looked up, a slight frown creasing his forehead,

"I can see your argument as being legitimate, but I feel that you underestimate the other clans. Perhaps they would see an alliance between our two tribes as proof that we can all live peacefully together." Curmer and Lenta exchanged worried glances while Eskara nodded thoughtfully, this new option had not occurred to him. "However," Remruc continued, "there is too much at stake to take such a chance. I will agree to this plan and to the obvious conditions that you have stated. Now I will go and organise my guards. We will have a lot of planning to do and Lord Eskara, I will require the assistance of your best Nemn trackers and guides. If we have to cross your lands, I would prefer to consult with someone who is familiar with every nook and cranny of the terrain." He rose before he had finished his thoughts and was halfway across the floor, a strong sense of purpose and determination in his step.

"It appears," said Curmer with a smile, "that the meeting is over." He and Lenta excused themselves, each moving off to carry out their pre-arranged plans. Eskara watched them go, pondering on their motives.

He had sensed in their thoughts that Lenta and Curmer had been trying to manoeuvre him into agreeing to their proposition and he was glad of this opportunity to correct his terrible mistake without losing face. He had a fairly good idea as to why they so desperately wanted to postpone the wedding and he felt that they were correct in their judgement. Eskara sighed, he was getting old. All this intrigue and secrecy tired him out, he motioned to his elder, and they left the great hall to its own brooding silence.

The warriors of the Chai and Nemn were more than eager to volunteer for this dangerous mission. They had been becoming increasingly bored with the routine drills and uneventful patrols, with not so much as a Cuc encounter to add excitement to their duties. Remruc was concerned with this unusual phenomena. Not a single Cuc had been sighted anywhere near their lands since they had driven the winged beast from the smallholding. It was popular belief that all of the Cuc were now terrified to venture near the San mountains, but Remruc was not so sure, there was still a nagging doubt in the back of his mind that this was the calm before the storm. It took a few weeks to draw up a rota system for communications and exploration parties. The Nemn were familiar with the land that bordered the Tarl territory, while the Chai decided to contact the Doona. The Nemn did not care much for the Tarl, and they had never bothered to send raiding parties into their small lands. According to the Nemn elders, the Tarl had nothing of value and were obsessed with making strange things from metal that they called machines. The Nemn records and traditional stories told of this unusual clan of the San who were totally against any form of violence. They were intent on discovering new ways of making their life easier, by making metal machines that could do their work for them. No Chai had ever met a Tarl and as far as Remruc could make out the Nemn were not keen on their company either. They said that they were a strange clan, quiet and unobtrusive and as cold as their machines.

It was the bravest of the Nemn warriors that volunteered to venture into the Tarl lands. They would not be frightened easily by any strange behaviour or sights.

The Doona, Remruc was familiar with. When he was young Storn had led a raiding party into their lands. He had been allowed to tag along, for experience and fun. The Doona were only interested in their animals. They had perfected breeding techniques for a variety of different kinds of creatures that had once roamed the plains of Surn when the planet was young. These creatures had been adapted for different uses; food, transport, clothing, animals etc. Normally if left unprovoked, the Doona would keep themselves to themselves, but if their families or beloved animals were threatened, they could be a formidable opponent.

Remruc remembered his first experience of the Doona well; the Chai raiding party were trying to obtain better livestock to replenish their own.

They had chosen a remote settlement on the fringe of the Doona territory; for even the most remote or poor settlements of the Doona had better animals than the most wealthy of Chai families. Storn had chosen an impressive mantel, from the milling herds on the edge of the settlement cavern, to be his new work beast. The mantelo had been bred from the smaller grazing animals that had evolved on the Surn plains. They were developed for speed, with slim slender legs, long elastic backs, small narrow heads and a very long tail acted as a counter balance. The mantelo could not be ridden, but they could pull sleds and carts at high speeds, they were surefooted and nimble along underground passages, their vision was well adapted for poor light, with a form of echo-location that came into play in total darkness.

This made them invaluable for the San, who could rely on them to guide a sled accurately home.

The Chai raiders had managed to creep among the herds, singling which of the tame animals they wanted and were slowly slipping them out of the cavern, thinking that they had succeeded in their raid, when the alarm was raised. The Doona were quick to respond, the Chai raiders hurriedly ushered the beasts into the passage way and Remruc was given the responsibility of driving them back to the Chai lands, while the warriors guarded their backs and held off the attack. The Doona were growling with fury, their minds throwing out all manner of curses on their hated enemies. They fell upon the fierce Chai with suicidal intensity, the battle was grim and the screams of the dying sickened Remruc as he tried to close his mind.

He had just managed to drive the frightened mantelos almost to the limits of their territory when an unexpected attacker struck him from a hidden passage. He had fallen to the ground with blood seeping from a gash in his arm, instinctively rolling to avoid a second strike, he stood up slowly and had been amazed to see a single Doona youngster, not much older than himself, standing between him and the mantelos. The Doona's mind was a confusing mixture of fear, anger and hatred. Remruc had been taken aback by the intensity of the emotions showered upon him.

It was obvious that the Doona would not let him pass and so a duel began in that dark and lonely passage, a duel to the death. The Doona was older than Remruc, but less experienced in fighting techniques. Remruc's skill with a blade was the only reason he succeeded in defeating his opponent. Several times he was beaten back by the furious desperation of the youth in front of him, the suicidal efforts by the boy had frightened him more than anything. Eventually the Doona made a fatal mistake and left himself unguarded for Remruc to pounce with a killing thrust deep into his side. As the Doona died, Remruc heard his thoughts and it had left a deep impression of respect for these people.

The boy had told him to please love and care for his mantelo. Nothing else had mattered to him except the safety of his beloved beasts. Remruc had carried the body back to his city with him. When the rest of the raiding party finally caught up with him they did not question his wish to give this unknown Doona a proper Chai burial. Storn had nodded slowly with an understanding that was uncharacteristic. Remruc had always wondered what the boy's name was.

Remruc was jolted from his thoughts and back to the present by the urgent request by his guard to oversee the final preparations for the first contact party of Chai to go into Doona lands. He marched swiftly to the far side of the city, taking a mental note at how busy and full the buildings were. A far cry from the emptiness of a few months ago.

Remruc had chosen his party carefully. He needed several strong, aggressive warriors in case the Doona were not as easy to convince as the Nemn but, more importantly, he needed a group leader that had the respect of the other soldiers, but who would be sensitive and diplomatic. He had chosen Rarl, the guard who had befriended the Nemn hunter and who had helped to change Remruc's opinion on the Nemn people.

Among the party of warriors were several Nemn. They were all very good trackers and had offered their services to Remruc, knowing that they would probably be safer among Chai warriors than with their own party heading into Tarl territory. All were present and they were busily checking their weapons and equipment. The Nemn hunters had taken to wearing Chai clothing and although they had brightened up the plain uniforms with a few decorations, it was most pleasing to Remruc that they would not be as conspicuous in the dull outfits. Final briefs were given, then the party headed off, out through the west gate of the city on a long journey through the eerie and deserted Chai homeland.

It was a frustratingly slow process. Relays of runners and communication posts were set up along the proposed routes; these sent constantly updated information back to the main city and headquarters. The drain on manpower was becoming more noticeable as the parties ventured further and further away from base. As the communication runners were positioned two days away from each other but still only bringing them close enough for maximum range telepathy, the depletion on the city's resources was lessened. The news that was filtering back was not encouraging. The Nemn did not know the location of the Tarl main city and so were conducting a sweep search up and down the mountain ranges, their minds open for any hint of Tarl thought.

The Chai were in the same predicament with the Doona. Although several locations of small holdings and outposts were known these were proving to be completely deserted, with plenty of animal carcasses lying around. Remruc and Curmer were becoming increasingly worried about the Doona. If all of their beasts had perished, it was not inconceivable that the surviving Doona had committed suicide.

Eskara, on hearing their thoughts on the matter was quite distressed. The Nemn, unlike the Chai, seldom carried out such an act and he was shocked that an entire clan could do such a thing. Fortunately, the Chai patrol encountered an inhabited outpost, barely scraping a living from their animals.

The initial contact sent a wave of hope surging through the searchers and they renewed their efforts. When the Chai patrol moved into the settlement, they were shocked at the condition of the carefully tended beasts. The Doona themselves were too weak and sick to put up any resistance and they were expecting no mercy from what they took to be raiders. The patrol treated those they could with serum they were carrying and explained the reason behind their journey.

To their surprise, the survivors were most grateful for help and begged them to aid their sick animals, some even denying their own treatment until a favourite mantelo had been inoculated. The patrol complied with their pleas, carefully trying to build up a certain amount of trust. Extra help was sent for and the Doona were taken back to the Chai city. The patrol continued their search, following the directions given to them by one of the settlers. Thus the pattern developed. Several Doona smallholdings had been saved in this way before the Nemn discovered the main and only city of the Tarl.

Herka was the leader of the search party for the Nemn. They found the metal city dead centre of the Tarl territory. At first it appeared totally deserted, the sharp edged buildings, cold and harsh to the eye. The reports of the first sighting of a Tarl dwelling were quickly relayed back to the Chai city. Eskara was fascinated by the reports of the method of lighting used in the city. Apparently there were no torches to be seen, but long strips of glowing rods lined the cavern roof, shedding a blue tinged light across a grey, hard city.

The Nemn patrol moved very slowly and carefully along perfectly straight and geometric streets all reflecting the blue light back from the buildings towering above them. As they ventured up the main thoroughfare, a sudden noise sent them scattering, seeking cover. A metal box was moving slowly along the street, every so often it paused, an opening would appear in one side and metal arms would reach out to pick up or straighten something that was out of place. This task done it would continue along the street till it met another offending article.

Herka gripped his axe tightly, he knew the blade was sharp, but he was not sure if it would even dent this metal monster. He leapt from his hiding place and stood directly in front of the oncoming box. His axe swung high in the air and landed with a dull thud on the roof of the metal casing. The box, completely ignoring his attack, neatly moved around the Nemn and continued its tidying duty along the main road.

The other members of the patrol stood up and gazed after the vehicle in amazement. They were so engrossed in the obsessive behaviour of this unusual item that they did not see or hear the diminutive figure emerge from one of the buildings.

"Have you come to kill us?" the timid thought sent them all spinning round to stare at one of the city's inhabitants.

The Tarl, although fully grown, was small and slender, dressed in a strange material that gave off a metallic sheen and nervously twisting his hands. Herka stepped forward, he towered above the Tarl, his muscular frame highlighting the frailty of the other. He tried to form a reply that would calm this terrified man, using a gentle, inquiring mood to colour his thoughts, "I am Herka. Leader of the Chai-Nemn search patrol. We have come to help your people, and offer you refuge from the sickness." Herka offered what he hoped was an encouraging smile.

The shock in the Tarl's mind at the mention of both the Chai and Nemn clans was obvious and Herka thought for a moment that the small figure was going to faint with fright.

"Did... did you say Chai and Nemn search patrol?" was the

whispered reply, barely felt in their minds.

"Yes. Our clans have joined together to try to cure the plague. You have had the plague here haven't you?" Herka frowned and the Tarl cringed in fear.

"Oh, yes definitely, but I am afraid you are too late. You see we have managed to save only a handful of our people and those of us who have survived... well, what I mean is... we have our own medicine and, it was really too late to do anything for anyone else... you see we thought that everyone would be... oh, I'm not explaining this very well...", the utter desperation in the Tarl was obvious to a mind numb Cuc and Herka decided to stop him there

"Perhaps Tarl, you should let me speak to who is in charge. Where is your Chief?" The small man was confused for a moment, then realisation dawned on him.

"Chief? You still have Chiefs? We do not have such a hierarchy anymore. Our voted leader is Tahlm and he is working with the other technicians on a new project. If you follow me I will take you to see him." The Tarl nervously bowed and nodded his way along the road, beckoning the patrol to follow him.

Herka glanced at the other patrol members, talking to them on a private line. "What do you think? Should we trust him? I do not understand half of what he says, but the half I do understand I don't like. He seems to have let slip a bit too much about the plague, share your thoughts with me. Oh, and Kartu, send a relay message quickly back to Lords Remruc, Curmer and Eskara. I think they should give me orders before I offer the Tarl sanctuary with our people." The general consensus from the patrol was that they were not going to learn any more if they did not follow this Tarl. All agreed that should anything happen, they should attack first and ask questions later.

Chapter Nine

The last of the surviving Doona were still journeying back to the Chai lands, when the message from Herka was relayed to Remruc at the guard hall.

"More trouble," thought Remruc to himself as he listened quietly to the runner. The Doona had not been as easy to convince as the Nemn, and there had been several skirmishes and ambushes on the search patrol. Fortunately no one had been seriously injured, the Doona were still far too weak from plague to be able to put up any real resistance, but the patrol was becoming increasingly more frustrated as their attempts at peaceful contact were being thwarted.

They had finally reached the main settlement of the Doona only to find a handful of survivors caring for their remaining animals. The carcasses of the dead were all piled into one building and according to Rarl, the stench of the decaying bodies would have made the mouth of a Cuc water.

The Doona in the main settlement were leaderless, the Chief and all of his kin had perished and those left alive remained only to care for their animals. Barely one hundred of the entire Doona population had survived, but to their credit they had managed to save more than three hundred of their beasts. The survivors were dispirited and shattered, the general feeling among them was that they were being taken prisoner along with their animals and no amount of convincing or reassuring by their Chai escorts would change their opinions. The only thing that kept the Doona from fighting and resisting moving was the promise that all of their animals would have better food and care in the now thriving Chai city.

It was the sudden and surprising appearance of Nemn that gave the weak survivors hope.

They met the incoming parties at the west gate and welcomed them into the city, the Nemn were good at organising food, clothing and accommodation for the refugees and understood the concern they had for the beasts that had been brought along with them.

Remruc was more than grateful for their competence at filtering the incoming bodies into the now bustling city and for organising their animals into grazing herds. They had to use food caverns from the closest settlements to the main city, to accommodate the influx of beasts, helping to keep the city food cavern dedicated to grain.

Curmer and Lenta had been in charge of the medicinal supplies and serum production, with Sorta working closely as team organiser. Eriya had been very quiet over the last few weeks; she had hardly been seen out of her rooms in the healer hall, her duties being confined to recording and stock taking. Remruc felt sorry for her. It must have been quite a blow to her ego to find that there were some things more important than her wedding. He knew now that Curmer did not want to marry her and was planning to announce his betrothal to Sorta as soon as things quietened down, this pleased him immensely. Eriya was far too proud to take the place of a second mate and it was now common knowledge that the Doona Chief along with his family had perished. That would leave his competitors down to the Tarl, who the Nemn despised anyway, or the Jenta.

Jenta, Remruc almost thought the word in his public mind. They were an unknown quantity. The Chai and Nemn had never come into contact with this tribe that inhabited the opposite side of their world. He would have to learn all he could from their neighbours the Doona and Tarl. That thought brought him back to the message the guard had given him. He knew he could trust Herka's judgement, he was as shrewd a diplomat as he was hunter! If he was wary and suspicious of these Tarl then there was a good reason. Remruc stood up from his desk, sending his knife skittering along its surface. He pulled a face at the writing slates strewn over the end of the desk.

"I hate all this boring work, I need some action," he mused, "perhaps I should visit these Tarl and judge them for myself." He moved swiftly out of the room, heading directly to the healing hall, his stride long, his steps urgent.

Curmer and Sorta were pouring over the details of the latest batch of Doona refugees. "Their animals are healthy enough, but they are in a sorry state," Sorta thought irritably. "I do not understand these people, they don't care if they live or die, just as long as their animals are alright," she continued, her mind swirling with varied colours of mood and urgency.

Curmer smiled and gave her a playful shove nearly sending her flying. "Stop moaning! This is the second last party, our patrol is coming back with the others and our work is almost finished." He grabbed her on his last thought and held her close as she put up a half-hearted struggle, "then we can get on with our lives."

Sorta gave up trying to get away and smiled back at Curmer, "what on Surn will Eriya say?" she mused, "she will not be pleased at being passed over for plain old me."

Curmer growled softly between his teeth. "She can say and think what she likes. Eskara is no fool; he did not want her to choose me, he knows her better than anyone else and I know that Eriya will eventually see her own heart. Now that I think about it, I haven't seen so much as a hair of her since we announced the search plan."

Sorta laughed and slipped from Curmer's grasp. "Ah," she thought cunningly, "Lenta and I have been putting a little distance between you and her. We decided that the less she saw of you and the more of Remruc the better things would be."

Curmer looked at her inquiringly a smile playing on his lips, "What have you two been up to? I thought Remruc was too busy with his guards to talk to me, but it seems he has been thrown into the clutches of Eriya." He growled menacingly at the mention of her name and made a mock grab at Sorta.

She quickly swatted him away and made her escape through the open door, her final thoughts came floating back to him. "Remember all that boring slate work that Remruc has been compiling? Well Eriya is cataloguing and filing, that means she has to liaise with the writer."

Curmer watched her disappear down the corridor. He fervently hoped that their little scheme did not push his brother and Eriya together too quickly. Turning back to the list he continued to check off the names of the Doona next to their animals and belongings. He was almost finished when Remruc surged through the door his body communicating his anxiety before his mind.

"I have just received a report from the Nemn patrol, they have finally found the Tarl and are establishing contact." He flopped down in a convenient chair before he had finished. Not waiting for a response from Curmer he continued, "Herka has spoken with one of them and is not at all sure of their reliability. He seems to think they know more about this plague than they should, something about this Tarl saying that they didn't have time to do anything for anyone else. What do you think?" he looked at his brother, a frown on his face.

Curmer moved slowly into the chair opposite, his mind covering all sorts of possibilities. "Surely, Herka does not think that the Tarl deliberately caused the sickness?"

Remruc's expression was grim. "He doesn't say, but he will

not offer our help nor invite them into our lands until we give him further instructions." Remruc continued to frown, biting his lip, deep in thought. "Should we bring this to the attention of Eskara?" he asked.

"No. Eskara has not been well, he is old and I think very tired of this life. We will deal with this matter, there is no need to give him any cause for concern. What do you suggest Remruc? I know that you have a plan, I can see it in your face."

Remruc smiled and leaned back in his chair. "Well, it is obvious that one of us should go out there and assess the situation. You are far too busy with the organisation of the refugees, therefore I will go. The message has taken eight days to reach us, I can send advance warning of my journey and get there as quickly as possible. Herka probably already knows the truth by now, so I will take a full complement of guards, just in case." Remruc stood determined to leave the room before Curmer could think of a good reason to keep him in the city. Instead Curmer surprised him.

"You are right brother, much as it troubles me to let you go. I will inform Lenta and Eriya of our decision."

"Eriya?", Remruc's sharp thought flashed across, "Why must you say anything to Eriya?"

Curmer carefully toned his thoughts to a neutral mood. "She is Eskara's daughter, and has been taking more and more responsibility for governing the Nemn as her father deteriorates. It is our duty to tell her." He saw Remruc relax.

"In that case, would it not be better if I informed her? After all, I will be going into the Tarl lands."

Curmer smiled and hurriedly tided his desk, turning his back on Remruc. "That would be a great help Remruc, as long as you do not mind and it doesn't take you out of your way." Curmer was careful to keep his mind neutral.

But Remruc gave him a second, suspicious look as he made his way out of the door. "Not at all Curmer, it will not take me long."

Eriya placed the bowl of half-finished soup on the table. Lord Eskara was resting in his sleeping chamber and he had done well to eat even a little of what she had given him. Eriya had been a healer long enough to know that there was nothing she could do to help her father but that knowledge didn't take away the desperation inside her.

She left his quarters and made her way along the corridor to her rooms, running her hand along the cool wall, delighting in the texture of the stone. She had come to appreciate the subtle beauty of the interior of the Chai dwellings and was no longer afraid to touch their sensuous surfaces. Opposite her rooms was a large balcony that viewed the entire marvellous city. She was drawn to the balcony, hoping to free her thoughts and worries and let them fly across the cavern to soak up the infectious joy emanating from the mixed tribes.

There she stood, alone at last, wrapped in her private mind, a different person from the haughty woman that had first entered the gates. Eriya had been humbled at last. The confidence in her beauty and ability to bend any male to her will was gone. She realised that the expedition to the other tribes had been an excuse, perhaps the only excuse for Curmer to avoid their marriage. She had not known Sorta and Curmer were lovers, but it had shocked her to find that for the first time in her life she could not take what she wanted. Eriya smiled a slow sad smile and chided herself.

She had not really wanted Curmer, yes he was handsome both in body and mind, but she did not love him. The image of Sorta and Curmer slipped into her head, she had seen and felt the feelings that had leaked from their private thoughts and into their public minds, Eriya had never experienced such an intensity of emotion, perhaps this was what she wanted more than anything else. To feel this way about someone else; to care more for them than for herself. A stab of grief sliced her heart. She felt this way for her father. She had not known her mother who had died to give her life. Her older brothers and Eskara's mates were all now dead from the plague and it had been Eriya that Eskara had showered with love and devotion. She had taken it all but given very little back. Eriya looked at herself as though for the first time and as all of her memories came flooding back she saw her little selfish ways, arrogant behaviour and cutting remarks. How proud she had been. How spoilt.

She rested her hands on the ledge of the balcony and as the shell of her former self was slowly stripped away, a new and better Eriya was revealed, like a soft, silky butterfly emerging from it's ugly cocoon, eager to dry itself and become the beautiful creature it was destined to be. A figure moved out from the shadow of the corridor and moved towards her. She turned in surprise, hurriedly closing her mind and composing herself. To her dismay she recognised Remruc, she cringed inside with humiliation as she imagined how much he must be enjoying her situation considering how much he disliked her.

"Lady Eriya," he said softly, "I am sorry to disturb you, but I have important news." Remruc was trying to control the ache in his heart. He had been in the corridor long enough to have picked up the pain in Eriya and to sense her loneliness. A rare glimpse had been given of the real Eriya and he was more determined than ever to win her love. She moved away from him as he approached, unwilling to let him get too close. Remruc stopped a knot of frustration within him.

"Lord Remruc. What can the news be that concerns me?" Her thoughts were strained, her mind tense.

"Lady Eriya. I am aware of the condition of Lord Eskara

and I feel that you are better able to deal with what I have to say." Remruc continued to use neutral tones, mellowed slightly to a light softness. The quick flash of pain across Eriya's face at the mention of her father was not lost on him and he was determined to keep the conversation as optimistic as possible. They seated themselves on one of the wall benches, each conspicuously at either end. Remruc dared not risk getting any closer for fear of upsetting her.

She listened quietly to his thoughts, analysing with her diplomatic mind all possibilities for the suspicions of the patrol. The leader Herka was known to her and, for once, she had to agree with Remruc's choice of commander and trust in his abilities. There was a long silence as she considered his response to the problem.

"Lord Remruc," she finally said, her mind tinged with curiosity and determination, "I think that you must travel to these Tarl and decide for us all the best course of action. If what you suspect turns out to be true, then I know we can trust you to deal with them accordingly." She looked at the determined Chieftain at the other end of the bench. If nothing else, she thought to herself, you are a very capable leader.

Remruc smiled and rose from the bench, "I am glad that you agree Lady Eriya. We will leave at sunset."

Chapter Ten

The troop of armed warriors swept across the night desert led by a Nemn tracker. They seemed to move as a single giant body that flowed over the rocky surface, moving with liquid steps towards the nearest entrance to the Nemn caverns. Eyes glowing faintly in the blackness of night, the company marched in silence, minds alert for incoming Cuc, rearguards watching the skies. The tracker stopped and motioned for them to enter the barely disguised entrance tunnel, this they did, pouring down the open mouth, armour clicking ominously under their cloaks. They passed the first communication post, manned by three runners. One was already a day ahead of them, warning Herka of their approach, another had just returned with a relay message which he quickly passed on to Remruc.

"Herka has met their leader, Tahlm and other survivors. He says that the Tarl are very strange, weak in body but strong of will. The report states that the Tarl are accepting responsibility for the plague although Herka does not understand their excuses or explanations. He urges you to come quickly, the other warriors want to wreak revenge on the Tarl and their city." The runner gasped for breath as he relayed the ominous news.

Remruc gave the order to continue to his troops, they would have to do without rest, at least until they reached the second communication post. It was a frustrating journey. Remruc was desperate to reach the Tarl lands before it was too late, but he could not push his troops too hard or they would be in no fit state to fight at the end of the journey.

The Nemn were not as efficient in their communication tunnels as the Chai and it was often the case that they had to go above ground for a few miles before connecting with the next settlement system. Often, Remruc and the guards would reach the end of the tunnels just as Rume and Emur were reaching midday. They then would have an afternoon of waiting for the cool of the evening before venturing out into the open.

This allowed the hard pushed warriors a welcome rest, but it was driving Remruc to distraction. They reached the fourth and last communication post, before the two day journey to the Tarl city, just as an exhausted runner arrived. His tired mind passed on his message while his straining lungs heaved for breath.

"Lord Remruc. Herka has managed to understand what the Tarl have been saying. They claim they are responsible for the plague, but it was the Jenta who caused it. Herka was given a lengthy explanation as to how it happened, but he does not understand some of the terms they are using. His patrol have calmed down, but are now intent on continuing into the Jenta territory, to see what they have to say for themselves. The Tarl get most distraught at the mere mention of Jenta and they are preventing the patrol from leaving."

Remruc clenched his teeth in anger. "Tell me how such a reputedly weak tribe can restrain strong warriors?" He moved over to the runner and pulled him to his feet.

"Lord Remruc, they are not stopping them by force, but they keep stealing their weapons, or closing off exit tunnels. Herka is finding it most frustrating." Remruc put the runner down, a low growl in his throat. He was really beginning to dislike the Tarl. The company set off again, even more determined to reach their goal.

Herka spun round, his teeth bared, his hackles raised, "Tahlm! Where are my weapons!" The diminutive figure crouched even lower into the metal chair, a look of sheer terror on his face and blind desperation in his mind.

"Please, please warrior Herka, try to understand. We dare not let your people leave here and journey into the Jenta's territory.

They would be most upset and may wreak terrible revenge on us!" Tahlm's mind almost screeched the last thought as Herka grabbed him by the metal clothing he wore and lifted him out of the chair.

"Do you realise what Lord Remruc will do to you when he finds out that you are preventing us from leaving? Did I not tell you that he is Chieftain of the Chai?" He watched with satisfaction as the small man, legs dangling in the air, almost fainted at the mere mention of the ferocious warrior clan. Somewhere in his heart Herka pitied the Tarl leader, he could imagine the almost constant state of terror this timid man must be in. To be faced with the Nemn warriors must be bad enough, but to know that he will probably meet a painful and slow death at the hands of the Chai must be driving him insane.

"What kind of tribe are the Jenta, to have you so afraid of them that you will risk torture and death by the Chai? Are they a warrior tribe also? Do you think that they could defeat us?" The curiosity in Herka's mind dispelled his anger as he considered his thoughts. This change of mood encouraged Tahlm and he quickly and eagerly gave a description of the Jenta.

"The Jenta would be no match for you and your noble warriors Herka. They would cringe in terror to be faced with an army of Chai, but they are very clever and secretive clan, they would plot and plan revenge, carefully scheming an attack on your people. Oh no, warrior Herka, they would not attack physically, they would instead poison the minds of your people and set them against each other. That is the real danger of the Jenta. Their ability to encourage people into

155

self-destruction."

The sorrow in the Tarl's mind as he finished his thoughts gave Herka a jolt and he gently put the small man down. He sat down in the metal chair opposite the shrunken figure and leaned on the table.

"Our people have always fought each other. It has always been this way." Herka thought.

Tahlm looked up slowly and shook his head, "no, warrior Herka, it was not always this way. In the past the San lived happily with one another. The world was young then and the people lived above the ground wandering free, but as we retreated underground and competition for space and food became important, the Jenta grew jealous of the other clans. They were not a large or powerful tribe. They could not compete openly and fairly for space, so they spread poisonous thoughts among the clans, turning one against the other, creating ideas and beliefs that have kept our people apart for thousands of years. You see, warrior Herka, the Jenta knew that if the other clans were busy fighting amongst themselves then they would never have time to attack their lands." Tahlm looked at the ground, his eyes blank, his mind depressed.

"Why did they not try to conquer you Tahlm? Please do not be offended, but your people would be easily defeated in battle."

"They tried once, but we are not as defenceless as we seem. You have seen the machines that clean our city? Well, we are capable of making other machines that can kill." Tahlm hurriedly continued as he saw the instant alertness on the Nemn's face. "Do not worry, warrior Herka, that was long ago, the machines have been dismantled and put to other use. The Jenta needed only to be taught a lesson once. They did not try again. We decided that it would be better to try to help their people to improve their living conditions and so we struck a bargain with them. If they left us alone, we would give them the occasional gift, something that would benefit their society and it has been this way for many centuries."

Herka nodded in agreement to the logic of this situation, it was a small price to pay for peace. He carefully arranged his thoughts then presented his proposal to Tahlm. "Let me take a small section of my guards into the Jenta lands. I know that your people have an agreement with them, but they would never find out that you had anything to do with it. My mission is to seek survivors of the plague and offer help. Much as I dislike the description of the Jenta you have given me, I must carry out my orders to completion, even if that means helping this unworthy tribe."

The Tarl leader became anxious and nervous once more, he wriggled uncomfortably in his seat, his eyes flicking across the room in uncertainty. "Warrior Herka, let me try to explain once more. Our people are responsible for this plague, but it was the Jenta who created and caused it. The latest gift that we sent their Chieftain was a preserving liquid that could be used as an additive to all manner of foods and would prevent them from spoiling over long periods of time. I know that you do not understand the details of what I am saying, but try to grasp the basic concept. The Jenta must have been tampering with this liquid, for what reason only they can tell you, but the formula they accidentally stumbled on caused a normally harmless bacteria present in our water to mutate into the plague. That was how the plague was spread. Through the water systems that run under all of our lands. As you have seen, a fraction of our tribe has survived. It did not take us long to create an antidote, but our lifestyle has become so sanitised and sterile that we are very sensitive to new strains of disease. I was not quick enough to save my people and I assumed that the rest of the San had suffered the same fate. I am sorry. Perhaps we could have helped you instead." He paused and sighed, "the point that I am trying to make, warrior Herka, is that since the plague we have heard nothing from the Jenta. This can only mean that in their warped and twisted minds they blame us for their misfortune and are plotting revenge on us."

"Or perhaps they are all dead." The strange thought burst into Tahlm and Herka's minds and they both spun round in surprise to see the formidable figure of Remruc standing in the doorway. Herka rose, a smile of greeting on his face while Tahlm turned pale with fear, his body trembling uncontrollably.

"Lord Remruc! I am glad that you are here. Have you been listening long?"

"I have heard enough to know what to do, Herka. I am grateful that you sent word and I am sure that we will be able to sort this troublesome tribe out." Remruc directed his stern gaze at the almost paralysed figure of Tahlm as he advanced across the room. The surprise at seeing so young a leader was lost in the sheer terror of Tahlm's mind, his heart racing he rose unsteadily to his feet, bowing to Remruc.

"Lord of the Chai, I am honoured to be in your presence." The thoughts tumbled over one another in their urgency as the Tarl desperately tried to appease this fearful warrior. "I beg you to let me explain..." his thoughts were cut short as Remruc, towering above him, lifted him up with one arm by the scruff of his neck.

"You will come with me!" he thundered, the anger in his mind cutting into the Tarl. It was all too much for poor Tahlm, with a frightened squeak he fainted, his body swinging limply from Remruc's grasp.

Herka could not contain the amusement in his mind as he apologised for this unusual behaviour. He explained how he had painted a black and vicious picture of the Chai Lord to try to intimidate Tahlm.

With a low growl of irritation, Remruc dragged the Tarl out into the main courtyard of the building.

There he dumped him unceremoniously onto the ground and surveyed the cowering crowd of Tarl gathered there surrounded by the Chai warriors. "Is this all of them?" he asked one of his guards.

"These are all that is left of the Tarl, Lord Remruc. The Nemn patrol has confirmed this."

Remruc nodded his approval. The pathetic people in front of him were clutching each other in fear, convinced that the Chai had killed their leader.

Herka gave Tahlm a prod with his foot and he slowly began to come around. Herka gave him a helping hand to his feet and dusted him down, giving him time to get his bearings.

"Leader of the Tarl." Remruc began, his thoughts stern. "You have deliberately hindered the warriors of the Nemn and prevented them from carrying out their assigned duties. Considering that we came to you to offer our help I find this behaviour unacceptable. You will return all of the hidden weapons immediately and begin to clear your exits into the Jenta's lands. If you do not do this," Remruc turned round and looked menacingly at Tahlm, "then we will kill one Tarl for every weapon that is missing."

There was an electric current of fear and shock that ran through all of the Tarl in the courtyard. They looked at their leader desperately, their minds appealing for him to obey. Tahlm and Remruc locked eyes. For all that this Tarl leader was timid, he was determined to prevent the Chai and Nemn from provoking the Jenta. He considered his options. There was no doubt in his mind that Remruc would carry out his threat, after all he was a Chai and considering the number of weapons confiscated he would literally kill all but a handful of his people. Tahlm was torn between two decisions. If he did not obey his people would die, if he did then he risked retaliation by the Jenta. Then it suddenly occurred to him that if the Chai and Nemn were so angry with the Jenta then it was possible that they would destroy their armies and warriors.

At the moment, however, Tahlm had no choice but to comply, on an unseen and unheard command the street cleaning machines slowly filed through a gateway into the courtyard. The Chai warriors, although unnerved by such unusual contraptions, remained where they were, alert for any sudden attack. The machines opened a hatch in their sides and began to neatly lay the stolen weapons down on the ground. Their task complete they silently left.

Remruc smiled to himself and continued. "Now with regards to the matter of the plague. You have openly and freely admitted responsibility for this disaster. This is a very serious admission. Normally such an admission would have to be punished by execution, but you have not admitted to actually causing the illness. In view of these circumstances and after listening to your leader's explanation I am willing to be merciful. Instead, you will return to our city and be set to work for us."

There was a frightened mental murmur from the crowd at the thought of leaving their metal city.

"Leave our home and go with you to live like savages!" Tahlm's mind exploded uncontrollably. Remruc whirled round and grabbed him by the throat pulling him close, "savages we may be, but at least we did not play a part in destroying the entire San race!"

Tahlm sputtered and choked, his mind frantically trying to appease the Lord. "I am sorry... what I meant to say was that em... em... your lifestyle will seem strange to my people. We are not used to hard physical work or plain living. We are a very delicate tribe." He breathed a sigh of relief as Remruc released him and regarded him with disgust.

"DELICATE! NO! You are soft and unfit. Our youngest children who can barely walk are more useful than you. But you will learn. You are clever people and we can make use of your inventions, in this way you may pay back the debt you owe the San nation. It must be made clear, that as of now you have no status, no rights, no wealth and no names you will all be called by your tribe's name, Tarl. You are no people."

There was an outcry from the gathered Tarl and they moved forward. The warriors instantly drew their weapons stopping the oncoming crowd in their tracks. "Would you rather we executed you now?" The crowd was silent, but Remruc sensed that they may well prefer death to slavery and tried a different approach. "I see. You believe us to be savages, below your intelligence and unworthy. Think. This is your opportunity to change that. You can teach us what you know, help us to improve our way of life, create a new society. I will grant you this concession, your children born in our city will be granted equal status in our tribe. It is you who must pay the price for the disaster you helped to cause." He paused and gave the Tarl time to think about what he had said. He had been more than merciful, he had offered them a new lease of life and they realised his generosity. "You have a short time to gather what belongings you wish to take, we will deal with the Jenta ourselves." His speech finished Remruc turned on his heels and left behind the stunned and deflated tribe, grateful at least for their lives.

Herka bade Remruc farewell and rounded up the last stragglers of Tarl. His search patrol was returning home to a welcome rest and good natural food. He did not like this dry and unnatural tasting mulch that the Tarl consumed, but it was nutritious and would suffice till his hunters reached the city.

The Tarl were listless and dejected. The fear in their minds could be felt by every Nemn that guarded them as they were driven at a slow pace along the tunnels towards the Nemn mountains. These survivors were too frail of limb and unfit to be pushed at a decent travelling speed, so for the Nemn hunters this seemed like a pleasant stroll.

Herka glanced back towards the Tarl city cavern, his eyes flicking nervously along the corridor, his mind unable to disperse the anxious feeling within him. Somewhere at the back of his mind was a gnawing fear, a sense of foreboding that something terrible was going to happen, not to him or his patrol, but to Remruc and the company of guards. He had tried to warn Remruc of his fears and the Chai leader had listened patiently to his worries, but despite Herka's insistence that he return with the Tarl prisoners, he had opted to carry on determined to punish the Jenta. The Tarl had not been much help in giving details of the Jenta clan, although the precise location of their main city was finally prised from their minds, they had been unable to give a detailed description of the nature, weaponry and ferociousness of their neighbours. This was due mainly to the fact that the Tarl had not been in physical contact with the Jenta for several centuries, all transactions between the two tribes had been handled by the machines that maintained the city. With a deep sigh and heavy heart Herka turned and walked along with his patrol determined at least to reach the Chai city and send out re-enforcements for Remruc.

The general mood of the guards was that of intense excitement. It had been a long time since there had been the promise of a good fight and now they were eager to be off. Remruc looked with pride at the awesome company of warriors. They may not be strong in number, but the Chai were more than a match for any of the other San tribes. Herka's words were rattling in the back of his mind as he gave the order to move out and as a young warrior marched past, he caught his passing thought, "this will be my first real battle." Unbidden a reply came into his private mind, "it may also be your last."

Shocked, Remruc searched inside, the mind he had felt had been so like Cupe, but he knew in his heart that is was only his own subconscious voicing the fear that Herka had prompted into awareness.

It was not often that Remruc felt this way, he was not normally sensitive to such instinct; in fact the last time that this feeling preyed on his mind was back in the deserted Chai settlement when his patrol was attacked by the winged Cuc. Remruc stopped in his tracks. "Of course," he thought to himself, "Cucs. I have always felt anxious like this when they are about." He sent a public message to all of the guards. "All of you, open your minds and listen for any sign of Cucs. There may be some prowling about close to us." The column of troops continued in slightly subdued silence, using torches to light the dark tunnel and sending scouts out to search ahead. They were within four sharr of the Jenta city and two days into their journey when it happened.

Remruc was at the back of the column organising the distribution and rationing of the rapidly diminishing torches, checking on any minor injuries that were being treated by the three healers accompanying them. There was nothing major, a few cuts and bruises on troops inattentive enough to stumble on the rocky path. He was making his way back along the line of warriors, his mind enquiring of the head guard the status of the scouts when the alarm was raised. A piercing mental scream, brightly coloured in panic shattered the minds and nerves of every Chai in the company. They were instantly alert, weapons drawn, their formation changed from straight line to scatter along the walkway.

The strangled scream frantically shouted its warning of Cuc before it was abruptly silenced, causing a shudder to pass through Remruc's heart, "Which scout was that!" he demanded of his head guard as he made his way quickly along the tunnel.

"Casn, Lord Remruc," was the prompt reply, "sent one sharr ahead of the main body."

"Recall all scouts, YOU!" he pointed sternly at a young warrior, face pale and obviously shaken, "take two others and search back for the nearest offshoot tunnel. NOW!" He growled to emphasise his thought and this spurred the boy into action. Remruc was furious. It was bad enough to be caught out in the open by Cuc, but to be trapped here in this narrow tunnel could be lethal. "If there are Cuc ahead of us and so close to the city of the Jenta then I doubt if any of them survived the plague." He thought to himself, grimacing at the image of a Cuc infested city.

By the time Remruc reached the head of the column, a second scout yelled his warning, "I can hear a lot of Cuc coming towards me. They're moving fast. How can they see where they are going?" Panic started to fill the scout's mind.

Remruc quickly searched for the Chai and tuned into his thoughts. "Stay calm and move quickly. Can you find any off-shoot tunnels?"

"No Lord Remruc, there are none along this stretch..." his mind echoed the pain as he stumbled and fell on the rough ground, "I can't outrun them... they're getting closer..."

Remruc quickly interrupted his thoughts. "How far away are you?"

"About half a sharr, Lord Remruc."

Remruc winced. The scout was too far away for them to help it was only a matter of time before the Cuc caught up with him and that would bring the foul creatures closer to the main complement of warriors. A sudden thought came into his private mind, "the Cuc cannot possibly see the scout, they must be using scent and hearing." He quickly regained contact with the almost exhausted Chai, "listen to me carefully. How high are the ceilings above you?" Remruc waited patiently as the scout mentally scanned the surrounding terrain.

"About five Chai high, Lord."

Remruc glanced at the rough walls and ceilings around him and hoped for the scout's sake that they were the same where he was.

"Take out your field rations. You should have some Tnsta bulbs amongst the herbs. Break up the bulb with a stone and smear yourself with the juice, I know that it stinks, but it will cover up most of your scent. Now climb up the walls and try to find a ledge, preferably near the ceiling and hold on. With luck the Cuc will pass beneath you and be disorientated by the smell of Tnsta. Our scent will be more noticeable than yours. Good luck scout."

"My name is Danrka, Lord Remruc." Was the grateful reply.

Remruc smiled, "good luck then Danrka." He turned and motioned to his head guard to follow, running quickly they moved down the line, repeating the instructions to use the Tnsta bulbs.

They were halfway down the line when the young warrior returned, gasping for breath, "Lord Remruc, there are two offshoot tunnels opposite each other, about a quarter of a sharr back."

Remruc looked at the anxious face and smiled his approval. "Well done." He sent the head guard back down the line passing on his orders while he made his way to the head of the column. The Chai company split into four sections. Three moved quickly back towards the offshoot tunnels, digging torches into the rocky floor to light the way. One section branched off into each of the off-shoots and the third section climbed up the walls, clinging to the ceiling with a steel grip and balancing on almost invisible ledges. The fourth section was led by Remruc and they remained where they were - living bait to draw the Cuc into the trap behind them. The message was passed that everyone was ready and silence fell among the warriors as they patiently waited.

Danrka quickly climbed up to the ceiling, his arms shaking with fear, but his grip strong with desperation. He could hear the hissing and gurgling of the rapidly advancing Cucs, their progress seemingly unhindered by the pitch blackness. He closed his eyes and prepared himself for the worst. The stench of Tnsta bulb did little to mask the foul presence of the mass of Cuc beneath him. They halted in their tracks, hissing confusion at the new scent that clung to the walls of the tunnel around them. Their intended prey had seemingly vanished; they listened intently for any sound of it scurrying away. The larger of the Cuc squealed its fury and frustration, the squeal choking to silence as a new, faint, even more tantalising aroma filtered through their mucous filled nostrils. More San. A little further on, but in a quantity that may even satisfy the group's ferocious appetite. They charged on through the tunnel, their bulky bodies not adapted for such travel making their movements clumsy and noisy.

Danrka waited for a long time after they had passed before slipping slowly down the walls and onto the ground. Every muscle in his body trembled from the effort of clinging to the rough stone and through fear. He had never encountered as many Cuc travelling together and the confined space had made their awesome stink almost overpowering. He quickly sent a message to Remruc, "Lord Remruc, the Cuc have passed me and cannot be too far away from you now. There are at least ten of them - no less I think. It was difficult to sense how many, they were moving around and their thoughts were jumbled."

Remruc replied swiftly, "Danrka! I am pleased that you are still with us. We can just about hear the Cuc making their way towards us. Don't worry! They are in for a very nasty surprise. Wait till I give the all clear before you make your way back to us, in case any of them escape and run over you." He quickly cut contact with the scout as he prepared to draw the Cuc into the trap.

Danrka smiled to himself and slowly settled his weapon on the ground. He would wait until he heard any Cuc advancing before climbing back up the wall. A chill crept up his legs, moved with icy fingers to the top of his spine and set his hair on end. He was slowly becoming aware of a presence behind him. Turning cautiously, his mind searching for a thought, his nose still unable to smell anything but Tnsta bulb and Cuc, his eyes staring uselessly into the pitch black he waited for any sign of an approach. A soft breath blew its hot and fetid air down into his face, looking upwards Danrka saw two huge glowing red orbs and suddenly, sickeningly realised that the blackness was not the dark of the tunnel, but the black form of an enormous body that filled the entire space.

Danrka switched his eyes to full night vision, although he knew that if he managed to see anything it would terrify him. Danrka's mind searched for Remruc, found him and locked their minds together. Remruc stopped in his tracks, his body paralysed his eyes and mind seeing and feeling what was before Danrka. The two red orbs grew larger as a massive head swung down closer to its prey. Danrka gasped in shock and pain as a large tongue, barbed with many hooks, rasped its way up his body, ripping the clothes and skin from his frame. He fell to his knees, blood pouring onto the rocky floor, his eyes locked in the burning glare of the red orbs and, as the massive mouth opened to gently nibble one of his arms from his body, a primitive mind forced its ugly thoughts into his head, "Here... Cuc... nest... you... go... die."

The intent of the thought was clear, but they were accompanied by a multitude of violent, repugnant visions and feelings of crawling Cuc young, eggs being hatched and rotting forms of San dead. The most chilling vision was that of the nest Leader, a gigantic winged Cuc that hissed and flapped his wings above the shattered city of the Jenta. The link with Danrka was abruptly broken and Remruc winced as he felt the agony of the scout as the Cuc continued its meal. He hoped that death would come quick to the unfortunate Chai, but his heart was chilled as the vision of the winged Cuc stayed in his mind. He had seen the ragged scar that ran along its side and one of its wings. He knew that it was the Cuc that killed Cupe.

A rough shake brought him back to his senses as one of his guards pulled him along the tunnel, "Lord Remruc, the Cuc are almost upon us, we must move!"

"Danrka is dead. One of the Cuc must have stayed and waited for him to come out of his hiding place." Remruc's shaken mind was more than enough explanation for the guard as they ran with the rest of the section back to the waiting Chai. By the time they had neared the trap, the Cuc were hot on their heels and Remruc had fully recovered his senses.

He quickly organised his section and positioned them just beyond the junction of tunnels. They watched the flames of the torches lick happily up the walls of the tunnel in front of them, where the torches stopped an ominous black shroud of darkness hung like a physical barrier. Remruc's section, along with the section clinging to the roof, were just beyond the welcoming light, an unseen and hopefully unheard danger waiting in the shadows. The crunching of rocks and babble of the Cucs was almost deafening as they approached the lit tunnel junction, but it was the stench that announced their imminent arrival to the waiting San. Suddenly the Cucs stopped, just beyond the glare of the torches.

All of the Chai tensed, each warrior hoping that the Cuc would possibly be too frightened to continue. The squealing and hissing curdled the blood of even the most hardened warriors as the Cucs uncertain what to do milled around on the edge of the pool of light. One creature, marginally braver than the rest, crept slowly forward, its ugly head swinging from side to side, searching for a scent of San, instead, the repugnant smell of Tnsta cloyed along the walls and floor. It snorted and wiped its nose on a powerful foreleg. The Chai watching the beast shrunk back in awe. It was probably one of the largest Cuc they had ever seen, its normally lean frame was bloated from excessive eating, dried blood and gore flecked the flanks and belly, its jaws and fearsome teeth clicking together in distaste.

It was obvious that the creature was not going to advance any further without some sort of prompt. Remruc stood up and walked into the pool of light. The Cuc was instantly alert, it hissed in fury and was about to advance on its prey when its head suddenly jerked upwards and its eyes became glazed.

Remruc waited. He knew that what one Cuc saw they all saw, what one knew they all knew and with a sinking feeling in his heart he suspected that this Cuc was showing its leader this scene. A grim smile cracked Remruc's face. "So", he thought to himself, "you want to see what is going on". He walked further into the centre of the circle of torches, just beyond striking distance of the Cuc. The massive head lowered and the glazed eyes slowly focused on him. Remruc recognised those eyes and he growled a warning to the far distant leader. His mind shouted the words, but he doubted if the Cuc could understand, "We meet again. If you were brave enough to face me yourself I would not let you live!"

Far away, in the city of the Jenta on a mound of rotting flesh the nest Leader of the Cuc screamed his fury. The walls of the desolate building trembled with the resonating force of this creature's frustration. Here at last was his hated enemy and he could not reach him. The Cuc leader sent an order to all of his children. "Kill every San, but bring me this one alive."

He would enjoy killing this one very slowly and listening to its screams. Before the Cuc in front of Remruc could regain full control over its body, Remruc struck with his sword deep into one red eye, penetrating past the optic nerve and entering its brain. The creature screamed in agony, pulling the weapon from Remruc's grip and throwing its head wildly, trying to rid itself of the source of its pain. Remruc turned and ran back into the shadows his warriors still silent, waiting for their commands. The remaining Cuc charged forward, throwing the injured creature to one side and crushing it in their haste to obey their leader. When the group was in the centre of the junction the Chai struck. The section from the roof dropped onto the heavily armoured backs, confusing and distracting the creatures.

As the Cucs reared up to try to dislodge the warriors from their backs, the three other sections attacked the revealed and vulnerable underbellies. The screams of fury and pain from the Cucs was deafening, they thrashed around the confined space killing any Chai caught within the arc of their raking claws.

It was the systematic and coordinated strikes of the warriors that defeated the unprepared and dull witted creatures. Even so, more than half of the company of San fell beneath the flailing bodies of Cuc, either crushed by staggering, dying beasts, or sliced by lethal claws. It was a bloody victory that was won in a matter of minutes. At the nest, the leader disembowelled two of the nearest Cuc to him in his fury and swore his revenge. Even if he had to hunt the San across the entire continent he would find and kill his enemy.

Remruc viewed the gory scene. A few of the Cuc were still barely alive, their massive flanks heaving, limbs twitching as their internal organs slowly slipped out of their bodies to lie on the ground. Two of the healers had been killed in the attack, and the third was quickly enlisting the help of more able bodied warriors to bind the stumps of severed limbs. Remruc moved over to the body of the young warrior he had seen earlier.

The boy looked up and smiled at his Chieftain. "We won Lord Remruc. Didn't we?"

"Yes warrior. We won." His mind almost choked as he saw the glazed expression and fixed smile fade along with the mind, disappearing into the void. Walking quickly over to the healer he demanded a report.

"Lord Remruc. Half the company are dead, a quarter of those left are injured; a few seriously enough to die within a few hours." The healer's face was ashen and exhaustion slowed his movements.

"We have no time to wait for the injured to die. How many can walk."

The healer looked shocked for a moment then answered his Lord. "All of the injured can walk, except for the fatally wounded."

Remruc nodded his acknowledgement and called the remainder of his guards to him.

"We have no time to take the dead back with us we must deal with them here. I want all of the torches gathered together and a fire lit. I will not leave my warriors to be eaten by Cuc."

The sombre troops carried out his instructions and as the flames of the massive funeral pyre consumed the dead the remaining warriors, carrying their badly wounded and dying comrades, made their way back to the city of the Tarl and on towards home.

"We must rest Lord Remruc!" The healer frantically tugged at Remruc's tunic sleeve to emphasise his thoughts, "the warriors are near collapse, you cannot drive us at such a pace!"

Remruc whirled round, almost throwing the startled man against the wall. "Do you think the Cuc will rest? They will search relentlessly till they find us. We must go on. I will give them time to recover in the city of the Tarl and time to bury those who have died along the way."

His tired mind was tinged with regret at the heart stopping pace he was setting, but resoluteness in his manner prompted the healer to refrain from any further demands.

The journey that had initially taken the company two days to complete was finished in just over one. As they entered the deserted Tarl city, the automatic lighting systems, their sensors indicating life forms, illuminated the cavern shedding a cold light on the deserted city and giving small comfort to the shattered Chai. Out of the full company of warriors, only thirty remained, some badly wounded, all demoralised and exhausted. The ten bodies of their comrades who had not survived the journey back were taken to the central square of the city to be cremated. As the troops lit the gruesome fire they formed a ring around its perimeter, all lost in their private thoughts watching with empty, unseeing eyes.

On some unspoken and unheard cue, the automatic cleaning machines appeared from nowhere and systematically began to advance on the funeral pyre, determined to put out the flames. As they neared their target small jets of water rained down upon the remaining troops. Furious, Remruc ordered the Chai nearest the machines to stop them, but the metal casings were impervious to the clanging axes and swords that rained down on them. The warriors tried a different tactic and pushed the heavy boxes away from the fire. No sooner had they turned them than the jet of water appeared again at the side nearest the flames. Despite the best efforts and persistence of the warriors, the machines did not succeed in extinguishing the flames before the bodies were reduced to crumbling ashes. Once the fire had gone out as wisps of smoke curled up to the vaulted ceilings, the machines dutifully scooped up the gory dust and cleaned the square till it gleamed in the unnatural light. Remruc watched the scene with dispassionate eyes. Slowly, an idea formed in his mind. These boxes of metal were heavy, and obviously opposed to anything that was not clean or tidy, they were persistent and relentless in their duty and could not be frightened.

"Staken! Bring two others and follow me," he ordered, spinning on his heels, hope giving him the energy to complete his task. The three warriors and Remruc gathered as much junk and rubbish as they could carry and made their way back to the square. The machines were still there, silently crouching in the corners, ready to pounce on anything that soiled their gleaming handiwork. Remruc dropped a piece of metal onto the floor, the sharp clang as it hit the ground echoing around the buildings. Instantly a box moved forward, eagerly seeking the offending article it stopped at Remruc's feet and neatly disposed of the junk. The rest of the warriors watched with fascination, a few of them considering the possibility that Remruc was going slightly mad. Encouraged, the Chief walked a few paces back and dropped another small item, the machine followed suite. He nodded to the other guards, their arms full of tiny pieces of scrap and they each moved to a box and started to coax them along the roadway. By the time their arms were empty they had reached the exit gateways and the machines had parked themselves most effectively across the open mouths blocking the tunnels in and out.

A crowd of warriors had followed the quartet and on seeing the results of their labour cheered encouragement. "I am glad that you are all here. If we use these machines to block the tunnels it may prevent the Cucs from following us into the city, with luck these contraptions will try to tidy up the scruffy Cucs." There was a burst of mental laughter at his comments and those who were able began to search for more bait to lure as many of the boxes they could find.

Once all of the exits from the city into the Jenta lands were barricaded the completely exhausted troops rested. Despite his eagerness to leave these strange and desolate lands, Remruc was willing to let them stay, at least until nightfall. The Tarl did not have ventilation shafts like those in the other San cities, so Remruc was relying on his own inbuilt senses to remind him of the passing hours, a trait that was well adapted and had been used often on raiding missions.

A slow anxiety niggled him as he slept and prompting him to wakefulness warned of the approaching Cucs. They were still a long way off, but nearing with every passing hour, randomly searching for their prey through the tunnels that riddled the mountains. Remruc climbed wearily to his feet, stiff muscles complaining with every movement. "On your feet!" he commanded to the still sleeping forms around him, "remember, do not move anything or drop anything, I don't want those metal boxes to leave the exits." The warriors quickly complied with his orders, moving with deliberate steps towards the Nemn lands in hushed silence. Remruc withdrew into his private mind as they mechanically retraced their steps, coldly cursing the hated Cuc and all of its offspring.

"Those metal boxes will not stop the Cuc for long," he thought to himself, a cold dread in his heart. "It seems that our attempt to avenge our people has only resulted in provoking yet another danger, a sort of bitter irony I think." a grim smile flitted across his lips as he marched along.

By the end of the second day from the Tarl City, the weary warriors walked to the end of the first tunnel complex of the Nemn. They paused in the grey shade just within the entrance, avoiding the stifling heat of late afternoon and squinting against the glare of the red rocks. "We will rest here until nightfall," commanded Remruc, his mind echoing the fatigue in his body. "Be ready to move out quickly and make as little noise as possible."

"Lord Remruc," the healer stepped forward and drew him to one side, making room for the resting guards, "do you still think that the Cuc will follow us?" His anxious thoughts were irritating Remruc's exhaustion sensitive mind and he had to struggle to keep his reply in neutral tones.

"These Cuc are different from others of their kind. Danrka managed to relay to me the images of the nest leader he gleaned from the mind of the Cuc that killed him. It was the same creature that attacked my patrol in the deserted holding. The same Cuc responsible for the death of my father's mate." He paused, the pain from that memory was almost too much to bear. The healer waited patiently for him to continue, understanding the emotion his Chieftain must be fighting to control.

"This particular Cuc seems to remember our encounter most vividly and has a natural tenacity, a vicious determination to destroy us. Yes. The Cuc will follow us, although it may take some time for them to track us down, I am sure that we will be forced to finish our battle, one way or another."

On those grim thoughts Remruc moved to one side and sat down, his back against the rock, warmed by the intense suns despite its sheltered location. Even before Rume and Emur had slipped below the horizon, Remruc was pushing his troops out into the dusty landscape, hoods up, cloaks down protecting them from the latent heat of day. They jogged in silence, each warrior concentrating on staying on his feet, trying to forget the long miles of unprotected ground that lay ahead of them. As the sky was turning to a violet hue and the light of day was fading into dusk the rear guard sent a warning, flashing through even the most tired mind.

"Find cover! Flying Cuc on the horizon!" The column scattered as each individual sought the safety of a black shaded overhang or boulder. Remruc lay as still as the protecting rock, his eyes protected from the red glare of dying sunlight by his inner lids. He watched anxiously as the formation of black dots in the sky grew larger. Each warrior unconsciously shrunk further into their hiding places, pulling their black clothing over bare skin, hoping to merge into the shadows unseen by the sharp eyed enemy. The dots remained high in the sky as they appeared to circle the surface of the Tarl lands.

Fortunately, due to Remruc's murderous pace, the Chai warriors were well over the borderline, and heading deep into the Nemn mountains.

It seems, mused Remruc to himself, that the Cuc have underestimated the endurance of the San. It was obvious that the winged Cuc were setting up an ambush along the border; waiting for their prey to run from the tunnels of the Tarl, right into their waiting claws. Suddenly each of the black silhouettes dropped down to a convenient perch spread out along the mountain ridge and giving them an excellent view of the Tarl tunnel entrances. Remruc called his head guard on a discreet mental line, "how far is it to the first of the Nemn tunnels?"

"Less than half a day at a good jog Lord Remruc," was the subdued reply, tinged with barely controlled anxiety.

"Good. We will wait until total darkness then move swiftly and silently on. The Cuc must have broken into the Tarl city. It will take them some time to negotiate that metal land and deal with those metal boxes, perhaps giving us the time we need to make our escape. Those winged Cuc are waiting in ambush, but their attention is on the wrong side of the mountain. Stress to the rest of the warriors that there must be total silence. The slightest noise will alert those vile creatures to their mistake."

The guard confirmed his lord's commands and began to pass the message round the remaining troops. Once more the brave band of Chai waited, watching the winged messengers of death, wondering what fate had in store.

Night spread it's velvet folds across the burning mountains, cooling the rocks with ear splitting cracks as it draped itself like a cold sheet across their contours.

The faint blue glow of the San's eyes were all that could be seen as the warriors moved out of their hiding places slipping into formation and moving in a silent mass along the mountain paths. The pace was set at a slow jog until they were well out of hearing range of the still vigilant sentinels; then a cracking ground-eating run was initiated. The well-rested troops moving with ease, their strength fuelled by the knowledge of what was behind them. As a result they reached the next Nemn tunnel well ahead of schedule. They did not pause. All were determined to put as much distance between themselves and the foul forces of the Cuc as possible and they ran till they were exhausted. Then they walked, staggering along the dark tunnel, bumping into the rough walls and stumbling over the loose stones on the floor. It was well into morning on the surface of the planet before the weary warriors swayed unsteadily into the first main campsite of the Nemn caverns.

The familiar light from the ventilation shafts were a comfort to the troops who were near collapse. Remruc halted, his breathing ragged, his heart heaving in his chest. "Now we can afford to rest." The long awaited thoughts caused the warriors to drop where they stood and lie, almost comatose, on the hard, dusty floor. That was how they remained for the rest of the day. A few had enough strength to nibble on field rations, giving them renewed energy. Those that were able helped others to force food and water down their throats. It was vital that they maintained their fast pace and to do this their bodies required food.

The light was fading in the cavern when Remruc finally roused himself. He searched his mind for any niggling warning of Cuc. There was none. They had managed to confuse and lose the following beasts, but Remruc knew that they would not give up their search and that eventually they would find the Nemn tunnels. Still, it would take them a long time to search these mountains and the remaining San would have several nasty surprises and traps waiting for them.

A sudden and sobering thought came into his mind. The

leader of the Cuc has been in the Chai lands before. What if he remembers how to get back. What if he has already sent his winged workers on ahead to wait for us? Remruc's heart fell, but he was determined not to lose faith and with even greater resolve he motioned for the Chai warriors to move out.

They carried on without rest for the remainder of the day and through the night, their steps becoming slow and faltering by morning. They had passed through several of the Nemn caverns and moved across the dark planet's surface twice in their journey, covering half of the Nemn territory in that short period of time.

They stopped at a tunnel junction, unable to continue, fatigue holding the limbs of all to the ground, even Remruc was forced to admit that his warriors desperately needed rest. He gave the order and slumped down against the wall, his body gratefully slipping into unguarded slumber.

A persistent murmur of thought and a hand shaking his body roused the sleeping Chief. Blearily, he opened his eyes to see the face of a Nemn bending anxiously over him. With elation he recognised Herka and his tired mind opened to receive the thoughts of the faithful hunter.

"Lord Remruc. I thought you were dead."

Remruc struggled to collect his thoughts and reply but before he could do so, Herka interrupted him.

"No. Explanations can be given later, once you are safely home. I have brought a complement of guards, Nemn and Chai with me. There are Doona volunteers driving the sleds, we will have you back home by sunset."

His short explanations were more than enough for Remruc who slowly slipped back into unconsciousness, his body's desire for rest overcoming his demanding brain.

All of the survivors were in a similar state and Herka was

grateful to his intuition and the Doona volunteers that they had brought five sleds drawn by the swift mantelos. The creatures had responded quickly to the good feeding and medication supplied by the Chai people, growing strong in a short space of time, eager to serve their masters. The sleds were sent ahead and the Nemn and Chai warriors, led by Herka, followed quickly, bringing up the rear, unaware of the danger edging ever closer across the continent.

Chapter Eleven

The muffled sounds of movement and soft mental murmurings of conversation filtered slowly into his mind. His body seemed to be cocooned in a soft, tight fluffy material, making movement impossible in his leaden limbs. He inhaled deeply and the mouth-watering aroma of steamy broth filled his mind, altering his dull senses to gnawing hunger in his belly. With an effort Remruc forced his eyes open and struggled to focus his thoughts into some coherent structure. The soft subdued light of his sleeping quarters warmed the stone chamber, the flickering orange plumes licked their way to the ceiling, wisps of scented blue smoke seeking the ventilation holes, but lingering long enough to leave their sweet aroma to mingle with the now tantalising smell of food.

"So, you have finally decided to awaken Lord Remruc."

The gentle tones dispelled any hint of harshness in the thoughts that slipped into his head. He shifted his gaze to one side to see Eriya sitting quietly in the corner, hands clasped around a small hide, the needle and beads she had been embroidering onto its surface gleaming on the side table. She put down her work and deftly lifted a tray adorned with a plate of broth, meat and sweet delicacies over to his sleeping platform. It was then that he noticed the rich soft fur blanket wrapped tightly about his form and he stretched lazily, enjoying the warmth and touch of this unusual luxury.

With a sigh he started to sit up only to find to his surprise that his arms seemed incapable of supporting his weight. A firm grip under his arm and around his shoulders eased him into a more comfortable position, but it was the electric response of his skin to the touch of her hands that surprised Remruc and he quickly settled himself against the back rest to his sleeping platform, thinking desperately for something to say.

"Thank you Lady Eriya. I must apologise for my weakness." Remruc resisted the urge to shake his head and try to clear the fuzziness that still lingered inside his skull. "Even my thoughts seem tired." He whispered to himself.

"Such a condition is to be expected from any San silly enough to run himself and his company almost to death." Eriya smiled to soften the chiding in her tone. It had come as a complete shock to her to find how concerned she was over the condition of the Chieftain, taking all responsibility to ensure his quick recovery. Her heart had almost missed a beat when the sleds had come careering into the city, charging headlong towards the Healer hall. It had been Lenta who had summoned her to aid the exhausted warriors lying on the sleds, Eriya was learned in dealing with such a condition, it had not been uncommon for a Nemn hunter to run himself into such a state while chasing prey.

Two of the remaining Chai warriors had not recovered. They had slowly slipped deeper into a coma till death silenced their minds. Remruc himself had been dangerously close to following that pattern, fortunately, Eriya had maintained a constant vigil, forcing revitalising herbal liquids down his throat while he slept.

"How long have I been unconscious?" Remruc suddenly asked, still swallowing the warm soup in hungry gulps. Eriya patiently handed him a protein rich meat cake before answering.

"Rume and Emur have passed the sky three times since you were brought back Lord Remruc."

"Three days!" he exploded, almost choking on the roll. "Why was I not woken? Never mind, Lady Eriya, please call your elders to a meeting, I will inform Curmer, I hope we still have time to protect ourselves." Remruc paused in his remonstrating to look at Eriya who remained sitting by his side, a look of amusement on her face as she watched the Chieftain stuffing food down his throat as his urgent demands were relayed to her.

"May I ask Lord, if you are concerned about the Cucs that attacked your company and followed you to the borders of the Nemn lands?" she replied calmly. He stared at her dumbfounded.

"How…?"

"Nantra, the surviving healer that accompanied you had the good sense to take some of the Reeesa stimulant as you dragged the warriors homewards. He was able to disclose what had happened to the company and also your fears of an imminent Cuc attack. Lord Curmer has begun organising defensive measures against such a possibility." She watched with satisfaction as Remruc relaxed at the news, his face still drawn with fatigue but beginning to regain its colour. "Now, if you have finished eating, I suggest you get more rest. I think it will take another day yet before you will be on your feet." Eriya rose to leave and on an impulse Remruc lightly grabbed her wrist.

"Stay a while and tell me of what has happened in the city since I have been gone. Please?" He was careful to tone his thoughts to neutral, but he could not hide the hopefulness in his eyes. Eirya inhaled sharply, glancing at his hand and then his eyes. She heard his thoughts but sensed another underlying question as yet unclear.

"Perhaps Remruc wishes to call a truce on our mutual antagonism", she mused to herself. "I too am weary of constant niggling, it is time that we at least tolerated each other." She smiled lightly and sat back onto the sleeping platform. "What would Lord Remruc like to hear?"

He grinned back and lay against the backrest, "everything. Start when I left the city and finish on my return." He closed his eyes and concentrated on Eriya's quiet thoughts, a sense of achievement warming him from the inside out.

"My Lord Remruc does not wish to hear much," was her quick reply, the humour in her mind a joy to feel.

Eriya paused in her monologue. She had been relating all of the city's events for over an hour and at last Remruc appeared to have fallen asleep. She watched him carefully with the eyes of a healer. Yes, she said to herself, you are very strong Remruc, you will be on your feet by tomorrow.

Then she looked at him again with the eyes of a Chieftain's daughter and this time she saw the handsome face that was identical to Curmer, but the slumbering mind mumbled with an identity that was as different as night and day. She could appreciate now how the two Chieftains complimented each other, Remruc's nature was as important as Curmer's and each created a balance of mind that could tackle and overcome virtually any problem. Eriya no longer resented Remruc's direct nature and fearless criticism. She had realised that he was as hard on himself as he could be on others and it was partly due to his thoughts that had caused her to look into herself and see the true Eriya, not the reflected face shown to the rest of the world. She smiled. "You and I are very similar Remruc," she said, "we each understand the others failings and perhaps appreciate the virtues." She frowned. It was possible that Remruc would never really like her, but Eriya was determined to try to at least win his respect. She rose quietly, the deep breathing of her patient satisfying to her healer's ears, and left the room.

Sorta hurriedly announced her presence before hurtling through Eriya's door, "I am most sorry Lady Eriya, but healer Lenta requires your expertise on the appropriate storage for medicines." She gasped for breath, her mind relaying the urgency of the request. Eriya smiled warmly at her, she no longer resented the object of Curmer's adoration and love and in fact had developed a healthy respect for the girl, she was a very capable healer.

"I will be along as soon as I have changed into my healer robes, please relay to Lord Curmer for me that Remruc is well and I expect him on his feet by tomorrow morning."

Eriya watched with satisfaction as Sorta's eyes became unfocussed as she sought Curmer's mind, her face becoming radiant as she passed on the message along with a more personal comment. Sorta broke the link with Curmer to find to her surprise that Eriya was already dressed and waiting patiently.

"Oh... I am sorry Lady Eriya, I didn't realise how long we had been speaking... I..." she faltered, embarrassment clouding her mind.

Eriya smiled indulgently and ushered her out of the room, making haste to the Healer hall. Curmer was there to meet them on the steps, his tired face lighting up when he saw their approach.

"Lady Eriya," he performed a courteous bow, "I am most grateful for your invaluable help in treating my brother, I do not know how I can possibly repay you." He took Sorta's arm and led them into the hall as his thought, tinged with relief, flowed into Eriya's mind.

"You can repay me, Lord Curmer, by ensuring that you do not end up in the same condition as Lord Remruc." She stabbed a finger at him to emphasise her point, humour dispelling the terseness of her reply.

"Do not worry, Lady Eriya, if he does I will follow your example and nurse him back to health," Sorta quipped, playfully tugging at Curmer's hair. All three laughed amiably as they walked briskly down towards the store cellars.

Lenta turned as the three figures trooped into the cold interior of the stairwell, she bowed to Curmer and Eriya. "Thank you for coming so quickly, Lady Eriya, and I am pleased to see you Lord Curmer. Tell me, how are the defensive precautions coming along."

They were steadily descending the wide stone stairs that led to the deepest and coldest area of the city as she made her inquiry, the rows of torches doing little to warm the freezing air. Moisture clung to the walls with white furred fingers, gleaming in the torch light, not daring to come too close to the flames.

As they moved deeper into the bowls of the mountains, Curmer was filling Lenta in on some of the traps and barricades the warriors of the city were laying and Eriya allowed her mind to concentrate on the activity around her. The steps she noticed were designed like small trays, filled with loose gravel, this gave them a more reliable footing than ice covered stone flags.

The troupe reached the first level which spanned out into an immense cellar, supporting pillars spiralling up to the ceiling, storage shelves and alcoves hewn out of the rock by many centuries of hard work. Around her were the dried herbs and less perishable medicines and solutions used by the healers. Many of the shelves had been emptied, their contents used up when the plague was at its peak, but now, slowly, the San were replenishing their supplies with items either brought in by the refugees, or with newly grown and made products. A commotion at one end of the room drew their attention,

"No! No! Put it over there and be careful!", the irritation in the mind was blatantly clear, as was the condescending manner. Curmer moved swiftly across followed closely by the others. There, directing a group of young healer trainees was a

Tarl. She was coordinating the installation of new light fittings, similar to those in the Tarl city. It was obvious by her manner that she considered her helpers to be stupid fools, incapable of comprehending the simplest of commands.

"Is there a problem?" asked Curmer coolly. The Tarl whirled round, visibly cringing when she saw the Chieftain.

"Oh... Lord Remruc, I did not realise..."

"That much is obvious Tarl. You are not here to give orders or to take advantage of our younger students. They may be children, but at least they can recognise which of their Chieftains is Lord Remruc and which is Lord Curmer!"

As the reply thundered into the Tarl, she let out a frightened whimper, crouching low to the ground, begging his forgiveness. "Please... please, I am sorry... it will not happen again I assure you."

Curmer stepped back in disgust. Herka had warned him about the nature of the Tarl, but this was the first direct contact he had had with them. He had given the responsibility of their management to the Nemn hunters who patrolled the city maintaining order and the Nemn were more than able to deal with this cowardly clan, putting them to good use repairing and improving the standard of living for all of the citizens.

"You." Curmer pointed to the oldest of the group, "make sure that this Tarl does what she is told, any more problems and you report her to a Nemn patrol, understand?"

The youth nodded, relieved that the order had come from the Chieftain, he did not want to be responsible for the woman to be punished. Lenta, Eriya, Sorta and Curmer continued on their journey down to the main cellar, Curmer in irritated silence and Lenta trying to think of something to say to dispel his dark mood.

"As you can see Lord Curmer, the Tarl have been busy

down here." She began, indicating the artificial lighting, "we have found these light sticks as the Tarl call them, most beneficial. They allow us to work safely while keeping the temperature of the lower caverns well below freezing point The torches always managed to lift the temperature somewhat, I think that we will find our stores will keep much longer." Lenta smiled, her breath rising in white plumes to condense and freeze on the icicle decorated ceiling lofting above them. "However, I think we may need to clear the ceiling more often." She laughed as the others smiled at her mock annoyance.

Eriya shivered, the warm healer robes and movement doing little to defend her flesh from the freezing air. She exchanged glances with Sorta, who was thinking the same thing and winked at her. "Healer Lenta," she said, "do your workers huddle together down here to stop themselves from freezing solid?", her innocent inquiry coloured with humour.

Lenta stopped, horrified with herself for forgetting their sparse mode of dress. "I must apologise. I completely forgot to give you extra clothing." Lenta stopped three passing workers making their way back up to the first level. "Give us your cloaks please and get yourselves new ones from the store."

The three quickly complied with her request, honoured at the privilege and continue with extra speed up to the warmer levels. After what seemed an eternity of descending they reached the lowest cellar. Eriya had never been into the stores before, and she inhaled sharply, feeling the cold air sting its way into her lungs. The light sticks gave an eerie blue tinge to the white room around her. Sound muffled by the ice encrusted walls, vast pillars of white furred support beams stretching into the distance letting powder fine ice crystals fall gently as unfelt vibrations from above dislodged them. They lay on the already cold carpeted floor giving a snowing affect to the air.

"It is beautiful." Eriya's mind finally managed to whisper.

"It is practical," replied Lenta smiling at the awe on the Nemn's face, "we also have similar chambers for storing food. Grain, meat, and such like. Perhaps you should visit them sometime," she continued. "Be careful!" was her urgent request as Eriya reached out to touch the frame of a storage rack. "Cold such as this can burn as easily as fire."

Eriya instantly snatched her hand away in surprise.

"Cold that can burn. I have never heard or seen such a thing." She wondered.

"Well it can happen, believe me," smiled Sorta, "Here, try these." She handed the group warm gloves and strange spiked straps. Eriya looked at her confused. "Put the spikes on your feet like this. See? It will help you walk without slipping." The four healers walked between the racks of medicine until they came to the latest batch that had been sent in by refugees.

Lenta picked up a bundle of weeds, crystallising in the cold air, "we were told by the Doona woman who gave us these that they can be stored in this manner, but I am not sure. Will the plant not spoil? I am afraid I do not recognise it."

Eriya picked up a sample and studied it closely. "These are fresh Dnatn. They are used for stomach ailments in manetols, but can only be used when well-rotted. It will not matter if you freeze them fresh and they begin to rot, in fact you will find that they store longer." She and Lenta became engrossed in sorting and allocating the medicinal herbs within the bundle and did not notice Sorta and Curmer slip away.

"I am freezing," moaned Sorta, using it as an excuse for wrapping her arms around Curmer's waist.

"Are you my beautiful one. Then I will have to think of a way to warm you up," was the mischievous reply as he returned her embrace. She smiled in anticipation for what he might suggest when he suddenly grabbed two ice shovels from the rack behind her. "Here get shovelling, that will soon warm you up."

"Oh! You!" she swatted him for his cheek and took the shovel from his grasp. "You can help me then!"

He laughed and they went over to join the other workers who were busily clearing one of the aisles.

It was late afternoon, almost evening by the time Eriya and Lenta had finished overseeing the storage of the herbs. Curmer and Sorta were almost exhausted by their efforts of clearing ice, but the work gang they were helping gave them both an appreciative appraisal.

"Lord Curmer," said one bold man, "if you ever grow tired of being a Cheiftain, then I will gladly give you a place on my work team." There was an explosion of mental laughter from all who had heard and Curmer bowed low as he replied.

"I am honoured by your offer." With that as a parting gesture the four healers made their way back up the steep stairs. The journey up was conducted in silence as each concentrated their efforts, the warm clothing soon becoming uncomfortable and in fact by the time they had reached the first level all had removed their over-cloaks and were breathing deeply from the effort.

"You are all invited to dine in my personal quarters this evening," said Curmer as he gave his cloak to a passing student healer. "Then I will give you all detailed instructions as to the defence plan of our city." There was a flurry of agreement and acceptance as each made their way back to their quarters to bathe and change.

Curmer detoured slightly along the corridor, making his way to Remruc's rooms. He noticed with a sense of satisfaction the sentry guards posted at every junction, their uniforms smart, their swords and axes gleaming. It felt like the old days once more, but there were several distinct differences. One out of three guards were Nemn hunters, dressed in the traditional Chai manner, but their light coloured, beaded hair a tell-tale sign of their origins. A feeling of satisfaction washed over him, they had succeeded in uniting the warring clans of the San with almost no conflict, giving the survivors hope for the future and ensuring the continuation of their race.

A sudden dread dispelled his mood. What if the Cucs do attack us, will we be able to withstand such an awesome and relentless enemy? His mind conjured up several disturbing scenarios of the vile Cucs laying waste to their beautiful city. No, we will not let that happen, ever! That determined thought shattered the horrifying image in his mind as he reached Remruc's door. Composing himself he announced his presence and entered. The main room was empty and the sleeping platform unoccupied. Curmer cursed to himself, with purposeful steps he burst into the bathing chamber adjoining the sleeping alcove. There, submerged to his chin in fragrant water, steam rising to form a haze around the pit was Remruc.

"If Lenta or Eriya find you up and about before they give you clearance dear brother, they will skin you and decorate the hide with some Nemn beads!"

Remruc opened one eye to see his brother's grinning face and lazily extended one arm to pick up a glass of brightly coloured liquid.

"Do not worry Healer Lord. I am taking my medicine even as we speak." With that Remruc drained the remainder of the glass, smacking his lips in mock satisfaction. "Mmm... I feel better already."

Curmer laughed, picking up a scrubbing rock he lobbed it into the pool, the splashing water causing Remruc to sit upright spluttering.

"I am going back to my quarters to wash and change. If you feel up to it, Remruc, you may join Sorta, Eriya, Lenta and I for dinner. But don't say I didn't warn you if the gaggle of females punish you for getting up too soon." On those parting thoughts Curmer left Remruc to dress.

The meal was rich and lighthearted. After the initial shock and subsequent remonstrations from the healers, when they found Remruc in their midst, all relaxed into a congenial conversation, humorous banter flying round the table. Once sufficiently stuffed they retired into the main communal room reserved for private guests of the Chieftains.

The most dominant feature was the circular fireplace in the centre of the room ringed by stone benches with cunningly carved backrests that, despite the hard material they were made of, provided comfortable seating. Placed round the wide rim of the fireplace were various tasty and succulent portions of food, warmed by the fire and ideal for nibbling should their meeting continue into the night.

Lenta picked up a soft cushion from one of the storage chests and gave another to Eriya, "I don't know about you, but I feel that the fire just doesn't warm those benches enough."

Eriya smiled in agreement and gratefully took the proffered cushion. Once all were seated Curmer produced a large hide, obviously new and donated by one of the Nemn traders. He unfolded and placed it on the wide hearth, careful not to have its edges too near the fire. Inscribed in neat lines and fresh ink was the most detailed map of the Chai city and surrounding lands, both above and below ground that had ever been produced. There was an exclamation of awe at such a fine example of art work from the audience and each reverently touched the soft hide, marvelling at its texture.

"This is beautiful Curmer," Lenta said, "where did you get

it?"

"The hide or the drawing?" asked Curmer nonchalantly.

"Both silly!" exclaimed Sorta annoyed by his deliberate teasing.

"The hide and the art work are the creations of craftmaster Natorl, formerly of the main campsite of the Nemn and now residing in our Artistic Halls. He is as you can see a most gifted man and is more than worthy of the title master."

Curmer swept his hand across the map as he communicated his respect for the old man. "I requested a detailed map of our city and tunnel systems leading to the nearest four settlements, but I did not expect anything as excellent as this." There was a flurry of agreements from the others as they all studied the fine drawing, showing views from above and cross sections.

Remruc lent forward, concentration creasing his brow. "I take it brother, that you have organised some unpleasant surprises along the main entrance tunnels and surrounding surface land."

Curmer smiled craftily. "Where would you place traps Remruc?" He asked innocently.

Remruc grunted, throwing him a sideways glance, amusement on his face. He looked studiously at the drawing once more. After what seemed an age he sat up, the suspense on the faces of the others almost making him laugh.

"Well," he began, "I can see no point in trying to block any of the Nemn caverns or tunnels, the more that are open, the more time the Cucs will take searching. However, I do think it would be useful to send out patrols to dig pits at the main tunnel junctions. If they are covered over with dust covered cloth, the stupid Cucs will run right into them. All of the nearest abandoned settlements should have their boreholes covered and disguised. Special attention must be paid to the small holding that had been invaded by that winged creature and the entrance securely sealed. We need traps set at intervals along the larger four tunnel systems, pits similar to those we will build in the Nemn tunnels, but this time filled with dka, to burn the Cucs. If we cover the tops with metal sheeting that the Tarl can make for us, we can use the tunnels until the last possible moment should the Cucs find us." Remruc watched his brother's face and waited for his reply.

"I have sent out the patrols as you suggested to the Nemn lands. So far they have managed to dig the pits at all of the main junctions from halfway into the territory to within a few sharr of our borders. The abandoned settlements have been sealed from the tunnels, but I didn't think it was necessary to seal the boreholes. What I have done though, is to also send out patrols into Doona territory, they are laying similar traps, as well as blocking tunnels. Now that is something you didn't think about Remruc." He smiled at his brother's look of satisfaction.

"I have underestimated you Curmer. Well done." Remruc picked up a glass of the potent Nemn brew and toasted his brother. "Now I will help you organise the final preparations. I feel that it is vital we disguise as much as possible, any evidence of ventilation shafts throughout the Chai territory. I do not want the Cucs to even begin to think that these mountains are hollow and occupied. The only thing I am worried about is we may well be sealing ourselves in only to be slaughtered if trapped." A worried frown creased his brow.

Sorta chose this moment to interrupt. "I have thought of that also Lord Remruc and I think I may have the solution." She balked slightly as all eyes were turned on her, nerves making her uncertain of their thoughts. A private message of encouragement from Curmer was all she needed to boost her confidence, and, with a nervous swallow, she continued. "If we keep the main exit tunnels to the northernmost settlements clear it will at least give us a backdoor should the Cuc break through our defences." She indicated on the map the routes she intended to be used. "These are all of the smaller tunnels, too small for a normal sized Cuc to follow us into. Even if they try to track us from above ground they will find the air cold. This hopefully will make them sluggish and unwilling to follow. I know that these northern settlements were abandoned because of the inhospitable, poor quality land available underground, but, our records show that it is cold enough to live close to the surface and water lies just below ground level. Further down there is a permanent frost and the water is solid like the store cellars below the city. If the worst comes to the worst at least we may be able to escape to the relative safety of these smallholdings, but I cannot say how long the land could support our increasing population." Her thoughts trailed off into her private mind as she considered how drastic this exodus may be.

"That is a very desperate solution to our problem Sorta," Remruc finally replied, "but it is the only one available to us. Well done. Now we must consider how we can make those northern retreats more hospitable." He smiled encouragement as they continued their discussion, considering alternatives and methodology well into the night.

It was a very tired but hopeful quartet that left the guest rooms later that evening, the future of their civilisation now resting on the actions of the Cuc forces.

Chapter Twelve

It took less than a week for the remaining traps to be set in the Nemn territory and work was beginning on the Chai tunnel systems. All of the remaining boreholes in the surrounding settlements not occupied were closed, the ones in use were heavily disguised. The animals that the Doona had brought with them were now in peak condition and provided swift travel between the main city and some of the now occupied lesser caverns. A patrol was sent north to assess the standard of the long abandoned settlements and their access tunnels.

They were supplied with thick warm furs from the Nemn and walking spikes from the store caverns in case underground ice lakes had to be crossed and, with their mantelos wrapped in warm felt material, they set off in grim determination.

Theirs was a journey that would prove to be the turning point in luck for the San. There was tension in the air as all awaited the coming of the Cucs.

Curmer strode back to the Chieftains hall taking note of the nervous apprehension that shadowed the minds and faces of all he passed. The people would need something to occupy their minds and to distract them from this terrible tension and helpless waiting. Smiling to himself he skipped up the steps, through the main doorway and along to the audience hall, there was something that just might do the trick.

Gathered around the main seating area and dais in the hall was a large number of masters and elders from virtually every profession in all of the San clans. Each in turn was giving an up to date report as to their readiness for the now expected Cuc attack. The air was thick with conversation and it was difficult to find a wavelength that was not already occupied with private discussion.

Curmer moved towards the central dais where Lenta and Eriya were coordinating information and trying to keep the mental noise at an acceptable level. The crowd tried their best to move aside for the Chieftain but the audience hall was almost filled to capacity, restricting even the slightest movement, Curmer, smiling politely, pushed his way forward trying to locate the correct line for Lenta.

"A moment of your time please healer Lenta," he finally announced on a crowded public line, she looked up smiling and waved her hands in exasperation at the jostling elders pushing reports and facts into her face.

"Outside in the hallway Lord Curmer, I cannot hear myself think amongst this babble."

Curmer nodded and made his way back out of the hall. He had to wait for quite a while as Lenta struggled to push her way out, appealing to the manners of the surrounding crowd and assuring them that all would be heard that day.

Eriya gamefully carried on, apparently unruffled by the commotion around her. Eventually she appeared round the door, closing it in mock exhaustion. "I never thought I would see this number of elders and masters again. They are noisy, frustrating and infuriating at times, but I love them all. They are the essence of life for our race and the image of a prosperous successful future. Thank you Lord Curmer and your brother for your determination against all odds to realise this goal. Sadelna was right. You were and are the saviours of not only the Chai, but the San nation." Lenta flashed a radiant smile at him and he hugged her in return.

"We could not have achieved anything without your help and support, Lenta. Thank you." They stood in silence for a while, each lost in their own thoughts.

Finally Curmer sighed and continued. "Lenta, the people need a brief respite from these frantic preparations, something to take their minds off the fight that lies ahead of us." Lenta tensed at this thought.

"Yes Lenta, I believe, and so does Remruc, that the Cuc will find us and we will have to face them once and for all." She turned pale and moved over to a nearby wall bench.

"I thought that with these precautions we would be safe. That they would never find us and would leave us alone." She placed her head in her hands, suddenly looking old and tired. "Why are the San destined to suffer so much?" She looked at him pleadingly and he moved to her side,

"Storn always said that it took a hard life to breed a hard warrior. The trials and tests that our people suffer today will prepare them for the future, it will instil a toughness and flexibility into our offspring that will make our people great one day. We will all have journeyed into the void long before then, our bodies dust on the ground, but our descendants will never forget these beginnings, we will always be remembered and thanked. Believe this Lenta. For the sake of our people, believe this!" He took her hands as he spoke and felt her radiance from within reach out and touch his heart. She smiled and nodded, too emotional to communicate anything more.

Curmer rose and pulled her to her feet. "Now, about this distraction. I am going to officially announce my marriage to Sorta. I want city wide celebrations to mark the occasion and representatives from all of the San clans when I take my first mate. It may well be the last big celebration before the final battle with the Cuc." Lenta beamed her joy and rushed away to prepare the city for the first marriage of one of their Chieftains.

It took another two weeks to organise the event properly. All work patrols were called back for that day, sentries working in shifts so that all could at least enjoy part of the celebrations. The city was alive with excitement; the happy couple had received gifts large and small from almost every citizen - the mixture of cultures giving a rich and exotic flavour to their collection. The day before the ceremony two runners returned from the north patrol their faces grim, their message urgent. Quickly they were ushered into Remruc's private quarters and he listened to what they had to say, sitting half dressed in his best uniform his mind frantically interpreting their thoughts.

"Lord Remruc, we have reached the largest northern outpost in Chai territory. The settlement has been well preserved although primitive in construction. The field cavern next to it seems large enough to support our grazing animals, but there is nowhere we can grow crops. The Tarl that was with us seemed to think that the air above ground is cold enough to allow for our hardier dry weather grains to grow, but only in the winter, by summer they would shrivel to dust. What Sorta told us is correct. The freezing level below ground is much closer to the surface, the settlement seems to make good use of that and is situated about one sharr below ground level. Further down, below the settlement, is a massive glacier sheet that is completely impenetrable. The Chai who lived there had been using this as a source of water, either chipping blocks off of the surface or using dka torches to melt it. The Tarl suggested that we use this natural phenomenon to store any extra food and grain produced in this city. It can be transported to the settlement in a matter of weeks and would be preserved in this icy cavern. If we take supplies out to this post, we could survive there for almost seven weeks, maybe more, there is enough room in the settlement and surrounding caverns for some rough living, but I wouldn't want to stay there permanently."

The runner sat down, tired by his exertions. Remruc continued dressing in silence, considering what had been said. He looked round at the other runner who had remained standing.

"What do you have to report?" The two runners exchanged glances, suddenly uneasy with their message.

"Well Lord Remruc," he began, "I am afraid I don't really understand the message so I will have to relay it to you exactly the way I heard it." Remruc grunted and sat down again.

"Report. Patrol Section Four, guards Kaenm and Gouar. On reconnaissance to the northern point, searching for other potential campsites. Entered cavern structure on second day out from main patrol. Floor very dusty and strewn with rubble. Small holding apparently situated at centre of cavern structure suitable for twenty people. Located remains of settlement. Only one building intact, the other had been dismantled." He paused in his monologue, glancing at Remruc.

"Dismantled?" asked Remruc, puzzled by the description, "how and by whom?"

The runner continued, "the method of removal unknown. Blocks of stone appear to have been cut..."

"Cut?" Remruc growled, "how?"

The runner winced and carried on, "they seem to have been sliced by an intense heat, the edges of the remaining blocks are melted."

Remruc stood up and began prowling around the room deep in thought. "What kind of tool can cut solid rock with heat?" the question clearly directed at himself. "Who would have such a thing and why would they want to take blocks of stone?"

The runner sat down beside his comrade and anxiously

interrupted Remruc's thoughts. "They did find tracks Lord Remruc." He flinched as Remruc spun round, looming over him.

"Tracks? What kind of tracks?"

"Now that, Lord Remruc is a mystery. Kaenm and Gouar had never seen anything like them before and whatever made them was almost as big as a Cuc. The tracks they had seen were about a decade old, but they requested that you send a Nemn hunter to investigate."

Remruc considered a moment, "take Herka back with you and find out what made these tracks and where they were going. Be careful! Keep men informed of the situation, the last thing I need are more complications." The two runners left to refresh themselves and then return to the north.

A wedding ceremony for the San was a very formal affair, more so if a Chieftain was being wed. There were more females than males in the San so it was practical for a male to have more than one wife. The first mate to be taken was the highest ranking position within the family, in many areas, especially social, a first wife would outrank her husband. It was her children who would inherit the majority of the wealth of the family and the family name. She would have authority over any other wives and would often have a say in choosing any further companions for her mate. It was also traditional to take a healer for a first mate, a warrior wife for a second (warrior women of the Chai seldom if ever had children) and a master in a prosperous trade as a third. Few males ever exceeded three wives, even Chieftains.

The day started early for Sorta. She was dressed in deep purple robes that announced her status as a healer, her head covered by a thin veil decorated by Eriya with small purple gemstones. Inlays of precious metals woven into the border of her over tunic complimented the otherwise plain garment. This was a time for the women. All family and friends were gathered in her apartments, to join her in a light breakfast. It was still dark on the planet's surface as they moved out into the streets lined with all the women from the city. Not a man was to be seen as they walked to the entrance platform, the crowd falling in behind her, murmurings of good wishes floating through the air.

People touched the hem of her dress as she passed to convey their wishes for luck into her life. The guards to escort her were all female warriors, their armour gleaming, their uniforms neat. The arrival of the procession on the surface was to correspond with the sunrise, for even when the San retreated underground away from the heat of those glowing orbs they retained their traditions that were born on the open plains of their nomadic days. The dawn heralded the birth of a new day and a first wife would greet Emur and Rume, asking them to bless her so that she may give birth to a new life the heir to her husband's family. All women secretly asked that their twin Suns would honour them with twin sons also, but few were granted that privilege.

While the women were on the surface conducting the birthing ceremony, the men emerged and gathered in the central circle of the city. Remruc was dressed in full armour, his Cuc scale mask decorated with precious stones and metal. All of the guards chosen for this special ceremony were heroes of the recent battles and hardships and it was pleasing for all those present to note that half of them were Nemn. This was a great honour for these warriors and hunters, it would give their families prestige for generations to come. All of the select few were gathered in a loose circle, the crowd of men behind them. Into the centre of the circle walked Curmer. He too was wearing armour, but a cape of deep purple adorned his back showing his rank as a healer. The Cuc scale mask was decorated like Remruc's subtle differences in design distinguishing who was who. The ceremony began. One by one the warriors came forward and a stylized form of fighting was conducted between Curmer and his opponents. Always Curmer defeated his attacker allowing them to escape to the safety of the crowd of cheering onlookers. Finally Remruc stepped up and they faced each other. The fight began similar to the others, but at the moment where Curmer would have defeated his opponent, he stopped and lay down his weapon. "I am Curmer, Chieftain of the Chai and member of the Leading council of the San. I will not kill you." Remruc laid his sword on the ground.

"I am Remruc, Chieftain of the Chai and member of the Leading Council of the San. I will never raise arms against you." There was a tumulus mental cheer from the crowd at this unusual event, it was fitting that neither Chieftain was defeated and both swore allegiance to each other. A silence descended and as the two brothers turned to face the crowd it parted slowly and reverently. Remruc and Curmer both removed their face masks as a chair was carried into the centre of the circle by three Nemn and three Chai. Seated on top was Lord Eskara. Dressed in his richest robes, his hair hidden completely by an elaborate headdress. The bearers gently lowered the old man to the ground and it was plain to everyone that he was making a great effort just to be there. Eskara drew on his fast failing strength and pulled himself upright in the chair, his eyes flashing with pride at the two Chieftains in front of him, one warrior, one healer, the perfect combination. He raised a trembling hand, shrunken with age, his mind still sharp and strong in this husk of a body.

"I am Lord Eskara, Chieftain of the Nemn, member of the Leading council of the San. I give you my blessing Lord Curmer. May your offspring be rich and plentiful, may your years be long and peaceful." He smiled, "I will not raise arms against you. Nor will my successor." There was a murmur of surprise at his last statement. They all knew the old Chief was almost ready to journey to the void, but it was unusual for a Chieftain to step down while he was still alive. "I will be here for no longer than one week, then I will journey to the void and join my mates once more. I have no sons left alive to inherit my wealth and position, but I do have a daughter and she is the equal of any son I have ever had. When she marries," Eskara gave a knowing look towards Remruc and he and Curmer exchanged smiles, "her mate will become Chieftain of the Nemn in name, but the responsibilities will remain with Lady Eriya, unless she chooses otherwise." Again a cheer went up from the crowd as they happily and readily accepted his decision. On the crest of that tumulus wave the bearers lifted up Eskara and carried him back to his quarters. He was exhausted by even this small exertion and needed to rest.

A signal was raised from the entrance platform announcing the return of the bride, there was some anxious fumbling by Curmer as he straightened his uniform, nervously awaiting the return of his beloved. Finally the crowd of men parted to allow Sorta, flanked by Eriya and Lenta to enter the circle. Curmer stepped forward ignoring Sorta, "Healer Lenta." She nodded. "Chieftain Eriya," there was a slight hesitation before she acknowledged her new title, it was obvious that she had no idea of her father's plan for that morning. "I am Chieftain Curmer of the Chai, I wish to take as my first mate this healer Sorta."

Lenta stepped forward between Curmer and Sorta with her

arms raised, "are you a strong enough warrior to defend her and your children?" The ceremonial warriors who had fought Curmer, unanimously 'shouted' their confirmation. Lenta stepped aside. Eriya moved forward.

"Will you grant her all of the rights of a first mate, abide by her decisions on your other mates?"

"Yes Chieftain Eriya." Both Eriya and Lenta turned to Sorta.

"Will you let this warrior Chief claim you?"

"He may wish to claim me, but let us see if he can keep me!" was the merry reply from Sorta as she took off her veil and overtunic handing them to Lenta.

Curmer removed his mask and armour body plates, giving them to Remruc. Then the game began. In the centre of the circle was a marble post set in a marble circle. Sorta moved to the post, while Curmer stayed on the edge of the circle. The object of the game was for the bridegroom to prevent his bride from escaping the circle. If she managed to get to the surrounding crowd then she was free to deny his claim for marriage. It was always good fun, the bride would tease her groom, making mock dashes for the crowd, but always being just slow enough to be caught and dragged back to the post. The excitement generated from the crowd spurred the contestants on as more daring leaps and escapes were attempted. If Curmer managed to catch her ten times then he could claim her and the feasting would begin. The crowd were ecstatic as Curmer finally swept her off her feet, dumping her unceremoniously into the circle for the last time.

"For every escape that you have made you will stay with me one year. At the end of that time you will have the choice to stand in the circle again." He said gasping for breath, his pretty Sorta had given him a run for his money.

"You have managed to keep me Lord Curmer and keep me

you will." She exclaimed as he lifted her to her feet, wrapping her arms around him as he kissed her. The cheering crowd rushed forward lifting the couple onto their shoulders and carrying them to the stone park where enough food had been prepared to satisfy everyone.

Remruc watched them leave for the park, joy in his heart for his brother, he would join them later, after he had listened to the report brought back by a third runner from the north. Herka had left yesterday along with the two Chai and he hoped they would make haste. "What do you have to report?" he said motioning for the runner to sit down.

"Kaenm and Gounar have followed the tracks to their source."

"And?"

"They lead into a large cavern in the centre of which stands a strange structure. It is made of blue crystals and, according to the Tarl who has examined it, it is generating its own power from light through the boreholes in the ceiling. The crystals are set in a ring and they seem to float in the air by themselves."

Remruc raised his eyebrows at this, but motioned for the runner to continue.

"Although the crystals are set in a ring, you cannot see through the centre, there is a mist that floats within the perimeters of the crystals, always swirling, but never dissipating."

"Have you seen this strange object?"

"Yes Lord Remruc."

"Then show me in your mind." The runner and Remruc linked minds and he saw this beautiful, unusual and frightening object appear before him.

"The Tarl is too frightened to continue his examination of

this object unless you specifically order him to. But, Lord Remruc, the most terrifying thing is the tracks. They lead directly to the centre of the ring then disappear. There is nothing on the other side."

"What kind of creature made these tracks?" asked Remruc."Could it have been a San?"

"No Lord. Whatever made the footprints moved on four legs, like a mantelo, not two like the San." Remruc sat back deep in thought.

"You may go," he said to the runner, "and join the celebrations. Mention this to no one, I will tell Curmer in my own time after I have visited this strange ring."

Several days after the wedding ceremony, Remruc excused himself from Curmer saying that he was needed to coordinate the preparations in the northern territory. With that he set out, making haste to reach the north as quickly as possible. When he did eventually arrive at the northern smallholding he was surprised to see the entire patrol at the entrance tunnel in the midst of a heated debate.

"Lord Remruc should be made aware of this immediately," Herka was saying, "it may be the only way to save our people."

"I am here Herka." Said Remruc stepping into their midst, a wave of surprise and relief washing over the gathered warriors. "What is it you wish to tell me?"

"Lord Remruc," Herka replied smiling, "I think you should see for yourself." After a brief meal and rest Herka, Remruc, the Tarl and four other guards set out for the deserted family dwelling. On the journey, Herka filled Remruc in on what had happened. "When I first arrived, Lord Remruc, I was completely bemused by the strange tracks; I have never seen anything like them before, the Nemn records give no mention of such a creature living on Surn."

"Can you tell what this animal looks like just by its tracks?"

"Roughly, Lord Remruc. It stands almost as large as a Cuc but it moves like a mantelo. The legs must be fairly long, judging by the stride, but as the tracks are not too deep I'd say it was lightly built, almost slender - nothing like a Cuc. There are some variations in the tracks; I therefore assume that there were more than one of these unusual creatures. The tracks leading back from the settlement were slightly deeper, as though the animals were carrying something."

"Is it possible that these were burden animals used by someone or something else?"

"That is possible Lord Remruc, but if they were then the owners did not leave any trace of their being there. The tracks themselves are strange. Our mantelos have four digits with blunt claws, these creatures walk on two toes with what must be very large blunt claws for support."

"So there is no chance that they were made by some large wild mantelos?"

"None whatsoever, Lord Remruc."

Remruc nodded and retreated to his private mind as they continued their journey.

Once they arrived at the dismantled smallholding the Tarl moved to the front of the group and Herka nodded at him giving him permission to speak.

"Lord Remruc," he began, nervously twisting his hands, "I have examined the ruins most thoroughly and it is apparent that a controlled beam of intense heat was used to slice blocks of the stone into bundles. These bundles, when fitted together would replicate the dwelling, the joins becoming almost invisible. Whatever was removing the stones must have been rebuilding the homestead somewhere else." Remruc grunted in slight disbelief at what the Tarl was suggesting but he did not interrupt him, the whole situation was too unusual to discount any explanation. The group moved forward, deeper into the cavern structure, towards the mysterious crystal ring. A faint glow from the cavern ahead indicated they had arrived. Remruc was awestruck when he set eyes on this incredible construction, and construction it was, nothing like this could ever have developed naturally, its symmetry was perfect, its form alien. The ring, (it was more like a hoop) stood in the centre of the cavern, directly beneath a borehole that cast a beam of light upon the subject, but the yellow orange light cast by the suns suddenly seemed to change to icy white as it neared the structure, falling to the floor in a blue reflection from the crystals. "As you can see Lord Remruc," The Tarl said moving forward, "the ring appears to be absorbing the light from above and emitting its own variation." Remruc moved around the ring, the centre, although obviously hollow, was filled with a swirling mist that never seemed to stray beyond the narrow confines of the crystals. It looked exactly the same from behind as it did from the front, but what really puzzled Remruc was the fact that the whole structure was not resting on the floor of the cavern, but at least a hand span above.

"How does it stay in the air?" he finally asked the Tarl.

"That, Lord Remruc, is a mystery. I have never encountered anything like it, although I can theorise as to the method."

"Well?"

"The ring itself seems to be generating some kind of force, possibly magnetic, that is repelling it from the natural magnetism within these very rocks. That is why it is in the centre of this cavern, you can see that the distance it sits from

the floor is identical to the distance it sits from the ceiling."
Remruc looked up to the top of the ring and, true enough, it
was a mere hand span away from the craggy roof. Herka
stepped forward.

"This is the most exciting part Lord Remruc. We tested the
ring to see what happened when we put a spear through." He
picked up a long spear and slowly walked forward to the ring
and pushed the weapon through the mist in the centre.
Remruc watched in amazement as the spear disappeared up to
Herka's hands, but did not, as it should have done, appear on
the other side. Herka withdrew the spear unharmed from the
mist.

"Where did it go?" asked Remruc.

"I wanted to find out too, so we tested first with a piece of
meat from our rations. We tied it to a rope and put it through
the ring, we dragged it back and it was unharmed so..." Herka
slowly smiled as Remruc began to put two and two together,
"...I went next."

Remruc growled in annoyance that this brave hunter
should try anything so foolhardy.

"The guards held onto the rope and I walked through the
ring. We had agreed to only let me go for a short while then I
would be pulled back through the ring. We communicated all
the time by jerking the rope every few moments and when I
came back I was unharmed."

"Well?" asked Remruc, barely concealing his excitement.

"I walked through the mist and it was as though I had
simply emerged on the other side of the ring, I thought at first
I had, but when I looked around all I could see was the ring
and no one else. Then I realised that I wasn't in the same
cavern, and, on the ground around me were tracks, the same
kind that we followed here. I moved a little bit into what
seemed to be a crystal cave, the same type of crystals as

these," he indicated the ring with his hand, "there was light at the end of a long tunnel, a bright light, not yellow like our suns, but white and a breeze of cool fresh air that smelt crisp. Then I came back."

Remruc was impressed and he turned to the Tarl who had been waiting. "What were your ideas?"

"We have concluded that this ring is some kind of portal or doorway leading to possibly a different part of our world or perhaps even another world, maybe even the void." There was a few anxious mutters from those gathered. "However, as Herka was unharmed we have concluded that wherever this leads to is safe for our people and we can survive there. We still don't know how large a complex this portal leads to or if there is another cavern at the end of the tunnel Herka saw, however, it may be able to accommodate some of us should we need refuge." Remruc nodded, picking up instantly what the Tarl was implying.

"This sounds like a possible escape route Tarl. If our people become trapped in these lands we will surely eventually die and I will not be food for any Cuc. Even if stepping into this ring will result in our death I know in my heart that the people of the San would rather choose this option. We will however, oppose the Cuc with all our will and strength and try our best to drive them from our lands. This," he pointed to the ring, "is our last resort, but an option we must keep open." There was a rousing 'cheer' from the warriors as they accepted their Chieftains thoughts. "You guards will remain here and protect this discovery. You", he grabbed the Tarl by the arm, "will come back with me and, with your friends, will try to work out what this thing is and who built it."

Chapter Thirteen

Remruc arrived back in the city on the morning of Lord Eskara's death. The city was in mourning, a stark contrast to the jubilation's of the previous week. Formal arrangements were being handled by Lenta, Eirya being too stricken with grief to do anything. He went directly to the quarters of the old Chieftain to pay his last respects and had to negotiate a large milling crowd of Nemn and Chai also attempting to enter the building.

"The old Chief certainly impressed a lot of people," thought Remruc to himself, "I will miss him too. He reminded me so much of Storn when I was a child and our people were great." Remruc corrected his thoughts, "Thanks to the cooperation of Eskara, our people will be great once more." He passed through the crowded corridors as the people of the San queued politely, waiting for their turn. As he neared the door into the private chambers of Eskara, the people moved aside, allowing him entry. The body lay on a stone table at the centre of the room, a circle of torches preventing people from touching him. The magnificent gown draped across the still form dazzled Remruc with its sparkling splendour; gemstones and precious metals glinting in the dancing light of the torches. Eskara's face was covered by a gold encrusted Cuc scale death mask and Remruc was glad. The old man had looked shrunken and grim at their last meeting, and Remruc was not keen on seeing the skeletal face in death. Behind the body, seated on a large ornate chair, was Eriya, her face ashen, her eyes reflecting the pain in her mind. She too was dressed in finery, the hide gown brightly clinging to her body. She was as still as her father and at first Remruc had feared the worst, but, as she drew breath, the clicking of the beads adorning the gown gave away the fact that she was still alive.

Now he moved forward and bowed to Eskara. "Farewell Lord Eskara, great Chieftain of the Nemn, you will be missed and mourned by all of our people." He then moved round to face Eriya. "Hail Lady Eriya, Chieftain of the Nemn, may you rule as wisely and strongly as your father."

Again he bowed and as he straightened he saw a glint of recognition stir her from her stupor.

"Lord... Remruc... I," she began, the thoughts broken by stabs of painful grief echoing the loss within her.

"I know Lady Eriya... I know," he said taking her hand, "if you wish, I can stay here and help you greet the people."

A grateful smile was the only reply she could manage and Remruc sat down quietly beside her an aching in his heart for her pain.

The funeral of Chief Eskara was much grander than that of Storn and although this may have irritated Curmer slightly to begin with, he quickly came to his senses when he set eyes on Eriya. She seemed to be in a daze and had to be guided by Lenta on one side and Remruc on the other. The Doona had provided a suitable sled for her as she accompanied her father to the ritual void of the Chai. Curmer feared that she may be so overcome with grief that she would follow her father into the yawning maw of the pit, but Eriya was strong and she knew what a responsibility her father had left on her shoulders, she was determined to prove herself and justify his actions.

Once the ceremony was over and as the mantelos drew her sled back from the void she seemed to grow stronger, as though Eskara was reaching out from his grave and instilling his strength of character and wisdom into her very soul. She became more aware of her surroundings and looking round, saw Remruc seated beside her. He saw her glance and smiled in encouragement, Eriya remembered his strong presence that had helped her through this day and she took his hand. "Thank you, Lord Remruc, for staying with me." Remruc's heart leaped at her touch and he struggled to control the emotion within him.

He was not entirely successful and Eriya, sensing the conflict within him, misinterpreted his reasons and quickly withdrew her hand, looking away in embarrassment and sorrow. Remruc was furious with himself and he too sat in stony silence, not daring to even look in her direction.

One year passed in the lives of the San before that fearfully dreaded day came about. In that year dramatic and subtle changes had occurred in the culture of the people. They were no longer this clan or that clan, but had begun to call themselves by their race name, San. The old clan names became formal titles that described a job or occupation. A Chai was a warrior and/or high ranking official, whether the person was Nemn, or Doona was irrelevant. A Nemn became the term used for the internal police force operating within the city, it was also used to refer to a lower ranking government official. All San involved in the care or breeding of livestock became known as Doona and of course the servants or technicians were Tarl. This was the beginning of the San civilisation, a civilisation that would exist and dominate for thousands of years. The population of the city had doubled, and everywhere there were youngsters and babes, life had returned once more. Sorta was expecting her first child and both she and Curmer positively glowed with anticipation.

She had a few more months of waiting ahead of her and Eriya (who had grown close to her) was constantly monitoring the situation.

Curmer and Lenta were becoming exasperated by Remruc and Eriya when they were in each other's company, a year since the unfortunate incident at Eskara's funeral had not dimmed the awkwardness. Lenta was ready to suggest a group mindmeld 'so that the two silly creatures' as she put it would realise their true feelings and this would probably have happened if it wasn't for the Cucs.

Such a long time had passed since the preparation for the Cuc attack had been made that many of the San doubted if they would ever be found, but they were wrong.

The winged leader of the Cucs had not been idle. His offspring had multiplied and had been raiding other Cuc nests, either killing or recruiting into their hordes the inhabitants. A new breed of Cuc had appeared. They were stronger, smarter and insanely violent. The winged leader maintained order within his ranks by fear and aggression. When they had eaten all the San corpses in the Jenta lands they fed on those killed in other Cuc nests. Once that source of food had been finished, the Cuc began to breed solely for selected offspring to provide food. They had no qualms, they had no conscience, only those worker types required as slaves were left alive the rest were fed, fattened and slaughtered, but the Leader was not stupid. He maintained a special guard force of male winged Cuc, their job was to protect him at all times, lest any of the minions become rebellious.

And their payment for this privilege? They were the only other Cucs allowed to breed. The Queen Cucs from every nest they had raided were kept apart from the workers and ferociously guarded. The females may have been Queens once but now they were kept as breeding slaves, their teeth and claws having been ripped from their bodies to reduce the chance of injury to the precious winged force. This Cuc knew that his success in destroying the San depended on the control he had over the winged males, for they would be his eyes and ears, directing the workers in their relentless search through the mountains for their intended prey.

A Chai sentry scanning the borders was first to raise the alarm. The message was sent by relay directly to Remruc. He was found on a Chai training ground sparring with an instructor who was hard pushed to keep up with the skilled Chieftain.

"Lord Remruc!" said the runner bowing hurriedly to both men, "Winged Cuc have been sighted scanning the bordering territory." Remruc nodded grimly.

"Alert two companies of Chai, we will be ready to move out at sunset." With that he spun on his heels and made his way to the council gathering of elders and masters of trade.

Healer Munta was chairing the meeting and he instantly called the group to attention when the Chieftain entered.

"Lord Remruc we are honoured by your presence, but I am afraid that we are merely discussing mundane day-to-day running procedures of the city, it may not prove an interesting debate for you."

"Thank you healer Munta but I am not here to listen." he stepped up onto the centre Dais. "Elders and Masters, today winged Cuc were sighted scanning the neighbouring territory. There will no doubt be more of their kind searching below ground. The traps we set one year ago may not be enough to deter them completely, so, with your help, I would like to begin the evacuation of all food, surplus livestock and people to the northern settlement."

"Do you not think Lord Remruc, that to evacuate now would be a bit premature?" said healer Munta sitting down with the shock of the news.

"More than one half of our population consists of babes and youngsters. I do not wish to leave anything to chance. If we must leave our city then we must be able to move quickly, this we cannot do with our offspring running around. No healer Munta, the children and expectant mothers must be moved to safety.

If and when we defeat the Cucs, they will be brought back. Now, there is a company of Chai guards at the settlement already and I will send another two patrols to accompany the evacuees. That should be enough for any unexpected encounters." Remruc turned to face the council. "I want everyone to send their able-bodied students over to the Nemn hall for training in basic defence against Cucs. The older members of all the trades must be evacuated along with the others. I want a fighting force only left in the city. Do you understand?" There was anxious confirmation from the council, their apprehension more than obvious.

Remruc nodded grimly to the now bustling bodies as they set about their appointed tasks and exited quickly, making straight for his home. He pondered on an excuse he could use to send Eriya along with the evacuees, but as she was a Chieftain and not old or pregnant or with young children he was stumped for a reason. Marching along the corridor he ordered the attendant guards posted at every junction to report back to the Chai halls for immediate reassignment, by the time he reached Curmer and Sorta's apartments the house was almost empty. With a slight pause to announce his presence before entering the room Remruc opened the door.

Sorta was seated next to the window, mixing herbs and labelling bottles, her face radiant, her complexion glowing.

"Lord Remruc," she thought warmly as she attempted to rise. Remruc hurriedly motioned for her to remain seated and made his way across the room.

"Sorta you look beautiful as ever. How is your son?" She laughed at his comments and replied,

"My son is fine Lord Remruc, it is still too early for him to think properly, but, if I listen carefully, I get these wonderful images of what he is seeing and feeling. Would you like to listen?" Remruc smiled, half-embarrassed at her offer and sat down beside her. She took his hand and laid it on her stomach, just above the bulge. He closed his eyes and 'searched' for his nephew. A sudden flash of brilliantly coloured emotion, warmth, comfort, security and curiosity at this other presence burst into his mind. Remruc took his hand away surprise on his face,

"Well! He certainly knew I was there, it will not be long before he starts to ask you questions." He smiled gently, "thank you Sorta, that was wonderful." She laughed and called for Curmer, offering Remruc some fruit. Curmer appeared, still dressing from the sleeping alcove, his hair ruffled, framing a face that bore the smug glow of a father-to-be. He sat down beside Sorta and studied Remruc's face.

"The Cuc have been sighted haven't they?" Remruc nodded. He heaved a heavy sigh and stroked Sorta's hair. "It is time for you to leave beloved," he said as she was about to argue. Remruc, sensing the conflict of emotions within Curmer quickly entered their discussion,

"I would like Lady Eriya to go with you Lady Sorta." His statement ended any conversation that Curmer and Sorta had been having and they looked at him, each with different expressions. Sorta was suddenly smiling again, Curmer had a cheeky, "why don't you just say it" look on his face. Remruc was puzzled by their reactions so he quickly added a somewhat lame explanation,

"Well, she is a healer and as all of the people journeying will either be old, very young, new born, expecting or first time mothers then it is appropriate that a senior healer accompany them. Besides, not only is she a healer, she is a Chief, and it is important that a figure be provided who can make decisions and give orders. Lady Eriya is a perfect choice."

"Are they the only reasons you want Lady Eriya out of the city, Remruc?" said Curmer, a sly grin on his face. Sorta promptly delivered a sharp kick to his ankle beneath the table and smiled courteously.

"Of course they are beloved, what other reasons do you need? I think it is a wonderful idea, Eriya can keep me company."

"Yes... quite... I see your point," replied Curmer, his body stiff, a fixed look on his face but managing to grin amiably. "I will begin preparations straight away." Remruc nodded his approval and made his way back to his own quarters, slightly perplexed at the odd behaviour he had just witnessed,

"Perhaps you are affected that way when your partner is expecting," he thought to himself scratching his head in puzzlement.

So it began. The evacuation of the city was, like most things organised by the San, quickly and efficiently done. It was completed within two days, the remaining San preparing to defend their territory.

Two Chai patrols left the city at sunset, their objective, to enter the nearest tunnel complex of the neighbouring lands and assess how far and extensive the Cuc search was. Only one patrol made it back. Their leader stood exhausted and filthy in front of the Chieftains, his news was grim. The missing patrol had encountered a massive, organised group of Cucs just ten sharr from the border.

They were wiped out instantly, the second patrol hearing their screams from their deserted section of tunnels. What the patrol leader saw when they examined one of the pits dug at an intersection turned his stomach. The pit had been full of the rotting carcasses of worker Cucs, their foul flesh being systematically eaten by larvae-like young. Apparently the Cucs had simply continued to throw themselves into the pit till it was full and their comrades could walk across, over their bodies. The pits then made ideal incubation chambers for the developing young of a new generation of beasts. It horrified the Chieftains to think of all of the pits full of a similar gory feast.

The Cucs, it appeared, were unstoppable. They were relentlessly driving their forces across the mountain ring reproducing more of their kind as they went, setting up new nests wherever they found an abandoned San settlement. Curmer sat with his head resting in his hands, the hopelessness of their predicament weighing heavily on his mind. Remruc paced around the room, frustration and anger pulsing through his thoughts. "I will not let them soil this city with their foul presence!" he thundered slamming his fist down onto the table causing the collection of writing slates to jump and tremble at his fury.

"You are right brother. We must prevent entry to our city at all costs - look!" Curmer picked up the hide map of all of their defences, "If we use one company to draw the Cucs here, well away from our main city and tunnel sections, the rest of us can begin to block the entrances to our city tunnels by collapsing the roofs. It must be engineered in such a way that if and when we return they can easily be unblocked from the inside. What do you think?" Remruc studied the map,

"It is possible, but how will the decoy company get through to retreat with us to the north?"

"If we leave the smallest access tunnels clear right to the very last moment, then they can return quickly from this old grazing cavern here." Curmer pointed, "I think we should set all of the pits in this area alight and burn the murderous beasts as they attack."

"You are right brother, but it will be dangerous, there is a good chance that the decoy company will not survive the encounter."

"Then the company must be made up from volunteers. We cannot force anyone to do such a thing."

"I will lead the company," said Remruc continuing as he saw Curmer's quick reaction to his thoughts, "You are needed here to organise the barricading of our city, besides, I know these smaller tunnels like the back of my hand, I will not get lost." He turned and left to organise his guards before Curmer could deny the logic of his choice.

Early that morning, before Emur and Rume crawled into the tired sky, the company of volunteers set out across the dusty mountains. They were all old, hard-bitten campaigners from the original Chai warriors, none had any surviving family, none had taken new mates, all were determined to destroy the Cucs at any cost. The rearguard laid strips of meat along the track, the scent of which would lure the Cucs into the waiting trap. They reached their goal just after sunrise; in the distance they could see the winged leaders rising slowly into the air, using the thermals to lift them high and allow them to view the terrain. Quickly and silently, the Chai slipped into the darkness of an entrance tunnel that had been unblocked for their purposes and with practised ease they descended into the depths of the mountain to wait for their prey.

Halfway round the continent, the supreme leader of the Cucs hissed his pleasure. San had been sighted and killed. He had joined his ferocious offspring in their minds as they finished off their kill, all the time he was searching for that one San that had plagued him throughout his days. The winged leader knew that they must be close to the Sans' nest and that was why they had emerged to challenge his mighty army. He called his most trusted ally to his side. The black skinned creature was the same one that had murdered Doorka in the ink dark passages of the mountains a long time since. He had grown since then, both in body and mind till he was almost as large and feared as the nest Leader himself.

The winged leader regarded his second with slightly suspicious eyes, although he had never been challenged by this Cuc, he knew that should his strength fail or should he lose control, this would be his successor and that knowledge burned within him with fiery red flames of jealousy. But if he wanted to destroy the San then he needed the co-operation of his second and all the other winged males. With a snort that sent mucous flying from his nostrils the Leader concentrated his mind towards this black, fearful figure. "Come. We... go... kill... SSSSSsssssan!" His thoughts were primitive, his mind diffused with yellow stabs of anger and revenge, but his second-in-command screamed in support and triumph for this long awaited moment. The Leader sat back on his haunches, his wings outstretched and flapping in the foul, stale air of the middle nest of his empire and screamed a resounding, thunderous encore to his second. The tight skin over the scar along his side and wing tingled with anticipation.

The Chai sentry at the entrance tunnel to the trap felt his heart stop in terror.

The very ground beneath his feet trembled with the resounding footfall of thousands upon thousands of Cuc workers. The horizon, wavering in a heat haze, slowly revealed the dark bronze line of advancing beasts, the brilliantly lit sky of Surn was growing darker as the massive winged forms of the controlling males flew above their hoards. The sentry's thoughts trembled slightly as he reported back his view of advancing death, but, like a true warrior, he held his ground, obeying his orders to remain in position till the last possible minute.

The eternal enemies of the San advanced till they stood on

the bordering range of mountains that marked the limits of the territory. With the evil winged males hovering above screaming abuse at their slaves, smaller, younger animals crept nervously forward, alert for any attack, seeking for any tracks that might give away the hiding place of the San. There was a blood curdling screech from beyond the ridge to the left of the sentry's hiding place as one of the Cucs found the scraps of meat that would lead them into the tunnel. The waiting hoards of worker Cucs tried to surge forward, but were instantly repelled by the slashing claws and whipping tails of the winged males. They were not as stupid and mindless as their minions; they sensed danger, they knew the San would never leave such an obvious sign or track. No. They would wait. It would not be long before the Nest Leader joined their ranks, then he would decide what should be done.

The massive males pushed their ranks of workers back onto the mountain top and there they remained, polluting the red earth with their foul presence. The Chai guard watched the unusual behaviour by the Cucs, relaying as best he could back to Lord Remruc waiting deep within the caverns. Frustrated Remruc told him to remain where he was and made his way back up the dark tunnel, towards the waiting jaws of death.

Hot air burned and whipped across his tough hide, even at this high altitude the stifling air was almost overpowering, as his massive wings beat in a steady rhythm echoed by his companions flanking his massive frame. He turned a glowing eye downward, scanning the jagged mountaintops of what was now his terrain. Clicking his teeth in satisfaction he noticed the abundance of Cuc workers swarming over the land, searching for the last remaining living creatures on Surn's burnt out surface. In the past prey as small as this would not be worth the effort of a Cuc, but now, any variation from cannibalism was a welcome treat.

The Leader hissed, saliva dripping from his lips to be whipped away and evaporated in the fast rushing air, as he anticipated the feast he and his fellows would enjoy when the San nest was found and destroyed. He did not notice the speculative look in his second-in-command's eyes as they covered the immense territory now occupied solely by Cuc. By late afternoon the most powerful and feared creatures on Surn arrived at their massed forces, causing a raucous roaring of greeting and terror from their minions. Instantly a young Cuc worker rushed forward, stopping a few paces from its Leader and enthusiastically ripping open its own throat. As the blood gushed into the dry ground, the Leader pounced on the still twitching body, ripping lumps of hot, quivering flesh and swallowing the tasty snack. He would, of course, have preferred well-rotted meat, but the long flight had stimulated his appetite. This signalled feeding time for the other winged males, but they did not find their food as willing and had to actively search among the terrified workers for a suitable meal. The Leader finished his meal quickly (the offering had been small) and moved over to the still eating male that had led this search. Forgetting his manners for a moment, the male hissed a warning at his leader as he neared the carcass.

He did not live long enough to regret his actions, enraged the Leader snapped out both of his front legs, back winging to maintain balance and with his massive meathook claws gouged two troughs of flesh along both sides of the offending males neck, grating along the bones and running up and over his eyes, the orbs popping out of their sockets and falling to the ground to be eagerly snapped up by the nearest Cuc workers. The body of the injured Cuc writhed in agony, the jaws snapping, trying to scream while the vocal chords swung uselessly in the open air. The nest Leader watched with satisfaction as the dying creature fell to the ground, he bored a demand straight into the pain-filled brain, "where... SSSsssssssan?" The male, blood filled lungs gurgling, used a mental picture of the strips of meat leading into the mountain to answer his executor. An excited squeal pierced the air as the nest Leader realised how close he was to destroying his hated enemy. With a snort he turned from the still writhing form before him and allowed the worker Cucs to feast on this unexpected treat. They shredded and stripped the corpse and the winged male within minutes, taking great pleasure in eating a creature that had dominated and terrified them for so long. The entire scenario was watched with interest by the other males; all except the black second had been impressed. The nest Leader was still a force to be reckoned with. The black Cuc, however, was more thoughtful. The nest Leader had shown a weakness that could be used against him with cunning and guile, he was easily angered and this anger would make him blind with hate and revenge and a blind leader was easily destroyed.

The black second was very careful to hide these rebellious thoughts and he shuffled and grovelled with the other males; the time was not right yet for him to strike, but it was getting closer. The Leader spread his wings, flapping them to stay cool and strode to the top of the ridge. He viewed the terrain before him, out there somewhere were the San and he was going to find them, but not until he had digested his meal.

Remruc felt a tightening in his gut as he watched the gargantuan winged Cuc shred and devour one of its own kind. He recognised the creature instantly and regretted not destroying it completely back in the deserted settlement when he had the chance. With horror he and the sentry witnessed the disciplinary action used by the Leader to maintain order in his ranks, the stench of blood and guts carrying across to them on the hot dry air.

Once it became apparent that the creatures meant to rest after their gory feast, Remruc motioned to the sentry to move back further into the tunnel. "We will have to use more than strips of meat to lure them into our trap. I want you to go round to the right, onto the ridge top, I will move over to the left. On my signal, stand up in full view of the Cucs, with luck they will be so incensed by our cheek they will attack instantly. Do not wait for an invitation to retreat, as soon as they move you run as fast as you can back down the tunnel. They are far enough away to give us time to get past the first set of traps before they enter the tunnel mouth. Understand?" The guard nodded quickly and they moved out into the dusk darkening sky.

An alarm was raised by one of the worker Cucs, breaking the languidity of the dozing males. They were instantly alert, their keen eyes scanning the mountains for the source of the worker's agitation. There, on the horizon, were two San standing watching them. The nest Leader sprang to his feet, the ground trembling as his massive frame bounded to the edge of the ridge, free falling into space till his enormous wings caught the updraft lifting him high into the sky. His body guards followed his example and as the Leader's keen eyesight viewed the two San before him his body vibrated with an ear-shattering howl. At last! He had found the San that had plagued him for so long. Before his massive army could mobilise, the Sans turned and ran, disappearing into one of their holes. The Leader circled the entrance ordering one of his winged servants to land first, in case there were any more San in hiding, waiting to pounce.

The Leader was not angry enough to risk further injury to his precious hide. The winged male landed and peered into the entrance tunnel.

The scent of San was strong, but he could hear the footfalls of the retreating prey with an affirmative snort to his Leader he announced the area was safe enough for him to land. This he did, almost causing a cave-in as his enormous weight settled above the entrance. But, as he moved forward to enter the tunnel system, his second-in-command blocked his path, striking a subservient pose he weaved his blunt-nosed head back and forward, "SSSsstill... not... sssssafe... for... ussss... let.... ssssslavesss... go... firsssst." There was initial fury within the Leader at this unorthodox action by his second, but as the coherent thoughts settled into his brain he realised the logic of his statement made sense. Irritated because he did not think of it the Leader swiped the face of the black second with the back of his forefoot, the claw carefully curved away.

The second's head was almost knocked from his neck by the force of the strike and he struggled to maintain his own temper, he must be careful, the time was not quite right to challenge the Leader. Grovelling in gratitude for being spared serious injury he backed off quietly to the side, muted thoughts of revenge mulling round his mind. The winged leaders waited, frustration fraying their already short tempers, as the hordes of workers raced across the mountains, a cloud of dust following their progress. It did not take long before all of the Cucs were gathered at the entrance tunnel. The Leader sent them forward, driving them into a killing frenzy with his murderous thoughts, while he and his winged companions waited impatiently to take up the rear.

Down at the first trap, Remruc and the sentry took up position. They carefully stretched the trip wire taut across the passageway. About two hundred paces behind the wire, rocks and boulders were positioned on carefully supporting platforms.

Once triggered, the rocks would fall, injuring and killing anything underneath them and effectively blocking the first section of the tunnel. Remruc wanted to let at least some of the Cucs through, with luck the nest leader would be stupid enough to lead the attack, then he would settle an old score. They could hear the thundering of the Cucs racing down towards them. Gripping the sentry's arm, Remruc pulled him up and they ran further down the passage, ready to lay their second trap. They had just finished pulling off the covers of the dry pit when the tripwire was triggered. Both warriors lay flat on the ground covering their faces as the dust caused by the rockfall billowed down towards them. They were almost deafened by the angry screams of the surprised and frightened Cucs trapped on their side of the blockage. The frantic sounds of digging could be heard as the trapped beasts tried to claw their way out and the rest, to dig their way in. Remruc frowned, the Cucs were not meant to escape, they were supposed to follow the passage down into this pit.

Even as he was thinking of an alternative plan of action the roars of triumph could be heard as the Cucs broke through the debris of boulders and mangled bodies. The sentry and Remruc looked at each other, "that didn't hold them long, Lord Remruc!"

"No, but hopefully this will." Together they pulled the last of the sheeting from the pit to reveal stone carved spikes lining its edge and covering the base.

"Nothing will get out of this one alive." They grinned at each other then turned and ran, just disappearing round a bend as the first of the Cucs charged into the pit. By now the enraged beasts were blind with fury and, as their comrades collapsed into the darkness beneath them to be skewered on the cruel spikes, more flung themselves on top, crushing those underneath and killing themselves. The San had been very careful in their design.

The pit was wider at the bottom than the top, the sides slanting to prevent any survivors from climbing out, the San reckoned without the enlarged size of this new breed of Cuc and a pit that normally would have claimed the lives of a hundred, only managed to destroy fifty or so. As had happened in the Nemn tunnels, the Cucs continued to throw themselves into the depths until the pit was full and the rest could walk over their crushed frames. By now Remruc and the sentry had reached the main trap set for this epic battle. The San had managed to destroy at least one hundred and fifty Cucs, but this was nothing when you considered the thousands of beasts still charging into the tunnel system. Here, in this old grazing cavern, a special surprise had been prepared for them. A deep trench had been dug round the entire perimeter of the cavern and filled with dka (the fuel used for torches), there was only one way that the Cucs could get into the cavern and that was through the main entrance. A metal sheet was covering the trench at this point to allow the Cucs easy access. The San were positioned on ledges around the wall each warrior within easy access to a narrow maintenance tunnel. These tunnels all congregated at the far side of the cavern and led, by a meandering route, back to the city of the Chai. The entire cavern was lit by hundreds of torches placed within easy reach of the warriors. The San waited, tension growing within them as they listened to the noisy approach of their enemies. Screaming their fury, the Cucs poured through the narrow entrance into the cavern and thundered across its dusty floor. They were dazzled and confused by the torches, but their eyes soon adjusted to the light and they began to search for their prey. One beast spied the San high up on the walls and ran towards the nearest, as it approached the San leisurely lifted a heavy hunting spear, took aim and threw it true to mark, directly down the Cucs throat.

The animal crumpled, blood spewing from it's jaws and rolled head over heels into the dust, legs scrabbling for a grip, eyes burning with pain and fury.

The other Cucs instantly began to run to the edges of the cavern, but as they approached the walls, they noticed the trenches filled with the strange-smelling liquid.

They hesitated and peered into the black liquid snorting at the unusual smell. The warriors carefully took aim, making each spear count and began to fell the confused creatures. Remruc had provided plenty of weapons for his company, but he knew that they would never have enough. Even as the first Cucs were slaughtered, hundreds more poured into the cavern in a seemingly endless stream. Finally the Cucs in desperation began to leap at the walls, their claws not able to grip the deliberately greased surface, they slipped down and fell into the tarry depths of the trench, struggling in vain as the thick liquid ooze pulled them slowly down. Remruc noted that virtually all of the spears were finished yet still the Cucs stormed into the now crowded and cramped cavern. He sent a command to the warriors positioned on either side of the entrance tunnel and they slipped down the wall, pulled the metal sheeting back from the edge of the trench and let it fall into the depths, taking any Cuc still on top along with it. There were at least two thousand Cucs crammed into the cavern, their disgusting odour hanging thick in the air, their raucous calling deafening the Chai warriors. Those beasts still in the tunnel system were trying to leap across the trench or throwing themselves into the slime. Remruc lifted his torch and his warriors followed suit. They paused for a moment and regarded the Cucs milling beneath them, climbing over the dead and dying forms of their siblings, still trying to reach the San. Suddenly they stopped and looked up at the warriors above them. The Cucs watched stupidly as the San threw the torches into the trench. Instantly the dka liquid flared up in red and yellow licking flames that climbed upwards towards the Chai. Panic filled the minions below at this circle of fire, the screams of those beasts still alive and struggling in the searing ooze filling the air.

Remruc ordered his troops to withdraw, within seconds the temperature of the cavern had risen above tolerance, he knew that within minutes the Cucs would begin to cook in their own skins and that the dka filled trench would burn for almost a day and a half. Not even the Cuc in that fearful trap could survive such temperatures.

Halfway down the tunnel system, the Leader of the nest screamed his frustration and fury, ordering his slaves to withdraw from the darkness. This they did with eager speed and back on the surface of the planet, in the coolness of night, the vengeful Cuc took careful stock of his losses. Nearly half of his workers had been slaughtered in the trap beneath the mountains, the rest of his army were tired and frustrated.

But, like him, they were furious at being defeated and more than eager to continue their pursuit. The black second sidled up to his leader, grovelling the entire way. He was not as stupid with rage as his fellow Cuc and his instinctively cautious nature was well-developed. "Sssssend ssssslavesss to sssssearch the holessss Leader." The Nest Leader was startled not by the suggestion made by his second, but by the coherent and fluid thoughts that had swarmed into his mind. The black second realised his error, he had been very careful not to attract attention to his more developed mind, it would be very risky at this time. He quickly continued,

"if... you... wish.. I... take... sssssssearch." This time the second was careful to allow uncontrolled visions of hatred, killing and violence to punctuate his thoughts. The Nest Leader relaxed, he was too filled with hate and revenge to take too much notice of his second's error, he acknowledged the suggestion and his second hastily moved out, grateful for the Leaders lack of attention.

The Chai warriors ran along the narrow passage way in single file, their mood grim, thoughts tinged with hopefulness, but also bearing the knowledge that they had not destroyed all of their enemies and that the Cucs would undoubtedly be searching for them. By dawn they reached the city, exhausted and battle weary they staggered into the waiting arms of healers, ready to administer reviving potions.

"Well?", asked Curmer once Remruc had recovered enough to think straight.

"I will show you brother." He linked minds with Curmer and replayed the entire nights events to him. Once he had finished Curmer sat down, shock and desperation on his face.

"It is to your credit brother that you did not lose a single warrior, but with those numbers against us we cannot possibly defend our city should they find it."

"I know. We must retreat now!" Remruc rose motioning to his guards, "mobilise all of the city we will leave at nightfall. Rarl ..." the senior Chai guard ran quickly to his Lords side, "...take a company and set all the traps we have lain around our City's perimeter. Uncover the pits, set trip wires to trigger the rock falls and rig up a wire that when released will drop a lighted torch into the dka pits, I want to burn, crush and destroy as many of these foul abominations as I can. Understand?" Rarl nodded quickly, running off to accomplish his task.

"We cannot take everything with us Remruc," said Curmer, "I will not be driven from my home, not by anything!"

"We are not leaving permanently, Curmer. I just want to prevent the Cucs from entering and spoiling our city. We will hide in the north settlement, once the Cucs have tired from searching we can return."

"They have followed us this far Remruc! What makes you think they will not pursue us to the limits of our planet!", replied Curmer, his thoughts ragged with fatigue and anger. "These beasts are determined to wipe us out. It is them or us, we must make a stand!" Remruc spun round and grabbed his brothers arms.

"HOW! You have seen the numbers we are up against, we do not have enough weapons to kill them! We must retreat and yes, I do know that the Cucs will follow but I have one final surprise for them." He let Curmer go, his eyes flashing with vengeance and made his way to the Chai training hall to organise the emptying of the stores. Curmer watched him go, fear in his heart, not only for the San but also for Remruc.

At sunset the last of the San from the city of the Chai stood at the north exit tunnel. Remruc and Curmer looked with sad, distraught eyes at the beautiful deserted city before them. "We tried so hard Remruc," whispered Curmer, his mind flooded with emotion, "why does fate do this to us?"

"Perhaps, Curmer, we are meant for greater things. At least we succeeded in uniting the San."

"That is not much consolation considering our probable destruction when the Cuc eventually find us."

"We are not dead yet and the San have one last trick up their sleeves."

Remruc turned and walked back the few hundred paces up the tunnel to where the rest of the San stood.

Curmer lingered a moment longer taking a good look at the City.

"I swear," he said to himself, "that my children and my children's children will always remember this jewel where ever they are." He followed his brother with reluctant steps, and once he was clear, Remruc gave the order for the roof of the tunnel to be collapsed, sealing the city forever in the heart of the mountains.

It was a silent, sad and depressed journey through the dark narrow tunnels towards the northern settlement, even the mantelos were caught up in the oppressive atmosphere and they moved with their heads hung in sadness. Despite the mood of the people they made good time, travelling as quickly as possible away from their home out into the colder north region. Rearguards covered their tracks, although none of the Cucs would have been able to follow them along such a small narrow passage. They reached their goal within a few days, a patrol of Chai being sent to greet them led by Herka. He had been responsible for organising the settlement and guarding the secret of the cavern and this he had done with skill and dedication. One look at the hollow faces was all the patrol needed to know the answer to their unspoken question. They smiled as reassuringly as they could but the mood of the company was infectious and they all returned to the settlement in sombre silence.

The original settlement was too small to cope with the large population so some of the Nemn tents had been restored and were in use in the adjacent caverns and caves. Most of the buildings had been rebuilt, but the dismantled remains were still conspicuously obvious at the centre of the group of huddled buildings and tents.

Remruc and Curmer strode to this empty space and waited patiently as the people were gathered and brought to the main settlement. Eriya pushed her way through the crowd, her healer gown covered by a heavy fur cloak. Even on this burnt out planet, the San could feel the cold of the North Pole. She looked with sad eyes at the shattered countenances of the twins and moved to them taking a hand each in hers. They looked so alike yet felt so different, even in their depression. Curmer was heartbroken and sorrowful, Remruc also heartbroken, but with a determination and hope within him. She smiled her support and confidence in them, squeezing their hands gently. They returned her smile, Remruc holding her hand just that little bit longer before letting go.

"Lord Curmer, you will be pleased to know that Lady Sorta is well," said Eriya in forced bright tones.

"I would not have believed anything else Lady Eriya, with her in your capable care," he returned, trying to brighten the mood. Remruc moved to one side to leave the two in private conversation and motioned to Herka to join him.

"Does anyone else know about the crystal ring?"

"No Lord Remruc, it has been carefully guarded as you commanded."

"Have any of the Tarl come up with answers yet?"

"Their latest suggestion is that it is a doorway of some kind that leads to a different world. They do understand the concept of such a thing, but not how it was engineered." Herka paused as he watched the thoughtful look on Remruc's face.

"Has anyone been through the ring since you went that day?"

"No Lord Remruc. We have left the cavern untouched since you left." Herka smiled softly, "Lord Remruc, I must tell someone," Remruc turned and looked at him. "My first mate Katcna has given birth to my son." Herka's eyes filled with pride his mind full of joy, despite their situation. Remruc smiled and slapped him on the shoulder. "Congratulations Herka. We may just be able to guarantee his future." They moved off together, leaving Curmer and Eriya to break the news of the desertion of the Chai City to the people.

Remruc stood in front of the ring. It was totally unchanged since the last time he had been there almost one and a half years ago. He motioned for Herka to join him and the two other guards. Behind the group stood a gaggle of Tarl, their heads bent in deep discussion, their fingers twitching nervously. One moved away and stood to the side of the group of warriors. Herka turned and motioned him to come forward.

"Lord Remruc. We have concluded that this is some kind of portal..."

"What is a portal?"

"A doorway, Lord Remruc," continued the Tarl bowing in apology, "that leads to a different world."

"You mean that if I step through this doorway that I will be on a different planet?"

"That is what we think Lord Remruc, but we do not know for sure." Remruc dismissed the Tarl and handed Herka the end of a rope he had just wrapped round his waist,

"Here, let us see what kind of a world lies beyond this ring." Herka grinned and, after wrapping the rope around his waist he handed the last lengths to the waiting guards. They took up the slack and slowly began to feed the twine between their fingers as Remruc and Herka stepped into the mist. They emerged into the crystal cave, the footsteps that Herka had made so long ago still clear on the floor. Herka grinned at Remruc as he looked behind him to see the ring and mist, but nothing else except the blue crystal walls. Herka motioned for him to follow and they made their way towards the light at the end of the tunnel. A cool refreshing breeze lifted the hair from their faces as they crept to the mouth of the crystal passage. Instinctively their protective third eyelid flipped across their pupils to protect them from the expected glare of the suns, instead what greeted their eyes was totally unexpected. A single yellow globe burned in the sky, the air was cool and clear, the sky tinged with green. What lay before them was a vast expanse of wilderness, plants thrived on the thin soil of the crystal mountain and living creatures roamed across the plains of purple waving grasses. The two San stood in awe, their sensitive skin fully exposed to the gentle warmth of the welcoming sun.

"It is like the legends and tales we were told as youngsters, about how Surn once was before Emur turned red." Herka finally managed to think.

"This is a world where our people could be safe." replied Remruc. "No Cuc could find us here and we could grow strong and multiply." He breathed deeply feeling the fresh cool air rush into his lungs with a sweetness he had never felt before.

"If we come here Lord Remruc, the Cuc will conquer the whole of Surn."

"Herka," replied Remruc sadly, "the Cuc have already taken over the planet, but we will destroy as many of them that we can before we leave." He turned to face him, "our planet is dead. We will survive." Herka smiled,

"You are right Lord Remruc, together we have given our children a future. There is however just one thing," Remruc look at him quizzically, "We haven't seen the creatures who made these footprints." Remruc grunted,

"We will deal with that problem if and when it arises." They returned to the crystal ring, hope in their hearts, joy in their steps, to tell their people of their discovery.

The people of the San listened carefully to what Remruc had to say as he told them of the mysterious ring, a faint hope growing in their hearts. Although his suggestion that the San should forsake this world and flee through the ring was unorthodox, it seemed to be the only logical answer. They set about organising the uprooting of their temporary camp, a company of Chai was first to go through the ring, their task was to clear an area just beyond the crystal cave suitable for a campsite. The Nemn co-ordinated the listing of items and goods that had been brought from the city, all people would receive their equal share once they had settled in the new lands.

Sorta and Lenta had directed the hardiest of the herbal plants to be seeded on the surface of the planet Surn. It was their responsibility to direct the uplifting of the seedlings and bring them back to the settlement. Katcna, Herka's first mate, who was trying to regain her normally fit and lean figure after the birth of her child, joined them.

"The exercise will do me good," she said cheerily smiling at Sorta, "and I can tell you all about the joy of birth, Sorta dear." Sorta laughed and hugged the loveable woman as they lifted their seedsacks and made their way to the planet's surface.

The black second spread his enormous wings and took to the air, leaving the Nest Leader to growl and vent his temper on those nearest him. He carefully selected five of the smaller Cucs who had been at the end of the line of creatures charging down the tunnel.

They would be less fatigued and more keen for a fight. He circled low lightly scraping his claws across their armoured backs indicating those he wished to follow. The workers dutifully replied to his summons squealing in suppressed excitement as they loped at high speed over the rocky mountains following the black shape in the sky. The second thought carefully. He knew the San could not tolerate the heat on the surface or further south that left the mountains where they were or north. The Nest Leader would search the mountains thoroughly so the second struck out northwards looking for signs of any San.

He flew for several days, it would have been less but the workers were getting hungry and needed rest. He isolated one and slaughtered it, letting the other four feast for a day.

After taking his share of the carcass he retired to a pinnacle of rock to clean his scaly hide, he was meticulous in his grooming, an unusual trait in a Cuc, the black second was the next step up in the evolution of the Cuc and he looked at the squabbling workers with their filthy hides and dull brains with contempt. He turned his gaze to the horizon and froze. There, far distant but there, were movements among the rocks. He flapped his wings, the warm flesh in his belly dispelling the sluggishness that he had been feeling since reaching the colder atmosphere. The workers were still feeding and too bloated to be moved, so the black second launched himself into the air to investigate his sighting.

Sorta laughed as she struggled to pick up the seedlings, trying to negotiate her swollen belly. The child within her chortled in response to her laughter, the contented emotion filled thoughts tickling her mind.

"The lump still stays there even when the space is unoccupied," smiled Katcna, "unless of course you do some exercise." She hefted a sack onto her back and strode down the slope towards the furthest seedling patch. The Nemn guard who had been helping them looked down the slope, puzzlement creasing his brow as he watched a dark shadow flit over the ground with horror he looked up and saw a winged Cuc diving out of the sky.

"Lady Sorta! Katcna! Look out!" he cried, lifting his spear. Lenta grabbed the nearest full sacks and threw them down the narrow entrance tunnel, turning she ran to help the Nemn. The winged Cuc made directly for Sorta, his huge claws glinting in the bright sun, as he was about to slice his prey, a heavy sack thumped into his nose, distracting him for a second.

Sorta tripped and fell, landing heavily, she rolled several paces over the stony rock strewn surface, hitting her head and losing consciousness.

Katcna ran, frantically towards the Cuc her arms swinging wildly, trying to distract him from the prone figure of Sorta. The black second looked round, anger in his eyes for the San that had dared to strike him, he swept round and low, his claws swinging in an arc, slicing Katcna's body in two. Lenta screamed; the Nemn guard grabbed Sorta's arms and pulled her back up the slope. The winged Cuc flipped up in the air, circling round to continue his attack. Lenta, coming to her senses, helped the guard lift Sorta and together they ran for the safety of the small tunnel. As they reached the open mouth the Cuc struck again, this time ripping the back off of the Nemn guard. He fell forward, throwing Sorta into Lenta's arms before he collapsed dead. Lenta's mind screamed for help as she dragged the still body of Sorta deeper into the tunnel system.

Curmer waited anxiously, his face drawn, his mind tense as the healers tended his mate. Remruc moved to his side, he had not needed to break the news of Katcna's death to Herka, her pain had been felt by him as her life had ended. He was in a drug induced stupor, the healers deciding this as the best remedy for his grief. Eriya emerged from the room. She was unable to look at Curmer, "Lady Sorta is alive and will recover."

"What about our son?"

"Your son is dead. Sorta can have no more children."

"NNNnoooo!" Curmer collapsed, his brother grabbing him before he hit the ground. Remruc's mind melded with his, trying desperately to ease the agony within the trembling form. A third mind joined them, it was Lenta,

"Curmer. Curmer! Listen to me," her mind echoed the grief he felt, "your mate needs you now. You must be strong for her. Go to her side, please."

Lenta gently eased him to his feet and led him to Sorta's room. Eriya gripped Remruc's arm,

"I tried Remruc, I really tried!" Remruc looked at her surprised at first by the informal use of his name, then he saw the agony in her eyes and on an impulse he took her in his arms.

She resisted at first, but the shock of what had happened was too much for her to bear and she was grateful for his strength.

"I know you did Eriya, I know that if anyone could save Sorta's child you would be you," he whispered gently

"Why are you being so kind to me, why do you not hate me for failing?"

"I do not know. Perhaps it is because I love you," he said holding her tighter. Eriya felt her heart miss a beat and she dared to look at him. She saw the truth in his eyes and felt the true feelings of her own heart emerge.

"I love you too, Remruc - I always have." They clung together, their joy a sad contrast to the sorrow in the next room.

It was a grey and tragic group that laid the small bundle to rest in those cold harsh lands. Herka had managed to fight the drugs enough to merit the healers allowing him to attend the funeral. He was a walking shadow of his former self, his face lined with the internal agony he felt. Slowly he walked to the front of the group, the wriggling bundle of his child in his arms. They had not found enough of his mate to bury. "Lord Curmer, Lady Sorta. I have a request."

Curmer looked up with understanding for the warrior's agony. "My mate died to save you and your son, Lady Sorta. She was only partly successful; I have no other mates to care for my son, I give him to you to replace the child you have lost. I will not leave Surn alive. I vow that I will protect the people of the San till they are safe in the new world." He turned to Remruc, "Lord Remruc. There are a few of the older Sans who do not wish to leave our world. I will lead them on a suicide mission, to distract the Cucs and lead them away from this settlement. It will buy you enough time to get our people to safety."

"Herka!", exclaimed Remruc, his emotions mixed. He was grateful for this brave action, but he had grown to admire this brave and loyal warrior, he did not want to lose this valued friend. Herka shook his head and thrust the child into Sorta's arms. She took the child unwillingly, the pain of her loss too great, but when the confused and inquiring thoughts of the babe drifted into her mind she relented. He was so like her own son. Curmer took Herka's arms.

"We will raise him as our own, Herka. You can pass into the void with the knowledge that he will be raised as a Chieftains son." Herka nodded and relaxed slightly. He moved away to prepare his patrol for their last battle.

The black second had left the workers in the northern hills and had flown directly back to his leader. Much to his surprise the mass of Cucs had been making their way north, their numbers depleted somewhat by the traps the San had lain in the mountains. They had not found the city of the Chai, but the scent of their prey had been leading them steadily up into these cold ranges. As soon as the Leader heard that the San had been found he pushed the slave Cucs at top speed towards his goal. He did not care if hundreds collapsed of exhaustion on the way, they either ran or they died.

His bodyguards of male Cucs were beginning to resent the relentless pursuit of this dangerous prey, but the black second sensed that none of them were ready yet to challenge the Nest Leader. As they finally neared the place where the second had attacked the San, their numbers had been reduced to a quarter of the original force. Those workers that were left were starving, cold and tired, they snapped at each other testing the weaker animals to see if they would resist being eaten.

The Leader was obsessed. With ruthless orders he forced the other males to search the mountains, making them direct the workers into digging teams. As one of the teams ranged far to the west it was attacked by Herka's patrol. A vicious fight ensued; Herka and his men taking great pleasure in slaughtering the weakened and vulnerable animals. They managed to destroy all of the ground Cuc and take down two winged males. Infuriated, the Leader sent all of his forces after them as they retreated west across the mountains, giving command to his black second. He however remained where he was; a strange niggling feeling in his dull brain told him to stay here; that perhaps he may just corner that hated San who had plagued him for so long. He kept two slave Cucs to dig, driving them almost to death, encouraged by the fresh smell of San so tantalisingly close. Finally, they came across the settlement that had just been evacuated. With a scream of triumph the Leader charged into the settlement leaving the workers at the entrance to their hole. It was empty. A few odds and ends scattered here and there were all that remained. The Leader howled his frustration.

"Looking for me?" The calm thought stabbed into his brain. He turned to see the face of that hated San that had dragged him over the entire surface of the planet. Remruc moved slowly to one side, a vicious growl in his throat, "This time I will make sure I finish the job."

"SSSSssssan... die... ssssslowly," grated the Cuc, the thoughts harsh and offensive to Remruc's mind.

"You can try you foul-bellied monstrosity!" Remruc threw one of his spears and it landed true to mark deep in the red eye of the Leader. He screamed again, this time in agony and his screams were answered by every Cuc on Surn. Snapping the end of the spear against a rock, the Leader tried to prise the stump from his socket. While he was distracted Remruc ran forward, jamming a second spear deep into the unprotected belly, he rolled quickly out of the way as the beast collapsed writhing on the ground, the whipping tail catching him across one leg as he rose. Remruc let out a gasp of agony as his leg was snapped by the force of the strike. But the Leader was not finished yet, blood spewed from the gaping wound in his chest as he struggled to his feet, vengeance lending him strength. He turned to see Remruc trying to crawl back out of the cavern. The Cuc hissed his fury, droplets of blood gurgling in his throat, teeth clicking in anticipation. The Leader crawled, slowly, painfully towards his enemy, Remruc inching back, unable to rise, his hand gripping his axe that had started this vendetta so long ago. His back hit the wall of one of the settlement buildings and he tried to stand, his shattered leg screaming its protest at the movement.

Trembling he raised the axe. The Leader was within striking distance, he lifted one foreleg, the slicing claw ready.

"NO!" The mind screamed from behind causing the Cuc to swivel his ugly head. Eriya stood in battle dress, a heavy spear in her hands, she hefted the weapon toward the monstrosity as the Leader hissed his anger. The spear met its mark and buried itself deep in the creatures throat. The Nest Leader's head thumped to the ground, inches away from Remruc, he swung the axe directly down between the Cuc's eyes, dealing a scale-shattering death blow. Every Cuc on Surn halted in their tracks, the Nest Leader was dead. The two Cuc workers who had been charging down to help their leader stopped, unsure what to do. The inherent cowardice in their nature caused them to retreat, hopefully to find the other Cucs in the process of killing the last of Herka's band of warriors.

Herka was the last of his brave San to die and he hit the ground as the Nest Leader breathed his last foul breath. All around them were the dead and dying bodies of Cuc workers, several winged males were among them. It was a testimony to the skill and dedication of Herka's band. The Black Second screamed in triumph. At last the San were all dead. At last the Leader had killed himself with his own obsession.

At last he was the new Leader. The supreme being on all of Surn. He quickly withdrew the surviving Cucs, they would make their way back to the warmer climates, to breed and thrive and begin a new era on Surn.

Eriya gently helped Remruc to the cavern with the crystal ring. He was trying desperately to remain conscious, but the pain in his body was clouding his mind. He did not remember passing through the ring, nor the waiting healers placing him on a sled and administering their potions. Exhaustion finally won and he fell into a deep, healing sleep.

Bright friendly sunshine warmed his face as he slowly roused himself. At first Remruc panicked. He must be on Surn's surface, exposed to Rume and Emur, he would die if he did not find shade. Then, slowly, the events of two days ago came back to him.

He opened his eyes to see a bright lemony-green sky above him, the flaps of the hide tent moving softly in the cool breeze. Noise of busily working people and their joyful happy thoughts wafted towards him.

Sorta appeared at the opening - a gurgling child strapped to her back. Her mind no longer shadowed with the loss of her own child but filled instead with love and devotion for the orphan in her care. She saw he was awake and joyfully called for Curmer and Eriya. They came so quickly that he suspected they must have been hovering outside. "Good day to you brother. Now that you have fully recovered your senses we can attend to some urgent business."

"Thank you Curmer, for being so patient and allowing me to rest," replied Remruc caustically, slightly annoyed that he was not even being granted a small break from his public duties.

"Now, now you pair, stop your squabbling." Lenta appeared in the tent, her face relaxed, a new flush of youth to her cheeks. "It is only fitting Remruc, that you make public your intentions for yourself and Eriya." Eriya flushed, and looked downwards, as Remruc's face lit up with a mischievous grin.

"Well Lady Eriya, what do you wish to do?", he said innocently. She smiled and countered his reply,

"Lord Remruc. It would be impossible for me to accept any position other than first mate. That limits my choices of appropriate suitors somewhat. Who do you have in mind?"

Remruc, for the first time in his life, became serious and true to his feelings for her,

"If it would please you Eriya, I would be honoured to accept you as first mate and heir to my title."

"There is nothing on Surn, or this new world that would please me more Remruc." She threw her arms around his neck and they kissed.

"Talking about this new world Eriya," said Curmer, "We must think of a name for this gem of a planet. Remruc, as soon as you are fit enough to move around, I must take you exploring. There is so much life and beauty here. I have never seen anything like it."

"We are beginning to build a new city Remruc," continued Sorta, "this time above ground for the world to see. We will use a mixture of architecture from every one of our original tribes, it will be the first truly united city of the San." Her enthusiasm for the project was dazzling to the minds of all who heard and she instilled her hope and joy into all around her. Remruc raised his hand.

"Listen to me, all of you. We have succeeded, together. We have united and saved our people. This is what we are destined for, this is the beginning of a new race, a powerful race that will flourish and spread our knowledge to every corner of this world and beyond. But we must never forget where we came from. Our children must never forget our struggle to survive, and one day I swear the San will return to Surn and reclaim our lost city, destroying the Cucs forever."

They all 'cheered' at his thoughts and each face reflected the determination to survive and continue the Sans of Surn.

The Idor watched in amazement as the strange two-legged creatures emerged from the Portal cavern. She scratched her nose, deep in thought. They must be the same animals that had built the odd living dens in that dead and burnt out world far across the galaxy, obviously their kind had not died when their world fried beneath the suns.

She stamped in annoyance at her own stupidity in leaving the Portal open, now she would have to explain how these audacious creatures had wandered into the Idor's domain, El would not be pleased. With a deep sigh she turned, never again would a Portal be left unattended while she delivered archaeological remains to the city.

There was some pity in her heart for the poor unfortunate animals below her, El would probably order their extermination. She jogged down the track and headed back to her city with the news of the discovery.

Chapter Fourteen

Purple fronds waved gently, stirred into action by a light cool breeze that wafted through the busy forest sending dappled light dancing across the hide boot. Stealthily the boot crept forward, the owner bending low beneath the thick, luxuriant foliage. A clearing among the tall vines was occupied by several of the slow moving, giant grazing animals that occupied this particular climate. The hunter paused, motioning to shadow figures behind him he edged forward, the others spreading out to surround the group of grazing creatures. On command, the hunters sprang forward, weapons raised, ready to strike down the expected rush of panicked animals. Instead, the grazers lifted their heads in mild interest, then returned to their daily business of gathering food. There was a general feeling of surprise through all of the hunters at this apparent lack of concern from their intended prey. They looked at each other in confused silence. Theirs was the first hunting party on this new world and they were unsure of the defence the gargantuan beasts had. The leader of the hunters stepped forward, his axe at the ready and edged closer to the bulky frame of the nearest grazer. As he approached, the creature nonchalantly grazed towards him, the long enormous head nodding in rhythm to the gnashing teeth. Once the hunter was within striking distance, the grazer lifted its head, planting its soft sensitive nose firmly on his chest and puffed a breath of inquiry at this unusual behaviour from an animal it had never seen before. The force of the exhale was enough to knock the hunter flat on his back, a muffled grunt escaping from him as he hit the ground. A deep rumble of concern was emitted from all of the group of grazers and the creature responsible, hurriedly tried to nuzzle the strange two legged animal to its feet. The hunter struggled to stand, hindered rather than helped by the grazer's clumsy dunts. The rest of the hunting party were doubled up with silent laughter, their antics intriguing the other grazers. The leader stared at the two enormous worried eyes above him, the soft nose wriggling across his chest, the annoyance in his mind was quickly replaced by amusement at what must be a ridiculous scene. He reached up with a tentative hand and returned the friendly scratch, a deep rumble of pleasure from the grazer vibrating through his body. "Come," he motioned to the other hunters, "we will leave these creatures in peace." They turned and left the clearing, making their way along the trail back to their base camp.

"Lord Curmer?" inquired one hunter, "Lord Remruc will not be pleased when he hears that you did not kill that animal for food?"

"We have our own food animals, we do not need to hurt the natural inhabitants of this world. Besides, it was obvious by their behaviour that they have no need to fear any carnivore, why should we instill fear into their lives when they could be more useful to us as friends?" His companions nodded at his logic, "we have never tasted the meat from the natural inhabitants, perhaps it would not be to our liking, then we would have killed for nothing. No. We will eat the animals we have always eaten and grow the crops that we know we can eat. That is what I will tell Lord Remruc."

They continued on in silence, each hunter taking personal delight in the novelty of moving above ground without fear of being burned by ferocious suns, or hunted by Cuc. The small party of San emerged from the thick forest of strange plants onto a vast plain of lilac and purple grass waving in undulating swirls in the gentle breeze. On the horizon, the different, dark forms of more grazers could be seen. So far, no San had been able to get close enough to them to get a good look. They could move with incredible speed, easily outpacing a mantelo drawn sleigh and disappearing into the vast plains of tall grass long before the San reached them. The party headed towards the gentle hills glinting in the sunlight, the crystal rocks reflecting the warm rays of the single sun. A shadow flashed across the ground and the hunters all instinctively crouched, spears at the ready, scanning the skies. Instead of the dreaded winged Cuc, small brightly coloured creatures flitted with ease through the air, their graceful wings outstretched to catch the wind, spiraling in dizzying circles of fun. Each of the hunters breathed a sigh of relief, a shamefaced and sheepish grin at their own nervousness flashing across their faces. As they neared the hills, the equally brightly coloured hides of their tents became clearer, a direct challenge to the beautiful flyers.

The grass plain had been sectioned into large acres of fields where the domestic animals of the San stuffed their faces in eagerness at this seemingly endless supply of food, the fat glossy hides of the docile lemaths shining in the midday light. A group of mantelos raced each other along another field, trumpeting a welcome to the returning party, their minds full of pleasure and joy. Curmer paused, raising a hand to his eyes to shield the gentle light from the sun, he scanned the newly cleared and planted crop field. The fast growing grains had wasted no time in the rich soil, they seemed as able to adapt to this alien environment as the domestic animals and once more Curmer was thankful that they had found such a beautiful, plentiful sanctuary. At last the luck of the San seemed to be turning.

Sounds and noises of the bustle of life filtered towards him on the light wind as the people of the San worked to improve their new homes. The tent structures designed by the Nemn councillors in charge of housing were by far the most suitable in this mild weather climate. They were based on the ancient designs used by the San nomads many thousands of years before, on a world light years distant, but they had been adapted and improved to allow the light and fresh air in and keep draughts out. They had been alarmed to find that they were running out of hides to make sufficient waterproof outer shells for the ever increasing demand, but a tough canvas like material, developed in the underground caverns on Surn by the Chai tribe was coated with a layer of gum from a native plant and had proved to be adaptable and suitable for both internal divisions and outer coverings for the main hide structures. Even so, there were more people than tents, and a great number of San were occupying the shallow crystal caves that pock-marked the hills. It had been agreed that the Chai warriors should be stationed in the caves, allowing the young families the luxury of their own private homes. Sufficient accommodation was still a high priority for the city designers.

The returning party were welcomed by a group of youngsters, who ran and danced around them in circles, their young undisciplined minds yelling inquiry on virtually every "frequency" available. They were quickly retrieved by older, more socially aware children and ushered out of range, stern warnings of unmentionable punishments that would be administered to any that would not follow. Curmer smiled, he knew what it was like to have a babe in the home, your mental shields had to be constantly at the ready, especially where Curmer's adopted son was concerned. It took several months before the babe could focus his thoughts effectively, but now that he had mastered the art of direct specific emotions, Curmer and Sorta were hard put to block out any unnecessary blinding flashes that ranged from ecstasy to fury. Everywhere there were children with nurses, babysitters or mothers. Many of the youngest babes had been born in this world and Curmer was both sad and relieved that they would have no memory of the San's home world, a bleak hard planet that had given them their tough nature, but which had also nearly destroyed their race. His companions were slowly filtering away from the group and wandering off towards their own tents, Curmer, his axe balanced casually on his shoulder, strolled further up the hill, heading for the last, large tent structure before the first of the crystal caves.

A green-yellow flash of sparkling frustration bombarded his mind before he had even pulled back the entrance flap. Ducking through he was just in time to see his son determinedly pulling himself up the side of a large silky cushion, his goal was the fascinating glass containers of healing herbs.

"Deyka!" shouted Curmer's mind sternly, "Don't you dare!" The shock of the unexpected thought frightened the toddler into mind blinding sobs of terror. Sorta came running quickly into the tent from the opposite direction, her hands full of newly picked plants.

"What has happened? What is wrong?" she said, her mind clouded with panic.

"Its alright Sorta, I just gave him a bit of a fright." smiled Curmer, the now placated Deyka in his arms. Sorta smiled in relief,

"Honestly, I just can't leave him alone for five minutes. Come here you trouble maker?" She picked up the now joyfully burbling boy and planting a kiss on Curmer's cheek, "Remruc is looking for you my brave and fearless child scarer." Deyka fascinated himself tearing the new leaves off of Sorta's plants while Curmer returned her kiss with more enthusiasm. "Hey! Stop that!" Said Sorta merrily, smacking Deyka's hands lightly and nudging Curmer away. He grinned and gently ruffled his son's hair,

"Don't let her bully you Deyka. Look what has happened to me!" He skilfully ducked away from her playful swipe and exited from the tent, continuing with light steps up into the first crystal cave.

The familiar outline of his twin brother was easily identifiable in the crowd of Chai guards watching a combat test being undertaken by hopeful new recruits. He was still on crutches, the broken leg mending, despite the ragged break he had suffered at the claws of the Leader of the Cucs. He was leaning on one and swinging the other about, mentally shouting instructions to the youths battling in the circle. Curmer had always disliked this ferocious side to the San nature, as a healer he found fighting repellent, still, at least now the combat tests were not to the death, but carefully refereed matches that tested the skill and natural abilities of every contestant. He peered over Remruc's shoulder into the circle. Three girls and two boys were stealthily creeping around the old trainer, trying to catch him unawares. A girl lunged forward, the blunt dagger lined with liquid dye slashing in an arc. The trainer easily dodged and parried the strike, sending the girl flying out of the circle and so out of the contest. He had turned and was ready for another strike before she had even hit the ground.

"An unfortunate mistake." said Remruc, acknowledging his brothers presence, "Still, she has shown promise. We will recruit her anyway." He turned and limped away, Curmer falling instep beside him. "So, how did your hunting expedition go?" The slight tinge of envy that coloured his enquiry was not missed by Curmer, he knew how frustrating it must be for his active brother to be so limited in a world that was begging to be explored.

"Well. We managed to get close to those large grazers that have been spotted in the forest, but..." Curmer smiled apologetically, "I couldn't bring myself to kill one." Remruc shook his head and grimaced, "They are so friendly Remruc, they have no fear of us. Think how much better it would be if we kept it this way. We hunted every living thing on our own planet. All creatures feared us, except the Cucs, this time we can make a new start." Remruc nodded a look of resignation on his face.

"Alright Curmer, alright, we will do as you suggest. I just hope that we don't find any large predators, they might not share your opinions when it comes to us." He smiled in greeting to Eriya as he and Curmer reached his temporary home. A larger cave provided their sleeping quarters and the entrance had been covered by a large and sectioned tent that gave living, cooking and entertaining areas. It was a successful combination of both systems and the Nemn designers were working on using this design for their planned city.

"Curmer, how are you?" welcomed Eriya, her mind brimming with happiness, "Was your expedition successful?"

"Yes and no Eriya," replied Curmer, "No we did not kill any creatures and yes I have finally convinced my stubborn brother that we should not harm the native animals." She laughed at his comments and ushered them into the main living section of their home. The ground cover was scattered with rich furs and silken cushions, the wall decorations a combination of Eriya's Nemn origins and Remruc's Chai heritage. A Tarl appeared from nowhere with a selection of freshly baked sweetmeats and spicy herb rolls. A beaker of cool, clear water was placed on the low centre table.

"Mmm...! I see the herbs have managed to adapt well to this world, they seem to have an even better flavour." commented Remruc as he stuffed another choice tit-bit into his mouth.

"Not only the herbs dear brother, but the grains as well. They all seem to thrive in this plentiful soil," replied Curmer, selecting a sweet loaf.

"Yes," joined Eriya, "that is true, but one of the Doona breeders was complaining about the difficulty the lemath's are having at digesting this tough grass."

"They look healthy enough to me," countered Remruc.

"Oh they are, the Doona are supplementing their feeding with extra grain. We have had to concentrate on growing feeding grain for the lemaths and mantelos first, any leftovers are used for rough food for workers. The only animals that have adapted well are the dak-tik, but then they prefer to eat the flowering heads of all of the plants." Eriya daintily licked her fingers as she finished her thoughts

"Perhaps there are some kind of natural plant extracts that you can use to aid the digestion of this tough herbage?", suggested Remruc, glancing at Curmer for a reply. He frowned deep in private thought,

"You may be right brother. I know that Lenta and Eriya here have been organising the analysis of all of the plant life in the surrounding area. So far there are no new plants that we can utilise effectively, but perhaps there are different species growing on the other side of that forest. Perhaps I should take a new team out with me tomorrow. We could plan a few days journey and try to reach the end of that dense growth of plants," Curmer hesitated as he realised that Remruc was watching him, a look of longing on his face. "Or perhaps it would be better if we waited till you were fit Remruc, then you could lead the expedition, after all you are better qualified to take care of yourself." Remruc smiled at Curmer's clumsy attempt at making him feel better,

"Nonsense Curmer. You are a healer, it is your expertise that is required to analyse different species of plants. There will be plenty of time for me to explore once my leg is healed. Stop fussing and start thinking." They all laughed.

"Thank you Remruc." said Curmer. Eriya gently squeezed her husband's hand, only she knew how much he wished to roam this planet and how hard it was for him to watch his brother adventuring. They all continued their meal, Eriya enquiring as to the health of Curmer's son, her own mind concentrating on the new life growing within her. It was too early yet for her to tell Remruc and she was fervently hoping for a son.

That evening, Lenta called round to speak to Curmer and Sorta. She found the happy couple in the main living area playing with Deyka. The air was alive with happy, joyful thoughts and it warmed the old woman's heart to see her favourite son of her mate content at last. She announced her presence and joined in the fun, little Deyka tottering towards her on unsteady legs, his arms outstretched, his mind a blinding fusion of merry colour. As they sat amusing Deyka, Lenta filled them in on her own daughter's latest escapades.

"Musi has grown so much since we came here Curmer," smiled Lenta. "She is under the constant attention of several prospective suitors, but you know Musi, she is far too fussy and not interested in what she calls silly little boys!" Curmer smiled, as the image of his beautiful half-sister, an irritated frown creasing her forehead, filled his mind. Sorta skilfully occupying Deyka's attention, chipped in,

"what career has she chosen Lenta? The last time we spoke she had opted out of healing and was looking towards Doona training."

"Ah, yes, well, you know how much she loves all animals, it seems that this training, specialising in mantelo breeding, is just what she wants to do," replied Lenta, waving a bright ball in front of Deyka. "She is young enough yet. I will let her do what she pleases till a suitable mate comes along."

"A career as a Doona is quite respectable Lenta. The successful breeding of our domestic livestock is vital to our survival, I see no need to dissuade her from this occupation, after all, she or her family should never be called upon to act as Chieftains," said Curmer, defending his little half-sister. Lenta nodded, a sad smile on her face,

"I know, I know, it is just that I wanted her so much to be a healer."

"You have me Lenta. You are as much my mother as Sadelna was - more even. You may not have given birth to me, but you have trained and taught me as a son and I am proud to carry on your knowledge and wisdom." Curmer hugged the old woman, a sudden fear in his heart as he saw the signs of age line her face. Deyka, sensing the change in atmosphere let forth a burst of worry and anxiety, the build up of sobs beginning in the back of his mind. Sorta quickly picked him up, reassuring him while Curmer planted a loving kiss on his cheek. Lenta smiled.

"Now then. Aren't you going to offer a visitor a bite to eat?" They all moved into the small separate tent that was used for cooking and Sorta quickly made them a meal of root vegetables and meat. Over supper Curmer, Sorta and Lenta discussed what types of plants were most needed by the San. All of their healing herbs and concoctions had been transported carefully, firstly to the northern settlement on Surn and then on through the portal to this new world. Because of the temperate climate however, it was difficult to keep the herbs fresh. Normally they were stored in deep underground caverns, where the temperature, even on Surn, was well below freezing, but here although the soil was rich, an impenetrable layer of crystal rock prevented any deep excavations.

The supplies of fresh healing herbs had been used up quickly, to prevent spoiling. Those that could be made into long lasting solutions or pastes had been stored in the darkest, coolest recesses of the caves. The dried medicines proved no problem with longevity and storage, but it was the fresh herbs that were most needed. Not all of them would grow here on this world. The most vital plant that was used in almost every healing salve, Dsrka, would not adapt. Despite numerous attempts at planting seedlings etc, the plants would wither and die. To find a replacement for this antiseptic herb was the most urgent goal of Curmer's mission. The Tarl scientists had brought with them an artificially made alternative, but they did not have the resources nor the facilities to reproduce their product. Instead, they were concentrating their efforts to analyse which herbage was edible and useful, firstly for the San's livestock and secondly for the San. The mantelo has a similar digestive system to the San and any new plant was fed first to them and their reactions watched carefully. The Doona carers were not very pleased that their precious animals were being used in this way and they monitored the Tarls' every movement, having the final say in what should be fed and what shouldn't.

This was irritating for the Tarl and they had complained to the council of elders that if they weren't allowed a free hand in this matter then the San may starve due to ignorance about their surroundings. Finally Remruc and Curmer had intervened, as the Chieftains of the San their word was law. It was decided that the Doona should be a little more lenient with the Tarl, but the Tarl were also reminded of their penance in servility that they owed the other San and were promptly told to stop complaining and get on with their work. By the end of the night, Curmer had compiled a list of the most urgent requirements for herbal remedies that must be found. He had a vast knowledge of the different types of fauna from his own world and, so far, the plants around them seemed to be basically of the same construction. It was only a matter of time before the San found the right plants that suited their needs and Curmer was determined to at least find an antiseptic alternative on his first journey.

The next morning Curmer set out to find his brother. He was told by Eriya that Remruc had been called to oversee an experiment in the construction area, so it was with an air of curiosity that Curmer wandered into the sectioned compound on the outskirts of the tent city. The compound was full of Nemn designers and builders. They had been coming under a lot of criticism by the rest of the San for their failed attempts at quarrying the tough crystal rocks. The vast number of people gathered in this temporary city had given the builders nightmares with regards to sanitation and fresh water supply. Basic facilities had been hurriedly dug out of the ground, but all families still had to share communal pumps for water and cold mountain river for bathing. The most frustrating thing of all for the designers was the tough crystal rocks. These rocks would be ideal for building but, due to their tough nature, the San had no tools sharp enough to cut through the stubborn material, even sharp crystal rocks refused to cut into the bedrock efficiently. Today Remruc had been called to witness the latest and, hopefully, successful experiment in creating adequate building materials.

Curmer saw him standing in front of a sectioned area of ground. Shallow pits had been dug in the shape of blocks and circles. These were lined with cross-sections of canvas strips that extended over the lip of the pits. To one side was a massive cauldron that was being stirred arduously by two youths. A greyish goo was bubbling ominously within the pot, a nose-wrinkling smell hanging in the air. Curmer moved to Remruc's side as the Nemn construction engineer began his explanation, he was assisted by a Tarl scientist. "Lords Remruc and Curmer," the engineer moved across to their side of the arena, a handful of the thick rubbery ground vines in his grasp. "This Tarl scientist discovered an interesting phenomenon while testing the feeding of these vines to mantelos. When it was broken down by the grinding action of the mantelo's teeth, it released a gum like substance. Once it had reached the fermenting stomach of the animal, the heat of its body turned this gum into the paste you see in the pot. Unfortunately for the mantelo concerned, some grains of crystal sand must have been mixed in with the vines. If you would like to follow me I will show you what happens to this paste when the combination is put into these moulds." The engineer walked across to the cauldron and ordered a quantity of the contents to be poured into the nearest mould. It oozed into the ground, the mixture cooling quickly once removed from the fire. It began to set in minutes into a concrete hard block. Once hardened, the block was lifted from the mould by the protruding canvas strips and the edges trimmed off. The result was a tough, lightweight building material that could be strengthened using more crystal sand and canvas strips. "The mixture started to set as it left the mantelo's stomach and moved into the lesser digestive tract. That was how we discovered this unusual substance," continued the engineer. Remruc looked up,

"What happened to the Mantelo?"

"Unfortunately Lord Remruc, the Mantelo did not survive," whispered the Tarl, hardly daring to look up as several of the construction workers who were once Doona glowered at him.

"Pity," said Remruc as he kicked the now solid block, "do

you think this material will be suitable for building?"

"I think it will be perfect, Lord Remruc," said the Tarl. "It is lightweight and we can seal the blocks together with a slightly more dilute form of this paste. The result will be an almost invisible join and a very tough weather resistant wall. We can build our city using these blocks, but it will take time, Lord Remruc."

"Time is, for once, a luxury we can afford Tarl," replied Remruc smiling with pleasure. Here was something he could put his energies into - organising the construction of the new San city. "Begin the preparations of plans and blocks. Use as many workers as you need, I am sure that some of the Doona field tenders and planters would be willing to help. I want to see working plans in my quarters tomorrow morning, understand?" There was a unanimous 'cheer' of approval and consent and the construction engineers busily set about their assigned duties.

"It looks good doesn't it?" smiled Curmer as he and his brother examined the concrete hard block. "I bet that mantelo had a nasty shock when it ate these vines, pity they could not save the beast."

"This is the beginning Curmer," Remruc said as they made their way back towards his tent, "I know we will be successful. We have finally found somewhere safe and beautiful to live, a world we can be proud of, a home for our children." Curmer looked at his brother, the powerful emotions clear from his thoughts,

"After all we have been through Remruc, we deserve nothing less. If anyone can organise and create this dream it is you and, as always, I will stand by your side." Remruc paused and grasped his brother's shoulder,

"No Curmer, this is our dream. We began this together back on Surn and we will complete it here on this new world."

Curmer smiled and returned his brothers embrace, nodding in agreement, his mind too happy for any clear thoughts.

Two days later Curmer was ready to leave on his exploration to the other side of the forest. A set of Chai warriors and Nemn healers made up the party, dried foods and provisions strapped to the backs of four mantelos. Two Doona handlers were present to care for the beasts and to advise on any herbage that may be suitable for animal treatments. The warriors were lightly armed, so far no predatory animals had been seen in the area, but noone knew what may be lurking in the depths of the forest. It was a happy, exciting occasion and most of the city had paused in their tasks to see the journeyers off on their expedition. Thoughts of goodwill and good luck filled the air as the travellers made their way across the grass plains, past the fields and towards the dense, dappled forest. All hearts were light and enthusiastic and Curmer, especially, was hopeful of a successful trip.

Chapter Fifteen

The party of explorers continued into the jungle of lush vegetation for the rest of the day. Their pace was slow as the healers and Doona paused to inspect any new or unusual fauna, the mantelos sampling any tasty looking leaves. They reached the clearing where Curmer's hunting party had encountered the large grazers, the family group was still there, munching contentedly in their favourite spot. The mantelo's had never seen any native animals up close and they were nervous and wary of the bulky forms slowly plodding round the clearing. As the group of San passed through the grassy circle, the large grazer that had knocked Curmer over moved towards them. The mantelo's were beside themselves with terror, the memory of Cuc's obviously still strong in their minds. The grazer halted and watched the unusual behaviour from the strange new animals in her territory and sent a low rumble of concern vibrating towards the frightened mantelos. They seemed to relax instantly, as if the large grazer had reassured them. The rest of the herd paused in their eating and watched with interest as Curmer walked towards the herd leader. The large Matriach lowered her head slightly, the soft nose whuffiling across his chest. Curmer returned the caress and sent his own thoughts of reassurance towards the creature. She seemed oblivious to his message, but when he let out a grunt of discomfort when her grooming became too enthusiastic, she instantly became alert, blowing gently into his face.

"It seems Lord Curmer that they communicate with sound. Rather like the lemaths and to a lesser extent the mantelos." said one Doona handler stepping forward to stroke the soft nose.

"Do you think they are totally mind numb Tantka?" asked

Curmer as they returned to their party, the Matriach rumbling a farewell.

"Probably, Lord Curmer. Most creatures that communicate with sound are, although the mantelos here can communicate emotions quite effectively," was the reply as the Doona patted his adoring burden beast on its slender neck.

"That doesn't make them any the less intelligent does it?"

"Oh no, Lord Curmer, although I would be dubious as to how bright these lumbering souls are. Size does not always equate with intelligence. You only have to look at a Cuc to see that." Curmer smiled at the Doona and motioned for them to continue. Now they really were entering unknown territory, even Curmer's hunting party had not ventured to the other side of the clearing.

They carried on till almost sunset, the diverse and fascinating life forms around them making the time fly past. The vegetation seemed to be very similar to those plants they had already discovered, although one of the Doona healers thought that a small fungi type plant would be beneficial to aid the digestion of the tough pampas grass on the plains for lemaths and mantelos. They had stored the plant carefully and one of the Nemn healers had carefully noted all the similarities the new fungi had with their own medicines. A space was cleared in the dense vegetation for the party to set up their lightweight tents.

This was done quickly and it wasn't long before the travellers were seated amiably around their campfire, a stew of dried meat and herbs bubbling merrily over the flames.

The second day took them deeper into the forest, the thick tough plants forming almost a solid wall before them. Their path was hacked out of the forest by the accompanying guards, the thick vines proving resistant to their blades. Every so often they had to pause for the guards to sharpen their axes and swords, muttering all the time about the damage to their precious weapons. Unexpectedly they stumbled onto a well-worn path, the size and width indicating that it was used by the large forest grazers; as it was heading in their general direction, Curmer motioned the party to follow him, the spacious walkway making their travelling easier. They camped that night on the path, their mood still light, their hopes high. Several new types of plants had been discovered by the Nemn healers, their uses and compatibility with the Sans nervous system and constitution still to be explored. It was a start. Slowly and surely the San were familiarising themselves with their new home.

Day three started as normal with the party of explorers leisurely moving along the path, chatting and discussing the vegetation around them. Relatives of the multi-coloured flyers from the planes flitted about them. Their movements more cautious and wary than their audacious cousins. Several times strange rustlings and noises whispered alongside the pathway as larger unseen creatures moved away from the strangers. The Chai guards would motion the party to stop, their weapons drawn, alert for any attack, but the secretive forest dwellers were merely creeping away from the unusual travellers. Quite unexpectedly, the pathway led them onto what Curmer at first thought was another open plain of grasslands but, when he looked closer, a dark band on the horizon showed where the forest began again. It was a large and lush clearing, the forms of forest grazers could be seen, dotted around in the distance, their true bulk and size dwarfed by the massive grassland. The mantelos were turned loose to feed and rest, the travellers pausing for their midday meal. The air was full of the buzz of insect life (fortunately for the San, the local insects were not partial to their blood) and the active conversations of the explorers. Curmer walked to the edge of their makeshift camp to watch the mantelos playing out on the flat expanse. In between mouthfuls of grass they would spin round and race across the open land, exercising their running muscles, enjoying the novelty of being wild and free. The beasts paused in their game and settled down to some serious grazing, they seemed to be motionless as they stuffed their faces with food. A slow chill crept through Curmers mind. The mantelos seemed to be motionless because they were. The mantelos were frozen in mid gulp, their jaws open, their eyes glazed. A silence closed in around Curmer. The insects were no longer buzzing around busily going about their business. A large beetle like creature was suspended in mid air before Curmer's eyes, the brightly coloured carapace spread out, the lace wings in a permanent downward swing. He spun round to stare dumbfounded at the rest of the group. Each one was as still as the mantelos. Tantka, a smile on his face, was leaning towards him, a freshly made meat roll in his hand. The flames of the fire were merrily stuck in the air, their orange-yellow tongues not daring to move.

One guard was cleaning his sword, another, suspended in the air in mid trip, forever waiting to hit the ground. Fear wrapped her cold fingers tight around Curmer's heart. He was the only moving, living creature on the vast plain and, for all he knew, on the entire planet. A soft sound behind him sent a chill along his spin, the hair on his neck standing on end. Something was watching him. Slowly, dreading what might be there, he turned around. There was a sudden flash of light in his eyes, his mind registered a sharp pain that was over before it really began, and darkness took him as he fell unconscious to the ground.

Remruc sat bolt upright sending the drawing slates balanced on his knees flying. He must have dozed off in the midday sun, but he was not warm, the cold, clammy grip of fear was still present in his heart. "Curmer is in trouble." He thought, rising as quickly as he could and grabbing his crutches. "Eriya!" he shouted, his thoughts tinged with fear. She came running from the tent, her eyes wide in panic,

"What is wrong Remruc? Have you fallen and hurt your leg again?" She reached out to steady him and help him into the tent.

"I am alright Eriya, thank you. But, I think Curmer is in trouble. I have this terrible feeling that he is in some kind of danger." Eriya remained calm, her thoughts cool and soothing in Remruc's distraught mind.

"Remruc, have you received any message or warning from your guards that accompany the party."

"No, everything is quiet."

"Did you not hand-pick the men yourself? Are they not your best warriors and did you not instruct them to send you regular updates as to their progress?"

"Yes Eriya, but perhaps they are out of range. Perhaps they cannot get a messenger to us."

"What possible danger is there on this world that a Chai cannot deal with? Your men have fought and defeated the fiercest Cucs, there is nothing they cannot battle and win. If there had been any sign of trouble, they would have sent you a warning somehow. You were just having a bad dream. A nightmare from the dreadful battles you faced against the Cuc. Search your heart now and tell me if there is any fear or worry about Curmer?" Remruc did what he was asked, and sure enough the fear that had clawed its way into his mind was gone.

"You are right Eriya, I am sorry. I cannot help but worry about Curmer, this world seems too good to be true, I can't help feeling that there is some kind of danger lurking in the background waiting to be discovered." Eriya laughed and ruffled his hair,

"You are becoming cynical in your old age my mate. After all the suffering our people have been through we deserve a paradise like this. Let go of your fear. We are safe here," Remruc nodded and pulled her close to him,

"Perhaps you can think of some way of occupying my mind?" Eriya giggled, a warm feeling growing inside her.

"Let me see..." she kissed him lightly, "that better?"

"I think I need an overdose," smiled Remruc as he flipped the flap over the doorway and led her into their sleeping chamber.

The pattern of leaves against sky spun round his head in a dizzying dance, prompting his confused mind back into awareness. Curmer slowly eased himself up off of the damp grass and looked around him. He was no longer in the clearing with the rest of his party, but was in the centre of a small, neatly cropped lawn, bordered by dense, tall thorny bushes. The bushes towered above him and were impenetrable, no light could be seen through them, only the pale sky above illuminated the tiny grove. There seemed to be no obvious way in or out of the enclosure.

"An impressive prison," mused Curmer as he surveyed his surroundings. "I suppose I could dig my way out if I was really determined." He continued digging his heel into the soft turf, but, a few inches below the surface he came into contact with the tough crystal rock that seemed to be everywhere on this planet, "cancel that idea." He paced around the enclosure, tentatively pressing against the daunting bushes. He was rewarded with several cuts from the needle sharp thorns and decided against trying to climb out. A gnawing hunger in his stomach reminded him that he had not eaten, as he still had his clothing and utility belt, he rummaged in his pouch to find some dry emergency rations. Munching slowly on the dry foodstuff he realised just how thirsty he was. There was no pool or stream for him to drink from and his hip flask had been left in the clearing in the forest. He examined the leaves of the thorn bush, they seemed to be quite thick and fleshy, with a waxy coat. Carefully he picked one of the leaves and broke it in half, sure enough it was full of moisture. Gingerly he put the leaf to his mouth, he would have preferred to test this new vegetation before attempting to eat it, but his thirst was too great and this small leaf could not possibly harm him. Before the leaf touched his lips, a blinding pain seared its way into his mind, causing him to reel backwards and drop the leaf. He fell to the ground unconscious again.

When Curmer finally came around, he found a large dished palm frond by his side full of clear water. He sat up quickly and looked around, the enclosure was the same as before, no way in or out. Judging by the light, he had not been unconscious for long and he slowly climbed to his feet. Cautiously he picked up the palm leaf and sipped the cool liquid. It tasted like water, no other flavours were noticeable so he drained the leaf, gratefully wiping his mouth. Curmer looked up. If there was no way into the enclosure from the ground, perhaps his captors could move in the air like the winged Cucs or the bright flyers. Whoever they were, they must have been watching him and they must be intelligent enough to realise what he needed. Casually he scanned the rim of the bush tops, looking for any signs of life, there was none. With a sigh he sat down again and collected his thoughts. Concentrating he sent a message out to his surroundings, trying to send it as far as possible. "Hello. My name is Curmer. I will not harm you. Show yourselves to me." He paused. Nothing.

Shortening the range and increasing the 'volume' of his message he tried again. Still nothing. With all of his will he sent another message, this time only to his immediate surroundings and at a frequency and strength that would have caused a terrible headache to any San receiving. Silence. Taking a deep breath he started to growl softly in his throat, he increased the volume and finished with an ear shattering roar. Annoyed by this lack of response he stood up and carefully paced around the perimeter once more. The thorns were needle sharp, but his hide boots would protect his feet adequately, and if he wrapped his shirt around his hands then he could attempt to climb up the treacherous surface. Quickly taking off his shirt and tearing it in two he started to ascend the thorn scrub. It was no easy task, the sharp thorns were merciless and tore at his bare skin at every opportunity and by the time he reached the top, his chest was cris-crossed with small scratches, blood stinging in the cuts. As he climbed to the top of the bush, he could not believe what he saw. There, stretching in every direction to the horizon was a solid rooftop of thorn scrub. The clearing below him seemed to be the only one in the vast forest. Gingerly he balanced himself on top of the bush and stood at his full height, scanning his surroundings in total disbelief. As he stood there a force, strong, powerful and totally unexpected, smacked into his body sending him toppling over the edge back into the clearing. Curmer's mind let out a frightened scream as he fell towards the ground, cringing inside he waited for the impact, knowing that he would be seriously injured falling from such a height. Instead, he felt his body slowing and halting just before he would have hit the ground and gently being lowered onto the turf. Breathing heavily Curmer rose, his limbs trembling from shock, his heart thumping wildly in his chest. As he watched the thorn bushes at the top of the clearing vanished and through the opening came the strangest creatures he had ever seen.

They walked on four very slender legs, were slim, almost skeletal in construction. They stood twice as tall as Curmer and their bodies were covered in short silver hair which grew long almost mane-like around their necks. Their heads were narrow, long and delicate, similar in appearance to the grazers that the San had already encountered, but it was their eyes that held Curmer spellbound. The eyes were large, protected by a bony ridge that extended out from the forehead. There appeared to be seven pupils in each eye. Three above and three below a large central one. These pupils glistened in the light as the six smaller pinpoints revolved around the central, dark orb. In a line up the centre of their heads ran a single row of very small horns, with one larger one protruding from the forehead. They were the Idor and this was their world.

Curmer stood tensely as the Idor circled around him. There were four present. They were the senior representatives of their race and the most powerful creatures on their world. The largest and oldest of the Idor, his hide pure white with age, stood directly in front of Curmer, he lowered his head, the pupils in his eyes whirling wildly as he studied this strange creature.

With a whuff of disinterest he turned and walked back a few paces, a large soft couch of moss appeared from thin air beneath him as he lowered his bulk onto its soft surface, folding his long legs neatly beneath him. The rest of the Idor followed their leaders example, all save the youngest and darkest relaxed on their magical moss beds. The standing Idor strode towards Curmer, her iron grey coat rippling in the sun's rays. Curmer backed away, suddenly very afraid of this towering powerful form. Instantly he was paralysed by a searing pain that bored its way into his mind, sending tendrils of fire coiling down his limbs holding him still, he tried to call out, but his thoughts were no longer under his control, his mind unable to focus on anything save the agony burning inside him. Unbelievably, Curmer became aware of a second pain, like white lighting flashing through his body, exploring firstly his physical structure then concentrating on his mind. He tried to resist, his mental barriers were swept aside as easily as the wind blows away fallen dried leaves. He was unable to prevent this torture from seeking out his own memories and when it found what it was looking for it paused then vanished, releasing Curmer from its grip. He fell to the ground, his body trembling, his mind reeling from the experience. He felt himself beginning to lose consciousness as his bruised and damaged brain tried to reduce the pain of controlled thought and heal itself. The same force that had knocked him from the top of the bushes carefully lifted his limp body off the ground, he felt his head being tilted back, but before he could sink gratefully into the beckoning blackness that was creeping into his mind the white lightning returned. It dragged him, painlessly this time, back to full awareness and he was lowered to his feet, his legs still shaking after the trauma. Curmer let out a soft moan and cradled his head in his hands. He slowly opened his eyes and looked at his captors, they were all apparently oblivious to his suffering and two were idly nibbling the short grass beneath them. The gap in the thorn hedge was still there and Curmer could see beyond a flat grassland, very different from the view he had witnessed on top of the hedge. Confused he looked again then desperation finished any further reasoning and he gathered the last of his strength. Leaping to his feet he sprinted for the opening. The Idor watched him as he ran past their couches, he had almost reached the gap when the burning pain slammed into his head and the powerful force knocked him on his back. He was dragged, struggling, by something invisible back to the centre of the enclosure and pinned to the ground. The sudden stab of energy directed at the memory centre of his brain paralysed him with pain, a strangled gasp escaping from his lips. Curmer lay motionless, unable to resist, unable to prevent this unknown force from sifting through his private mind. Once again he found himself on the planet Surn, the fierce twin suns burning brightly in the sky. All that he had seen and all that he had experienced as he grew up in the subterranean world of the San was extracted from his mind and viewed. Each feeling and emotion that had been experienced was relived by him now. Again he felt the pain of grief over the death of his father and the suicide of his natural mother, the fear and anxiety when his brother was in danger when he was attacked by the winged Cuc in the deserted settlement. The tension and hopelessness of trying to combat the plague while Remruc strived to reconcile the tribes of the San. The realisation of his love for Sorta, the joy and jubilation when the plague was finally destroyed and the peoples of the San united. The anger and frustration at the constant threat of the Cucs.

Curmer fought the inevitable, there were some things, some memories and feelings that he just did not want to remember, but, slowly and surely he was drawn towards them, a growing feeling of fear and anger in his mind. Suddenly he was there, once more he was ecstatic over the news of Sorta's pregnancy, hopefully waiting the birth of his son, he experienced the joy of 'listening' to his unborn son's thoughts and emotions in the safety of his mother's body. Again he stood in the cold crumbling settlement in the north of their territory, he felt the sudden pain as his mate cried out in fear and anguish. His eyes saw her limp and battered body being carried into the settlement by the healers and guards, he felt her cold hand and the faint murmur of her unconscious mind. Lenta was standing in front of him, the thoughts that he could not bear to hear filtered into his mind, "Your son is dead." The total devastation he had felt filled him once more, the comforting thoughts from his brother did little to ease the agony of the loss. These were memories that Curmer had tried to bury deep in his mind, memories that he could not bear to live with.

The anger and frustration that he felt at his own mind being violated in this way by these uncaring creatures fuelled his willpower. Curmer was crazed with grief and fury and, despite the power of the force holding him down, he attacked the mind that was probing his. This sudden and unexpected action caused the probe to retract in surprise, the moments hesitation giving Curmer the edge he needed. He fought his way to his feet, oblivious to the restraining pain of the force that held him, he was kill-crazy, determined to hurt the creature that had hurt him so badly. He turned snarling towards the dark grey creature that had been controlling the proceedings, a roar of fury in his throat. With eyes blazing in agony he sprang towards her, the fact that she was twice his height and four times his weight was irrelevant to him. The San were descended from fierce predators and they still had the strong canine teeth and hunting instincts of their ancestors, now Curmer was using this instinct to its maximum effect. His mind no longer capable of coherent, logical thought, the emotions that burned within him using the physical pain of the restraining force to double his efforts. The watching creature snorted in surprise, taking a step backwards. The others of her kind leapt to their feet, the moss couches disappearing as suddenly as they had arrived. Curmer was within inches of her throat, his teeth bared, his hands almost touching the silky hide when the white lightning flashed through his mind, paralysing his body in an arch of muscle tight tension and sending him spinning into the oblivion of unconsciousness.

"Wake up now." The soft voice whispered.

"Go away... leave me alone..." was the barely coherent reply.

"You are hungry." the voice persisted, a gnawing hunger beginning in Curmer's stomach as soon as the suggestion was made.

"I... do not want... to wake up ever again... let me die."

"No." said the insistent voice.

"My mind hurts... you have hurt me... why are you so cruel?"

"Wake up. There is no pain." The violent throbbing in Curmer's mind ceased as soon as the thoughts entered his head, but the despair and anguish still strong from the memory of the death of his son remained. Curmer was still confused, he was not sure of where he was, all he knew, all that he could remember was the grief for his dead son.

"Leave me alone... my... my... son. Why did they kill my son?" Curmer began to lose track of his thoughts as he drifted through a sea of anguish and despair.

"That was long ago. Wake up now. Talk to me," the voice said, becoming stronger, more commanding.

"It hurts so much..."

"What hurts? There is no pain."

"In my heart it hurts. I miss him so much. I will never see him grow." He was losing his mind now, unable to control the turmoil within himself.

"Open your eyes." The voice demanded. Unable to resist, Curmer's body obeyed the command even though his mind was still reeling in despair. Slowly he realised that there was darkness all around him. It was night. This fact became an anchor for his struggling mind, some tangible reality for him to focus his attention on. Slowly the cold feeling of reality dispelled the fuzziness of the semi-conscious state and Curmer was finally awake. His breathing was laboured. His injured mind was struggling to control his vital bodily functions, the injured nerve endings still screaming their message of damage to his brain, unknown to Curmer, the messages were being skilfully blocked by a mind more powerful than he could ever imagine. What the mind could not block was the pain in Curmer's heart. The San could not weep, perhaps this was what made their grief so intense, they had no way to demonstrate the feelings of their loss, they could only endure and survive. He was lying on a soft couch of the disappearing moss that had reformed itself beneath him, despite the cool air he was warm and comfortable. Hovering in space a few feet away from him were two huge glowing, spinning orbs, that seemed to light up the air around them with their iridescent blue glow. Curmer's eyes adjusted to his sensitive night vision and he saw, lying on a similar couch of moss, the creature that had lain next to the white haired one. This one was silver in colour, lighter than the others.

"That's better," crooned the thought in his head. Curmer blinked in confusion, the grove was empty save for himself and this creature. He tried to raise himself from the couch, but a searing pain in his limbs and trembling muscles caused him to gasp before the mind skilfully absorbed the pain from his body. "Do not move," was the stern command. "You have been injured; you must rest while I heal your body," continued the thought in gentler tones. Curmer felt himself beginning to drift away again with the shock of the pain. A soft tugging at his mind brought him back to full awareness and slowly the events of the day came back to him.

"Who are you?", he asked the large silver form.

"I am Thr. I will replace El when he fades."

"What are you?"

"We are the Idor and this is our world."

"Why did you torture me? I would not have hurt anyone, why did you not speak to me earlier? You are not mind numb."

"You ask a lot of questions. Which one would you like me to answer?"

"All of them." said Curmer, his breathing becoming easier as the Idor healed his damaged body and brain.

"We had no intentions of torturing you, but you resisted our probing, you are a very determined animal," was the cool reply.

"I am not an animal!" came Curmer's indignant reply, to which the Idor only snorted.

"You certainly gave a good impression of one when you attacked Yln." The thought was tinged with amusement.

"What Yln did to me was wrong. It is against our social customs to pry into another's private mind and memories. Do you not comprehend the agony you put me through?"

"We wished to know why you were here and where you came from. Your thoughts were interesting, we needed to know more."

"You could have asked me, I would have told you anything you wanted to know. You did not need to hurt me like that, the pain I felt over my son's death is still too strong, have you no idea what you put me through?"

"No," was the simple reply, "we do not understand. What is death and why does it distress you so?" Curmer stared at the Idor dumbfounded, he was lost for thoughts, how could he explain the concept of death to a creature so very different from himself.

"Do the Idor never die?"

"No." Curmer's mind conjured up all sorts of concepts as to the physical and social structure of these new creatures, how could they possibly understand his culture when there was not even the common ground of death from which to empathise with each other.

"It does not matter. It is over and forgotten," said Curmer, sighing deeply. The Idor lowered his head and peered into Curmer's face, the eyes whirling frantically.

"You are lying," teased the thought. "It matters a great deal to you and your people. Tell me what happened after your son died." Curmer felt the emotions well up inside him once more. "Or," said the Idor quickly, "with your permission," there was definitely a slight hint of mockery in the thought, "let me see the rest of your memories." Fear of the pain that he had experienced before made Curmer flinch and hesitate.

"Do not worry. Yln is young and inexperienced; she has not yet mastered the art of mind probing. I, however, am Thr, I will replace El when he fades; I know everything. Come with me Curmer ...let us walk together into your past ...."

Despite himself, Curmer felt his mind being led down the dusty corridor of time and once more he was standing by his son's grave. This time however, there were no emotions, no feelings of despair only a strange detached sensation, like an outsider watching through a window. He saw Herka handing over his own newborn son to Sorta; Herka's mate had died trying to save Sorta's life. Curmer swore to raise and love the child as his own and to honour the brave Herka who had sworn to die to give the San time to escape from the hoards of Cuc. Then they were in the land of the Idor, their people were safe and happy in this new world. As he watched the growing bond between Sorta, Deyka and himself he began to feel the warmth and love for his new son, the pain of his own child's death fading into his past. The rest of his experiences on this new world flashed past until he lay once more on the soft moss bed, the Idor still and thoughtful beside him. Curmer was tired, but the pangs of hunger continued to prompt him. Before he could form the thought, a bowl of fruit appeared hovering in mid-air beside him.

"This food is compatible with your physical structure, the leaf you tried to eat earlier is not. You would have ceased to function instantly," Thr said distractedly.

"Ceased to function?" asked Curmer.

"Hmm?"

"Ceased to function. You said I would have ceased to function?" persisted Curmer.

"Yes, the poison in the leaf would have systematically destroyed all of your neural processes, the damage would have been irreparable, your mind would have ceased to function." The Idor paused and looked at Curmer intently.

"Is that what death is?" Curmer smiled,

"I think so, or at least it is similar." He looked at the fruit, "Can I move my arm now?" Thr's eyes whizzed around even faster.

"Yes, yes, that's you all better. All damaged systems repaired. Oh by the way, Csjn sends his apologies, he did not mean to hit you so hard, but your body and mind is so frail and he doesn't have the required control yet."

"So it was Csjn that hit me with the lightning bolt." said Curmer, feeling more and more relaxed by the minute.

"Yes, I told them that I only had to hold you down, but as Yln persisted in her probing regardless to your physical discomfort I became distracted. That was how you escaped." The Idor's thoughts became tinged with mirth, "You certainly gave her a fright. I must say that you look very fierce when you are angry." Curmer was slightly irritated by Thr's apparent amusement about the whole incident.

He did not lose his temper often, as a healer violence was abhorrent to him, but Yln had pushed him beyond the realms of reason and he was squirming inside with humiliation regarding his behaviour.

"Please send my apologies to Yln. I really did not mean to lose my temper." Thr looked at Curmer, humour colouring his mind.

"You are a strange little animal aren't you." Curmer was completely offended and this seemed to amuse Thr even more. He put down the fruit he was eating and pushed himself up to a sitting position, bringing his eyes level with the Idor. Thr did not flinch.

"I am not an animal." he said

"Of course not," replied the Idor unconvincingly. "Lie down please, you must rest." Curmer obeyed the command but he wasn't entirely sure how much of the reaction was under his control.

"Where are the others?" he enquired, trying to change the subject.

"They are not here," said Thr irritatingly. Curmer gritted his teeth, was this creature deliberately teasing him.

"Obviously." His caustic reply seemed to go unnoticed by Thr.

"Have you any idea, little animal, how rare telepathy is in this universe?"

"What is telepathy?"

"Communication through the power of thought."

"People talk in their minds, only animal's use sound to communicate," replied Curmer uncertainly. The Idor looked at him intently. "Please stop that."

"Stop what?" asked Thr

"Stop looking at me like that, it is most disconcerting."

The Idor's answer barely concealed his mirth, "you are very irritable little animal, go to sleep." Instantly Curmer slipped into a deep slumber, Thr's parting thoughts echoing in his mind, "I find your kind most interesting, we must know more."

Curmer awoke to the sound of the bright flyers welcoming the dawn. He yawned and stretched, his sleeping fur slipping from his body.

"Good morning Lord Curmer!" came the Nemn healer's bright greeting as he entered the tent with a breakfast broth. Curmer smiled in response and rose, distractedly looking for his shirt. He grunted and removed another from his pack, no doubt the other would reappear.

He strode from the tent and surveyed the vast clearing they had camped on. The afternoon and evening of the day before seemed strangely hazy in his mind, he could not for the life of him think what they had been up to. He shook his head and shrugged, dispelling the strange fuzzy feeling inside his mind. They had work to do. There was a whole forest ahead of them to explore and lots of interesting new plants to discover. He motioned to the rest of his party to break up camp. He felt unusually fit and healthy, his body bubbling with energy despite the strange numbness somewhere in the back of his mind. In record time the camp was packed and the explorers ready to continue. With a light heart Curmer stepped out in front, leading them directly across the clearing, towards the beckoning forest.

Chapter Sixteen

The vegetation was different on the other side of the clearing, it was less dense and tropical, the plant forms more delicate, the open spaces between the tall tree-like palms allowing a gentle breeze to waft across the forest floor, disturbing the small, light feathery bushes and cool the travellers. "I like it here Lord Curmer," said Kurct one of the Nemn healers, "it is peaceful and quiet." Curmer smiled back in agreement as he pushed aside a cascade of lace fine moss that was draped across their path.

"Let's go this way, I can hear water running," Curmer replied.

"I cannot hear anything Lord Curmer," Kurct's puzzled thought confusing Curmer.

"Yes, listen." They all stood still, straining to hear.

"No Lord Curmer, I still don't hear anything."

"We may not hear anything Lord Curmer, but the mantelos can certainly smell the fresh water, look at them," laughed Tantka as he held on to the restraining leads of his beasts who were tugging excitedly in the direction Curmer had indicated. With a smile of satisfaction Curmer led the way to the place he knew there would be a large luxurious pool caught between two splashing waterfalls. Even before they reached the pool, Curmer was lifting his digging tools from the packs on the mantelos, a strange certainty in his mind telling him that here he would find the healing and antiseptic plants he was looking for. They emerged from the shady forest into a bright canyon, a thundering white splash of water tumbled into a deep emerald pool that stretched almost half a sharr before crashing down into the waiting river below. The party were spellbound, held in awe at the raw beauty of this forest jewel. The mantelos rushed to the clear pool and submerged their noses deep into the fresh water, drinking in deep gulps. The San relaxed, unpacked their belongings and settled down in the comfortable surroundings. Curmer stripped off and began to wade into the beckoning depths of the lagoon, the others, mistaking his intentions, did likewise and plunged into the water, enjoying the warmth of their own personal swimming pool, but Curmer had no intentions of swimming and enjoying himself, a strong sense within him was urging him on to the rocky overhang behind the waterfall. He walked through the silver curtain of spray wading in the chest deep water, his digging tools held above his head, a small water container slung around his shoulders. There, clinging onto the rough rocky ceiling were small, round, spongy orange-red plants, their fat bulbous bodies speckled with clear water drops from the spray beyond. Without hesitation Curmer reached up and cut through the tip of the nearest blob. He held the container beneath the cut as the red fluid wept out from the injured plant, as the fat bulb emptied itself of its precious contents, the sides of plant collapsed till it hung limp and thin from the rock. Curmer repeated this exercise till his carrier was full, he fastened the stopper and waded back to the now resting party on the smooth rock beach.

"Kurct! Kurct! Look what I have found!" Curmer's mind shouted excitedly as he breathlessly ran towards the healers.

His excitement was infectious and all of the travellers gathered around, even the warriors, to see his discovery. Carefully Curmer tipped out a small quantity of the red liquid onto the rock. The strong unmistakable pungent smell of antiseptic filled the air, Kurct dipped his finger in the solution and quickly withdrew it as the concentrated liquid stung his skin. As he quickly washed his hands in water, the red stain on his finger faded to yellow and vanished as it mixed with the neutral water. Kurct smiled,

"It looks very promising Lord Curmer, it definitely has an antiseptic quality, and it can be diluted with water to control its concentration. Now all we need to find out is if it is compatible with our physical structure."

"This liquid is perfectly suited to our physiological needs, it will not harm us in any way," said Curmer confidently beaming at the others. The healers frowned, and exchanged glances.

"I am sure it will be, Lord Curmer, but we must test it first just in case," continued Kurct. Curmer shook his head,

"no, we do not need to test this discovery, I know it will be alright. Look." Quickly Curmer picked up his cutting knife and slashed the palm of his hand, before the shocked onlookers could react he had rubbed the surface of the wound with water and red liquid mixed together inhaling sharply as it stung the open cut.

"Lord Curmer!", cried Kurct, quickly grabbing his medical pack and removing clean bandaging. He bound the wound, disapproval colouring his mind and face. "We do not know if this will produce any side affects, you should know better than to take such a risk, we may not be able to cure you should you become ill!" His thoughts tumbled one after the other as his fellow healers peered anxiously at their Chieftain. Despite his own amazement at his sudden and decisive action, Curmer laughed.

"I will be fine Kurct don't worry. I think that you will be impressed at the healing potential of this liquid."

"Lord Curmer," said Kurct exasperation sharpening his thoughts, "you do not know that for sure. This is a strange world, we must be cautious and careful, not everything is safe for us here, look what happened to that poor mantelo that ate the ground vines."

"Kurct." Curmer gripped the healer by the arms, his eyes

burning with intensity, "I know this is safe. I know this is what we have been searching for. Trust me!" The certainty in his thoughts caused Kurct to reel slightly, the rest of the group began to relax slightly. Kurct nodded, a slow smile spreading across his face,

"Alright. Alright. I will trust you, but if you fall sick remember that..."

"...you told me so," finished Curmer as laughter dispelled the last of the tension. He fastened the stopper on the flask of precious liquid and placed it carefully in his pack then returned to the others, the guards already beginning to prepare their midday meal. Tankta pulled Kurct to one side, switching to a private 'wavelength'.

"Healer Kurct, have you noticed anything strange about Lord Curmer recently?" Kurct looked puzzled and shook his head.

"Other than the foolhardiness of youth, no."

Tankta continued, "could you hear any water before Lord Curmer led us closer to this pool?" Kurct shook his head,

"No, but who is to say that Lord Curmer doesn't perhaps have sharper hearing than the rest of us."

"Why, out of all the places in this vast and diverse forest did Lord Curmer lead us directly to this place, go straight to the waterfall where he discovered this miracle liquid that we have been searching for? How did he know where to look? How did he know for sure that it will not harm us?"

"Perhaps it is just luck that he found this place and perhaps he is just lucky that he seems to be right about this antiseptic liquid," Kurct replied, uncertainty colouring his mind. Tankta shook his head,

"Once may be luck, but twice is not." Kurct looked unconvinced, so Tankta decided to ask the question that had been bothering him since yesterday, "Healer Kurct. Can you tell me what you did yesterday afternoon and evening?"

"Of course," replied Kurct bemused, "we made camp and prepared our meal then we..." his thoughts trailed off as suddenly the memory of yesterday became hazy and unclear, "...we... well, I suppose we just rested for the rest of the day then went to bed."

"You suppose. Can't you remember?"

"Now that you mention it, no. it all seems unclear," said Kurct in puzzlement. Tankta smiled, a little relieved,

"It may interest you to know, healer Kurct, that neither I nor any of the guards can remember what we did yesterday. Strange isn't it?"

"What do you think is happening?" said Kurct intrigued. Tankta frowned as he formed his thoughts.

"I don't know for sure, but I have a feeling that Lord Curmer has been affected in some way. I think we should keep a careful watch on him and inform Lord Remruc as soon as we return." Kurct nodded in agreement and they made their way back to the now happily eating group.

Remruc was surveying the mass of excavators, builders and engineers stolidly going about their business of creating a new San city when the runner came sprinting across the rough ground.

"Lord Remruc! Lord Remruc! Lord Curmer's party is returning." Remruc stepped down from the small platform and motioned for the Nemn councillor to continue the distribution of the volunteer workers consisting of Chai guards, a few Doona and several Tarl. He marched towards the outskirts of the tent city following the gentle flow of well wishers for the returning group. The travellers looked well and relaxed as they made their way into the main meeting circle in the centre of the cluster of tents, the mantelos jogging excitedly beside their handlers, their heads high, their steps light.

"Well?" thought Remruc, smiling warmly at his brother.

"Yes, we have found an alternative antiseptic plant, yes we have something to aid digestion of the grass for the lemaths and mantelos and yes we have several interesting native plants that may be useful as a supplement to our own herbal remedies."

"A very successful trip!" Remruc replied enthusiastically, "but wait till you see the progress that we have been making on the new city." Curmer laughed,

"Can't you even give me a minute to rest, refresh and eat!"

"Plenty of time for that later, come with me and see what we have been up to." Remruc pulled his brother away from the gaggle of healers discussing the new found remedies and swung himself expertly along at a fast pace on his crutches. Curmer found himself watching Remruc's injured limb, it was healing well, but a broken bone in an adult tended to heal slowly and was not as strong. The break had been ragged and bad, there was every possibility that Remruc would be left with a limp. It was possible (although Remruc had not been told) that he may always need the support of a stick or crutch. Curmer knew that this would devastate his active warrior brother and he fervently hoped that there would be no such complications. Suddenly, from somewhere in the back of his mind, an image of a dried withered looking plant appeared. It was crouched between large white salt encrusted rocks that huddled near a lake so wide that Curmer could not see the other shore. A certain knowledge that this plant would help to heal the bone quickly and efficiently crept into his soul. He also knew that the place in his vision was at least twenty days journey in a straight line to the east, beyond the open plains. How Curmer knew this was a mystery to himself and he felt somewhat afraid of this new found gift of vision.

"What's wrong?" Remruc's thought brought him back to

reality and he realised that he had been standing blank eyed for a few minutes.

"Nothing, I... I was just thinking that perhaps I should set out again, in the other direction this time and see what I can find."

"There is nothing to the east except grass," smiled Remruc,"come and see what we have been building." Curmer smiled and carried on, a determined thought forming in his mind that he would set out as soon as possible to find this mysterious bush.

They had reached the limits of the tent city, the last few hide homes flapping in the light breeze, the gentle hills, the crystal rocks flashing in the sunlight where the earth had exposed them, sat in front of them. There, extending from the open mouths of the cave quarters, several stone-like buildings had been erected. The blocks replacing the light tents that had once sheltered the occupants. The buildings were very much in keeping with the graceful curves and spirals of the original Chai city on Surn.

"This is just the surface," said Remruc, his thoughts tinged with pride. "Before we constructed the external coverings, we placed pipes made of the same substance into the ditches dug for sanitation. Pipes have also been used to bring water from the mountain lake, diverted directly into each home. Come with me," he motioned moving round the first hill, heading for the still wild tangle of plant life on the east side of their city. As they stood on the ridge, Curmer surveyed the slope below him. The wild fauna had been carefully organised and tidied into neat strips of selected plants. At the top of the ridge a waste pipe allowed a constant trickle of soiled water to seep into the ground and head through the different levels of plants. "Each species of plant extract different substances from the water." explained Remruc, "The end result is as you can see," he pointed into the distance," a reservoir of fresh re-cycled water."

"How fresh?" asked Curmer.

"Fresh enough for us to drink. We will store the water in the reservoir for a time before releasing it back into the river system. That way we will not contaminate our surroundings or destroy this beautiful planet." Curmer smiled and nodded his approval.

"Very good Remruc, this is most impressive. Who thought of this idea?"

"Believe it or not, a team of Tarl scientists have been noting the properties of these plants and they suggested that we put their theories to the test. We have and this is the result." Curmer turned round and viewed the city once more. The bright tents were a stark contrast to the dull grey, monotonous stone buildings and Curmer felt sorry to see the welcome splash of colour replaced by the beautiful but dull dwellings. Remruc smiled, reading his brother's mind before the thought had been formed.

"Don't worry brother. Come with me and look at the final plans." He led Curmer back towards one of the completed buildings. To his surprise, Curmer realised that this was the cavern/tent home of Remruc that he had left only a few days before. The doorway into the building was very large and this confused Curmer slightly, but all was revealed when he saw the final plans laid out in the main living area. Each building was designed to have a large sectioned tent expanding out from the doorway. This would allow a family the benefit of both summer living in the tents and winter warmth in their buildings.

The outsides of each house were decorated with more wall hangings, bringing colour and variety of texture to the new San city. "Once our population in this city becomes larger, we will start another further down the valley. Some of the Doona were interested in starting summer grazing camps for the animals with young at foot, and leave the grasses around our city for the winter. I know that if we were to begin such an exercise then we must have a tight control over each of the groups. The last thing I want is for the San to split into their tribal groups again, that will only lead to a situation we had on Surn."

Curmer nodded his agreement.

"We may find though brother, that the San have learned their lesson. I do not believe that we will ever be divided again. We have come so far and achieved so much together."

"I hope so Curmer, I hope so. One precaution that I have taken is to remain in complete command of all of the Chai warriors and guards. If there is only one army then we cannot fight each other. The Nemn patrols will maintain the everyday order and law within the city and they are answerable eventually to us."

"You have done as much as you can at this point Remruc. Now we can only finish our city and wait and see how our new culture develops." Curmer eased himself onto a wall bench and surveyed the spacious, intricately patterned interior. Eriya entered from another wide doorway, her arms full of eating herbs.

"Curmer! You are back so soon! Did everything go well?" She put down her bundle and embraced her brother-in-law.

"Yes! We have an antiseptic alternative, something to aid digestion for lemaths and several other interesting plants that we must spend time testing." Curmer was eager to tell Eriya more about his exciting discoveries, but he was also yearning to see his mate. Eriya sensed his feelings and quickly released him.

"You and Sorta are invited for evening meal. You can tell

me everything then." Curmer smiled gratefully and rose,

"We will be delighted to join you tonight; I will leave Deyka with Lenta for the evening," he turned and left, eagerness in his steps to see Sorta and his son.

Deyka was seated outside the tent on a large soft hide. A variety of bright objects lay around him but he was most interested in the texture of a small scrap of fur. He had already experimented with eating the fur, but it tickled his throat and tasted awful, now he was content to sit and stroke the soft surface, watching the hairs flick through his fingers, their colours dancing in the sunlight. He was so engrossed in his game that he did not hear Curmer approach.

As his father's shadow loomed over him he was fascinated at first by the strange dark creature that lay on the mat in front of him, then realising that it was a shadow cast by something behind him he turned round, protective lids flicking over his eyes to shield them from the sunlight, like in-built sunglasses. He burst into a mind blowing wave of ecstasy as he recognised the figure, the colours of emotion bouncing through Curmer's brain as he was almost floored by the welcome. He bent down and scooped up the small figure, hugging him close, a strange feeling of guilt somewhere inside his mind.

"I love you Deyka and I will never hurt you," he whispered softly as Deyka chortled amiably.

"Curmer you are back!" exclaimed Sorta who had emerged from the tent wondering why her son was so excited. She rushed over as Curmer put Deyka down and swung her off her feet holding her close.

"I missed you Sorta," he said.

"And I have missed you my mate." she replied her mind almost as ecstatic as Deyka's. The family moved into their home, Sorta heating some water for Curmer to bathe and refresh himself before evening meal. Curmer sat on one of the scatter cushions watching Deyka crawl around the living area amusing himself. Slowly his mind seemed to drift away and the room became unclear, like looking through a mist or a veil. His limbs were heavy, weighed down into the cushions, his breathing shallow. His body was not responding to his thoughts, it seemed distant somehow, he tried to blink away the strange mist from his vision, but nothing happened. Deyka stopped crawling around and sat staring in wonder at his father. His young mind could perceive things that the adults carefully shielded or ignored and he was staring in amazement at what he could see. With a smile and an inquiring thought he crawled over to the fascinating object. Curmer felt fear grip his heart, he did not know why, but he was terrified to let Deyka come near him, he tried to command him to stop, but his mind seemed numb and he knew that his thoughts were being blocked by something. He watched in horror as his arms reached out of their own accord, stretching towards the small figure gleefully crawling towards him, with all of his will power he tried to move, to no avail. In desperation his mind screamed a plea, to who or what he did not know.

"No! Please no! Do not hurt my son!" Instantly the strange feeling disappeared, his arms dropped down to his sides and his vision cleared, his mind snapping back into his head. Deyka stopped in his tracks a stab of disappointment coming from his young mind. Curmer was breathing heavily, the numbness in the back of his head seemed to be growing and spreading, creeping out of his unconscious mind into his conscious state. "What is happening to me?" he thought privately, "am I going mad?" The sound of Sorta's footsteps made him look round as she returned with bathing cloths.

"Are you alright?" she asked when she saw his pale and

shaken features.

"Yes. Yes, just tired," he thought hurriedly as he took the drying cloths from her hands and all but ran into their bathing section where a tub of steaming, scented water waited for him. Slowly he relaxed in the soothing warmth of the water, his mind drifting into his private thoughts as he reviewed the events of the last few days. He was having problems remembering what he and his party did on their first afternoon on the large clearing, but everything else was crystal clear in his memory. Curmer opened his eyes and almost died of shock. He was no longer lying in the tub, but had wandered, still naked, into the sleeping chamber, a variety of clothes and trinkets lay around the room, pulled from their storage caskets. His skin was almost dry, so he had been out of the tub, wandering around for some time. With shaking hands he picked up a drying cloth and rubbed himself down. "Why am I doing these things? What is happening to me?" his thoughts in his private mind trembled with his body, "I must talk to someone, but who will listen without thinking I am completely mad. Any healer would immediately instigate a mind meld to investigate, but I am afraid that this may cause me more anguish." Curmer knew in his heart that the only person he could turn to was his brother. Remruc would listen and analyse the events with a warriors logic, he would help him sort out this strange behaviour and Curmer knew that Remruc would keep this business to himself. He dressed quickly, spinning round guiltily as Sorta came into the chamber. She looked in amazement at the mess, a frown on her face,

"Curmer! What have you been doing?"

He smiled weakly and shrugged, "I couldn't find my things, have you been reorganising?"

"Your clothes are where they have always been Curmer.

Are you sure that you are alright?" Sorta's frown deepened, she knew that he was hiding something from her, what, she could not tell.

"I am fine, honestly. Here," he pushed her back out of the room, "you go and fix me something to eat while I tidy up." Reluctantly Sorta left, casting an anxious glance over her shoulder. Curmer was still pale when he returned to the living area, his smile forced, his eyes distant. Sorta decided to have a private word with Lenta, perhaps she could suggest what might be wrong. They ate their light snack in silence, Deyka's anxious inquiries oblivious to both. When his young mind screamed its protest at the tension in the atmosphere they snapped out of their private thoughts to reassure the toddler. Curmer felt a nagging urge to leave his tent and walk through the city of the San although his conscious thoughts told him that after being away from his family for so long, he should spend time with them and not go wandering about. But not matter how he reasoned, the insistent niggling remained and grew stronger. Sorta noticed the distracted colouring in his mind and cautiously began a light-hearted conversation.

"I think that Deyka will be walking soon, he can crawl quickly and I have seen him trying to stand by himself." Curmer forced his mind to focus his thoughts,

"Yes ...yes, I think you are right." He smiled at his son, a sudden vision of the grave of his natural son flashed into his mind, a sense of loss and guilt welling up quickly inside him, only to vanish suddenly.

"What is wrong?" asked Sorta, anxiety tingling her mind

"Nothing... I was just thinking, about our first son on Surn. I suddenly thought of his grave, I don't know why." Sorta's mind filled with sorrow, her feelings still strong for their lost child. Deyka reached out for his mother, his emotions fearful at her pain. She quickly picked him up, love for the child she now had replacing her grief.

"I am sorry Sorta, I didn't mean to..." Curmer was angry with himself for stirring such memories in his mate, he started to reach for her and Deyka but stopped, the urge to leave was strong, his body felt as though it was trying to move by itself. "I need a walk, I am sorry." He quickly rose and was about to disappear through the doorway when Sorta's thought stopped him.

"Curmer! Don't go!" He turned round, but it took all of his will power to do so, his body was leaning out of the tent, struggling to get away.

"I must Sorta. It would be better if I was alone for a while. Why don't you take Deyka over to Lenta for the night and join me later for evening meal at Remruc's house," he barely paused long enough for Sorta's reply,

"I love you Curmer."

Remruc sat back in his chair and viewed the expedition party that had accompanied Curmer. In front of him were his own personal guards. Hand picked by him and totally loyal to not only himself, but Curmer. He knew that he could rely on their judgement and integrity, that they were not prone to wild imaginings and yet here they were to all intents and purposes saying that Curmer was not his normal self. Eriya ground her teeth in concentration, she too was disturbed. The Nemn healers were known to her, Kurct especially was one of the senior healers about to be upgraded onto the council of the San, she knew that he would not risk the wrath of the Chieftain if he was not wholly convinced of his case. Remruc leaned forward, his elbows resting on his knees, his hands clasped under his chin. "Tell me Tankta," he began, "did anything unusual happen before you camped in the large clearing?" The Doona gulped nervously, Remruc's fearful temper and devotion to his brother was well known amongst the San,

"No, Lord Remruc, not that I noticed."

"Then everything seemed to start on the morning after you broke up camp?"

"Yes Lord Remruc."

"Can you remember anything of the afternoon and night in the clearing?" Remruc's eyes burned intently into Tankta's mind.

"None of us can remember what went on that day, Lord Remruc," interjected Kurct his thoughts carefully neutral.

"I did not ask you healer Kurct," was the cold reply that stabbed back, causing all in the room to wince. Eriya sent a private message,

"Patience my mate. Do not let your feelings interfere with your judgement." Remruc breathed deeply and replied on their private line.

"Eriya. I trust your Nemn healers as much as my Chai guards, the Nemn and Chai are united by their suffering as much as by our marriage, but the Doona are still an unknown quantity. They did not join us willingly but through necessity. The council have been constantly petitioned by groups of Doona for permission to set up their own grazing camps. They have of course been denied this privilege, but what better way to break up the San and return to their tribal ways than to spread rumours that one of the Chieftains is insane?"

"I think you are being paranoid Remruc. His thoughts bear no traces of deceit, only concern and fear," Eriya pursed her lips trying to control her own fiery temper.

"Let us see, Eriya, just how honest he is." Remruc sat back sending a quick command on a private wavelength to two of the guards nearest the door. "Tankta, would you agree to a mind meld. Just to see what really did happen that day?"

There was a gasp of surprise from everyone present, Tankta paling visibly at the prospect. The Doona did not wish his mind to be opened and all of his private thoughts examined by anyone, however, he realised that this may well be the only way to prove that he believed what he thought. He glanced down at his hands, they were trembling.

"Yes, Lord Remruc," came the quiet almost whispered reply. Eriya released the breath she had been unconsciously holding, the rest of the group also relaxing. She looked at Remruc, an amused eyebrow raised in his direction, "your move I think my mate," was her mocking private comment.

Remruc ignored her thought and smiled at Tankta. "You have answered well Tankta, if you had made any other decision you would have been executed immediately. I do not intend to have the healers carry out this mind meld, however, I have considered what you have told me and I think perhaps there may be some cause for concern. At the moment my brother does not seem to be behaving abnormally, he is not prone to mood swings or irrational behaviour. I think we should wait and watch. If anything should occur then the senior healers will be called in to deal with it immediately, agreed?" There was a nod of approval from the healers present and Tankta let out a sigh of relief. "I must also add that nothing of what was said within these four walls will be discussed. This is a most delicate matter and I wish it to remain confidential, if anyone else hears of this then I will find the culprit and personally choke the life from them, understand?" The group of San hastily agreed and hurriedly excused themselves leaving Remruc deep in thought.

Eriya patiently waited and watched the changing moods in her partner's mind. Eventually he spoke, "I did not sense anything wrong with Curmer nor did you. I will talk to him tonight about his expedition; try to probe deeper into the afternoon and evening on the large clearing. I cannot believe that Curmer is simply losing his mind, he is probably more stable and sensible than me, but I definitely think that there is a link with the loss of memory from the entire party and Curmer's behaviour." He looked at his mate, anger in his eyes, "I can sense a presence Eriya, the same way that I can sense Cuc. What it is and what it wants I do not know, but, I think we are about to meet the builders of the crystal ring."

Chapter Seventeen

"What manner of creatures are these?"

"They are so contradictory, so unpredictable."

"To feel such loyalty for some of their kind and yet distrust others who appear no different. How unusual."

"How dangerous."

"If they will not trust their own species how can we expect them to stay here and maintain the harmony?"

"If we destroy them we would extinguish a race with a very rare gift. It is obvious now that they are the only survivors of their kind."

"What use is such a gift to a species with so violent a nature. In time they may pose a real threat to this Universe."

"There are other races with more distasteful temperaments and they will arise to nothing."

"Their minds have so much potential, perhaps we can show them the correct way?"

"There is no point. They can be of no use to us. They came here uninvited and unwanted, they must leave or be destroyed."

"What can you see El?" The three Idor turned to their leader, their minds focussing within his, looking through one of his many eyes that viewed the possibilities of time past, present and future.

"We do not have the right to destroy this species, they came here by accident and have altered the pattern of time we have been following, now there may be alternatives open to us, we may be avenged. It is too early yet to see far along many of these new paths, but we must be cautious about how much knowledge we give to this child race. Thr, what do you feel through this animal?"

"I sense great compassion and love of all living things. It

would do anything to protect its people, especially its young and its mate. There is also, buried deep but still there, an aggressive streak that it cleverly channels into a determination to combat disease and heal others of it's kind. There is also an interesting feeling that this creature forms only one half of an even stronger, powerful presence. It has a brother who appears to be physically identical but whose nature completes the circle, rather a nice balance don't you think?" Amusement flicked through the combined minds at Thr's lighthearted quip.

"We must know more before we decide." Csjn interjected, "I suggest Thr takes complete control of the animal and interacts with the others."

"This creature finds it most distressing when I move into its body, perhaps there is some alternative?"

"There are no alternatives," thought El, "if you know enough of their simple behaviour patterns and you feel you will not be detected if you take full control, then do so now."

"As you command and wish El."

Curmer walked through the tent city smiling and returning the greetings of those citizens he passed, heading towards the large grazing fields on the outskirts of the city. He stopped by a gently sloping bank and settled himself down to watch the mantelos play and to relax in the warm sun. Suddenly an icy chill snatched at his very soul, he felt his thoughts spin around his head as a strange darkness covered his vision. When the darkness cleared he found himself in the circular grove surrounded by the tall thorn bushes. As he stood bemused, the memory of his encounter with the Idor slowly crept back.

"Hello Curmer." The echoing thought seemed to reverberate throughout his body. Curmer turned to see the Idor called Thr standing behind him. Panic filled his being,

"Why are you doing this to me! What do you want?"

Thr shook his long head, "have no fear, I will not hurt you."

"Why did you take away my memory of our meeting? What are you up to? What are you trying to hide?" Curmer's thoughts suddenly reached their own, disturbing conclusion. "It was you, wasn't it? Those times when I couldn't control my own body, it was you that was invading me."

"Yes. Well done! You are really quite bright little animal." Curmer was furious, he took a step towards Thr, a low growl in his throat. "Now, now, behave yourself." Curmer was instantly dumped unceremoniously on his back. "Listen to what I am going to tell you."

"You can't just snatch me away like this! People will notice and will search for me! Send me back at once, if you can't communicate with us face-to-face, then don't bother talking to us at all!" Thr crunched his teeth and sighed, watching Curmer's indignant outburst with benign good humour.

"Finished?"

Frustrated, Curmer nodded, falling into a sullen silence. Thr lowered his head and peered intently at him, "good. Now I want you to listen and try to understand. I have not snatched you away, you, or rather your body is still sitting on the grass bank on the outskirts of your settlement. What you can see is simply a picture that your own mind has created to ease the shock of being cut off from its physical self. You see me in my physical form, but I am not really here, I am communicating with you via your own mind, it is your thoughts that have created this image, to help you deal with this situation. Following me alright?"

"You mean," said Curmer, curiosity overcoming any fear or anger, "that all of this is inside my head."

"Yes, well done!"

"Was that how I met you before?"

"No, we brought your body and mind to our circle that time, that is why your mind shows you this picture now."

"What do you want Thr?"

"I would like to borrow your body for a while. We are fascinated by your people and I would like to communicate with them through you."

"Will they know that it is not me?"

"No."

"Then if you make a mistake or say something wrong they will assume that it is me that is behaving oddly. No, you cannot take over my body; I will not allow my people to be deceived in this way!"

Thr looked sadly at Curmer and shook his shaggy neck, "I am afraid, little animal, that you cannot stop me." With that parting thought the image of Thr vanished leaving Curmer standing alone in the thorn circle.

"Wait! Come back!" shouted Curmer, his thoughts ringing hollowly in his own imagination.

Thr stood up. "It certainly seems strange to walk on your hind legs", he mused, his body swaying slightly as he adjusted himself to the unusual sensation. Once he had regained his balance he turned and walked back to the city of the Chai those people he passed wondering at the serious expression on their Chieftain's face. He reached the dwelling of the animal's brother in time for evening meal. There to greet him was Sorta, the animal's mate, Remruc and his mate Eriya.

"Is anything wrong?" asked Sorta anxiously when she saw the rather blank expression on Curmer's face. Thr quickly smiled, suddenly remembering the use of facial and body gestures used by these creatures to compliment and emphasise their thoughts.

"I am fine Sorta, thank you." Thr was not quite used to having to move his face in such a way, his own body's structure limited virtually all visible expressions, as a result the smile he wore resembled an insane grin. Sorta felt her blood run cold. The person standing in front of her looked and communicated like her mate, but she knew that this was not Curmer. She flicked a glance to Remruc and Eriya. Remruc's face was like thunder, he could sense the alien presence as well. He threw a warning look to Sorta and gripped Eriya's hand. With a fixed smile he welcomed his brother into his home. Sorta switched to a private frequency and tried to question Remruc, but before she could put her fears into thoughts he quickly interrupted her,

"Curmer looks well Sorta, you really must give Eriya some of your delicious recipes, after all it wouldn't be fair if one Chieftain is healthier than the other," he led her by the arm into the dining area, Eriya, sensing his strategy, partnering Curmer.

Sorta looked confused for a moment, then she relaxed and winked at her brother-by-mate. They seated themselves, Thr feeling rather smug thinking that he had managed to fool them, let his face relax from the grin.

"Would you care for some of my spiced lemath meat Curmer? It's a new recipe I am trying, Remruc likes it?" smiled Eriya sweetly as she offered the plate, her eyes as cold and sharp as daggers of ice. Thr felt revulsion as the pile of steaming meat was presented to him, the Idor were strictly vegetarian and the smell of burnt flesh was abhorrent to him.

"No!" He checked himself, that thought was too strong, "Thank you," he added in softer tones, "I have already eaten my fill of meat, I will just nibble on some of your delicious herb rolls." Sorta struggled to control her fear, Curmer would never turn down an opportunity to try one of Eriya's new recipes.

"Very well Curmer, here, have some straaas cakes," continued Eriya undeterred. Remruc watched Curmer closely, his reaction to Eriya's offer would confirm if this was really Curmer or an impostor.

"Thank you Eriya," said Thr, smiling again. "I am beginning to get the hang of this," he thought to himself. There was shocked silence as Curmer/Thr munched his way through the cake. "Mmm, delicious. May I have another?" Eriya and Sorta looked to Remruc for direction. Curmer hated straaas herb and would never have eaten the cake. Remruc paused, quickly mulling over several possibilities,

"Certainly, Curmer, as you know, my home is your home." He forced himself to smile nonchalantly, throwing warning glances at the two women. Thr hesitated. Something was wrong; the two females were on their guard, their minds a turmoil of fear. He thought quickly. If he left the animal's body now and returned control to Curmer then he would obviously tell them what had happened. "Perhaps I should use another memory block on him." He quickly disregarded that thought. That would risk him losing contact with Curmer altogether. Thr decided to try to cover up whatever mistake he must have made. "Tell me Remruc," he said quickly changing the subject, "how long do you think it will take to complete the city?"

"As you know brother," replied Remruc carefully, "we San do not relax till we have completed out projects and fulfilled our dreams. Speaking of dreams, remember that day your party first entered the large clearing on the other side of the forest?"

"Yes..." said Thr slowly.

"I was sleeping in the sun that afternoon and I had a rather strange dream."

"Oh?" Thr was now on his guard.

"Yes. I awoke suddenly from a frightening vision that you and your party were being attacked by some strange creature." Remruc maintained the amiable smile as he studied the guarded features of his brother,

"Strange isn't it?"

"Very," replied Thr, "but then dreams usually are." As they had been talking, Remruc had slipped his hands underneath the table to clasp Eriya's and Sorta's, suddenly the two women grabbed Curmer/Thr's hands and all three instantly attempted a forced mind meld. Thr reeled in surprise at the force of the mental attack. Quickly regaining his senses, his skilled mind deflected their combined efforts, circling their thoughts with an offensive loop of will and dragged their conscious minds deep into the subconscious trap set in Curmer's brain.

Eriya was the first to become aware of her surroundings. Bending over her was Curmer, instinctively she backed away, fearing that she would be attacked again. "Its alright Eriya, Its me, Curmer, the real one that is." Recognising his presence she gratefully let him help her to her feet. Curmer received a similar reaction from Sorta and Remruc but, like Eriya, they quickly realised their mistake.

"Where are we Curmer?" asked Remruc as he looked around the circular enclosure and thorny hedges.

"Somewhere inside my mind." replied Curmer.

"What?"

"Thr explained it to me, it's like a picture inside my head."

"Who is Thr?" queried Sorta, a frown on her face.

"One of the Idor. This is their world that we have entered and I don't think they are very pleased about it."

"Then they are the builders of the crystal ring?" thought

Eriya, nodding to her mate.

"Just as I suspected," growled Remruc as he prowled around the enclosure, "I take it that this Thr was the one that attacked you in the clearing?"

"Yes. Remruc, I do not know what the Idor are up to but they have some sort of control over me. They keep taking over my body, or rather Thr does and I cannot stop him. They are incredibly powerful, both physically and mentally."

"You have seen these Idor?" Sorta asked clasping her mate's hand, "what do they look like?"

"Like this," came the thought from behind. They all spun round to see Thr standing quietly on the lawn. Immediately Remruc raced forward, to protect his family and friends from what he considered terrible danger. With no effort Thr halted him in his tracks and dumped him on the ground, pinning him there. "Have you noticed anything unusual yet, Remruc?", he asked with irritating good humour. Remruc growled and kicked out at the Idor. It was this action that caused Remruc and the others present to stare in shock.

"My leg," thought Remruc, "my leg is no longer broken." He stared in wonder, running his hand along the clean straight bone.

"That is because what you see is merely created by your own thoughts, not by your physical presence," answered Thr stepping forward and instantly changing into a ball of light. "I can look like this - or this." The ball of light stretched out into a flat black disk. "Or whatever I choose to think of." He finished, finally regaining his original form.

"And what, may I ask, is your true self?", asked Eriya, her double-edged question not going unnoticed by Thr. He studied her intently for a few moments before answering,

"Why my dear little creature, this is my real form." He released Remruc and allowed him to rise. Immediately

Curmer was by his side and the San Chieftains faced the Idor, their thoughts unconsciously mingling, their life essence joining in a harmonious unity that none but the Idor could see.

"Why have you attacked us? What do you want? Why are we here?" demanded Remruc, but before Thr could answer Curmer interrupted.

"You will have to ask one question at a time my brother, these Idor are very good at avoiding those questions they do not like." Curmer stepped closer to Thr and looked up at the towering form. Thr obligingly lowered his head to stare eye to eye with the San. "Thr, you know what our questions are; I think that you at least owe us an explanation." The Idor lifted his head high, a faraway look in his massive eyes. Remruc recognised that strange expression, it was very similar to the blank stare of a Cuc that was communicating with its nest leader. He walked forward and reached out to the silver giant, but the Idor were not like Cuc, their minds were more than capable of focusing on several different things simultaneously, as Remruc's hand reached forward, Thr suddenly lowered his head, the single large horn on his forehead barely touching Remruc's throat.

"It is not polite to make such advances," was the cool response. Curmer was outraged,

"You and your people have had very little regard for our customs and beliefs, why should we show any respect for yours!"

"Why should you worry?" said Sorta suddenly. She had been standing very quietly watching the Idor carefully, trying to assess its true motives, "after all you have already said that what we see are merely our thoughts turned into three dimensional pictures. Remruc could not have done you any harm, or could he?" Thr ground his teeth in annoyance, he had allowed these creatures to manoeuvre him into revealing a secret he would rather have kept.

"It is possible to damage a thought and mind as easily as a physical body. I would therefore prefer if you made no attempt to touch or harm me, I might react too quickly and you would cease to function." Thr backed off slowly as he spoke, his eyes whirling in agitation. Remruc looked at Curmer in confusion,

"He means he might kill you by accident," said Curmer in response. "You still haven't explained your actions, Thr," he continued. Thr had calmed himself, the other Idor were now in direct contact with him, watching the situation through his eyes.

"We needed to know why you had come to our world, by questioning Curmer we discovered the reason."

Curmer flinched slightly at the memory of such 'questioning'.

"You are very unusual creatures, with a very rare gift and we are trying to decide what to do with you."

"Do with us?", asked Eriya, her eyebrow raising in haughty response.

"Yes. If we decide that you cannot stay here then we will send you back to your own planet."

"Back to Surn!" cried Sorta in distress, "please, you cannot, would not, be so cruel as to place us at the mercy of the Cucs!" Eriya gripped Sorta's arm as she rushed forward.

"Sorta is right," said Remruc, "there is nowhere on Surn left for us to hide, believe me when I say that we came to your world as a last resort. We did not know that your people were here, we have tried not to change or pollute your lands, all we ask for is some space to live. We will not harm you or any other living creature on your planet."

Thr regarded them all solemnly for a very long time. "If we decide to send you back, what would you do?" He finally said.

Curmer looked at Remruc, the brothers were united in their feelings and their duties. They would not let their people face certain death at the claws of the Cucs. Eriya stepped forward, her head high, her proud bearing impressing even Thr. "Idor!" Thr jerked his head in surprise and irritation at her impetuous thought, "we have harmed no one. If your kind are too intolerant to abide with other intelligent species then that is your problem not ours. We are here now and we will not be sent anywhere against our will. We have had to fight the plague, we have had to fight starvation, we have had to fight the Cuc and now we may have to fight you. The San are not cowards, we would rather die here than back in the dark holes on Surn." As she finished, Sorta, Remruc and Curmer moved to her side, their silent action backing her thoughts. Thr was furious,

"Then little animals you may well have decided your own fate!" In the blink of an eye all save Curmer vanished from the enclosure.

"Where are they!" demanded Curmer as he advanced on Thr. He was ignored and thrown roughly back against the thorns, he gave a gasp of pain as the mental barbs tore his mind. Thr stared at him coldly, the orbs of his eyes spinning rapidly around the central pupil. Curmer felt himself being lifted and dragged back towards the towering Idor who lowered his horny head, threatening to impale him. Curmer braced himself for the impact, but, much to his relief Thr stopped him just as the horn tip touched his throat.

"You have invaded our world, reshaped and infested our lands and now you dare to threaten us!"

"Please Thr, listen to me," he gasped, "we are desperate. We do not want to have to fight anyone, if we had known that you lived on this planet then we would have asked your permission to come, as it turned out the Cucs forced our hand and we had to escape. You already know that, have you not explored every possible corridor within my mind? You can see that I am telling the truth, you can feel that I do not lie, so why are you torturing me?" Curmer felt despair fill his being, he knew that the fate of his people depended on him convincing this cold alien creature that lacked any noticeable form of mercy. The Idor's eyes bored deep into the mind of Curmer. Once again the alien presence filled his being, seeped into every crevice of his conscious state, absorbing his identity into its vast, fathomless intelligence. As he was drawn into Thr's mind, Curmer felt his own spirit fade as madness threatened to destroy him forever. Just as he reached the brink and his will to survive was almost broken, the Idor let him go. He fell back into the mind trap in his subconscious, awareness of the small enclosure offering an anchor to his unstable thoughts.

"You are very strong little animal. You could learn much and go far, but our people do not trust your kind and do not want them in our world." Thr watched in silence as Curmer's jumbled and confused thoughts formed a coherent reply,

"Trust? Far? You speak in riddles Thr. What more can I do or say to convince you of our good intentions?"

"Believe it or not Curmer, I am on your side. I like you, but my fellows are not so sure. They need more time to decide. I am going to give you back your body, I will not block this memory from you, but I have blocked the memories of your friends, so do not tell them anything or they will think you insane. It will be up to you Curmer to convince us that your people can live in harmony not only with our world, but with each other. Do you understand what I am saying?"

"I understand Thr, but I don't believe you. So far you have

humiliated, hurt and degraded me, how can I now trust you."

"Very well, when you wake up you will find a peace offering by your side, you will know how to use it." On that thought Thr vanished from Curmer's mind, leaving him alone and empty. A terrible weariness pulled at him and he slowly slipped into a deep sleep.

"Wake up Curmer! Your bath is ready, if you do not hurry we will be late for evening meal at Remruc's house!" Sorta's thoughts bubbled into his mind with cajoling good humour. Curmer sat up. He was seated on the large cushions in his living section of his tent, it was mid-afternoon and Deyka was playing on the mat in front of him. He rubbed his face vigorously, trying to dispel the terrible nightmare from his brain. He breathed deeply, "Thank goodness, it must have been a bad dream after all," he thought to himself. As he put his hand down to push himself from his resting place, the rough bark of a wizened twig scratched his skin. He looked down in surprise, a cold feeling of shock and fear seeping into his body. There on the cushion was a branch, the vision that he had earlier that day instantly flashed into his mind.

This was the gift that Thr had promised, this would heal Remruc's leg successfully, now all Curmer had to do was think up a convincing story as to how he had come by it.

"Good luck." The thought echoed around his head, the tone disturbingly familiar.

Chapter Eighteen

Remruc watched his brother carefully all through evening meal. It was obvious that he was distracted and perturbed about something, but there was no blatantly abnormal behaviour. Eriya was also watching for any signs and her probing questions did not go unnoticed by Curmer. He had ground the twig into a fine powder which he had added to a mild painkiller solution that Remruc still took and he fervently hoped that this strange plant would heal the ragged break and restore his brother. What really was disturbing him was his memory of their 'original' evening meal. It was as though time itself had been set back, thus his companions' had no knowledge of the experience with the Idor because for them the incident had never happened. Curmer was becoming increasingly afraid of these creatures, if they could control time itself then their powers must be awesome indeed.

Sorta noticed her mate's serious expression and anxious overtones to his thoughts. She sent a private inquiry to him, "are you not happy with the meal Curmer? Perhaps I could fix you something different when we go home?" Curmer's reply covered his inward anxiety and relaxed Sorta,

"I am fine Sorta. I am just worried about the Doona."

"The Doona?" she asked. Curmer switched to the 'frequency' that the rest of the group were using.

"Tell me again, in detail Remruc, about these Doona groups wanting to leave. It has been troubling me all night." Remruc smiled inwardly, "So that's what's bothering him," he thought to himself.

"Certain factions of the Doona have been petitioning the council of Elders requesting that they set up summer grazing camps, to save the grasslands around the city for the winter.

Now, I personally think that they have a valid and important point, but, I am wary of letting the tribes of the San revert back to their old traditional families." Sorta sat in silent thought for a few minutes, her brow furrowed. Eventually she rejoined the conversation,

"Remruc, if you continually refuse to let the Doona set up their camp then they will become restless. They will drum up support from their fellow clansmen and probably try to leave by force. The Nemn patrols that police the city will be more than able to deal with their efforts, but the unrest could disrupt the fragile social structure that we are building and prove disastrous to our efforts."

"I agree with you Sorta, but what else can we do?" asked Eirya.

"You could let a specially selected group of Doona move out to set up an experimental camp," suggested Curmer.

"Specially selected? In what way?" asked Remruc intrigued.

"Well, we have seen that more and more Nemn and Chai people have shown an interest in the Doona's traditional methods of animal husbandry. It has now reached a point where, although we call them Doona, there are almost as many of the other clans making up the profession. Now, I know that it has been the small pockets of "original" Doona who have been trying to break away, but what if we choose a careful mix of breeders and carers, selecting loyal Chai and Nemn people and break up the problem groups of old Doona. That way we show that the council is indeed fair and will listen to suggestions from every tribe that makes up the San and we ensure that those chosen will not cause any problems. We may be pleasantly surprised to find that the old Doona will settle down into our community if we give them this certain amount of freedom." Curmer sat back, slightly surprised himself at this wisdom he displayed and wondered if he was again being influenced by Thr.

The others stared at him in admiration. "That is a very good idea Curmer," Remruc finally ventured. "We will certainly try it." They continued their meal in amicable silence, once finished, the party moved into the main living section of the building, it was almost identical to Remruc's own quarters back in the Chai city on Surn and Curmer felt himself relax as old happy memories came flooding into his mind.

"I have an announcement to make." Eriya smiled as she seated herself, "You will be the first to know, I have not even told Remruc yet." Remruc watched her, a smile of anticipation playing on his lips, "I am expecting our first child."

"Ohh! Eriya that's wonderful!" exclaimed Sorta, her mind full of joy, "do you know if it will be a boy or a girl?"

"No Sorta, it is still too early to 'hear' anything," she replied as Remruc sat down beside her, the delight in his mind obvious to all, despite the private 'frequency' he was using. The topic of conversation was set for the rest of the night. Sorta and Eriya exchanged stories and notes on child care while Remruc, his mind still dizzy with joy, was warned with good humour about the "trials" of fatherhood by Curmer.

Later that night, after Curmer and Sorta had returned to their own home, they lay awake for a long time thinking about Eriya's child. Eventually Sorta rolled over and nudged Curmer. "Curmer?"

"Mmmm?"

"I am troubled. If Remruc and Eriya have a child, who will be the next clan Chieftain when we are gone? Deyka or their child?"

Curmer thought carefully before he answered, "the law

states that the firstborn child of the Chieftain, be it male or female, will be the next in line. That law is the same even if there are twin leaders."

"Yes Curmer, but Deyka is not our child."

"Deyka is our child, Sorta!" exclaimed Curmer, "as soon as I swore the oath to Herka on Surn he became our child, our flesh and blood. Have we not raised him as our son? The son of a Chieftain."

"Yes my mate, but remember that although to us he is our flesh and blood, he will never be the firstborn of true Chieftain blood line." Curmer was silent for a long time before he replied,

"He is our son Sorta, he will be the oldest child in the family, it is his right to be leader and leader he shall be." Curmer rolled onto his side and closed his eyes, but it was many hours before he managed to sleep, as a terrible sense of foreboding gnawed at his soul.

The next morning Curmer joined Remruc at the council of Elders to announce their decision about the Doona petitioners. As they walked to their seats, Curmer noticed how easily his brother moved the bound limb, occasionally putting his foot lightly on the ground. "How is your leg today brother?"

"It feels good Curmer, there is no pain today, in fact, perhaps I should stop taking the powders."

"I think you should use up the supply that you already have and then we will see how things go from there," smiled Curmer, inwardly hoping that this improvement was only the beginning of the ground twig's healing properties, and not the deadening of the nerve endings in a wasted limb. They sat side by side at the head of the council watching the group of Doona waiting for their decision. They made little attempt to hide their feelings of anticipated disappointment at what they expected to be a negative comment from the Chieftains, this disappointment also had distinctly angry undertones. The elders were shifting uncomfortably in their seats, their own thoughts trying to mask the insolent feelings from the Doona. Curmer and Remruc stood up and all in the room seemed to hold their breath. Their minds merged as one and their thoughts flowed in perfect unison, the strong undertones of Remruc complementing the light and easy line of Curmer.

"We are the Chieftains of the San. Our word is law. Our decision final. We have listened to your plea and have thought long and hard over what you have said. You are Doona. You are gifted in the rearing of our beasts, therefore we trust your knowledge and advice. We will allow groups of Doona to move the animals further across the plains for the summer grazing, your elders have been notified of the people who will make up these grazing camps. A patrol of Chai will also be sent, to protect you and your animals from any predators that may lurk beyond our city. This is our word and so it is law." They sat down and watched the dumbfounded expressions and happily astounded thoughts of the Doona with satisfaction.

"So," thought Curmer to himself, "it seems as though we have almost completed the first task set for us by the Idor. Are you listening Thr? I think you are. Perhaps now you can see the determination of the San, to survive anywhere and to learn to adapt and change." He was brought back from his private mind by Remruc tugging on his arm,

"Come brother, it is time to leave. The elders will coordinate the Nemn councillors and begin the relocation of the Doona camps, they will bring us a full report later, besides, I would like you to take a look at my leg." Remruc swung himself quickly onto his crutches and led the way out of the chamber.

They made their way to the privacy of Curmer's tent, it

being nearest to the Elder Chamber. Once inside Curmer began his inspection. The skin was beginning to lose its bruised and battered appearance, the swelling was definitely subsiding. The leg appeared to be straight, but Curmer wondered just how well the bones were knitting. "What do you think Curmer? It seems to look a lot better to me?"

"You are right Remruc, there is definitely an improvement."

"How long do you think before I can use it properly again?"

"That is difficult to say for sure, Remruc, I think that you should just take each day as it comes." Curmer smiled as his brother grunted in annoyance, the anticipation of being fit and whole again was almost too much for him to bear. A sudden image of Remruc flashed into Curmer's mind, not an image of a cripple, but an image of a strong and healthy warrior running towards him. The picture was gone in an instant and Curmer knew that it had come from Thr, as some form of reassurance perhaps? He did not know, he only hoped that it would indeed be true.

Time passed quickly for the San. The Doona camps were an unrivalled success, the people were happy and a sense of harmony and peace descended over the entire city. Remruc's leg was indeed healing well and, slowly but surely, his crutches were laid aside as the bone was able to take his body's weight. He still walked with a limp, but at least he was able to walk. Eriya's pregnancy was carefully monitored by all of the healers, old Lenta was almost beside herself with joy and the anticipation of the imminent birth was occupying all of her waking moments. Both Remruc and Eriya could "hear" their unborn child quite clearly, the contented thoughts bearing the unmistakable tones of a female.

It was Lenta who first began to ponder on the possible

dispute that may occur as to which of the Chieftains offspring would inherit the leadership. She first began to notice that certain members of the council of Elders were putting more importance to the imminent birth of the child when she sat in on major meetings. More and more of them were inquiring as to the birth date of the new Chieftain. They no longer asked after Deyka and this troubled Lenta greatly, for, like Curmer, she felt that Deyka was as much the son of Curmer and Sorta as their own dead child had been. What did it matter that he was adopted. Hadn't Herka more than proved himself an honourable warrior. Didn't his child deserve to be accepted as the next in line. Lenta was old enough and wise enough to keep her inner thoughts on the matter well hidden, but she could sense the growing unease in Curmer and Sorta as the opinions of the Elders became more and more obvious. As the day of her birth drew closer even Remruc began to look decidedly uneasy. He had at first been oblivious to the general feelings toward his child, too wrapped up in his own delight to notice anyone or anything else, but now he wrestled with his emotions, his love and loyalty to Curmer, his love and hope for his child and the fear that this difference of opinion as to who will inherit the leadership could possibly split the San's people forever. Curmer and Sorta had the support of the original members of the Nemn tribe, they had all known Herka and wished for his child to become their leader. There were also divided loyalties among the Nemn Elders. Should they side with Curmer and Deyka, or support Eriya and her unborn child. The harmony that had descended on the San for such as short time was being disturbed and threatened by this undercurrent of tension.

On the surface Curmer and Remruc showed a united front, but their conversations with each other was limited to official business only. Neither one wished to raise the question that was uppermost in their minds; neither one wanted to draw attention to the growing tension within their city and so they tried to ignore the problem in the hope that it might go away. But it did not go away.

In the autumn of their first year on the new planet, Eriya gave birth to her first child, Mora. She was a strong and healthy child, showered with gifts from every member of the San, blessed by all who saw her and the delight and anguish of her father Remruc. It was now that something must be said. It was now that he and Curmer could no longer deny the division within their people. Remruc sat alone in the great hall of the Elders desperately trying to marshal his thoughts. How could he put this to Curmer without hurting or upsetting him? He rose and walked slowly to one of the windows. Looking out across their now completed city he wished with all his heart that they would find a simple answer to their predicament.

"Good morning to you, Remruc." came the formal thought into his public mind. Remruc turned to see his brother standing in the doorway, the tension in his body echoed by the tension in his mind. Deliberately switching to their private frequency Remruc walked towards him,

"Good morning to you Curmer, I am glad that you have come to my summons."

Relaxing slightly Curmer moved into the hall and seated himself next to the fire. He absently poked at the burning rocks with a stick as Remruc joined him. They sat beside each other in silence for a long time, each one locked in their own thoughts, neither one wishing to say what must be said.

Remruc grunted. "Who would have thought that the day would come when you and I cannot speak to each other."

"There are some things brother that I dare not say."

"By not speaking, Curmer, do you think that they will go

away?"

"Obviously not, Remruc, or we would not be sitting here today." Curmer's terse response to his brother's gentle enquiry caused another long silence. Remruc's patience finally gave out and he turned sharply round to the quiet figure next to him.

"There is an unrest within our people Curmer, an unrest that may destroy all that we have built. I know that you have also noticed this and that you know the cause." Remruc sensed the anger that his statement stirred within his brother but he knew that they must resolve this situation quickly and that like it or not one of them must be hurt in the process. "There is a question of which of our children will inherit the right to be Chieftain."

"There is no question in my mind, Remruc! The first born of the Chieftains will inherit the responsibility of leadership whether the child is male or female. Deyka is older than Mora by almost two years. He will be Chieftain!" Curmer's face was dark with fury and he stared at Remruc, challenging him to deny his son's right.

"I agree with you Curmer. The first born of the Chieftains will be the heir. Mora is the first born by proxy, your child died Curmer, Deyka is not of the bloodline, he is not your true son." Remruc was taken unawares as Curmer flew at him in a rage. Taking the advantage, Curmer struck his brother squarely across the jaw, sending him flying from the bench. He landed awkwardly on his newly mended leg, there was an awful snap as the fragile bone cracked, but Remruc's scream of pain was drowned by Curmer's screem of anguish.

"Remruc... Remruc I am sorry!", he bent down to try to still his brother who now writhed in agony from the pain in his leg and the knowledge that now he would be crippled forever. "Lie still... do not move." Curmer's hands searched for the pressure points on the struggling form a turmoil of emotions within him threatening to erupt. Desperately he tried to meld with Remruc, to ease his pain, but his despair and guilt prevented him from concentrating sufficiently for even this simple exercise. With all of the force he could muster he screamed out in his own mind, "Thr...Thr...I know that you are there, I know that you are watching, help me, please. Help my brother. Only your kind can heal the damage that I have caused. Please, I beg you, help." Curmer opened his eyes to see the thorny hedge surrounding the clearing and neat lawn. He was alone. His mind reeled as he struggled to regain control of his emotions. Taking deep breaths he turned slowly round looking for Remruc. Instead he found the quiet gaze of Thr standing behind him.

"Dear, dear little animal, just when you were doing so well too."

"Thr,.." Curmer took a step forward and reached out to the Idor, then, remembering their dislike of being touched, he stopped short, unsure of what to do or say. "Remruc?" he managed to gasp.

"Yes, quite. I am afraid you handled that situation extremely badly. A nice mess you have made of your brothers leg. You understand of course that I am under no obligation to help either of you. In fact, I should not have even brought you here." A bed of disappearing moss appeared beneath Thr as he spoke and a similar couch materialised beneath Curmer. "Now sit down and listen to what I must tell you." Curmer obeyed, unwilling to annoy the only creature that would help him. His quick obedience did not go unnoticed by the Idor and he looked long at Curmer before he continued. "You and your brother have done well. My people are much happier about your presence. You have succeeded in maintaining the harmony in our world and we have all been impressed by your efforts. It is really unfortunate that this new situation has cropped up," he paused to nibble at the grass beneath him, Curmer shifted irritably in his seat, if the Idor could smile then Thr would have worn a grin from ear to ear, "patience little animal, patience."Again Thr noticed the lack of response to his gentle goading and unknown to Curmer the Idor looked deep into his mind, seeing the sorrow, guilt, anger and fear tearing him apart. Thr relented, "I will heal your brother Curmer, but I will not take away the memory of what happened, when I return you it will be to the moment just after you have struck him. It will be up to you to sort things out."

Relief and gratitude welled up inside Curmer, drowning out the words his mind was trying to form. As he watched, the unconscious form of Remruc appeared, hovering in the air between them. A brilliant blue haze surrounded his body the light being slowly absorbed through his skin. Once the glow was gone, Remruc vanished. Curmer was mildly surprised at how natural this appearing and disappearing was becoming. He stood up.

"Thr. You did not need to help me but you did. I will never forget that. I am sorry for the trouble that my people have caused your kind and I swear that somehow I will find a way to solve this new dilema. Personally Thr I am more than grateful, I owe you my brother's life. I will make this oath to you today and let it stand for all time, if by life or death I can help and repay you then I shall."

Thr stood silent and motionless before him, his many eyes seeing things that Curmer could not comprehend, vistas of time and chance spanned out before the Idor, all were viewed and contemplated, but this moment had not been foreseen and this was the moment for which the Idor had waited. Now they may be able to form an alliance that could build an empire that would span many universes, an empire that legends were made of.

"I know, Curmer, I understand. Thank you." Before the fact that Thr had thanked him had sunk in, Curmer found himself before the fireplace, Remruc was slowly picking himself up from the floor, a look of black fury on his face.

"You idiot, I could have hurt my leg!" Remruc's fury was soon replaced with puzzlement as his brother fell about laughing.

"I am sorry, Remruc, truly I am," he strode over and took Remruc's arms,"do you believe me when I say that I love you brother, more than life, more than my son's life." The desperation in his now sombre thoughts struck Remruc almost as hard as the blow on the jaw. He looked hard into the face that reflected himself and automatically placed his hands on the pressure points that were used in the mind meld.

They stood together in one mind, one thought, one heart. The single mind thought quietly to itself, reviewed the past misunderstandings, considered impassively how to resolve the unrest amongst their people and congratulated itself on the solution. Slowly, reluctantly the strong single mind split into its two separate components, promising to form itself again soon.

For a long time they just stood and looked at each other. All hurt between them healed, a new strength formed around their bond, a new power had been born.

Chapter Nineteen

Lenta muttered to herself as she eased her old bones out of her sleeping furs. Her Tarl servant quickly brought warm robes to keep out the night chill, anxiously fussing around her beloved mistress. Lenta caught the Tarl's hand as she readjusted the robe, "Go to bed now Karcha, there is no need for you to come with me to this untimely summons." The Tarl smiled gratefully at Lenta, she was one of the original Tarl that were still working off the debt they owed to the San people and as such had no status. The fact that Lenta spoke her true name meant more to her than anything else and served only to strengthen her bond of loyalty to her mistress.

"If it pleases you Lenta, I wish to come. What kind of a servant would I be to let you travel alone at such an hour?"

Lenta patted her hand and nodded, smiling at her concern. "As always Karcha you win. You may come with me and I know I can rely on your discretion." Together they left the warm building and walked along the starlight street. Lenta had lived her life below ground on Surn and still rejoiced inwardly at the spectacle of the dazzling display above her head. They passed a group of Nemn hunters patrolling their city. The Nemn were extremely efficient at maintaining order in the streets, any unruly behaviour (usually caused by slightly inebriated individuals) was soon put down and the offenders taken to their homes quickly and quietly. They recognised Lenta and her maid bowing low as approached.

"Healer Lenta. May we escort you on your business?" Their leader asked formally.

"Thank you for your kind offer, but I have been summoned to the house of the Chieftains and as you can see my Tarl servant is here to aid me."

"Safe journey healer Lenta, we will not delay you any

further." The patrol leader bowed again and the group continued on their nightly duties.

Curmer answered their knock on the main door of Remruc's house. He was surprised to see that Lenta was not alone but made no comment. He knew how fond she was of her servant and how faithful the Tarl was to both Lenta and Musi. They went to Remruc's private guest quarters, a small cosy room set apart from Remruc and Eriya's sleeping area. The fire was blazing well and a warm glow filled the room. Lenta gratefully eased herself into a padded seat, her eyes noting that Eriya was obvious by her absence, as was Sorta. She turned to her servant, "Go to the kitchen and prepare some refreshments for us." Quickly the Tarl rose and left the room. Lenta guessed that this discussion was going to be very important and very secret and she steeled herself, ready to receive bad news.

Remruc entered the room quietly, closing the heavy door to his sleeping area as gently as possible. He nodded to Curmer and they both sat down opposite Lenta. She studied the sons of her mate carefully, her trained eye and trained mind was surprised at the change she could sense, surprised and somewhat in awe of the awesome power that now sat before her. How they had grown, these children that she had helped nurse. Again she saw the frightened youths that had taken the weight and responsibility of leadership, the young men who had struggled to change the rigid, outdated laws of their clans, the brave Chieftains who had led their people to safety. Sadelna had been right when she had named them as the most powerful leaders their people had ever seen. "If only you could see your sons now Sadelna," thought Lenta to herself,"how proud you would be, for now truly are they mature in both body and spirit." With her years of training, Lenta could see almost as much as Thr, she could almost feel the power emanating from her beloved mate's sons. She knew that for whatever reason she had been called here at this late hour, their news would not be bad, their strength and unity told her that.

"Lenta, mate of my father, you have been as a mother to me always," began Curmer, "your wisdom is deep and your heart full of love. There is a task that must be undertaken, a task that will be difficult but not impossible, a task that we feel only you could perform."

"You are aware no doubt of the problem of succession to our leadership," continued Remruc, "Deyka is the oldest child, but Mora is of the Chieftains blood line. We know our people are divided, they await an answer and whichever child we choose will not please all of our people. The harmony of our city is threatened and so we seek your help."

"Lord Remruc and Curmer," gasped Lenta, "surely you do not wish me to choose who will succeed you!"

"Please Lenta, hear us out." said Curmer, a smile tugging at the corners of his mouth. "As you know, Remruc and I have not exactly stuck to our traditional ways,"

Lenta grunted her amusement at his quip.

"Since we have changed so many of our laws, why should we not change this?"

Curmer turned to Remruc who took up the line of thought, "we feel that in this new world, a new type of leadership is called for. It should not be up to us to decide who will succeed, but up to our children. We propose that until Deyka and Mora have reached maturity no final decision should be made. It will be up to them to prove their skills of leadership, to prove they are worthy of our people and to win the support of the San nation."

Lenta was stunned by their proposal, her mind reeling at the prospect.

"Of course," continued Curmer, "there is no guarantee that our people will support one or the other, there may still be a difference of opinion. That is why we feel that our children should be taught and educated in all skills and trades, should have a sound knowledge of politics and diplomacy and should receive equal and impartial tutoring by one person. It would not be fair if Remruc or I taught our own children, they must learn from a third party."

"And you want that third party to be me," finished an incredulous Lenta.

"Yes. Lenta, both Curmer and myself feel that you should be entrusted with the task of training the future Chieftain. Our children would then stand a fair chance, an equal opportunity to prove their worth as leaders of the San. When the time comes, they will decide who will succeed, and, if it comes down to it, why should they not both rule together? We have done so most successfully, why can our children not work together also?"

Lenta was lost for words, she mulled over what the possible reactions by the people would be. It was true that she would be a fair and neutral tutor, she would show no favouritism and would be able to see that their minds would not be corrupted by greed or envy. "It would be an honour." Her simple reply came slowly and carefully, "I hope that I live long enough to complete my task." The sombre statement was lightened somewhat by her smile. Both Remruc and Curmer relaxed, the hard part was over, now they simply had to inform their mates and the people of their decision. A light knock on the door heralded the arrival of refreshments as the Tarl entered quietly. "Put the tray down there Karcha and take some for yourself." The Tarl froze and looked quickly at Lenta then Remruc and Curmer, she was a Tarl and must be treated as a non-person with no rights, Lenta had made a mistake by naming her in front of the Chieftains and she feared their terrible wrath. What if they punished her mistress, without further thought she threw herself at the feet of the Cheiftains,

"Please Lords Remruc and Curmer, I beg you to forgive my mistress, she meant no harm, punish me, it was I that told her my true name, it was my fault not hers. I beg you to forgive her." Her anguished plea was stopped by Curmer as he gently pulled her to her feet,

"I heard nothing Tarl, neither did Lord Remruc. Now do what you have been instructed, the matter has been forgotten."

Lenta smiled at Remruc, she knew he was annoyed, after all it was he who had thought of the punishment that the Tarl were destined to serve.

"It is a new world Lord Remruc, perhaps it is time we changed more of the decisions made on Surn." She laughed at his grunt of amusement and placed a hand on her servants arm, "Do as you're told child and serve the drinks."

Chapter Twenty

The nights grew longer and the days colder for the San. Winter began to draw her soft white folds across the plains of their city. The novelty of cold snow and ice was not lost on the young and they found endless enjoyment in this new source of fun. The adults too (although few would admit it) were enjoying the bracing wind and weather, making excuses to be out of doors on the coldest of days. The spirits of the people were high and for a time at least there was peace amongst the San.

It was a bright morning and the fresh snow lay deep in the streets of the city. Curmer rolled over in his sleeping furs and nudged Sorta, she feigned sleep and snuggled deeper into the warmth. Undeterred Curmer vindictively blew softly onto the back of her neck, causing a chill to run down her spine. "You are an evil creature, mate of mine," she retorted digging him in the ribs with her elbow and rolling over to deliberately lie on top of him, "now that I'm awake I have you at my mercy." Curmer grinned at her wickedly,

"Have you ever thought about losing weight Sorta?" With a growl of mock annoyance she clamped her sharp teeth on the end of his nose slowly and surely increasing the pressure. Shaking with laughter Curmer tried desperately to plead for mercy and she enjoyed every minute of his torture.

"Deyka want to play!!!!" the sharp tone invaded their minds, followed closely by a solid little body hurtling onto their furs and laughing at this new game. Curmer grabbed the little form and swung him high into the air to be caught deftly by Sorta. There followed a few more minutes of mayhem, sleeping furs were tossed and turned, growls and laughter filled the air, at every opportunity Curmer tickled and nipped Sorta, she returned his attack with equal enthusiasm. Finally they collapsed breathless, Deyka standing on top of them in triumph, "I'm hungry." he said plaintively.

"Go into the eating rooms, you will find fresh greens and cold meat from last night." Sorta replied, giving him a little push. They watched him as he trotted off, intent on stuffing his face. Quickly Curmer sprang on her and pinned her down on the furs,

"Now that I'm awake I have you at my mercy!" he declared. He didn't find any resistance to his further suggestion.

Later that morning Sorta had some urgent business at the healer hall, she and Eriya had a minor emergency to deal with regarding the collapse of one of the storage roofs under the weight of snow. Curmer, having been nominated as babysitter, decided to take his fast growing son out for a walk down to the frozen river. Wrapping their feet well in furs and taking a small amount of food along, they set off, pausing now and then for fights in the snow.

They reached the river by midday and found it deserted. Most of the San were either helping to re-build the storage shed or watching the process for pure entertainment value as the workers struggled to keep their feet (and dignity) on the slippery ground. It was all carried out in the best of humour as the crowd shouted encouragements or roared with laughter at the appropriate times.

Curmer and Deyka walked along the bank (Deyka had been suitably warned not to stray onto the frozen surface of the river) marvelling and the silent beauty around them.

"Nice isn't it?" a familiar voice said behind them. Curmer turned quickly to see Thr walking down the small slope towards him. A momentary panic filled Curmer as his son ran towards the Idor arms outspread to greet this new and exciting creature.

"No Deyka Stop!" Curmer shouted, remembering the Idor's dislike of physical contact, but it was too late, Deyka had already grabbed hold of Thr's front leg, his head barely reaching the Idor's knee. Carefully Thr lifted his leg, a giggling and purring Deyka clinging onto his limb. "I'm sorry Thr, please forgive him!" Curmer was still in a state of panic, terrified that the Idor would kill his son.

"Calm down, Curmer, I won't hurt him," Thr said, "he is only a baby and means no harm." He lowered his great head and Deyka gasped in wonder at the massive face in front of him. With outstretched hands he grasped the Idor's face and stroked the soft hair of his hide, his little fingers examining the texture of the horn growing from the forehead. "Would you like to play with me, Deyka?" he asked.

"Deyka play! Yes Deyka play!" Curmer felt his anxiety slowly subside as he watched his son float off the ground and onto the back of Thr.

"Hold tight Deyka." said Thr, but Curmer knew that even if Deyka didn't hold on he was in no danger of falling off. With a tremendous burst of speed Thr set off up the slope and back down, running in circles around Curmer, knocking up great clouds of snow which sparkled in the air before settling back onto the ground. Gasping with pleasure Deyka screamed faster,faster as the Idor spun in dizzying spirals and leapt into the air. After a few minutes Thr returned to Curmer who was trying very hard not to laugh. "I believe this belongs to you." said Thr as Deyka floated off of his back and landed at his father's feet, his face radiant and eyes full of wonder.

"You look a little out of breath Thr," smiled Curmer, "perhaps your getting too old to run about like a young mantelo."

"I will never be too old Curmer," replied Thr, his thought tinged with amusement and good humour, "and I am most

332

certainly not a mantelo! Walk with me a while, I must speak to you." Obediently Curmer followed the Idor as they continued down the river with Deyka wandering along in front of them.

"What is it Thr? What have you come to tell me?"

"Yln and Csjn want us to take action against you and your people, Curmer. They wish you gone from our world."

"But why!" exclaimed Curmer, his mind frantic, "What have we done wrong? What more do they wish from us?"

"It is not a matter of what you have and haven't done Curmer, but what you and your people may do. They still do not trust you and feel that you may yet prove a threat to all that we have created." Thr paused and stared across the river towards the purple and white forest. "If it is any consolation Curmer I and the other members of the circle are on your side."

"Will this conflict ever end Thr? Will our people ever be left in peace, allowed to live our lives without the threat of attack?" Curmer's heart sank as the pressures weighed heavily on him.

"I think, Curmer, that a deal must be struck. Your people must show that they will work for and with us and not against us. Perhaps it is time that we announced our presence."

"Would Yln and Csjn be happy with that, Thr. Do you believe that a simple agreement will change their minds?"

"Maybe not, Curmer, but we can only try." Abruptly Thr vanished into thin air, startling Curmer and Deyka.

"I wish he wouldn't do that," thought Curmer to himself as he stilled his beating heart. Before he could turn back Thr re-appeared just as quickly.

"I forgot to say that I will be in touch with you soon, Curmer," the Idor added pleasantly.

"I thought that you never forgot anything Thr," said Curmer dryly. Thr winked at him and disappeared.

Chapter Twenty One

"It is time"

"When will we move?"

"Now, they are ready now."

"What if we do not succeed?"

"We will attain our objectives one way or another."

"They would not submit to force, you have seen the strength of their will, to break their will would remove their most useful attribute."

"Thr is correct, we need their minds intact."

"Will they trust us?"

"They fear us, that is enough for the present."

"Fear may destroy what we are trying to achieve."

"They only fear what they do not understand. In time they will understand."

"Time is on our side for once."

"What do you see El?"

"The paths are merging into one, the future is not yet set, we are not completely committed. If we choose we can destroy what we have started and begin again."

I would not like to destroy them. I will protect what I have built."

"That is you choice, Thr, and we will respect your wishes, but if we must start again you will have to remove them from our world."

"I understand."

"Shall I go first?"

"Watch your temper, Yln. Do not terrify them any more than necessary."

"The game has begun."

Lightning Source UK Ltd.
Milton Keynes UK
UKHW010518220822
407537UK00001B/21